A HIGHER EDUCATION

A MODERN RETELLING OF PRIDE & PREJUDICE

ROSALIE STANTON

ACKNOWLEDGMENTS

I cannot thank my beta readers Terri Meeker and Kim McCoy enough for their brutally honest comments. Together, they helped me identify the places that needed revising the most. They were absolutely right in every suggestion and didn't hold back to spare my feelings. In other words, everything an author could ever want in her beta readers.

Thank you to Brittany Hutzel for taking no prisoners during this edit. I'm so fortunate to have you on my team.

Thank you to Jane Austen for these wonderful characters. They haven't stopped intriguing me since I met them, and I hope they never do.

To my mother, even though she won't actually read this unless it's available in audio form.

Which makes this the best time to confess the following: Mom, the night we watched the BBC adaptation the first time, you said it was too late to start the second disc and I'd have to wait until the following night. I took that second disc into my room and watched the whole thing after you went to bed.

#SorryNotSorry

___

It wasn't that Elizabeth didn't like parties. In fact, she liked them just fine. But when parties included drunken assholes doing keg stands and staring pointedly at women's chests, they stopped being fun. Unfortunately, this was one of those parties.

"You're hating this, aren't you?"

Elizabeth turned a smile to her roommate Jane. She had only known the girl a few days, but they already felt like sisters.

Jane was the walking antithesis to the horror stories about college roommates. Plus, she was in her third year—*not* a fellow freshman—and Elizabeth would gladly offer sacrifices to the campus gods to keep whatever administrative error that had caused this happy accident from being corrected. Returning to college after a long break was hard enough. Starting over in your mid-twenties sucked beyond the telling of it. If Elizabeth had to do this, at least she had a leg-up with an early jackpot in the roommate department.

"I'm not hating this," Elizabeth said. "It's just been a while."

That was an understatement. In a sea of college freshmen, she felt a bit more like the den mother.

"Are you sure?" Jane tucked a fallen lock of brown hair

behind her ear. "Because if you're hating this, we can always head back. I bet Mary would be up for a round or two of Exploding Kittens."

Elizabeth shook her head. "I'm not leaving, so stop asking."

"But—"

"Jane, stop worrying about me. You've been talking about this party for three days. Relax, dammit."

Jane arched an eyebrow. "'Relax, dammit'? Has that ever worked on anyone?"

"There's a first time for everything." Elizabeth cracked a grin and turned her attention to the sea of sweat-glazed bodies. The frat house, she'd admit, was the nicest one she'd been in, or at least she'd guess so if it weren't crowded with tables of food and booze. But then, the Greggii House was an institution at Meryton College—established by the wealthy for the spawn of the wealthy so the dears didn't feel too lost among the plebeians.

Apparently this mixer was one that was thrown every semester by the trust fund crowd. Their way of saying *welcome* and *see how much better we are* to those here on scholarships and financial aid. Everything about this place—from the Corinthian columns to the ornate crown-molding medallions etched into the ceilings—screamed money, *old* money, and lots of it.

Peers they were not, but Elizabeth supposed inviting the have-nots over to gawk was about as charitable as some trust-funders ever got. They might even find a way to write off the experience on their taxes.

A guy who had either lost his shirt or forgotten to put one on stumbled as he attempted to navigate the swarm of people near them. He managed to save himself from face-planting, but the same could not be said for the beers he carried. Elizabeth tried not to squeal—she did—but the splash of cold, fizzy liquid on her skin forced her to lose all control over her vocal chords.

"Goddammit, watch where you're going," the guy spat, his

words an angry slur. "You have any idea how much a case of that costs?"

"You ran into us, fuzz butt," Jane snapped.

There was just something about the way Jane managed not to swear like a sailor while channeling her inner rage monkey that had caused Elizabeth to fall in instant like with her. This was no different.

The guy frowned, his brow furrowing. "What butt?"

Elizabeth just laughed and ignored him, hooking her arm through Jane's. "I need to find a bathroom," she said. "I smell like a mini-bar."

"But he was rude—"

"He's drunk. Some people are rude when they're drunk."

"Hey!" the guy shouted. "I'm not drunk."

"Okay, fine. Then he *is* rude," Elizabeth retorted, biting back a grin when his face tightened. "Excuse us, fuzz butt."

Elizabeth managed to steer Jane a safe distance away before the urge to laugh got the better of her. She'd forgotten how seriously college guys took their beer.

Will was not having a good time. Then again, he hadn't expected to—something Charlie would undoubtedly say was part of the problem. But he wasn't sure, exactly, how anyone was supposed to have a good time here. Every corner of the frat house was occupied, mostly by shiny guys who had run into a clothing shortage. Apparently all of the hosts had decided they would be more easily identified if they went topless.

If that wasn't enough, the music thundering from the speakers made it damn near impossible to hear himself talk, let alone anyone else. The air was thick with the scent of sweat, underscored with hints of beer. Not even good beer.

The second he'd stepped inside the frat house, Will had had to fight the urge to do an about-face and get as far away as his legs would take him. But he'd promised Charlie he'd go along for the ride, and he was determined to do that. Even if it killed him.

Which, honestly, it might.

How anyone, much less a guy he called his best friend, could look around with anything but a desire to flee was beyond him. Yet Will also admired that about Charlie, reluctant as he was to admit it. No matter where the man went, he found himself right at home, and rather happy to be there.

Case in point...

"I love this song!" Charlie screamed before starting some hopping motion that made him look like the Easter Bunny on steroids.

Will had long ago decided that he had been born at the ripe old age of seventy-seven. There were so many things he didn't understand—not in a *to each their own* way, but in the *how does anyone* capacity. He wasn't sure he'd call whatever was offending the air at the moment *music*.

Yet Charlie was bounding up and down, a dopey grin on his face. Granted, the dopey grin faltered a bit when Charlie realized Will was not joining his excursion into aerodynamics. After a few prolonged seconds, he stopped hopping, a fine layer of sweat lining his brow and molding his curly blond hair to his forehead, which wrinkled as he frowned.

"Come on, Will," Charlie whined. "Can't you pretend to have fun just for one night?"

"I said I'd come. I made no promises about enjoying myself."

Charlie rolled his eyes and released a dramatic sigh. "You could suck the fun out of just about anything. You know that, right?"

Will shrugged. "And yet you still insist I come along."

"'Cause you need to learn how to cut loose. I'm not going to be around forever, you know."

Will paused and seized Charlie by the shoulder. "Wait. You didn't bring me here to tell me you're dying, did you? I'd think you'd at least have the decency to get me a drink first."

There was a moment where Charlie was very clearly struggling to keep a straight face—a feat that had never been easy for him. When the serious moments came, he could usually pull himself together long enough to absorb the important stuff, but he was happier in the space between them. In that regard, he was Will's polar opposite. It was likely one of the reasons they had managed to stay friends as long as they had. Will was there to translate when it seemed that Charlie never took anything seriously, and Charlie was there to explain that Will had been born in a bad mood and never grown out of it.

Charlie attempted to glare at him a few seconds longer, then gave up with a wry smile. "Fine," he said, and turned, scouring the room. "Drinks are—oh, yes. Let's go get one. Now. Let's go now. Over there. To get drinks. Now."

Translation: Charlie had seen a woman he found attractive.

Will sighed and clapped his friend on the shoulder again. "Lead the way, will you?"

"Gladly."

And then he was off, and Will followed, weaving between bouncing frat boys and grinding, practically nude couples, and a few giggling girls who looked just barely out of high school. Charlie didn't spare them a glance, much to Will's relief. Instead, he continued in a solid beeline toward the table spread with the night's alcoholic offerings.

Two girls were standing next to an ice-filled bucket, which crested with the bottlenecks of subpar beer, and Will knew immediately who had caught his friend's eye. The girl on the right wore a cream sweater, a pair of hip-hugging slacks of the same color, and the contrast to her rich, dark skin created the illusion of a perpetual spotlight. Her brown hair had been pulled from her face and pinned at her nape in an elegant twist. She was, in a word, stunning, and every bit Charlie's type.

Her friend was laughing so hard her body seemed to be caving in on itself for support. Her eyes were squeezed shut, her face sparkling with tears. She wore black leggings paired with boots that wrapped around her calves, and a vibrant red blouse that was shorter in the front than the back. Her skin was the color of moonlight—a beacon in a sea of spray tans. Her long brown hair fell in tumbles around her shoulders, a bit wild but in such a way he could tell it was intentional. And the earnest way she laughed made her shine.

For a moment, Will felt like he had been sucker punched. His chest tightened, a ball of pressure collapsing somewhere in the vicinity of his gut. The air seemed to pulse, pulling on him until his feet gave way and he found himself moving closer. It had been a long time, a damn long time, since he'd had such a visceral reaction to a woman. Since his skin had hummed and his palms had dampened, and his tongue had found itself stuck to the roof of his mouth.

He didn't like it. Especially here. He was too old for coeds. Didn't matter that he was one himself—the unexpected break he'd taken from finishing his degree meant the students who were his peers also happened to be dramatically younger, and he had no interest in getting involved with someone who couldn't yet legally drink.

Or at all with anyone from Meryton. They had a reputation.

He knew this, yet knowing it didn't magically make the woman he was looking at—no, the girl; she couldn't be a woman yet—less appealing.

It just made her dangerous.

Charlie nudged him hard on the shoulder, breaking Will out of his stupor. "Come on. Introduce me."

Will blinked. "What do you mean, introduce you?"

"What do you think I mean?"

"I think if I'm going to introduce you to someone, I should know who that someone is first."

Charlie pointed as though it was obvious. "Her," he said. Will noted that his eyes had taken on a somewhat dreamy, faraway look.

"Yes," he said, torn between irritation and amusement. "I put that together."

"So what's the problem? Introduce me."

"The problem is *I* don't know her. An introduction from me isn't going to mean much, is it?"

That seemed to snap Charlie out of his stupor. He blinked and gave his head a shake, then favored Will with a skeptical look.

"What?" Will asked.

"Everyone on campus knows who you are and you know it."

Ah. There it was. The curse of his family legacy surfaced again. Will sighed heavily. "I still don't know them, so I'm not going to—"

"Do that thing from *How I Met Your Mother*."

"The old sitcom?"

Charlie nodded with barely contained enthusiasm. His attention had returned fully to his target again, and the dreamy look was back.

Will refused to follow suit. He didn't need to find the brunette any more intriguing than he already did. It was bad enough that he could hear her talking, her voice animated, and the few words that cut through the noise were not only multi-syllabic, but used in the correct context.

"Just walk up to them," Charlie instructed, "and ask if they've met me."

"Why on earth would I do that?"

"Because you're a good friend and that's what good friends do."

"Make asses out of themselves?"

"When necessary."

"Why can't you introduce yourself?"

Charlie broke away from salivating over the pair long enough to favor Will with a smirk. "'Cause I have you here to do it for me."

Will rolled his eyes. "You're a grown man, Charlie. You pay your taxes and everything. Go introduce yourself."

"That's boring." But Charlie didn't need any actual encouragement, it seemed, because he had stumbled forward without further prompting.

Will would have been annoyed if he weren't amused, because that was his friend all over.

Charlie didn't need help with women. He enjoyed getting it where he could, and even further enjoyed pushing Will hard against his own boundaries to see if his comfort level had any give. On occasion it did, but not by much and not often. And when push came to shove, Charlie thankfully knew when to knock it off and respect that the line.

But not tonight, apparently.

Will watched Charlie approach the women, the one on the right—the one he seemed most interested in—noticed him first. She flashed him a smile and extended her hand to his.

"Jane," he heard her say. "Pre-law."

"Of course you are!" Charlie boomed enthusiastically. "Excuse me while I take the fifth on everything."

She laughed, and it was a sweet, pleasant sound that seemed authentic, as though his joke was actually clever.

"What year?"

"Third," Jane replied, beaming wider still. "You?"

"Same. Though in nothing as exciting as law." He looked to Jane's friend briefly, then flashed the same smile that had gotten him laid throughout high school. "Business."

"That's exciting," Jane said.

"You're sweet to say so," he replied, grinning at her.

Finally, Jane's friend stepped forward and decided to insert herself into the conversation. "I'm Elizabeth."

"Of course you are!" Charlie boomed again. "Elizabeth, I want you to meet a friend of mine." Then he turned and grinned at Will.

Don't do it. Don't—

"Will, stop being antisocial and get over here."

There was every chance he would murder Charlie when they were alone again. Will drew in a deep breath, tried to resurrect the polite smile he'd always worn at his parents' various functions, and marched over with all the enthusiasm of a man headed toward the gallows.

"This is Will," Charlie said loudly, throwing an arm around him once he was within arm-throwing range. "Now, don't let his soulful eighty-six year old eyes fool you. He is only a bit older than me..." His voice dropped conspiratorially. "And a *freshman.*"

If ever a hole were to spontaneously appear beneath his feet, now would be the time. Either to drag him into the pits of the underworld or provide him some sort of weapon with which to bash over his so-called best friend's blond head—either would be appropriate.

"I am too, actually," Elizabeth said. "Glad to know I won't be the oldest freshman in the class."

"That remains to be seen," Will said immediately, his mouth acting of its own accord. "How old are you?"

Elizabeth cocked an eyebrow. "Pretty sure that's one of those questions you're never supposed to ask, isn't it? How old are *you*?"

"Twenty-five."

She blinked. "Wow. You *are* an old freshman."

Yes, like he needed a reminder of that.

She looked at him expectantly, the way everyone did when they learned he wasn't a doe-eyed recent graduate of a preppy high school. Of course, once they learned his name, most people were smart enough to keep their stupid mouths shut. Somehow he didn't think that tactic would work on her.

Finally, Will realized the conversation wasn't going to change without help, and cleared his throat. "There were circumstances."

"What kind?"

The none-of-your-business kind. "My mother died."

That was actually just the tip of the iceberg, but he didn't need to say more. Elizabeth looked rather abashed. Served her right for prying.

"Do you live on campus?" Charlie asked, his gaze pinned on Jane. The guy had never once learned how to be subtle.

"Yes," Jane said, a pretty blush staining her cheeks. "Elizabeth and I are roommates, actually. We're at the Longbourn dormitory."

They might as well be rooming on the moon. That proclamation alone told Will everything he needed to know.

Meryton had a reputation—the sort of reputation grounded more in truth than gossip. It was twenty miles outside of New Hertfordshire, where some of the oldest families in the damn country still called home and the income discrepancy was dramatic. Many of the families, particularly those set in tradition and slow to adapt—had lost everything as the world around them changed. After the housing bubble had popped, those who had been struggling to remain ahead, or spending extravagantly with money they didn't have in order to look like they still belonged, had long-since crashed and burned.

But those families still sent their kids to Meryton. Some riding the school's scholarship program, if their children were bright enough to qualify, and others taking out exorbitant student loans to keep up appearances. Second and even third mortgages taken out on old estate homes just so the neighbors didn't gossip.

Pride didn't have a price for these families.

Because Meryton was a family legacy for most of New Hertfordshire. Because more US presidents had graduated from Meryton than any other college. Because that was where the money was.

Where New Hertfordshire's elite still sent their eligible sons.

Where New Hertfordshire's struggling but prideful poor sent their daughters.

And *that* was the exact reputation Longbourn dormitory had. Right or wrong, fair or not. It was the catch-all dorm for students who didn't have rich parents to pull strings.

"Longbourn," Will said shortly. He tried to catch Charlie's eye, but his friend was too enraptured with Jane.

"Yes," Elizabeth replied. "Why? Where are you guys?"

The question was enough to peg her as a scholarship student rather than someone relying on loans. Student loan recipients at least knew enough to try and fake it for the first few days.

"Netherfield Heights."

Something flashed in Elizabeth's eyes. "Ah."

Will arched a brow. "Ah?"

"Yes. It's a noncommittal sound people make when they have something they want to say but aren't sure it's appropriate for polite company."

Jane's jaw fell. She elbowed her friend hard enough to earn a croaky wheeze. "Lizzie!"

"Ow."

"That was rude."

"So was trying to pry apart my ribs with your elbow." She made a face and rubbed at her side. "Remind me not to panic if we ever lose the can opener. Your bones can cut through steel."

"What inappropriate comment did you want to make about Netherfield Heights?" Will asked.

"Nothing," Jane said. "She's just kidding."

Elizabeth, though, wasn't paying attention. "You guys are snobs."

Charlie burst out laughing, and Jane followed with a nervous titter.

"You're funny," Charlie said, slapping Elizabeth hard on the back and flashing a good natured grin. "Isn't she funny, Will?"

"Hysterical."

"You guys should talk more." Charlie seized Jane's hand and she didn't put up a fight. Not that Will had expected her to; if she did, she'd be the first. "Come on," his friend said, tugging. "Let's let them talk."

Jane nodded, her face brightening—either at the prospect of leaving the conversation or getting some alone-time with Charlie, or both.

Elizabeth watched her friend disappear into a mass of people, a small smirk playing with her lips. It was, he conceded, a pleasant smirk, and a pleasant set of lips. But then, he'd known that across the room.

What he hadn't known when he'd been across the room? She was a pain in the ass.

Not surprising. Somewhat disappointing. Overall, a blessing in disguise. Because if she wasn't a pain in the ass, he might be tempted to do something stupid like ask for her number or follow Charlie's example, and the last thing he needed was another goddamn complication.

"I haven't known Jane long," Elizabeth said after a long moment. "Just long enough to understand she's one of the nicest people on the planet. So I'm not sure if your friend is just dicking her around or not, but she isn't the casual fuck sorta girl."

Will's jaw became entangled with a sudden, embroiled battle with gravity. "Excuse me?"

"I'm just saying. Your friend hurts my friend in any way and I'm going to become his least favorite person in the world." She favored him with a smile. "I've been away for a while, but I do remember that trust-funders rarely had anything to do with us mere mortals unless it was to get their dicks wet. And I really have no patience for that kind of thing anymore."

Heat flared and began straining up his neck until he thought his ears might blow steam. "Are you always this crude?"

Her eyes—perfect, almond-shaped eyes—narrowed. "Do you always have a stick up your ass?"

"Well, I suppose that answers one question."

"I'm just looking out for my friend."

"They're just dancing." Though, from the glance he stole across the room, their version of dancing was apparently simulated sex. He'd never understood how two people could go from not knowing each other's name to ready to fuck in the span of ten minutes. Perhaps why he'd never fit in here, even with his last name credentials. "She doesn't look like a hostage, does she?"

"Again," Elizabeth said, her tone annoyingly measured. "I'm just looking out for my friend."

"By implying mine's an asshole."

"Rich boys used to getting what they want and damn the consequences. Sound familiar?"

Will swore hotly under his breath. He needed to get away from this woman. Now.

Though the thing that really pissed him off was that she wasn't too far off the mark. Charlie liked everyone. Hell, he was an equal opportunity man-whore. He fell in and out of love faster than a hormonal teenager, and while he never meant to cause anyone harm or heartache, there had been the notable scorned ex or two who didn't realize his attention was on the fleeting side. He was just so damn nice that people rarely called him on it.

But truth had nothing on loyalty. Charlie was the best friend a man could ask for, and Will would not stand by as anyone, especially a woman he'd just met, dragged him through the mud.

Except when he opened his mouth to fire back at her, his eyes connected with hers and his stomach dropped. He saw his own fire reflected back at him—the same drive to protect and defend—and the part of him that was hard with anger began to soften.

He didn't think he'd ever meet a girl here who wouldn't go out of her way to kiss his ass.

It didn't help when she released a long sigh and seemed to deflate. "Look," she said. "I'm really not some psychotic mega-bitch. Not that, you know, you'd know it from this conversation. I'm just..." She trailed off, seeming to consider her words, then shook her head. "Never mind."

Will forced a small smile. "I don't think anyone could blame you for being protective."

"As long as *protective* isn't mistaken for *rabid*." Elizabeth smiled, and this time it lit up her face. Brown eyes had never stood out to him before, but there was something both mischievous and sincere in her look, more expressive and telling than anything he'd seen before.

Elizabeth waved at the throng of writhing coeds. "You wanna..."

"Ahh, no," Will said shortly. The words came before his brain could catch up, so it occurred to him after the fact that he might have sounded more clipped than he intended. He couldn't help it—it was a visceral reaction to the suggestion of entering any swarm of sweaty, half-naked people. He'd been groped a time too many, thank you very much.

The smile that had begun to brighten Elizabeth's face fell just as quickly. "Oh. Well, I'll just..." She waved magnanimously. "Leave you to it, then."

A thousand synapses in his brain began firing at once, screaming at him to do something, say something, to clarify what he'd meant. His tongue, overwhelmed with options, was rendered motionless. He wound up staring at her as she turned and disappeared into a sea of people.

For a few dumbfounded seconds, Will stood completely still, trying to make sense of what had just happened. Though he regretted not being more eloquent in his refusal, he couldn't help but feel that perhaps his brain's lack of preparation had been for the best. Because the last thing he needed—the very last thing—was to get involved now.

His father had known returning to college would be an issue after the funeral, which was why he'd stubbornly made Will's education a stipulation of his inheriting the Darcy Media empire. Still, the old man hadn't known the funeral would be the easy part. He couldn't have.

Now that he was here, Will needed to remain focused.

And something told him that Elizabeth, or any woman like her, would not help with that goal.

In the end, this had to be for the best.

2

Ugh. She really hated this party.

Elizabeth didn't know who she was angrier with—herself for getting into a situation in which she could be rejected—or Will for doing the actual rejecting. It was the third random surge of uncontrollable emotion she'd experienced since Mr. Charming Pants had decided to insert himself into her conversation and begin his quest of *charming the pants* off Jane. Hence his name. Mr. Charming Pants.

But that Charlie guy had at least been personable. His friend, Will, had looked like he'd rather be getting a root canal sans Novocain. His holier than thou expression throughout their entire conversation had given Elizabeth the distinct impression that he was a massive tool. Something in the way his chin seemed gravity-resistant.

And that would have been fine—she could have laughed at that had the guy not been so much fun to look at. Elizabeth had a natural mistrust of pretty men, but Will was a step beyond pretty. He didn't have the new penny shine that Charlie exuded, or the rather, the puppy-like enthusiasm. No, he looked...older, if not physically then certainly in spirit. Like he hated this scene even more than she did.

He also wasn't built like a brick-house, which was a small thing, but something she couldn't help but admire. Elizabeth had never been the type to go gaga over beefy dudes. Muscles she liked, but not the sort that made her think the guy lived at the gym. More like Will, whose shoulders looked firm and arms defined without being obnoxious. He also sported killer cheekbones, a strong jawline, and deeply intense brown eyes that made the verbal sparring almost worth it. His hair was not super short or shaggy, and had just enough wave in it to make her think about running her hand through it.

Which was an impulse she didn't need or want, so she'd lashed out. But hey, at least she recognized her own bad behavior enough to try and walk it back. Even if the gesture ended up failing in a big ole way.

It wasn't even that he'd turned her down—Elizabeth wasn't one to shake her groove thang anyway. Not at parties like this. Give her a hairbrush and a mirror and she could karaoke with the best of them. And she wasn't allergic to fun, but she did have to try a bit harder when pressed from all sides by sweaty, therefore smelly, naked man-flesh. Still, she'd been known to kick back, imbibe a few, and even adapt an *if you can't beat 'em* attitude—every now and then.

Yeah. She was a certified fun-haver.

The crux of the insult where Mr. Tight Ass was concerned was that he hadn't made an apology or even attempted to look rueful. It had been quick and curt, and damn her, she was human. That much *did* hurt.

The jackass.

Elizabeth got about twenty feet before realizing what she really wanted was a drink, and she'd just left the place where she might get one. Thankfully, being that it was a college party—another table wasn't too far off.

A few grunts, shoves, and several unwanted touches later, and she was pouring herself a liberal amount of beer, which promptly went down the pipe. Then she poured herself another.

Perhaps she should just call it a night. After all, she'd done what she said she would. The Greggii House welcoming party was everything she'd thought it would be, and yet she'd come anyway because she liked Jane.

Only now Jane was gone, likely in some dark corner with Charlie's tongue stuck down her throat, and Elizabeth had polished off a beer and was considering the virtues of drunkenness.

Yeah. Perfect way to restart her life.

What she needed was a moment away from this party to collect herself.

Elizabeth looked around for an exit point and spotted one almost instantly—a door tucked into a corner. Hopefully one that led to a room that wasn't occupied with people fucking.

Only one way to find out.

She managed to get to it without getting trampled in a sea of hormones, announced herself with a tentative knock, then pushed the door open. The space behind it turned out to be a coat closet.

Elizabeth heaved a sigh—one that she felt all the way to her toes—and pushed herself into the confined space. Shutting the door muffled some of the noise, but not enough to matter too much. She had just enough space in her brain to think.

And pull her phone out of her bra to see if it was late enough to bail without looking like a killjoy.

There was a text waiting for her. One from Mom.

I don't know how you could do this to me. You're a hateful child.

Elizabeth inhaled a sharp breath, hating that her first instinct was still to cry. She should be numb to this sort of thing.

But there wasn't enough numb in the world to soothe this ache.

It took a moment longer to compose herself than she would have liked. Elizabeth wasn't a fan of breaking down in public, and though most everyone on the other side of the door was too drunk to notice and unlikely to remember her if they did, the threat of being seen emotionally compromised had her combating tears longer than normal. After she was certain she wouldn't dissolve into a blubbering mess, she stuffed her phone back into her bra, straightened her shoulders, and grabbed the closet doorknob.

"No, Will, I'm not leaving yet."

And promptly froze.

"You have a seven a.m. class," came the reply from Snooty McSnoot. "Don't give me that look. You all but commanded me to drag you out of here after two hours."

Their voices were surprisingly clear, given all the sound competition. They must have stopped right outside the door. Elizabeth held her breath.

"Well, I changed my mind," Charlie replied.

She let it out and decided that, in the interest of full disclosure, she really should make herself known. It wasn't polite to listen in on other people's conversations.

"Uh huh," Will drawled, sounding about as enthusiastic as Elizabeth felt. "More likely you're looking to get laid. You might as well forget it—her friend's decided to nominate herself Chief Cockblocker, so she's more trouble than she's worth."

Elizabeth froze, her hand still on the doorknob, now clammy and slick. The desire to announce herself dissipated in a blink.

"I don't think I've ever heard you use the word *cockblocker*," Charlie said. "I assume you're talking about the friend."

Will grunted.

"And here I thought you two had gotten chummy."

"She's obnoxious," Will replied forcefully. "And vulgar."

"Jokes aside, man, are you *actually* ninety or something?"

"You left me alone with her."

"I didn't realize you needed a babysitter, Will."

"You know I don't like these things." He sighed—one of those sighs that originates somewhere in the bottom of the stomach and emerges with a growl. It damn near rattled the door. "And you always do this. You always beg me to come along—"

"Begging is a strong word, I think."

"Then take off the moment you see a girl you want to fuck."

"I don't think you understand how this whole *wingman* thing works," Charlie replied. "And don't talk like that about Jane."

"So you *don't* want to fuck her?"

"I'm just saying I... I think I like this one."

Will groaned. "Don't tell me. She's not like other girls."

"She's really not. And from what she told me about her friend... What was her name again?"

"Elizabeth."

"Yes."

"Well," Charlie said, "from what Jane said, she's really nice."

Will barked a short laugh. "Nice. Perhaps when her fangs aren't showing."

"You're not exactly a people person yourself, you know."

"I don't go biting the heads off of random strangers."

"Well, no. That'd be hell on your teeth."

"It's just... I don't know." He paused, seeming to struggle to find the right words. "Not attractive."

A pang struck Elizabeth in the center of her chest—hard, unforgiving, and familiar. Just as familiar as the resounding swell of anger that rippled from the impact, rolling hard toward a boiling hot explosion.

Not attractive. Not fucking attractive?

That was so it.

Stifling a growl, she jerked the door open. It caught Will in the shin on the out swing, and he released a woof of pain before his eyes found hers.

And the color promptly drained from his pompous face.

"And here I so badly wanted you to like me," she spat.

"I... I..."

Charlie picked his jaw up from the floor and started to laugh. Elizabeth ignored him.

"This might come as a shock to you, assface," Elizabeth continued, slamming the door shut with enough force that a few heads turned, "but my self-worth is not dependent on whether men find me attractive. Especially not over-important douchebags like you. So you can take that 1950s attitude of yours, ball it up real nice, and shove it up your ass."

She didn't wait to for his response. The residual heat of her anger had started to melt into something uglier and less manageable, and those damn tears were threatening again. It'd be a cold day in hell before she let any rich asshole see her cry.

Elizabeth spun on her heels and took off at a rapid pace.

This time, the crowd parted like the freaking Red Sea.

Good. There had to be some perks to losing one's shit at a party.

3

By the time Will dragged himself over the threshold at Nether-field Heights, he felt like complete shit.

His mind, the helpful asshole that it was, kept dragging him back to that space. To the indignation on her face, the fire in her eyes.

The hurt.

That was what hit him the hardest. In his world, pissing people off was just part of being alive. No one liked the stuck up rich kid, and those who did typically had their own interests at heart. People wondered why the wealthy stuck to each other—in Will's case, it was because he knew Charlie was a true friend, not someone looking for a loan or a favor. While Will hardly went out of his way to be an ass to anyone, he knew that *ass* was how he came across. It was a defense mechanism, one passed down through generations of Darcy men.

At the moment, though, he was hard pressed to remember a time when he'd said something that had hurt someone on a personal level. Not just someone—a woman he...

Just say it, you coward.

A woman he found attractive. That seemed safe enough.

Not that he'd gone out of his way to hurt her. How the hell had he been supposed to know that she was in the coat closet? That she could *hear* him over the mesh of screaming lyrics, ear-blasting chords, and general chatter that made up any decent college party?

Apparently, he'd backslid into anger.

Will stood still for a moment, not knowing where to go. If the Netherfield workout room had anything practical—more than the five-pound weights and the shiny machines—he might have been tempted to burn off some of this frustration.

As though triggered by his thoughts, he heard a door open from down the hall. A moment later, Charlie's sister Caroline strolled into view, wearing practically nothing, which he supposed was the point.

"Will? You're back early." Caroline paused, her hip jutting at an angle that couldn't be comfortable. Her blonde hair was pulled into a ponytail that managed to be both messy and elegant, and her eyes—the same blue as her brother's—were round with concern.

Concern Will could see right through. And though he didn't think he had the patience to deal with her tonight, he managed to find it all the same. "You too," he said, gesturing. "I thought you'd still be out there."

Caroline wrinkled her not-unattractive forehead and made a face. "No. I've never been one for those parties."

That wasn't the story Charlie had told, but Will decided not to call her on it.

"You seemed to be having fun, though," she said, her eyebrows winging up. "You and Charles both. Did he really go home with her?"

"Which one?"

"Don't play dumb, Will. The girl from that trashy dorm. What's it called?"

Will sighed. "Longbourn. I—I don't know if he went home with her." Though smart money was on the bet that he had. Will just didn't want to go there—he didn't like the idea of Caroline passing judgment on Jane, though he wasn't sure why in the world he should care either way.

Except that wasn't true. He knew why he cared.

"What about you?" Caroline asked, her eyes sparkling with interest.

"What about me?"

"You and that girl—I saw you talking with her. She was with..." Caroline gestured as though doing so was an acceptable substitute for a name. "That black girl."

Will's jaw tightened and he forced himself to bite his tongue. "That was her roommate, apparently." And just thinking about her made him feel things he didn't want to feel. Before his brain could catch up with his tongue, he heard himself saying, "Elizabeth. She's a pill."

And that was a mistake. There was nothing Caroline Bingley loved more than a reason to hate someone. Particularly if that someone, Will had noticed, happened to be a pretty woman in his line of sight.

"I'm glad you said so," Caroline said, her practiced smile blooming on her lips—the one that feigned compassion in place of the real thing. "I didn't want to say anything rude in case you liked her."

"No," Will replied, forcing a smile. "No, I don't. She's...*passionate,* I suppose. Really outspoken."

Caroline nodded eagerly. "She seemed to be dressing you down when I saw her."

The smile on his face nearly became authentic, which startled him. "Ah...yes. She's very protective of her friend. She wanted me to know that if Charlie hurt Jane, she had a shovel with his name on it."

Caroline snorted and rolled her eyes. "Classy," she replied.

The door behind him crashed open the next moment, and the air filled with the rich baritone of slurred singing.

Saved by the drunk.

Will turned around just in time to catch Charlie as he stumbled to a halt beside him, a dopey, lovesick look on his face.

"Will!" he exclaimed, grabbing Will by the upper arm. "You...you will not *beliefth* the *angel* I met tonight."

"God, Charles." Caroline scowled and stepped away from him. "You smell like a brewery."

Charlie beamed. "Thankth you."

"What happened to you?" Will asked.

"I was gonna askth you the sthame thing." Charlie staggered a step, which was impressive given he hadn't moved. "You tisappeared on me."

Charlie had a tendency to morph into Daffy Duck when drunk.

"And you got wasted in the span of, what, twenty minutes?"

"Twenty *goooood* minutes." He turned to Caroline. "She's an angel."

"So I heard," Caroline replied dryly.

"You'll luff her, Carrie." Charlie moved forward a few feet. "She's soooo schmart. And pretty. And schmart. She knowths all the things."

"You did shots, didn't you?" Will asked. "Charlie..."

"Shots!" Charlie yelled, pumping a victorious hand into the air. "I am the winner!"

Will heaved a long sigh and exchanged what he hoped was a suitably apologetic look with Caroline. "I better get this moron to bed."

"Don't know what we'd do without you, Will."

Charlie seemed in full agreement. He swirled around and slung an arm over Will's shoulder. "Willth's my favorite," he proclaimed, then planted a wet, slobbering kiss on Will's cheek. "You're my favorite, Will."

"Thank you."

"Am I your favorite?"

"At the moment, no. But ask again tomorrow."

Charlie sighed happily. "Okay. But remind me."

"I will."

Will managed to get Charlie upstairs, which was no small feat, given Charlie attempted to escape more than once. By the time Will had maneuvered his way into his friend's room, Charlie was on the seventh verse of "One Hundred Bottles of Beer on the Wall" and gave no indication of quieting down.

"I like Jane, Willth," Charlie said dreamily as he reclined on his bed, his face contorted into what must have been the world's dopiest smile. "I think she might be the one."

Will grunted to indicate he'd heard and pulled off Charlie's right shoe.

"She'th gonna be a lawyer, you know."

"Did you let her see you this drunk? Because that might have been a deal breaker for her."

Charlie didn't answer. Instead, he went back to humming to himself.

"Sleep on your side," Will said, then, realizing he might as well have spoken to the wall, heaved his friend off the mattress as best he could to position him appropriately. Once Charlie was on his side, a stack of pillows against his back and the waste-basket within reach, Will drew back and wiped his brow with his sleeve. "All right. Stay like that, okay?"

"Mmm..."

Charlie's eyes had fallen shut, and the next second, his loud snores filled the room.

When Will returned to his own room, he felt like he'd won a personal war. Every inch in his body screamed for sleep, his mind becoming sluggish. He went through the rituals of getting ready for bed on autopilot. Once under the sheets, he was certain he'd be dead to the world the moment his head hit the pillow.

Except that didn't happen. Will found himself staring at the ceiling, his uncooperative mind lulling like an overheated engine, then abruptly taking off again. In an instant, he was back at the party—that stupid party he should never have let Charlie drag him to—watching Elizabeth laugh at whatever Jane had said.

The girls he'd been raised with had a certain museum-like quality to them, and anyone else knew who he was—at least back home—and was always on their best behavior. Even the other girls at the party hadn't looked that free. They'd looked like starving artists desperate for validation.

Elizabeth either hadn't known or hadn't cared. Or if she had, she'd done a very good job hiding it.

As it had earlier, his mind pulled the emergency brake.

This way lies danger, Will.

He knew it. Just as he'd known the second he'd seen her. He was not the sort of guy to get distracted from an objective easily, and dating wasn't anywhere on the list.

Which was why the fact that a very real part of him had wanted to rewrite the damn list after just looking at Elizabeth scared the shit out of him. That fire hadn't burned out after she'd all but verbally assaulted him, and the way her face had fallen when he'd turned down her peace offering might as well have landed a physical blow.

But it was what had come after that would haunt him for days to come. In his desperation to create distance between his thoughts and his reality, he'd said things he'd never meant her to overhear.

He'd never meant her to...

Well, the damage was done. And if fate was fair at all, he'd never have to see her again. He figured she typically wasn't the sort for those types of parties, given that she'd ignored the main attractions of getting drunk and making out with a stranger. Odds of them sharing classes weren't great, so aside from possibly passing her on campus, their paths would never again cross.

His brain had been fixed on the mental image of her for so long that other parts of his anatomy were getting ideas. Elizabeth's face was so clear in his mind. Those beautiful dancing eyes, the way her lips curved into a smile. The damn near melodious sound of her laughter.

His cock tented against his boxer shorts. Will stifled a groan, scrubbing a hand down his face. Wrong it might be, but that didn't do much to kill his boner, and though his brain was in conflict, his hand lacked any such reservations. He popped open the front flap of his boxers and drew his cock out before his stupid mind had the chance to catch up. His length strained toward the ceiling, begging for release, and he was too weak-willed to fight it.

Instead, Will gripped his shaft and began to stroke. And *goddamn* if that wasn't the perfect answer to everything. The clouds in his head parted, the strain of the evening fading back, and all he could see was Elizabeth.

Elizabeth and her laughter. The fire in her eyes.

The image of her on her knees before him, her lips parted, her tongue darting out to lick the head of his cock.

A hard moan rolled through his body, chased by a wave of guilt, but it was too weak to make much of an impact.

Emboldened, his mind upped the ante.

Elizabeth taking his cock into her mouth, those big brown eyes fixed on him. Elizabeth pulling hard, cupping his balls as her tongue massaged him, her head bobbing, her hair flying around him. He imagined hitting the back of her throat, of her moaning and gripping his ass to hold him there. Of her eyes telling him *it's okay. Do it.*

Then of her abruptly releasing him, flashing him a wicked smile as she pushed him onto the bed. She became naked—miraculously, because that was how fantasies worked—and he admired the smooth lines of her perfect milky skin as she straddled his waist and positioned his cock at the mouth of her sex.

And then she sank down, and he felt her clamp around him, slippery with excitement. She steadied her hands on his shoulders and began to move, leaving him with the breathtaking image of her bouncing breasts, of his cock disappearing inside her over and over again. And her eyes—on him. Demanding. Needy. And—

Will hissed, his hips jerking, and then he was coming. Pleasure shot wild through his veins as ropey strings of semen met the air before landing on his shirt. It went on forever, it seemed, because the image was so real he could almost see it. Almost *taste her.* And god, how he wanted to taste her.

Will lay still for several long seconds, gulping air as though he'd been lost at sea. The falling sensation continued, well past self-disgust and into the heart of unadulterated shame. At once, he felt dirty in a way that a thousand showers couldn't fix.

He'd used the thought of a woman he'd hurt to get himself off like a horny teenager.

And now he was covered in his own semen.

Fuck. One night out with Charlie—one night away from home—and he was acting no better than Wickham.

Don't think that name.

Will cursed and rolled out of bed, stripped off his boxers and tossed them into the corner with the rest of the dirty laundry.

Perhaps he'd try a shower after all. Get the sick feeling off him.

Tomorrow would be better. It had to be.

And hopefully he'd manage to get through it without thinking about things—*people*—he shouldn't think about.

4

Elizabeth knew before she entered the building that she was the first one back. Well, except for Mary, but Mary hadn't left to begin with, as she wasn't the social type. Kitty and Lydia, from what Elizabeth had gleaned, would likely be the last of the party to return for the evening, if either returned at all. Those girls were both in the running for most annoying housemates. It was a small miracle that their rooms were on the other side of the dormitory, else Elizabeth would accomplish very little.

The downstairs was empty, save an abandoned pizza box lying across the table. There was no noise coming from upstairs, either, so Mary had either retired early—smart thing to do—or was having another overwrought, hushed phone conversation with her girlfriend. Elizabeth sighed and shook her head. Poor Mary. Long distance just didn't work.

Every muscle in Elizabeth's body seemed to have fallen asleep without her permission. The act of dragging her ass upstairs became a herculean effort. Her ears were still ringing with the thumping base of the music, and every time she blinked, it seemed, Will's face was waiting for her. Like a bad flip book.

Elizabeth was a firm believer in the philosophy that the only people that could hurt you were the ones you allowed to do so. She certainly didn't give a shit what a pompous little rich boy thought of her. Except for whatever reason, his words remained on an endless loop.

And she should have known better than to extend an olive branch to a trust-funder who could likely pose for GQ on the side.

Fucker.

Elizabeth sighed, kicking off her boots, then her leggings before finally stripping her blouse over her head. Jane was a bit of a neat-freak, but hopefully she'd be too preoccupied on cloud nine to notice that her roommate's clothes, however temporarily, were scattered across the floor.

If Jane even came back tonight.

Elizabeth wrestled herself into an oversized tee and tried not to frown. Tomorrow was a busy day for both of them, and Jane didn't seem the type to shirk responsibility for a quick lay, even if she and that Charlie guy had been all over each other.

She shook her head to dispel the image and meandered over to her bookshelf. There was little to no chance she'd get any sleep until Jane got back—Elizabeth's overactive brain couldn't be bothered with a full night's sleep when there was a problem to be solved.

"No time like the present," she muttered, and grabbed *The Gunslinger* off her shelf. Might as well try to get into this for the seven thousandth time, though usually her eyes started to glaze over right around page ten.

Elizabeth climbed into bed, propped a pillow behind her, and cracked the book open.

No sooner had she read the first line—for the seven thousand and first time—did the whine of the front door echo from downstairs. The sound of giggling did not follow, so Elizabeth assumed it was Jane.

She focused harder on the book and tried to look engrossed. She didn't want Jane to know she'd waited up for her.

Not that Jane would have noticed, necessarily. After a minute or so, the dorm room door exploded inward, and a tired but blissful Jane waltzed over the threshold.

"Hi Lizzie," she said, dropping her keys on the dresser.

"Hey," Elizabeth said, keeping her eyes glued on the book.

"How long have you been home?"

"A while." Not technically a lie. A while was a loose enough term to apply to any measure of time. "How are you?"

"I'm...*perfect*."

"That's nice."

"Charlie is..." Jane stared off into space for a moment. "I have no words for him."

"I can think of a few," Elizabeth muttered. Jane, thankfully, didn't hear.

"He was just so sweet." She pulled her sweater off and—to Elizabeth's shock—tossed it over her shoulder. "We talked all night."

"You talked?"

"Well, he talked. I listened, but he's so much fun to talk to. And he's not bad on the eyes, either." Jane giggled. "Apparently, his father owns some corporation out of New York and insisted Charlie get an education before he took over."

Elizabeth tilted her head, somewhat impressed in spite of herself. "Really?"

Jane nodded, her eyes bright with enthusiasm. "Yes. And he's adamant about climbing the ladder. He wants to start small and prove to the shareholders that he belongs in the job and that his advancement, whenever it comes, isn't nepotism. He was really passionate about it, Lizzie."

Hmm. Good for him. Elizabeth thought it might be necessary to revisit her inner scorecard and evaluate the marks she'd given him.

"So did he try anything?" she asked instead. This would be the real test of character.

Jane shook her head. "No. We just danced. His hands remained above the waist at all times."

"You know what else is above the waist." Elizabeth pointed at Jane's considerable rack and arched an eyebrow.

"Lizzie!"

"Tell me I'm wrong."

"You're wrong. He didn't so much as look at my breasts all night."

She found that hard to believe, but decided not to challenge her friend. Instead, she changed tactics. "Did he ask for your phone number or anything?"

"He texted himself from my phone." Jane pulled her phone out of her bra as she kicked off her pants. If possible, her face brightened even further. "Oh! He's already texted!"

"Yeah?"

Jane beamed and tossed her the phone.

Elizabeth looked at the screen and blinked. It wasn't just one text message. Apparently, Charlie was a drunk texter.

Charlie: U mite be the prettiest girl Ive ever met. Thot u shld know.

Charlie: I miss u alrdy.

Charlie: Do u belief in love in first seeing?

Charlie: Plz. Must c u. 2morrow?

Charlie: Wil put me 2 bed. Cant stop thking bout u. Hope ur real.

Elizabeth wrinkled her nose, handing back the phone. "So... he's wasted."

"He offered to walk me back here but a few friends were going to do shots. I practically had to sign a permission slip to get him to go with them." Jane shrugged. "I think he really likes me."

"If not Charlie, then certainly drunk Charlie."

Jane's smile dimmed by a fraction. "Do you not like him?"

"I don't know him. I like *you* a lot and I'm probably going to be super suspicious of any guy who so much as looks at you." Not to mention some rather uncharitable thoughts she'd been having, mostly as an offshoot from her mind's preoccupation with Will. The last thing sweet Jane needed was to be some rich guy's idea of slumming.

But that was Jane's business. If she wasn't worried about Charlie's motives, then Elizabeth wouldn't be either.

"Sorry. That's my emotional baggage showing. The truth is, Charlie was fun to be around, and you clearly made an impression." She waved at the phone. "And that his go-to when super drunk was to send you sweet messages speaks volumes, I think. Unless you deleted a dick pic or twelve before you came in here."

Jane laughed and shook her head. "No dick pics," she said. "Hell, he didn't even go for the goodnight kiss until I asked him if it'd be all right if *I* kissed *him*. Even then, he was...sweet. Like he thought he'd break me."

"Then I can't think of any reason not to give him the Elizabeth Bennet stamp of approval."

"Really?"

"Really. That said, I reserve the right to decide he's an assface when and if I'm presented with conflicting evidence."

"That seems perfectly fair."

"I like to think so."

Jane grinned and started humming. She hummed all the way through her bedtime ritual—eventually picking up her clothes and therein proving she wasn't a pod-person. She

hummed as she brushed her teeth—which had to be messy—
and as she set her alarm.

Elizabeth was too awake to consider switching off her lamp
—due to both the thoughts churning in her head and Jane's
unending humming. In fact, were it not for the fact that Jane
seemed three seconds away from breaking into song amidst
chore-completing woodland creatures, Elizabeth might have
been tempted to scream something like, "Shut the hell up."

Alas, Jane *was* three seconds away from a Disney number.
She couldn't stop smiling, and Jane's smile was infectious.

"Oh, and he's *funny*," Jane said as she came back into the
room, dressed in a virginal white gown that would have looked
ridiculous on anyone else. "I don't think I've ever laughed
that much."

"He definitely knows the right things to say," Elizabeth
agreed, glancing back to the open book in her lap. Not that it
mattered. She still hadn't retained a word.

"His friend though...I didn't get as good a read on him."

Elizabeth pursed her lips and didn't look up. "Hmm."

"Did you? I should have asked." She paused. "I mean, aside
from the way you practically flayed him alive within the first ten
seconds."

"I did no such flaying. I just...*remember* what it was like when
I was here before. The trust-funders acted like they were royalty
while we were lucky to be breathing the same air." She shuddered. "Will was just entitlement personified."

"Charlie says he's a really good guy."

"Well, Charlie's a dude. Dudes have each other's backs. And
maybe Will's a good guy when he's around others who have
extra zeros in their bank account. From what I saw, he's an ass."
Elizabeth slammed her book closed. Definitely time to give up—
she wasn't going to finish the chapter tonight. "Also, if Will's a
freshman, there's a chance he and Charlie haven't hung around

each other much in the last few years. Maybe Will only recently got that stick up his ass."

"Did he say anything specifically? You seem to...*really* not like him."

Elizabeth wrapped her arms around her legs, trying and failing not to think about the horrified *oh god no* look he'd given her when she'd asked if he wanted to dance. "I tried to make nice after you guys left," she said. "Because even I can admit when I'm an asshole. He seemed to accept that and we went our separate ways. Then I took a breather for a moment—found a closet to decompress. It's been a while since I've peopled to this extent."

"Are you okay?" Jane asked at once. "If you were having a bad time, I—"

"I'm fine," Elizabeth said. "Tonight was good. *Promise.* I just needed a moment. But I heard Charlie and Will talking before I could come out. Charlie was nice," she added quickly at the curious and somewhat terrified look on Jane's face. "And yeah, he was gushing about you."

"Really?"

"I think we could have drawn cartoon hearts around him." She smiled weakly. "He asked Will about me and Will was... Well, not charitable."

Jane's expression went stony. "What did he say?"

"That my attitude sucks and I'm not attractive."

"What! That jerk!"

Elizabeth shrugged, hoping she came off as blasé. The last thing she needed was Jane or anyone thinking she gave a damn what Will thought of her. Because she didn't. At all. "What pissed me off isn't that," she said. "It's just...he dismissed me as a person because I'm *not attractive*. This is something that only happens to women. Men think they can rate our worth based on how *attractive* we are. You know, having a dirty mouth has been scientifically linked to higher intelligence, but if we drop a few expletives here or there—as the *fairer sex*—we're crude and *not ladylike* and all that bullshit."

Jane inclined her head. "Yeah, I think that attitude is pretty prevalent around here. But if we're gonna challenge the system, we need our beauty rest. Tomorrow's going to be a loooong day."

"I take it the professors here still haven't embraced the culture of handing out syllabuses on the first day and going over coursework in lieu of an actual class?"

Jane shook her head. "Sorry, hon. Be prepared to actually learn things tomorrow."

"Damn."

"You'll do fine."

"I'm going to be the old lady among a bunch of kids." Elizabeth wrinkled her nose and began edging down the mattress. Time to get some zs. "Remind me again that I don't want to drop out."

"You *don't* want to drop out." Jane climbed into her bed and pulled her blanket close. "Good night, Lizzie."

"'Night, Jane."

5

Of course.

Elizabeth stood in the doorway of the morning's first class, staring dumbfounded at the last face she wanted to see. To his credit, Will didn't look much happier to see her. Rather, the second their eyes connected, he coughed and shuffled in his seat, casting his gaze about the modest-sized classroom as though desperate for a diversion. It was just her freaking luck that the only available seat in the room was next to him.

Because obviously the universe hated her.

Also, somewhat served her right for not getting to bed until late. Then getting to class late, and clearly having the last pick of the seating.

Curse her for attending a college with a student roster that could probably fit on a postage stamp. If she were going to a larger school, this likely wouldn't have happened. But Meryton was small, tiny, even, and so were its classes—this factor being one of the key selling points to most.

And right now, a major thorn in her side.

Elizabeth heaved a sigh, shifted her book bag on her shoulder, and pressed through. She caught Lydia and Mary's eyes before she reached her desk, and gave them both a good glower for not saving her a seat.

Oh well. She could ignore Will today and make a point to get here earlier before the class met next.

Yet as she settled into her seat, she became aware of just *how* aware she was of his presence. And how aware he was of her. Though she didn't want to give him too much attention, she could feel him sneaking glances at her from the corner of his eye.

This was going to be a long hour.

"Good morning, everyone," came from the head of the room. A woman with graying blonde hair, glasses, and dressed in a conservative brown skirt with a matching cardigan stood next to a whiteboard.

Elizabeth reached over to dig out a notebook and pen.

"Welcome to Introduction to Ethics," the woman continued. "I'll be playing the part of your professor, Sally Greenfield. As the course name suggests, this is an introductory class designed to help you get a better understanding of the subjectivity of ethics in the modern world. If you decide to stick with it—which I very much recommend—you'll find that Meryton has a great selection of more career-based courses depending on your major or post-college plans as you advance."

The professor stopped for a moment, ostensibly to see if she'd lost anyone yet.

"We cover a lot of broad ground in this course," she continued, "and because of that, no topic is off limits. It's my goal to help you frame every substantive issue you encounter with its ethical virtues or faults. More than that, understand that your personal ethics"—she pointed at a student sitting near the back —"and yours"—she pointed at Will—"are not necessarily going to match, or if they do, not precisely. Understanding your own ethics, and being able to empathize with alternative views, will help you forge stronger relationships both in business and elsewhere."

Professor Greenfield deposited a briefcase across the table at the head of the class, popped it open, and pulled out a thin stack of paper. "Then we'll move on to the syllabus."

The professor divided the stack appropriately and issued one chunk to each row, horizontally rather than vertically, denying Elizabeth the opportunity to get out of this class without acknowledging Will's presence. She resolved to avoid eye contact with him regardless.

Yet she felt Will's gaze on her like it was a physical thing, and found she couldn't keep from looking at him. When their eyes connected, her breath caught and her face flushed with heat. His expression was both unreadable and tense, and in spite of herself, she felt something inside her seize.

"Here," she said, tearing her gaze from his and shoving the remaining syllabi into his outstretched hand.

"Thanks," he replied shortly.

Elizabeth released a long, calming breath before turning her attention to the syllabus. Overall, it looked fairly standard. Course required reading included *Fundamentals of Ethics, The Elements of Moral Philosophy,* and *Justice: What's the Right Thing to Do?* as well as a handful of essays. There were several debates scattered throughout the semester, with a team debate scheduled for the midterm. The final would consist of a term paper.

Easy peasy, lemon-squeezy.

"As you can see, we're going to do a lot of arguing," Professor Greenfield said. Her comment earned a collective smile. She grinned and inclined her head. "Who all took debate in high school?"

Elizabeth raised her hand and noted, not without a smirk, that Will did not. No matter that high school was nearly seven years behind her—she considered that a win in her book.

And yes, she was being petty. But she felt she'd earned it.

"Excellent." The professor nodded her approval at the show of hands. "Then this will come easy for you. You will not always find yourself on the side of an argument that you agree with. Investigating and understanding alternative views and their ethical arguments is a big part of what I expect you to take away from this class. But don't get too comfortable—if you *do* find yourself assigned to the side of a particular argument that you agree with, you must be *absolutely prepared* to make your case. The readings we do between these debates should help frame your arguments as much as possible. These arguments are intended to be persuasive, but every good debater comes prepared with sources to back them up. And no, not including Wikipedia."

"Dammit!" came a voice from the back. Elizabeth was fairly certain it belonged to Lydia.

"Before we leave today, I'm going to assign debate teams," Professor Greenfield said, apparently choosing to ignore the outburst. "Not every exercise will be a group effort, but for those that are, your team will be your defacto family throughout the rest of the semester."

At that, Elizabeth's heart plummeted. *Fuck. No.*

Will tensed as well and threw her a somewhat panicked look that only served to piss her off more. Because he obviously found even the possibility of having to work with her insulting.

God, this guy.

"So..." The professor reached into her briefcase and pulled out a single loose sheet of paper. "I don't take attendance," she informed them. "You're paying to be here. It's not my job to make sure you make every class. And that might mean that it takes me a bit to learn your names, because this is the one time you're going to see me refer to the class roster." She glanced at the roll call. "Elizabeth Bennet."

Elizabeth shot her hand into the air. "Yes, ma'am."

Greenfield nodded. "Okay. Why don't you pair up with Miss Wikipedia-lover in the back there?"

"Think that's Lydia," Elizabeth supplied.

Lydia answered by bursting out into giggles. The girl seemed incapable of other reactions.

"Oh." The professor's brows arched. "You know each other?"

"We live in the Longbourn dormitory." Elizabeth glanced sideways at Will, daring him to say something. She looked straight forward again. "Lydia, Mary and I do."

"Which one's Mary?"

"Right here," came the response from the back.

"Perfect. You're team one." Professor Greenfield beamed. "I'm good but not usually *that* good. Now none of you will be able to tell me you couldn't reach one of your teammates for whatever reason."

Elizabeth released a long breath, tension leaving her shoulders. Thank *god*.

"All right, moving on. Randall Brown, Penelope Crown, and Fitzwilliam Darcy will be team two." The professor paused, frowning at the roster. "Fitzwilliam Darcy," she echoed and looked up, scanning the students. "Where's Fitzwilliam Darcy?"

Will cleared his throat and waved a hand. "Here, Professor. And just *Will*, please."

"All right," she said, "Will, then. Is this Darcy as in Darcy Media Group? Darcy Foundation? The Fitzwilliam Darcy Scholarship?"

"Ah..." Will shifted a bit in his seat, and Elizabeth couldn't help but look at him. It wasn't conspicuous at least—everyone else was.

"Yes," he said.

Professor Greenfield's eyes rounded in sympathy. "I was sorry to hear about your father."

Will's jaw tensed, but his expression remained otherwise neutral. "Thank you. I appreciate it."

"That happened—what? Two, three years ago?"

He gave a clipped nod.

"And your mother..."

"She died before my father."

Despite everything, Elizabeth felt her insides start to thaw. The guy was clearly uncomfortable, and the professor, who seemed to be an otherwise intelligent woman, was either oblivious or uncaring of the fact.

"And you're just starting school now?"

"Yes."

"You're a little old."

"Yes," he said, shifting. "But I'm here."

"You seem to have taken your time."

"My sister needed me," he replied shortly.

And that was what did it. Those four words made something in Elizabeth's chest twist. Combined with the whispers that had sprouted around the room and the appraising, dollar-sign looks some of the coeds were shooting his way, Will was either on the fast track to being a piece of meat or a social pariah.

Most likely the former with the women and the latter with the straight men. Even Elizabeth had heard of Darcy Media.

"He's not the only old freshman here," Elizabeth volunteered loudly. The room fell silent again as attention diverted to her. "I think we're the same age." She turned to Will. "Twenty-four?"

He studied her a long moment, his face still inscrutable, but she thought she saw the corner of his mouth tick up. "Twenty-five," he said. "So I guess I am. The oldest."

"Not by much." She turned back to the professor, her pulse spiking. "My parents had a messy divorce that prevented me from completing my first semester here."

A round of giggles exploded from Lydia in the back. Others

were glaring at her as though she'd announced she kicked puppies in her spare time, and it didn't take much to guess why. Her unsolicited proclamation probably looked like an attempt to cozy up to the wealthiest guy in the class.

Though her cheeks burned, she forced herself not to blink. No one deserved to have their life put on display in front of a room of strangers.

"Oh," Professor Greenfield said, looking somewhat bewildered. "Well then. Thank you, Elizabeth. And welcome back."

Elizabeth shrugged. "You just seemed so interested in his personal life, I thought I'd share some of mine."

The professor gaped at her, a wild streak of red creeping up her throat as others joined in Lydia's gigglefest. Elizabeth held Professor Greenfield's gaze until the other woman bit the inside of her cheek and returned her attention to the roster.

She waited a long moment, then looked down and released a long breath.

Oh well. It wasn't like life here was going to be easy, anyway.

Elizabeth busied herself taking notes. The class was still in a stage of chatter, Professor Greenfield having seemingly lost her footing, though she managed to get through the rest of the team assignments as well as the chapters that were to be read before class next met. By the time the hour was over, Elizabeth was practically buzzing to shoot out the door.

But she didn't. She knew how that would look. Instead, she deftly packed her supplies, doing her best to seem unbothered by the glances the other students shot her way. Let them think what they wanted—none of it mattered. She wasn't here to make friends, after all, so whatever.

If she could sound half as confident in the real world as she did in her head, she'd take the university by storm.

"Lizzie!" Lydia came bursting up the aisle, her face flush

from giggling. "You know who he is, right? I mean, what *Darcy Media* is?"

Elizabeth cast a quick look to Will's chair. Thankfully empty. She'd been so focused on getting her own things together she hadn't noticed him escape. "Well," she said slowly, "I guess I do now."

"Do you have any *idea* how much money he's worth?" Lydia was practically bouncing on her toes. "Never mind, of course you do. Why'd you say that stuff about your parents?"

Mary stopped beside Lydia, her expression a solemn mask, as Elizabeth had come to expect. She adjusted her glasses and tucked a clump of brown hair behind her ear. "People often try to forge relationships through commonalities," she told Lydia. "Elizabeth was making it clear that Will was not alone and could—"

"That's not what I was doing at all," Elizabeth said shortly, swinging her backpack over her shoulder. She glanced toward the head of the room, where Professor Greenfield still stood. They made eye contact and for a second, Elizabeth anticipated an explosion, but none came. Instead, the professor clamped her briefcase shut and made for the door without a word.

"Then what were you doing?" Mary asked, tilting her head. "It seemed rather...abrupt."

Elizabeth sighed and began moving toward the door. "It was obvious she was making him uncomfortable," she said. "She stopped in the middle of class and started asking all sorts of personal questions, just because he has a famous name."

"And a lot of money," Lydia gushed. "I need to look up how much he's worth. He's kinda cute, in a boring kinda way. Don't you think, Lizzie?"

"No," she said shortly, though she felt her cheeks going warm. "And it doesn't matter. The professor shouldn't parade his or anyone's personal life out in front of everyone."

Lydia frowned. "But *you* did."

"I did to make a point."

"Did it work?"

"Obviously not."

The air burst with Pink Floyd's "Mother" before Lydia could bombard her with a new round of questions. If possible, Elizabeth's mood plummeted further south. She stopped and pulled out her cell phone. "You guys go on," she said. "I need to take this."

Lydia shrugged and practically skipped out of the room. Mary favored her with a curious look, but didn't say anything as she followed suit.

Elizabeth inhaled and swiped to accept. "Hi, Mom."

"What took you so long?" came the answering squawk. "Are you hurt?"

"No, Mom. I'm at class. Or I just got out of one, and I'm going to be late to the next so I can't talk long."

"Oh." A sniff. "I should've known you wouldn't have time for me."

Elizabeth took a measured breath, her stomach clenching. By the time this day was over, she would have aged about a decade. "We've talked about this, remember? It's not that I don't have time for you—it's that I can't answer every time you call. I need to—"

"Well, *excuse me* for needing help."

"Mom—"

"I'm sorry to be such a nasty inconvenience."

"I didn't say that. Don't put words in my mouth." She waited a moment, then continued in a gentler tone. "Do you remember what you promised me before I left?"

Another long beat passed, then the line erupted in a pitiful wail. "I'm such a bad mother."

Elizabeth sank behind a desk and slammed her forehead against her palm. "Mom, stop."

"I just can't do this by myself. I don't know how..." She dissolved into sobs that might as well have been daggers. "I can't get anyone to stay. Everyone leaves me."

"I'm right here."

"You couldn't wait to get out of here," her mother spat. "I've just been holding you back."

"Don't say things like that."

"Why not? It's true, isn't it? I know you've been telling your friends how awful I am. How glad you are to be rid of me."

Elizabeth blinked; her eyes were stinging. God, she hated it that her mother could get under her skin so easily, especially when she knew the words weren't born out of something genuine. This was the voice of the ugly, twisted entity that had consumed her mind, and made her a caricature of herself.

It had always been there, though had become more vocal and boisterous in recent years, worsened by resistance to doctors and medication and provoked by intense, unpleasant emotions. Elizabeth's failure to answer the previous night's text must have triggered an episode. Or Lynette Bennet had been snooping on her ex-husband's Facebook account again.

Elizabeth's mother was difficult to talk to on good days. On days like today, communicating was damn near impossible.

"Mom," Elizabeth said slowly. "Have you been to see Dr. Henderson?"

"I don't need Dr. Henderson. I need a daughter who cares about me."

"You promised me before I left that you'd make an appointment with Dr. Henderson. You told me I didn't need to take you. That you'd go on your own." A pause. "It might be time to have your medication adjusted again."

"I don't like those pills!"

Her breath caught. "You are taking them, aren't you?"

"The pills don't do anything. And neither will that doctor. He won't make your father leave that whore, will he?"

"Mom—"

"Or you any less selfish."

"It's not selfish of me to want to get an education," Elizabeth said firmly. "Please make an appointment with Dr. Henderson."

"Elizabeth..." A choked sob seized the line. "He's getting *married*."

Her stomach dropped. "Huh?"

"Your father...he... They're getting married. I saw it. I saw it on Facebook." Then she dissolved into hard sobs.

Elizabeth held her breath and squeezed her eyes shut. No, her father would not do this to her—leave her to find out something huge through the grapevine.

Would he?

Doubt and panic joined forces, familiar and toxic.

"Mom," she said, praying her voice was steady, "make an appointment with Dr. Henderson."

"Did you hear me? He's getting *married*. Married!"

"Yeah." There was that panic again. "You need to make that appointment. You're going to make yourself sick if you go on like this."

"How can he be getting married?"

Elizabeth expelled a deep breath. "I don't know. But he is, apparently, and that's his decision." She flicked her gaze to the clock at the head of the class and groaned. "Mom, I'm sorry, but I really need to go."

"You're just gonna leave me like this?"

"I'm not leaving you. I just need to go to class."

"I need you to help me!"

Anger was so much easier to navigate than heartache, so when it came again, Elizabeth embraced it. She slid to her feet once more and readjusted the bag on her shoulder. "I am helping you. After I get out of class, I'm going to call Dr. Henderson and schedule an appointment. Then I'll call a taxi and schedule them to pick you up."

"I don't need—"

"Mom. You. Promised. You're going to go. What you do when you get there is up to you, but you promised me you'd go and that's what's going to happen." She hoped. Without someone there to physically drag her mother to the doctor's office, it was anyone's guess as to whether or not she'd show up. "But I need to go now. I love you. I'll text you the details after I get your appointment booked."

"Elizabeth Bennet, don't you dare—"

Elizabeth ended the call, shaking. She waited for the pounding in her head to subside, the jittery feeling to start to normalize. Once she felt reasonably certain her legs wouldn't fail her, she bound out of the classroom and cut a quick left to haul ass out of the building.

And nearly plowed into Will, who stood beside the door. Who had clearly heard every freaking word.

Because *of course.*

"What the hell do you think you're doing?" Elizabeth sputtered, stepping back on reflex.

To his credit, he'd gone instantly pale, his eyes wide and filled with an emotion she didn't want to name, mostly because it looked a lot like pity. But fuck *to his credit.* What the hell was he doing, lurking outside an otherwise empty classroom, listening to a private conversation?

"I...I just wanted..." He looked around as though searching for signs of life, but there were none to be found. "I... Never mind."

"You wanted what? To spy on me?"

"No," he said emphatically, almost angrily, which was

fucking rich considering she'd caught him doing just that. "I wasn't spying—"

"Oh yeah." She made a show of looking up and down the hallway. "Clearly."

"I only wanted a word and thought I'd wait. I didn't know you'd be having such a..." But he looked as though he didn't know how to finish. Which was just as well. She was in no mood to hear it.

"You know what? Fuck you."

Elizabeth didn't wait for a response—she needed to get the hell out of there. Now. She bolted around him and all but flew down the corridor, her heart begging her feet to carry her back to the dormitory, but her brain retaining enough control to aim her where she needed to go.

The first day of class was sucking spectacularly.

But dammit, she would *not* give up without a fight.

6

Will blinked slowly, and realized for the fourth or fifth time that he must have spaced out. The blonde seated across from him—whose name had flitted out of his mind—was practicing one of those *don't look as pissed as you are* faces that he'd grown up around. He found this expression was almost exclusively in use by people who admired the fact that he or his family had a lot of money. Wealth had a way of excusing rude behavior.

"Sorry," he said in a flat tone. "I drifted off again."

She sighed and stretched a hand across the café table. "I understand," she said in one of those offensively fake tones. "It must be hard...talking about your father."

He didn't know about *hard*, but it definitely wasn't his favorite topic, especially with people he'd known for less than an hour. "It's fine," he said, hoping she'd read between the lines and spare him from having to be even blunter. He checked his watch. "It's been nearly a half hour. I thought you said our, ah, third was joining us."

She smiled and flipped her hair in a move so obviously practiced, that he had to wonder if it worked on anyone else. "Randall's on his way. He just likes to take his time. We went to high school together, you know."

No, he hadn't known. Nor did he care. "Well, I have a class at ten-thirty, so—"

"Can I just tell you how *brave* I think you are?" She smiled, tilting her head. "You said you took those years off to take care of your sister?"

"Ah, yes." Will turned to glance to the door again, willing someone he knew to arrive. At this point, he'd even settle for Caroline.

"That is *so sweet.*"

He forced a smile as he debated swearing off caffeine for life. He'd ducked into the campus coffee house after his last class for a much needed pick-me-up. The blonde had been waiting, introduced herself as someone from his new debate team in Greenfield's class, and asked if he'd like to join her and their third for a quick meet-and-greet. Randall was on his way, she'd said. He'd be there in a moment and they could discuss what their team roles would be for the semester.

Stupidly, Will had agreed. And it had become very clear after a few minutes that Randall and the class was the furthest thing from this girl's mind.

At least the blonde was achieving one thing—he didn't have much time to think about Elizabeth while contemplating escape routes.

"Oh my god," the girl said, looking over his shoulder, her nose wrinkling. "Is that...is that the girl from our class? The one who started talking about her parents?"

Will froze.

No.

"It *is* her. I remember thinking those shoes screamed thrift shop." The blonde rolled her eyes. "What was her deal?"

He counted to ten, then hazarded a glance over his shoulder.

Sure enough, Elizabeth was in line, her gaze fixed on the menu but bearing a certain quality that made him think she wasn't reading it at all.

He turned back to the blonde. The last thing he needed at the moment was to be spotted. They'd run into each other enough to last a lifetime.

"It's funny," the blonde said, trailing her fingers over his knuckles in a way that was undoubtedly supposed to be seductive, but just made her look like a little kid trying to act like an adult.

"What's funny?"

"She was ignoring you all through class. Well, ignoring is a bit tame—she seemed, I don't know, angry."

"You were watching her that closely?"

The blonde shrugged. "She looked too old to be in there, and her body language was not what I'd call friendly."

Will fought the urge to look over his shoulder. Old?

Then again, perhaps it was a matter of perception. The blonde barely looked old enough to drive, which in turn made *him* feel old because that time seemed so far away from where he was now.

He realized the blonde was looking at him expectantly and fought for something to say. "She's younger than I am."

"I think guys just wear it better. Anyway," the blonde said, leaning in, "she changed her tune almost immediately after the professor let it slip who you are."

Yeah, he'd noticed that too. Elizabeth had been dead-set on ignoring him until the professor started prying. Then she'd broadcast her own situation to the class, and he hadn't known why. Not at first. He'd wondered if it was a compulsion with her —to be loud and brass and volunteer information or make blunt, abrasive demands of people she'd just met.

It hadn't been until she'd met his eyes that he'd understood she'd been doing it *for* him.

He'd wanted to thank her afterward, and see, possibly, if they could start over. Well, start over insofar as apologize for his rude behavior and determine if it was possible to get through a semester in the same class. That surprise had been quite the ugly wakeup call this morning.

One way or another, Elizabeth seemed determined to occupy his thoughts. He figured he owed it to her, and himself, to see if he could make nice, just so the times where they were forced to interact wouldn't be so awkward. He didn't think he could stomach more classes like the one they'd shared today, and there was no telling how many other subjects they might have together over the course of their respective academic careers.

He hadn't meant to overhear her conversation with her mother. It had just happened.

"Will?" The blonde across from him waved a hand in front of his face. "Are you all right?"

He blinked and snapped back to himself, then flashed her what he hoped was a decently apologetic smile. "Sorry," he said. "Wandered off a bit."

"I don't blame you," she cooed, sliding forward in her chair. "Today must have been rough, reliving all that about your dad."

He felt his smile turn acidic. She seemed determined to talk about his parents. Or get him worked up so she could provide some comfort. Too damn bad. "Yeah, well," he said at length, "it's not something you forget or anything."

She nodded. "Well, do you have plans tonight? I thought we could...get started on the reading. See how we might tackle our assignments. Since we're going to be working together and all."

"With Randall, right?"

Her grin faded a bit. "Yes, with Randall."

"Who was supposed to meet us here."

"I told you. He's running late."

Will sighed heavily, but it did no good—he felt his temper steadily rising, and he couldn't afford to go off on her. He very much doubted the professor would allow him to switch groups. Or maybe she would, given that she'd seemed equally enthralled with the size of his bank account.

This was why Will didn't care for making friends.

"Well, I have a class here shortly and can't wait," Will said. "And we probably don't need to get together before we know what our assignment is, anyway. So I think we hold off meeting for now. I don't know yet how much work I'll have to do tonight and I need to make sure I have time to get all my reading in."

To her credit, the blonde didn't object, though her eyes lost the flirtatious shine and the corners of her mouth tipped downward. She nodded and rose to her feet, collecting her purse as she went. "Sounds good," she said. "I better get going too."

He couldn't help himself. "Not going to wait for Randall then?"

A light blush flickered across her cheeks. "Ah. No. He might have forgotten, and like you, I can't stay around here. My next class is across campus."

Will nodded. "Right."

"Well...umm...bye." She walked around him in a hurry, leaving him blessedly alone at last.

He waited for a moment, debated heading toward the lecture hall where his next class was being held, then decided his system could use another shot of caffeine. He hadn't exactly gotten much in the way of sleep last night.

His decision to linger, he told himself, had nothing to do with the fact that Elizabeth was nearby.

Nothing whatsoever.

She'd chosen a public place on purpose for this phone call. Hopefully, being around others would keep her from flying off the freaking handle.

After buying a blueberry muffin and the largest cup of coffee the Meryton Mudhouse offered, Elizabeth tucked herself into a corner booth, which provided a nice illusion of privacy. She still had a view of the bustling café, though, and the chatter around her was loud enough that she wouldn't forget herself.

Plus she'd spied Will across the room. Because he just had to be everywhere, apparently.

Elizabeth forced a sigh. It would do her no good to focus on that at the moment. Not when she had a call to make. She pulled out her phone and drew up her father's contact information, then hit the call button.

Her father answered on the second ring. "Lizzie, so good to hear from you."

"Hi Dad."

Two syllables. That was all it took. Two little syllables for her father to know this wasn't an ordinary call.

"What's wrong?" he asked. "Did something happen? Are you okay? I can be there in four hours."

"No," Elizabeth blurted, wiping at her eyes, which had started to sting. "No, I'm fine. Everything here is fine."

"You know I can tell when you're lying to me, don't you?"

"I talked to Mom today."

A beat. "Oh? Is she doing... How is she doing?"

"About as well as you'd expect. She told me she'd go see a psychiatrist before I left. It was somewhat conditional... Well, not really. I was going to leave regardless."

"Of course. You needed to. It was well past time."

"Right." She swallowed. "Anyway, she's reneged."

A long sigh filled the line. She could picture her father running his hands through his salt-and-pepper hair, stalking the familiar strip of carpet that had prematurely aged due to his pacing habit.

"Elizabeth," he said at last, "you tried. I know you love your mother. I do too. But she's... You can't make people get better who don't want to get better."

And then she couldn't help it. The question pushed against her lips until she had no choice but to let it come tumbling out. "Are you getting married?"

The line fell quiet for a long moment, so long that she checked to see if the call had been dropped. It hadn't.

"Dad? Are you still there?"

"I... Yes, I'm here. Did you just ask me if I'm getting married?"

"Mom saw something on Facebook. About you being engaged."

"Your mother's on Facebook again?"

"Answer the question, Dad."

"Do you really think I would get engaged and let you find out on social media?"

She tried her best to keep those damn stupid tears that had gathered in her eyes from falling, but she was just one person and couldn't compete with gravity. "I didn't know. I didn't check. I was too afraid that it was true and I wanted to ask you first."

"Sweetheart, no. Of course not. I don't know..." He paused. "Wait. Theresa went to a bridal shop with her sister, who *is* getting married in five months. There were pictures and—"

And now Elizabeth couldn't help herself—she started crying in earnest, feeling embarrassed and hating that she couldn't stop. The relief his words provided was immeasurable and intense.

At one point, the relationship she had with her father had

been sacrosanct, but she was still sorting through the debris left from the bomb he'd lobbed into her life after high school graduation. While her mother had always been difficult, Elizabeth had grown up believing wholeheartedly that her father was a man madly in love with his wife. Come to find that had been a lie. He'd stayed with her mother until he'd figured it would be safe to leave, which turned out to be about five minutes after Elizabeth had collected her diploma.

The past few years had been an exercise in reconciling the fact that her father was a remarkable actor, and trying to find her way back to the relationship they'd had before. It wasn't easy, and she'd never quite gotten to the point where she trusted there wasn't another bomb waiting to explode.

In fact, the entire experience had prompted her to reconsider the childish convictions about romance at all. If a good man like her father could have her so thoroughly snowed, what did that say about other men? What the hell use was there in trusting anyone?

Pretty much none.

She gave another choked sob.

"Oh, Lizzie." Her father sounded heartbroken, which only served to make her tears harder to stop. "I'm so sorry. I would never let you find out that way."

"Sorry, Dad," she said at last, getting a hold of herself. She cast her gaze around the café, feeling at once horribly self-conscious and foolish. Thankfully, Will's back remained to her, and no one else seemed to be paying her any attention.

"I won't deny I'm a little shocked you thought I could do something like that."

Guilt collided with resentment, but she shoved it back. "It's been a long day," Elizabeth said, wiping her eyes with the back of her hand.

"It's not even ten yet."

"Yeah. *That* long a day." She fixed her gaze on the back of Will's head, and before she knew what was happening, the events of the last twenty-four hours were spilling from her lips, up to the enemy she'd made of her first professor of the day. "I probably should have kept my mouth shut. God knows he's an asshole, but that just seemed wrong."

"You absolutely should not have kept your mouth shut," her father replied, his voice soft, and she could almost see him smiling at her. "Sure, this Will guy is a jerk, but the daughter I raised stands up for everyone when the time is right. I'm very proud of you."

"Thanks," she said, somewhat hoarse. "That makes me feel a little less like an idiot. I might need another pep talk when the grades are posted."

"It won't be as bad as all that. Professors like students with spirit."

"Yeah, that's not how the world works anymore, Dad. I'm not sure if it ever did."

"Then fuck 'em."

Elizabeth burst out laughing, and this was enough to earn a few surprised glances. Even Will turned in his seat. Her mirth faded the second their eyes connected, and what was quick becoming a familiar sense of intense dislike took its place.

"Been spotted by an asshole," she muttered into the phone. "I better go. Still need to eat and I don't want to be late to my next class."

"All right. Well, it was so good to hear from you, sweetie. Call me this weekend?"

Maybe.

"Yeah. Will do. Say hi to Theresa for me."

"And Lizzie—don't be so hard on your mother. I know she... She's just not well."

"I know. That's not what gets to me about her." It was that she flat out refused to seek help.

"I know." Her father sighed. "Love you, precious."

"Love you too."

She disconnected the call, feeling minutely better, though the cry had helped. Crying, Elizabeth had learned, was very cathartic. Negative emotions seemed less threatening after they had been properly exhausted.

As she knew from experience, it would take a bit for her emotions to reset where her father was concerned, but she didn't have time to ruminate and plenty to keep her mind occupied. Picking at her muffin, Elizabeth forced her thoughts back to the things she *could* control. She considered sending a quick apology to Professor Greenfield just to officially get her semester back on track—at least before it could derail too spectacularly—but decided the conversation might be one better had after some time had passed.

Then, because she couldn't help it, Elizabeth found herself thinking about her mother again. The text message she'd sent confirming her doctor appointment hadn't been answered, nor had the one about the taxi being on its way over. The cab driver might be in for a shock—Lynette Bennet wasn't above throwing things at unwanted visitors. If she didn't receive an angry message from the cab company, Elizabeth would consider it a personal victory.

A glance at her phone told her she had about twenty minutes to find her next class. Elizabeth packed up and made her way out.

She'd gotten a few paces away from the coffee shop when he called after her.

"Elizabeth."

The easiest thing to do would be to pretend she hadn't heard, but given the way her feet had decided to go funny at his voice, she doubted that excuse would fly. Elizabeth stopped, swallowed. "I don't have anything to say to you."

"I just wanted—"

"Seriously." She whirled around, pinning Will with an angry glare. "Are you just so not used to hearing the word *no* that you don't understand it?"

"Look, I didn't mean to listen in on your conversation earlier."

"You can see where people might be confused."

Will scowled, but continued chugging along like the freakin' little engine. "I was there because I wanted to talk to you." He paused. "To thank you for what you said to Greenfield."

On a rational level, Elizabeth knew he meant this sincerely. On an irrational level—otherwise known as crossing the Lynette Bennet Line—she didn't care. She'd hit the level of bullshit she could take in a day. "Yes, well, I probably screwed myself in doing so, but at least I know I got an eavesdropper out of the deal."

His scowl deepened. "I didn't ask for that, you know."

"Oh, I know," she replied. "It was just one of my crazy impulses."

"For which I was going to thank you, but I see now that would have been a waste of time."

"I don't need pats on the back or atta girl's for doing the right thing. I was not brought up in a house of participation trophies."

A swell of righteous energy expanded in her chest. And she realized, belatedly, that she was enjoying this.

"Well," Will said in his most assholey voice, "I won't make that mistake again."

"Smart money's not riding on that bet, but thanks."

"Judging by your people skills, I doubt this was the first or will be the last your mouth got you in trouble."

Pleasant shivers shot down her spine, her insides fluttering.

It wasn't just that unloading felt good—because it did—but she hadn't had a sincere argument with anyone in a long time. Venting her negative emotions had never been an option at home, and *god,* she'd forgotten how cathartic this could be. That plus the fact that Will was still standing in front of her, his annoyingly handsome face contorted with frustration, did something to her that she would have never thought possible.

It turned her on.

And that was a big ole red flag.

"And judging by recent experience," she said, hoping her voice didn't sound as shaky as it felt, "your foot likes to live in your mouth. So I'm not sure how, exactly, you have room to talk."

Elizabeth whirled around the next minute and commanded her feet to start walking. Her nerves were on fire and her body felt more alive than it had in years, which would have been nice if it weren't so damned disconcerting.

She didn't want to walk away. She wanted to keep arguing.

What did it say about her if arguing was what did it for her?

No, that couldn't be it. Had to be a fluke. A symptom of an otherwise crappy day, overflowing from a previous crappy evening. Her body was not to be held responsible for what it did under the influence of sleep deprivation and Mom-induced stress.

But the way his eyes had sparked with challenge, the way he hadn't backed down, the way he'd fired back...

She liked that. A lot.

And if that wasn't disturbing as all get out, she didn't know what was.

7

The rest of the week, fortunately, passed without nearly as much excitement as the first day, and the second class with Professor Greenfield was uneventful. Elizabeth had gone in expecting the worst, but it seemed the instructor was determined to put the incident behind them and press onward. Even more wondrous, the call she'd asked the check-in nurse to place if Lynette didn't show for her appointment had never come. When Elizabeth had phoned to make sure this wasn't an oversight, the nurse had confirmed that her mother had in fact shown up.

That was one heck of a huge win.

Will had evidently decided to ignore her, which was fine by her. She was still a little wigged by how their last chat had left her feeling hot for reasons not due to anger. Arguing shouldn't be one of her buttons. Childhood issues or not, that one was just weird.

On Thursday afternoon, Elizabeth staggered into the dorm room she shared with Jane. She had several chapters to read and a few short essays to write, but the adrenaline she'd used up on the first day had left her woefully unprepared for a full work-week. Her bed had her name written all over it.

For a couple hours. Then she'd get busy with all the things she needed to have done tomorrow.

"Oh, Lizzie! Thank god you're here."

Elizabeth deposited her book bag on the ground beside her bed, then turned toward the open closet, where stood Jane wearing nothing but a pair of sleek leggings and a beige lacey bra.

"Whoa, hot mama alert."

Jane stuck her tongue out at her before turning back to her selection of blouses. "I'm going over to see Charlie," she announced, grinning. "He has a class he'd like some help in."

Elizabeth snorted. "Ah. That old chestnut."

"I could use some help too. I think he took the Econ class I'm in. I just need to find the appropriate shirt for flash cards."

"Yes, that is quite a dilemma." Elizabeth flopped onto her bed, and immediately regretted it, as these dorm beds were not made for flopping. On the plus side, it jolted a bit more awareness into her. She sat up, wincing. "So is this an all night study group? Is Charlie going to get rewarded for knowing all the answers?"

"If you're asking if I'm going to sleep with him, the answer is no," Jane replied coolly. "I told him I don't sleep with guys I just met, even if they are adorable and sweet and send me encouraging text messages throughout the week. We're just going to help each other out with some work."

"And make out a little."

Jane shrugged. "It helps break up the monotony." She pulled a royal blue blouse from her selection of clothes and held it up to her neck. "What do you think? Does this say...'flirty but determined to not get distracted', or 'hurry up so you can feel me up'?"

"Whichever one is the one you're going for is obviously the right answer."

"You're no help."

"In my defense, I never claimed to be." Elizabeth stifled a yawn—or tried to—and stretched out along the bed, her tired muscles sending her a silent thank you. "Do you think you'll be late?"

"I hope not. I have class at some unreasonable hour tomorrow morning. But Charlie did say he wanted to introduce me to his sister. She's a year behind him and the president of the Realis Society for Women."

"The what society?"

"It's a Meryton institution," she replied, and Elizabeth could tell that her ignorance where this was concerned was unusual. "It's a group dedicated to helping women network and integrate into the business world throughout our years here so we will have a better idea of how to handle negotiations and other common interactions once we graduate. They also have proper conduct guidelines and—"

"Conduct?"

"Yeah. Sort of like George Washington's *Rules of Civility*, but modernized and catered to women."

"That...doesn't sound outdated at all."

At that, Jane turned to her with a frown. "This would mean a lot to me, Lizzie. The Realis Society is one of the oldest female-focused societies in the country. Outdated or not, it's helped women open doors that are otherwise closed."

Elizabeth inclined her head, the fight in her dying. There was a lot in what Jane wasn't saying that was frighteningly easy for her to forget at times. "Well, if that is the case, I will champion your membership to the...whatever society of whatever."

"Realis Society for Women."

"Yes, that one. I predict you'll dazzle all of them until they're as in love with you as Charlie seems to be."

Jane grinned what Elizabeth had dubbed her Charlie-grin. "He is rather lovey-dovey at the moment, isn't he?"

"And for someone who knows he's not getting laid anytime soon, he gets a gold star." Elizabeth glanced toward her desk, where sat the reading she needed to have done by tomorrow, then to the backpack which held the assignments due early next week. It was likely a good thing Jane had plans for the evening, as she'd have no excuse but to dive right in to schoolwork. "What time are you heading over?"

"As soon as I figure out what I'm going to wear." Though it looked like Jane had decided, having pulled on a pink tee, which looked phenomenal on her.

"I think we have a winner," Elizabeth said. "You'll knock him out."

"Let's hope not, as I do actually want to get some studying done."

Elizabeth arched an eyebrow and Jane giggled again.

"Well," she amended, her cheeks reddening, "it's way less creepy if I make out with him when he's conscious."

"Consent is very important."

Jane checked herself in the mirror hanging on the back of the closet then, seemingly satisfied, pulled out a windbreaker. "All right. I'm going to head over," she said, zipping up.

"Walking?"

"Biking. If it's late, I'd rather not walk."

"Does Charlie have a car? He could drive you back."

"He does, but it's parked on the other side of campus in a private garage. I'm pretty sure he only gets it out on weekends." She shrugged. "There's the campus shuttle too, but I think it stops running at nine."

"Lame ass public shuttle."

Jane shrugged. "Meryton is advanced in many ways but not so much in others. So I'll just make sure I'm back before then."

"Or you could pack a change of clothes."

"Ha ha. No. Not having sex yet."

Elizabeth brought her hands up. "Hey, *I* didn't say anything about sex. Seems your mind's in the gutter."

Jane blew a raspberry, then busied herself with fitting various books and folders into her backpack. "All right," she said, "I think that's everything. You going to be okay tonight?"

"I see a large pizza in my future, so the short answer is yes."

"Save me some."

"Psh. Pizza's for dateless losers like yours truly, not for chicks who are leaving to go neck with their rich boyfriend."

"He's not my boyfriend," Jane said, totally unconvincingly. She hiked her backpack over her shoulders. "But I see your point."

"Have fun. And remember to make him wear a condom."

Jane looked scandalized. "Lizzie! We're not going to sleep together!"

"It's just an expression," Elizabeth replied, all innocence. "You know... 'Bye, have fun! Wear a condom!' All the kids are saying it."

"You're awful." Jane flipped her the bird, then hurried out the door before Elizabeth could think of a rejoinder.

Which was just as well—she didn't want to hold her friend up any longer, and the sooner the dorm room was empty, the quicker she could get started on the work she had due. The nap she'd intended to take had been shoved aside, chased away by a wave of alertness, and while it lasted, she was determined to make every second count.

Plus, once she was finished, she could reward herself with pizza. Or possibly one of those mythical early nights. Elizabeth definitely considered herself more of a night-owl—the best ideas occurred when no one was awake to appreciate them—but this week had run amok with her internal clock. She could use a couple extra hours, and finding sleep would be a tad easier without a roommate around, since Jane, sweet as she was, snored hard enough the sounds could be mistaken for a wood-chipper.

That would be the true testament of Charlie's feelings for her, Elizabeth decided. The man who could sleep through that and still love her in the morning was a man to freaking marry.

Elizabeth dug into her reading, opting for the desk rather than the bed, as it was harder to fall asleep while sitting up—though not impossible, as she had discovered a time or two. Thankfully, the books she'd been assigned in Greenfield's class were interesting enough to keep her focus. By the time she checked her phone, dusk was around the corner.

And she had an unread text message from Jane.

SOS! I completely forgot my period was going to start today. There are no women around. HELP ME!

Elizabeth checked the time-stamp. The text had arrived about ten minutes earlier.

On my way, she fired back, and immediately got to work.

Another ding.

Jane: THANK YOU THANK YOU THANK YOU!!!! When you get here, we're in Charlie's room. Third door on the right. Also, can you bring me some spare underwear? Just in case.

Elizabeth: You say that like I've never needed a tampon. What do you take me for?

She pushed herself off the bed and set about gathering supplies. A handful of tampons—just in case—a pair of spare undies, and one of the textbooks by Jane's bed. She doubted Jane wanted it broadcasted that she'd forgotten a girl-essential, and Elizabeth needed some reason to be at Netherfield.

After emptying her backpack and stuffing the SOS kit inside, she checked the shuttle schedule, did some mental math, and decided that with the time it'd take the shuttle to arrive, plus all its other stops, she was better off just walking. Netherfield Heights was about two miles away, but Elizabeth knew how to motor when properly motivated.

And if she started now, she could get there and back before the last vestiges of sunlight had disappeared for the day.

Maybe she'd order her pizza from Netherfield. With any luck, it'd be waiting for her by the time she got back.

Had it not been for the weather alert that had hit his phone ten minutes prior, Will might have thought someone was trying to pound their way through the roof. Netherfield Heights had been modeled after some of the grand tour homes in the South, and built in much the same way. The result was an echo chamber, and it filled him with a swift longing for home.

If there was any saving grace, it was that tomorrow was Friday and he'd have two full days to gather his bearings. He needed to prioritize, get his mind back on the things that mattered and off a certain annoying brunette.

Will sighed and scrubbed a hand down his face, then tried to refocus on the sentence he'd already read four times.

The trouble was, he'd decided, that he liked her. He'd kept waiting for her to say or do something that would magically make her repulsive, but it hadn't happened.

A hard knock on his door forced him out of his thoughts, and his eyes off the page he had yet to complete. He cursed and swung his legs over the bed.

If Charlie was here in search of condoms, he was barking up the wrong tree.

Will tossed his book onto his desk and tore a hand through his unkempt hair. Then he threw the door open, and froze.

Elizabeth stood shivering on the other side, her arms folded, every bit of her looking like a water nymph. Or someone who had just ridden Splash Mountain seven or eight times. Her drenched brown hair was half in a pony-tail, half plastered to her skin, which, rather than creamy, looked downright pale. Her shirt clung to her midsection, so wet it might as well have been transparent, and giving him a spectacular view of her nipples. Her jeans molded to her shapely legs, and her shoes—what was left of them—stood in the middle of a small puddle.

"What happened to you?" Will asked, completely dumbstruck. Other questions, such as *what are you doing here* flitted through his mind, but they didn't seem as important.

Elizabeth's teeth were chattering too hard for her to get a word out. At least, not a word he could understand.

Then his brain switched gears and the part of him that had grown up a gentleman came rushing out.

"Come in here," he said, throwing the door open wider. "I'll go get some towels."

Elizabeth's eyes rounded and she shook her head. "J-J-Jane," she said after a long moment.

Will frowned. "She's in Charlie's room. He's down the hall on the other side of the staircase."

Elizabeth shook her head again, perplexed. "Sh-she said it w-was the th-third door on the right."

"It is, but you go left from the stairs."

"She l-l-left out that part." She turned to start down the way he'd indicated, but he grabbed her by the shoulder before she could put more than a step between them.

"You're freezing," Will said. "I have clean clothes and towels. Whatever it is can wait."

For a moment she looked uncertain, but she gave him a nod and what looked like the hint of a grateful smile and let him lead her into his room.

"What happened?" Will asked again as soon as the door was

closed. It was a stupid question, he knew—the rain beating down on the roof didn't leave much to the imagination, but his mind was still stuck on the reality that the woman he'd spent all week thinking about was suddenly *here.*

"Jane...forgot a book. I brought it." Elizabeth indicated the backpack strapped to her back. "Apparently...during the middle of a typhoon."

"Yeah, it came on without any warning." Will hurried to the bathroom and retrieved three large, fluffy towels. When he returned, he found Elizabeth glowering at him.

"What?"

"You have...an attached bath?"

He looked over his shoulder as if to verify that was in fact where he'd come from. "Uh, yes."

"And your own room."

He shrugged. "Netherfield Heights was built for comfort."

"Of course." She offered a flat smile, which turned a smidgeon warmer when he handed her the towel. "Thanks."

Will watched her for a moment, caught somewhere between transfixed and struck stupid. Watching her bury her face into the towel he'd provided was a bit more satisfying that it ought to be, as was the small pleasure sound she released as she covered herself. It wasn't until her eyes met his that he jolted from awkward voyeur to helpful citizen again. His feet carried him toward his dresser without waiting for his mind to catch up, and the next thing he knew, he was digging through clothes.

"Thank—"

He turned and held out a pair of flannel bottoms and an oversized sweater. "You should put these on," he said.

She regarded the clothing as a child might regard a cup of liquid medicine. "I'm fine."

"You're not fine. You're gonna freeze if you stay in what you're wearing, and those towels can only do so much." He stalked his way back to the bathroom and tossed the clothes onto the toilet. "Don't argue—you know I'm right."

When he reentered the room, it was to the sight of Elizabeth chewing on her cheek, her brow furrowed, and her eyes alight with fire. She wanted to fight, he saw, but knew she couldn't. There was stubborn and there was stupid, and Elizabeth was definitely not the latter.

He watched, then, with a measure of satisfaction as she carried herself into his bathroom and shut the door behind her. Almost the second the latch caught, his mind began bombarding him with images of Elizabeth peeling the clingy shirt off her body, baring her breasts in a space where he had, just a few hours ago, jerked himself to orgasm while fantasizing about wrapping his mouth around one of those puckered nipples.

Will cursed himself, glanced down, and cursed again. The last thing he needed was for her to see him sporting a hard-on. She'd get the wrong idea—or worse, the right idea—and he'd never be able to look at her again.

A moment later, the bathroom door swung open and Elizabeth stepped out. Will had to force his throat to work.

He'd heard that some men took pleasure in the sight of a woman dressed in their clothes. Like many things, Will had accepted this at face value but dismissed the notion that it could apply to him. Granted, that had been before he'd had such a strong physical reaction to a woman—a reaction that had gone beyond scaring him.

Because, yeah, right now he was soaking up the sight of her dressed in clothes that belonged to him.

Elizabeth made her way forward, doing her best not to trip over the pant-legs, which dragged along the floor by a few inches. She'd obviously tried to roll them up, but the material wasn't very forgiving, and they hadn't remained in place for long. The sweatshirt he'd given her was one that was large on him—on her, it came down to her knees, and the sleeves, also rolled up, still dwarfed her hands.

She made a face. "I feel like a kid who just tried on Dad's clothes."

"At least they're dry," he offered.

"Yeah. Umm, thank you." It could have been a trick of the lighting in his room, but Will would have sworn he spied a hint of red on her cheeks. "I already feel a thousand percent better. And hey—sleeves." She clapped her arm sleeves together in demonstration.

He laughed. "It was the least I could do."

Elizabeth swallowed and lowered her arms, her eyes finding his. Will's throat went tight.

"I—ahh—you came here for Jane."

"Yeah." She hurried back to the bathroom, presumably to hunt through her backpack. A sound somewhere between disgust and dismay tickled the air before she returned with a bloated text book, cushioned within one of the towels he'd provided. "Ugh. I guess...the words are still good?"

"I've seen worse," Will agreed. "Just give it some time to air out."

"I'm going to have to replace this, aren't I?"

"Almost definitely, but she'll be able to use it until then."

Elizabeth cracked a small smile, which felt like a personal victory.

"I'll—ahh—take you to Charlie's room, if you like," Will said. "And then throw your clothes in the wash."

"You don't have to—"

"No, I want to. Least I can do."

Elizabeth considered him. "I really don't want to put you out. You've already been nice enough to...well...save me from self-inflicted hypothermia."

"That's not nice, it's just decent."

"Even so, please don't inconvenience yourself for me. If you show me where the laundry room is, I'll take it from there." She paused, then smiled again, and it transformed her whole face. "Really, thanks. And thanks for the loaner clothes. I'm already getting the feeling back in my toes."

Will nodded, a smile tickling the corners of his mouth. "Good." He glanced down, searching for words. "Come on. Let's go find Jane."

Elizabeth cast a dubious look at the ruined textbook in her hands, then nodded and let him guide her into the hallway.

8

It was downright impossible to concentrate with Elizabeth Bennet at Netherfield Heights. Every time Will cracked a book to catch up on reading, his mind would drag him on a tour of the building, picturing her in various rooms or tucked into various corners.

He knew she was still here, even without stalking the halls to find her, because the storm, rather than wearing out, had become more aggressive. Well, it wasn't so much a single storm as a series of storms, one right after the other, and each seemingly determined to show-up their predecessors. The lights had flickered once or twice, which in itself was disconcerting considering Netherfield Heights had been updated with enough protections to outlast a nuclear fallout—or so the stories went.

Also, Elizabeth couldn't leave yet because she'd left her backpack in his room. Plus her clothes were currently being laundered and he didn't think she'd want to wander back to Longbourn, storm or no storm, while wearing his pants.

Though he certainly didn't mind the idea at all.

Will scowled at his textbook for not being more interesting.

If it could just hook him, he'd be able to put her out of his head for a while. But with Elizabeth so near—in his space—the likelihood of making a dent in his coursework was about as high as Caroline doing a nice thing for someone with no ulterior motive.

He snorted at that and officially gave up. In the span of a blink, he sprung to his feet and was out the door.

The door to Charlie's room was cracked wide enough to get a good look inside, but Will knew at once that she wasn't in there. Charlie was in full flirt mode, which didn't mean much by itself, but the fact that he was speaking in low tones meant he didn't want to be overheard, which he wouldn't do if someone else were in the room. Charlie didn't have much patience for people who excluded others from the conversation—he felt it was rude, and always did his best to bring those around him together.

It was an admirable quality—one Will tried to adopt in theory, if not in practice.

He turned at the staircase and headed to the first floor. Elizabeth wasn't in the game area or channel surfing. He cast a glance out one of the large bay windows, but couldn't see much beyond the sheets of rain pouring down, even amid the occasional streak of lightning. While he was confident she wouldn't have left in such awful weather—especially with no fast way to get back—he'd made an ass out of himself by assuming things before.

The laundry room was deserted, though a quick glance informed him that Elizabeth's clothes had finished drying. They had been neatly folded and placed on a folding card table along the wall opposite the machines—something Will had seen Caroline do a time or two when she was attempting to make a point to the other housemates. Roughly, *you're an adult now so pick up your own goddamn laundry.*

His best guess was that Caroline wanted to shame anyone

who came to collect their clothes into finding out who had folded them. It hadn't worked. Charlie, the most obnoxious offender, had responded by giving her tips on how he most preferred his socks bundled. Had Caroline not had an audience, Will imagined she likely would have ripped her brother apart.

Will wandered into the back hall. He passed the library, which was empty, and the aerobics room, also empty. To his knowledge, Elizabeth hadn't brought any homework with her, having assumed that she'd be able to return after dropping off Jane's book. He wasn't surprised, therefore, to discover the study room vacant.

The unmistakable crack of pool balls colliding, and his heart gave another funny lurch.

He found Elizabeth bent over the pool table, her brow furrowed in concentration as she studied the colorful layout of balls spread across a rich green surface. She straightened, grabbed the cue, and bent again, this time armed.

"Lurking in the doorway," she said without glancing up. "How very ominous of you."

"You're holding your cue wrong."

Elizabeth smirked. "No kidding?"

"You knew."

"Well, if I had managed to do it right, I'd have been shocked." She punched the cue forward jerkily. It scraped against the green felt, but the cue-ball managed to knock a target or two. "I've only ever seen this done in the movies."

"I'm sure you could find a tutorial on YouTube."

"Yeah, but my way's more fun."

"Your way isn't a way."

Elizabeth straightened and lifted her eyes to his.

"So I'm not playing pool," she said, shrugging. "Do the rules matter if I don't give a crap?"

Will frowned. "What's the point of playing if you're not going to follow any rules?"

"Who says there are *no* rules?" Elizabeth retorted. "If I decide what the game is, I decide what the rules are. In the end, I have fun and kill some time. What's the harm?"

"That's not pool."

She shrugged again, then repositioned herself to take another strike at the cue-ball. "Right. Like I said, I'm not playing pool."

"I could teach you how to play, if you like."

"Nope," Elizabeth said, letting the cue fly. "Not interested."

"I—"

"This is really bothering you, isn't it?"

Will fought back a grin as she rose to full height again and flashed him a challenging look. He couldn't tell at the moment if she was being sincere or obstinate for the hell of it, and despite the warning sirens that started howling in his head, he knew he was beginning to cross the threshold from physical attraction to something more.

If he was being honest with himself, he'd passed that barrier the second she opened her mouth in Professor Greenfield's class.

Which was entirely inconvenient.

"No," he replied. "I just thought you might enjoy the challenge."

"The challenge," she deadpanned.

"Of learning something new, or perhaps you're worried about not being very good at it."

Elizabeth rolled her eyes. "Yeah, that's not gonna work on me."

"What a shame."

"Mmm." She set the pool cue across the table before looking

at him again. "Let me guess...you never broke the rules once when you were a kid."

"And I suppose you were a serial rule-breaker."

"How else do you learn?"

"By paying attention."

"Yeah. I bet you got beat up at school a lot."

Will tilted his head. "Sorry to disappoint you, but no. By conventional standards, I would have been considered a jock at my school."

"Conventional meaning *public*."

He shrugged. "If you like."

She stared at him for a long moment before breaking away with a laugh. "So you went from elite private schools to living in a dormitory that likely costs more in utilities alone than most people make in a year. It's really the hard-knock life for you."

"I suppose there's something wrong with private schools?"

"No." Elizabeth shook her head. "Not with the education part, but the students tend to be snobs."

"Do you paint everything with such a wide brush?"

"I'm speaking from experience. It's all I have to go on."

"And your experience..."

"Private school for three years," she replied. "Then money became tight and my family couldn't afford the tuition anymore. When I informed my friends that I'd be going to public school the next year, you'd have thought I just announced I had cancer."

Will winced. "They're not all like that."

"Uh huh. Does that have its own hashtag? 'Not all men'? 'Not all private schools'?"

"What?"

Elizabeth bristled. "Never mind." She turned her face from him, sighing. "So, who else lives here? The only people I've seen are you and Charlie."

"Charlie's sister lives here too."

"That's it? Just three of you?"

"There aren't that many rooms," he said defensively. "Well, that are ready. Third floor's mainly storage right now."

"And this is why people hate the rich. Thousands of students on campus and the three wealthiest have their own McMansion."

"Charlie's father did donate the money that got this built." He left out the condition that Charles Bingley IV had gotten in writing that anytime a Bingley attended Meryton, they and they alone would call the place home.

"Yes, and it was put to spectacular use."

He had no idea how the conversation had derailed so dramatically, but he could see, from the way she held herself, that she was annoyed. Not a flirty annoyed, but rather something genuine and deep. He wasn't sure how they had gotten there, but he thought it best not to stay. This was the longest they had gone without fighting since he'd met her.

So in his haste to continue speaking, he blurted, "Did Jane give you too much trouble?"

Her eyebrows winged upward. "Jane?"

"About the book being ruined."

"Oh, no. She was horrified that I was here, though. Apparently the weather alerts started coming in about ten minutes after I left. She'd texted, but the text didn't arrive until I was almost here and it was too late to turn back."

"I'm surprised she didn't volunteer to come keep you company," Will stated, though that wasn't true. He'd seen Charlie break up his share of friendships by being overly friendly with someone he should have steered clear from. Jane seemed nice, but they all did at first—until they realized that their girlfriends could double as competition.

"Don't let her hear you say that," Elizabeth said. "Jane could feel guilty because the sky is blue, so when I say she was horrified that I came here in this weather, I freaking mean it. Seriously, I pretty much had to make her leave me alone."

"And why did you?"

"Because I wasn't born yesterday and I didn't want to be the third wheel in her date. No sense ruining both our nights."

"So being here ruined your night?"

"It wasn't on my bucket list, no," Elizabeth replied dryly. "And by the time the storm calms down enough that I can head home, I'm going to be too wiped to get any reading done."

And there it was. An opening.

"I was about to head back upstairs," Will said quickly, "to continue studying, myself. Ethics?"

She nodded. "Don't let me keep you. I'll go back to poke-ball."

"Poke-ball?"

"Mmm. The game I invented." Elizabeth tapped the pool table, grinning. "And I saw a big ole room full of books down the hall, so if I get bored I'm sure I can—"

"I was going to say, you're welcome to come with me."

She stared at him.

"For the reading. We have the same course."

She still didn't say anything for a beat, and what might have been a grin started to tug on her lips. "Thank you. That's—"

"Will?" came a lilting voice from behind.

The next moment, Caroline was beside him, her flawless stage smile in place. She leaned against the doorway, not bothering to acknowledge the presence of anyone else.

"I thought that was you," she said. "How long have you been down here? I wanted to see if you wanted me to make you something to eat."

Elizabeth coughed, but Will was fairly certain it was to mask a snicker.

"Excuse you," Caroline said, turning to Elizabeth at last, her eyes cold, even if her smile remained in place.

"Many people have tried," she retorted, grabbing the pool cue off the table again.

Caroline watched her for a moment before sliding her gaze back to Will. "Well?" she said softly. "Hungry for anything?"

"No, not at the moment," Will replied. "Thanks."

The crack of pool balls colliding broke through the air again, followed by a hard thud. Caroline hissed and grabbed onto Will for support, throwing her full weight onto him without warning so that he tumbled back and had no option but to seize her about the waist.

Instantly, he was closer to Caroline than he'd ever been or ever cared to be. And while her eyes were alight with anger—he saw recognition flash bright behind them.

"Oops." Elizabeth placed the cue down again. "Did I get you?"

It was then that Will noticed the eight ball lying on the floor beside Caroline's foot.

"Sorry," Elizabeth continued impishly. "That's the risk you run when you walk into a high stakes game of poke-ball."

His first and most primal instinct was to laugh, but one look at the rage that flooded Caroline's eyes and his mirth died an abrupt death. Caroline Bingley was not someone most people would test—she had destroyed reputations and even taken down a company or two because she'd felt she'd been wronged.

"Are you stupid?" Caroline asked bluntly. Her tone wasn't outright menacing, but it didn't need to be.

Elizabeth blinked. "No. Are you?"

"What?"

"What? I thought we were doing a thing where we asked each other rude questions."

Caroline's face grew stony, which was never a good sign. Also not good—she was still plastered to Will, and he didn't know how to indicate that he wanted to be released without shoving her away. Caroline had never had much respect for his personal space, but this was pushing it.

"Well," she said at last, some of her southern drawl leaking into her voice. Like Charlie and himself, Caroline had worked at eradicating any hint of accent, though she knew when to pull it out. At times it worked for her, whereas it never worked for Will. "Aren't you just full of moxie?"

Elizabeth arched an eyebrow. "Seriously? People still talk like that?"

"In civilized circles, yes," Caroline replied coolly. Then she turned to Will and favored him with a cheeky grin. "Go on. Have fun with her. I'll still be here when you're done."

Will stared at her, his body too warm—unpleasantly warm —from her closeness. "Caroline—"

"I know, I know." At last she drew back, the unpleasant smile broadening a bit. "But you know where to find me."

Then, thankfully, she turned and headed down the hall toward the kitchen. Will didn't let out the breath he'd been holding until he saw her turn the corner.

"So," Elizabeth said, drawing him back. "Casual fuck who thinks something more serious is going on?"

Will's heart stuttered and his brain—a little sluggish now— had to work through what she'd said a few times to determine she hadn't just propositioned him. "Excuse me?"

"Am I close?" Elizabeth nodded in the direction Caroline had disappeared. "I swear, she was three seconds from pissing around you to mark her territory."

"I... That is...I'm not..." Great. He felt his cheeks heating. This was something he didn't need. "I'm not...*like that.*"

"Like what? Heterosexual? Cool. I didn't get that vibe from you, but—"

"No, that's not what I—" A surge of irritation heated his veins, aimed both at himself for fumbling all over the damn place and her for putting him in a position to fumble. "I don't do casual relationships."

"Ah." Elizabeth thought for a moment, then shrugged. "Well, good news for Caroline, then. She definitely doesn't want anything casual."

"Yes, she's made that perfectly clear over the years."

"Uh huh. And I bet you just hate the attention."

Will frowned. There was an edge to her voice, something like anger but not quite there. "I don't care for it, no."

"Yet you drew no boundaries." She waved at him. "She was ready to climb you like a jungle gym and you just stood and let her do it."

"What would you have me do?"

"Tell her that you're not into her."

"Just like that?"

Elizabeth shrugged. "Direct and to the point. Guys can do this thing where they drag a girl along. Well, I say *guys,* but women do it too. Let's say people. *People* do this thing where they don't tell someone how they actually feel, especially when the way they actually feel is *go away.* It's partly fear and partly because hey, it feels good to have someone giving you all that attention. Little boost for the ego does wonders."

"That's not what I'm doing."

"Oh please. That's what *everyone* is doing."

"She's Charlie's sister."

"Even more reason to be upfront." She paused. "And wow. Poor Charlie."

"So your solution to unwanted advances is to hurt the person's feelings."

"No," Elizabeth replied, drawing out the word. "My solution

is to be honest. Feelings might be hurt, embarrassment might be had, but it's better than the long-term harm."

Will arched an eyebrow. "And what is the long-term harm?"

"Hurting their feelings and making them doubt their worth by constantly making them think they *might* have a chance, but never giving them one."

"Hmm. And here I didn't think you cared for Caroline."

Elizabeth held a hand up to her ear. "Hear that? It's the sound of you missing the point."

Will chuckled. "What do you do, then," he said, "if you *do* like someone."

"I think the term *don't be a dick* pretty much covers it."

"That is nice and vague."

"It doesn't take much to not be a dick. I don't see what's vague about it."

Will inclined his head. "What about you, Elizabeth?"

"What about me?"

"What would a man need to do to get your interest? Beyond, ahh, not being a dick?"

A pretty frown crossed her face, and she narrowed her eyes at him, suspicious. "Why?"

"Just curious," he said. "You are the first woman I can remember meeting that wasn't...ahh...*overt*."

"Meaning I haven't thrown myself at you because you're apparently worth millions."

If nothing else, one had to appreciate Elizabeth's candor.

"Yes," Will replied.

"You seriously have never met a woman who hasn't drooled all over you?"

"I wouldn't put it like that, but—"

She barked a laugh, then immediately tried to sober. "Sorry," she said, but her face was twitching, her mouth seemingly determined to break into a smile. After a handful of seconds, she lost the battle and began laughing in earnest. "Sorry," she repeated between giggles. "It's not funny, but it's...*so* funny."

"That women find me attractive?"

"That *this* is what you'd call a problem."

"I never said it was a problem."

"Of course not," she replied, trying again for a straight face. "It's just...the very definition of a first world issue. You meet someone who doesn't fall all over herself to kiss your ass and you go, *hmm,* what's wrong with that one?"

Will cocked his head, torn between amusement and offense. "You're good at that."

"At what?"

"Taking something someone said and twisting it around."

"I'm not twisting anything. You just asked what it takes to get my motor revving because I'm the first girl you've met who isn't turned on by dollar signs."

"That isn't what I said at all." The seesaw landed firmly on *offense*, and a bubble of irritation bloomed in the middle of his chest. "I was just wondering—"

"Yeah, I know what you were wondering." Elizabeth shook her head. "The answer is being honest. Kind. Compassionate. Empathetic. And, while we're at it, I'll add smart and funny to the list. Must *not* be arrogant or cruel or think that he's God's freaking gift. In other words, you gotta be a unicorn."

"A unicorn?"

"Mythical creature. That's what does it for me. The mythical creature known as the genuine good guy."

Some of the irritation began to ebb. "There are good guys out there."

Elizabeth snorted. "Yeah. They're fantastic. So good they'll catcall you or send you dick pics, then follow-up with rape threats when you don't thank them for their attention."

"I think your definition of *good guy* might need some revisions."

"Will, I have met exactly *zero* self-proclaimed *good guys* who are actually that. And *believe* me, every man-creature out there is bound and determined to prove they're just a good guy who can't catch a break. Those exact words, in fact. If I had a penny for every time I'd heard them, I'd have more money than you." She broke off, sighing. "That's just part of being a girl. Turn down a guy when he asks you out. Leave a comment on a news article. Exist on the internet at all. This is what we get. And we're the lucky ones. Too many women get much, much worse."

Will recoiled, irritation fully gone now, replaced with shock. If this was true, there was a nice doorless tower in Georgiana's future. He didn't think he could go through the Wickham ordeal with her again. It would send him to the grave sixty years early.

"That's awful," he said for lack of anything more profound. Because it was awful, and more than that—it was terrifying.

Elizabeth nodded. "That's life. And one of the many reasons why I'm off relationships. Too much bullshit to wade through to find someone even kinda decent."

"Off...relationships? That sounds a little extreme."

"Depends on your point of view."

"But the men I'd assume you'd be with aren't like those you mentioned," he replied, frowning. "So what does this actually achieve? You weren't going to give them the time of day anyway."

Elizabeth was quiet for a moment, her expression softening. "Avoidance of pain."

"What?"

"That's what I achieve."

Will swallowed. "Not all relationships are pain, you know. Some people even make it work."

"In your universe?"

"My folks were happily married, so yes."

She nodded, pressing her lips into a solemn line. "Good for them. Seriously. But that's the exception, not the rule. Believe me when I say I've seen it go the other way and *no thank you*. I'll stick to my no-relationship diet."

"Even if the right guy comes along?"

"Especially if the right guy comes along."

He waited for his heart to catch up with his mind, for everything he'd just learned about her to cement. He wasn't even sure she knew how much she'd revealed about herself.

It didn't take much to put together why she felt the way she did—from what he'd overheard of her call with her mother combined with what she'd shared that first day of class, things at home were not idyllic. While Will had never been in the front row of a marriage dissolution, he certainly had enough friends and relatives whose families had been torn apart. The example in his home had been the opposite—for the right person, love was worth everything.

Even the pain that came with saying goodbye.

"So that," Elizabeth said, returning the cue to its place, "is about the full of it. Have any more questions?"

Yes. About five hundred, but Will knew when to wave a white flag, and now was that moment. He cleared his throat and shook his head. "No."

"Then I'm going to go see what the forecast is." She started toward him—or rather the door. He happened to be in the way. "'Cause it's going to be past my bedtime soon." Elizabeth paused when she reached him, and for the first time, he saw a glimmer of uncertainty enter her eyes. "Umm, I don't want to be a nuisance, but I'm going to gnaw off my arm if I don't get some food in me."

"Help yourself to whatever's in the kitchen."

She offered him a small smile. "Thanks."

Then she was gone, moving down the hall, and around a

corner toward the front. Will watched her but didn't follow. Not yet. His head, allowed a free moment, began to flood with everything he'd learned—everything she'd said. And the fact that, despite everything, the feelings he'd realized he had hadn't gone away.

If anything, they were stronger than they had been. That couldn't be a good sign.

He was fucked.

9

Apparently, Elizabeth had done something to piss off the weather gods. Rather than tapering off, the storm system seemed to get uglier the older the night became. Concerns about getting back to Longbourn in time to get any of her work done had been exchanged for worry that she might not get back at all tonight. The most optimistic reports showed the storms finally crying uncle in the neighborhood of three in the morning.

Elizabeth blew out a breath and placed her phone back on the couch's arm. After wolfing down a turkey sandwich, she had asked Will if he would mind letting her borrow his books. The temptation had been there to remind him of his earlier offer of studying together, but the fact that she found herself wanting to hang around him more—even a little—meant she was edging into dodgy territory. Because she'd enjoyed talking with him. Watching him. While their conversation had been charged, it hadn't been hostile, and the fact that she'd had just as much fun doing that as she had arguing could only lead to very bad things.

As it was, Will hadn't repeated his offer to study with her.

He'd given her the textbook and gone back to whatever it was he'd been doing and she'd tried to not be disappointed.

And she wasn't disappointed. Nope. Not her.

Elizabeth sighed and tore a hand through her hair, which was still damp in places from her cross-campus mid-monsoon hike. Thick hair was envied by many, but it could be a genuine pain in the ass. She was already dreading her next date with a hairbrush, being that she wasn't the hugest fan of scalp torture. The tangles her fingers encountered were painful enough.

She cast a glance toward the windows that overlooked the common area just in time to see a menacing bolt of lightning zigzag to the ground. Three seconds later came the crack of thunder, booming with such intensity the walls shook and the lights flickered.

Yeah, she wasn't going anywhere tonight.

"This is where I'm going to die," Elizabeth muttered, dropping her face into her hands. "And Jane is never getting another favor from me ever again."

Especially considering the utter futility of this favor. Not only had the tampons been useless by the time Elizabeth had made it here, Caroline had arrived in the interim and helped Jane to her supply. So Elizabeth had lost an evening of studying for no good reason, and she'd been stuck with no one for company but Will...and she hadn't minded that as much as she should.

Will had surprised her. A lot. And she'd found herself warming to him in ways she didn't want to warm to anyone. Anytime she'd found someone mildly interesting, she'd find whatever reason she could to run hard and fast in the opposite direction, because if something seemed too good to be true, it typically was.

Will didn't seem too good to be true, and that actually scared her more. Rather, he seemed real.

Elizabeth forced herself to her feet, grabbed the book Will had lent her, and started for the stairs. Once outside his door, she hesitated only a moment before knocking. There was a chance he was already in bed asleep, but she didn't think so. Will didn't strike her as the type to fall into bed before resolving immediate problems, and her continued presence here certainly qualified.

Sure enough, after he opened the door, she saw the lights in his room were on and the television was playing in the background. He likewise hadn't changed out of his jeans.

"Hi," he said simply.

"Hi." Elizabeth licked her lips and pushed the book forward. "Thanks. For letting me borrow that."

He accepted it with a nod. "Of course."

"And...well, I'm not sure if you have any spare gopher wood lying around, because it's Ark time."

"Ark time?"

She nodded. "The rain hasn't stopped. I... I don't want to be an imposition, but would it be okay if I crashed on the couch?"

Understanding lit his eyes. "Oh. Of course, yes."

"Thanks." She crossed her arms, her cheeks heating, though she had no idea why and found this irritating. "Is there—"

But Will was already in motion. "Come in," he said as he stepped back into his room. "Let me get you set up."

Elizabeth swallowed, not sure for a moment if he meant in his room or elsewhere, and she didn't want to chance his hospitality by asking. But Will was harmless, so if he got the wrong idea, she could set him straight. She drew in a breath and stepped over the threshold for the second time that day.

Will had disappeared into the attached bath. When he returned, his arms were full of quilts and one fluffy looking pillow.

"You keep all that in your bathroom?"

"In the linen cupboard."

Of course he had a linen cupboard. Wonder of wonders the toilet wasn't carved out of solid gold.

Elizabeth bit her tongue. "You must've been a boy scout."

"Why's that?"

"I've never known a college guy to have that much bedding just on hand."

"I'm not most college guys."

Understatement of the year.

Will shifted his weight and tipped forward. "Can you grab the pillow? I've got the rest."

She did as asked, then followed him back downstairs and to the common area. The storm outside was still raging, flooding the area with the occasional stab of light before the ground shook with thunder. Will led her straight to the plush couch she'd parked at earlier and began setting up her makeshift bed.

"What time's your first class?"

"Seven," she said, watching him work. "Hey, I can do that—"

"You're a guest," he replied. "And seven?"

"I have my phone. I'll set an alarm for six so I can start on the way back to Longbourn to grab a shower and my things."

Will frowned and looked up. "I'll take you."

Elizabeth's brow furrowed. "No, you can't."

"If it's still storming, you'll be stuck here anyway. The campus shuttle pick up is nearby, but it'll take forever to get around to Longbourn, and you'll likely be late."

"I'll get up earlier."

"Elizabeth, I'll take you. You can shower here to save time, and we can swing by your dorm after. I have to be at class by eight, anyway."

"How exactly are you going to take me? Aren't you parked in the garage on the other side of the world?"

"Yes," he said. "But I am resourceful."

"Resourceful enough to get your vehicle here overnight?"

"Resourceful enough to have Lyft programmed on my phone. I'll have them pick us up here; we'll swing by Longbourn so you can get your things and do what you need to do, and then get to class."

Elizabeth stared at him for a long moment, unsure of what to say. "I...that's...you really don't have to do that."

"No," he agreed, "but I was going to anyway, so you might as well take advantage. This will be easier."

"You weren't planning on going by Longbourn," she said. "It's out of the way—"

"It's a favor, Elizabeth."

Yes, she knew. She didn't like favors. The ones she'd been dealt in the past came attached to all sorts of strings. But she couldn't deny his solution sounded a lot easier than whatever she'd have come up with at the ass-crack of dawn, particularly with a rough night ahead. If she didn't have a plan worked out, she was liable to keep herself awake worrying about sleeping too late or not having enough time to get to class, and she didn't sleep well on couches to begin with.

"Okay," she said at last.

Will smiled. "Okay." He looked down at the sofa, now made up with the quilt he had brought down. "Do you need anything else?"

Elizabeth shook her head, rubbing her arms. "No. You've been...very nice."

"Don't sound so surprised."

She felt her mouth twitch. "Thanks for all this. Seriously. I showed up unannounced and kinda ruined your afternoon."

"You didn't ruin anything except the game of pool."

She snickered at that and pressed forward, suddenly exhausted. The long day had caught up with her and she was ready to lie down. "My way was better."

Will studied her a moment, then moved out of the way and around the coffee table. "Let me know if you need anything else."

"I think I'm set," she replied, dropping onto the couch. "'Night, Will."

He looked at her a moment longer—a moment that seemed to stretch into hours. The wheels behind his eyes were in motion, the desire to say something else palpable. His mouth opened and his brow furrowed, and she found she felt his presence in a way not unlike that first day in class. He seemed to dominate the space around him, which she found surprising and more than a little unnerving.

At last, though, the silence broke. "Good night," he said, then turned on his heel and walked away.

10

Elizabeth awoke in Will's bed. This was cause for alarm. She distinctly remembered *not* going to sleep in Will's bed, rather having spent the better part of an hour trying to get sleeping-comfortable on an otherwise perfectly comfortable sofa.

But she knew before she opened her eyes that she was not on the sofa anymore. The pillow smelled like Will—which also alarmed her, as she hadn't been aware that she knew him well enough to pick his scent out of a lineup. When she forced her eyes open, she found herself staring at the navy paint that made up the colors of his dorm room. Other sensory details began to filter in, like the beep of the clock beside her head and the sound of running water.

Will was in the shower.

Elizabeth rolled over, her legs tangled in his blankets. She gave the room a thorough once over—yep, this was not the downstairs—and slammed her palm on the clock's snooze function.

Then the fogginess in her head lifted and she remembered.

The storm had lasted forever. Elizabeth had slept fitfully for a couple hours, drifting in that awful place that didn't feel like sleep or wakefulness. After midnight, she'd started panicking about falling asleep at all. Worrying about falling asleep was not the best sleeping aid, as she knew all too well, but telling her brain to knock it off with the worry had never been effective.

Her inner dialogue had been interrupted by noise from the floor above. A few minutes later, Will had plodded downstairs. She'd thought his destination the kitchen at first, but he'd made a beeline straight for her the second his feet hit the floor.

"Have you slept?" he'd asked.

Elizabeth had shaken her head.

He'd looked at her hard, his mouth a firm line. "Okay," he'd said, and held out his hand. "Come with me."

It was either a testament to how surprised or sleepy she'd been that she hadn't argued. That was, until, Will had marched her across the threshold of his dorm room and told her to take the bed. He'd said something else, something that had appeased the immediate protest that had bubbled inside her at the thought. Not that it would have taken much—her sleepy brain had been too enchanted by the sight of an actual bed to put up much of a fight.

She'd tumbled onto the mattress and fallen asleep the second her eyes closed.

And now she was in his room. In his bed. And he was showering.

A thrill raced down Elizabeth's spine as she racked her mind to recall whether or not Will had slipped into bed beside her. Given the fact that she was not pressed against the wall, she didn't think so. He would have had to climb over her to get to the bathroom. And she had apparently burritoed herself with the blankets thoroughly enough that anyone who would have thought to share them would have had a fight on their hands.

The shower in the other room shut off, leaving a void where sound had once been. Elizabeth began struggling to un-burrito herself. While smart money was on the bet that Will, while definitely in possession of douche characteristics, wasn't a sex offender, she preferred to not be incapacitated by bedding while in a relative stranger's bedroom. Had she been thinking clearly last night, she wouldn't have followed him up here in the first place.

She had just managed to detangle her legs when the bathroom door opened and a shirtless Will stepped into the room.

Elizabeth abruptly froze.

The man-appreciating heterosexual woman inside her had assessed Will the night they met and declared him a babe. Then he'd opened his mouth and the man-appreciating heterosexual woman inside of her head been shoved aside by the anti-relationship-feminist. Granted, the reason he'd opened his mouth was that she'd opened hers, but she'd at least had the good sense to realize she was being an asshat. Still, ever since that night, the part of her that recognized Will was indeed attractive had been shouted down by more rational voices.

Now, though, those rational voices were hoarse. Because as nice as Will looked in clothes, he looked infinitely better out of them. The shirts he favored, she now saw, were on the baggy side, which had the unfortunate side-effect of concealing his hard chest and lean, wiry build. His arms came with defined muscle, his abdomen with one of those six-packs she'd seen in magazines but had never witnessed in real life. Every part of him was entirely lickable, which had the man-appreciating heterosexual woman alert in ways Elizabeth hadn't been alert in years.

But she wasn't superficial. Mostly. She didn't think.

That didn't mean she couldn't enjoy the view.

"Elizabeth."

She jerked her head and forced her eyes to his, and was instantly annoyed when she saw he was amused. Couldn't a girl ogle in peace?

"I asked if you wanted to use the shower." He indicated the room behind him as though she might need a diorama. "You mentioned taking one this morning, and I thought it might save some time if you—"

"Where did you sleep?" she asked, needing to reclaim control.

"Downstairs."

Her throat tightened. "Why?"

"I told you last night." He ran a towel over his head, mussing his normally unmussed brown hair, and inspiring her ovaries to do another happy dance. It was way too early to be presented with man candy. Her rational, regulated side didn't wake up until after at least three cups of coffee.

"I don't remember much of last night," she said. Then hurriedly added, "After making up the couch, at least. I was running on fumes."

"Yeah. You have the earlier class, and I never sleep well in a new place. I thought this was better."

Elizabeth stared at him, swallowed.

Okay, maybe she had underestimated how much trouble this guy could be. Because now the jury was in and the verdict was that Will was not the enormous asshole she'd pegged him for the first night. Maybe he'd just been an asshole *that* night. Hell knows she hadn't been on her best behavior. The nerves associated with coming back to school, combined with her determination to save someone—anyone—from the heartbreak she'd witnessed at home had made her a not so pleasant version of herself. If that could happen to her, it could happen to anyone.

And if she dismissed that first night entirely, then his biggest flaw was that he was rich.

"Thanks," Elizabeth said at last, heat blooming across her skin. "That was... That was nice of you."

"I do have my moments." He smirked. "Anyway, shower?"

She motioned to the rat's nest that was her head. "Kinda doubt you have a brush that'll salvage this mess."

Will held up a finger. "Wait here," he said, then dashed back inside the bathroom. A moment later, he strolled back into view, wielding a hairbrush. "Will this work?"

"Thank god for old girlfriends," Elizabeth agreed, swinging her legs over the side of the bed. She was still wearing the clothes Will had given her the day before. She'd slept in his bed and in his clothes. They were already much further along than her previous two relationships.

"Try sister," Will said, handing over the brush. "I packed it by mistake."

Elizabeth didn't move for a moment.

"It's not going to bite you," Will prompted.

"Well, obviously." Still, she felt her cheeks heat as she accepted his offering. "Thanks. And my apologies to your sister."

His eyebrows rose.

Elizabeth gestured at her head. "My hair is where brushes go to die."

That earned a frown, and a long, assessing look as though Will were trying to determine if some gnarly creature was about to pop out of her rat's nest. Well, she wouldn't be surprised. When her hair *felt* like a tangled mess, it meant that it had reached disastrous proportions. The only option might well be to shave it all off.

"Looks normal enough to me," he said.

"That's because I'm willing to bet *your* hair has never so much as curled around your ears, much less your ass." Thankfully, Elizabeth had grown out of the weird hippie phase in high school, but over the past few months, her hair had gotten longer than she'd grown accustomed to keeping it. She fisted a sloppy handful and held it up for inspection. "Also, I'm half Wookiee. Believe me, this is going to be a nightmare."

Will looked like he didn't know what to say to that, which was likely for the best. She was stalling, anyway, doing her best to stop noticing his annoyingly perfect skin and magazine-model abs. Honestly, hadn't the guy ever heard of a shirt?

He cleared his throat. "Well, did you want to shower here? Offer stands from last night. It'll—"

Get her out of this conversation, that's what it would do. Elizabeth bounced to her feet. "Yes," she said. "I will. Thanks."

She was almost to the bathroom before an obvious problem occurred to her. She paused, but didn't turn around. *No more drooling over the man-candy.* "Ahh, my clothes. Are they—"

"I'll get them," he answered promptly. "Towels are in the third drawer."

"Thanks." And she all but flew the rest of the way to safety, then closed the door behind her.

Will pulled his phone out of his pocket the second he stepped out of the dorm room and contacted Lyft about a ride. Perhaps he was being overly optimistic to assume Elizabeth could be ready in thirty minutes, but if she wanted to run by her dorm and make her class, he needed to get things in motion now.

Once done, he headed to the laundry room on the floor below, where he found Elizabeth's clothes still neatly folded atop the dryer. He picked up the small pile and started back for the stairs, his mind tumbling all over itself in a frenzy to decode the conversation he'd just left. Moreover, the borderline famished look that had fallen over Elizabeth's face the moment he'd stepped into the room. It was the first time that she'd regarded him with open female interest, and it had been blatant to the point that he knew, without a doubt, anything he might have thought he'd seen before had been an illusion. Elizabeth was not a subtle woman. It was one of the many things he appreciated about her.

Right now, he appreciated the fact that she was in his room —in his shower—rubbing his soap onto her hands, then running those hands over her naked body. In fact, he might appreciate it too much, given the way his cock twitched every time that particular image entered his mind, which had been approximately every five seconds since he'd stepped into the hall.

Will shook his head to clear it—not that it worked—and started back up the stairs.

When he arrived in his room, he noticed the shower was no longer running, which lent him pause. Living with Georgiana most of his life had instilled in him an understanding that women took twice as long doing pretty much everything, especially when it came to anything involving the bathroom.

Apparently, Elizabeth was the exception to that particular rule.

But as he was learning, she was the exception to a lot of things.

"Shitshitshitshit!" erupted from behind the bathroom door, followed by an odd rip that sounded like Velcro being pried apart.

"Elizabeth?"

"Yeah," she replied weakly. "Just doing battle. I won't lie, Darcy. It doesn't look good."

"Is everything—"

"I'm going to be bald. Literally bald." She sighed. "I knew I should've tackled this monstrosity before getting in the shower."

"You're..."

"Brushing my hair—ow, *mother-fuck nugget!*"

Will bit the inside of his cheek to keep from laughing. "You all right?"

"Getting there," she replied. "You have my clothes?"

He glanced down, then felt stupid for needing to verify that yes, her clothes were still in his hands. And then his cock jumped back in the game because he realized, belatedly, that the item on top of the pile was her underwear.

Will inhaled sharply. Had she been wearing his clothes without underwear?

The thought made his spine tingle.

"Will?"

"Oh, yes," he said, nearly stumbling over his feet in his eagerness to get to the door. "It's here."

The door edged open and a pink-faced Elizabeth peeked through the crack. Her towel-clad body was completely visible in the mirror behind her, though he forced himself to keep his eyes on hers.

She extended a hand. "Thanks."

He blinked, almost asked for what, then cursed inwardly and shoved her clothing forward. She snatched them as though afraid he'd keep them from her and slammed the door shut— but not before taking another long look at his naked chest.

Which he should probably do something about. He turned to his dresser and tugged free the first thing he saw.

A few minutes later, Elizabeth emerged from the bathroom, dressed in the yoga pants and long-sleeve tee from the day before. Her hair was, thankfully, still attached, straight and visibly damp. She looked...

Beautiful.

Will swallowed. Yeah, she was beautiful. Denying it didn't make it any less true. If the past week had taught him anything, it was running from his attraction to Elizabeth had done nothing to kill it. Perhaps if she'd been a different person...but she wasn't.

Elizabeth held something up that looked like a cross between a microphone and road kill on a stick.

"Benefit of having money is your sister can afford some sturdier accessories," she said. "The handles usually break off mine when my hair gets that bad."

He blinked, comprehension dawning. "God, that must've been..." Well, at least the Velcro sounds made sense now.

"Painful," she supplied. "You'd think for as often as I have to do this, I'd get used to it, but I'm a big weenie when it comes to pain. My mom used to say I had a tender scalp." She nudged said scalp with her free hand, a somewhat wistful expression falling over her face. It didn't last. "Anyway, the brush survived, but I don't know if it's salvageable. I'll do my best to pull the hair out and get it back to you." Elizabeth raised her eyes to his. "Don't be fooled, Will. Thick hair is a real sumbitch."

"I like your hair." The comment left his lips before his brain could sign off. Will felt his cheeks heat almost at once.

"Oh." She looked discomfited too, which only made the moment more awkward. "Umm. Thanks."

A thick silence fell between them. That was until Will's pocket vibrated with what he was sure was notification that their driver had arrived.

"Ah, better get going, then," Will said, kneeling over to pluck Elizabeth's backpack off the floor. It was still slightly damp from the previous day's downpour, but seemed otherwise to be in working order.

She snatched it. "Yeah, thanks. For this." She jostled the backpack. "And for the bed."

He nodded. "Anytime." Well, that didn't sound forward at all, did it? "I mean—"

"We should go," she said before fleeing into the hallway.

For a moment, he stood still, watching the empty space she'd vacated. Then his brain kicked on and remembered that she wouldn't get very far without him, and he started after her.

11

Will refused to let her walk from Longbourn to her first class, which she supposed others would consider chivalrous. For Elizabeth, it was downright confusing. Still, she knew she was liable to spend less time arguing with him about her method of transportation than she would traipsing across campus, so ultimately she agreed to return to the car after grabbing her things for her first morning class.

As soon as the driver pulled up outside the appropriate lecture hall, Elizabeth all but dived out of the vehicle, full arms fumbling to keep hold of all her books. Her backpack was stuffed to the brim and she intended to sequester herself in the library later to catch up on everything she'd missed the night before.

"Thank you for the ride," she sputtered, not looking at Will. "This wasn't necessary but thanks."

"Do you need any help?"

"No," Elizabeth said, forcing her eyes to his. He had a foot out of the car like he was about to spring into action, but paused at her word which, she realized, had been more barked than spoken. Forcing herself to calm, Elizabeth summoned a smile from somewhere deep down and hoped it looked at least somewhat convincing. "No. I've got it from here."

Will withdrew, situating himself back within the car. Still, the door didn't close. "If you're sure."

"Yes. I gotta go." She glanced toward the lecture hall. "Umm, see ya."

And then she was off at a brisk pace, desperate to get her mind off Will Darcy and onto other things.

Because she was feeling things. Things she'd sworn she wouldn't feel. Granted, it had been a long time since she'd gotten excited over any guy—like before she'd graduated high school. Even her last two boyfriends hadn't elicited this much jitteriness, and she'd liked them both just fine. They'd been nice guys. Safe. A little on the boring side, but otherwise fine and dandy. Breaking up with them hadn't been fun—the last one had been a crier—but also hadn't broken her heart, and she'd thought then that perhaps that was because her heart, still gunshy from her parents' divorce, had known better than to get involved.

This had led her to the brilliant no-relationship plan. It made more sense to keep *anyone* from getting hurt. She hadn't loved being the person who broke hearts, especially when it hadn't been on purpose.

No relationships. Safe and sound.

Her heart had been in it to win it until she'd met Will. And even that first night when he'd been a total tool, she'd felt something.

Now...

She seriously needed to nip this in the bud.

The next thing Elizabeth knew, she had bounced off something warm and firm and landed on her ass amid a shower of text books. She blinked dumbly to clear the cobwebs, then looked up to see what the hell had run into her.

The *what* was a guy. A guy with a furrowed brow and worried eyes. "Are you all right?" He paused. "No, of course you're not. Here..."

He offered her a hand, which she took without thinking, and he pulled her to her feet in a swift move that looked way more effortless than it was.

"Are you hurt?" He looked her up and down in a way that made her feel naked, but not in a sexy way, rather a *I'm wearing yesterday's clothes and it's obvious* way. "Sorry—you came out of nowhere."

"Serves me right for being in my own little world," Elizabeth said, offering a small smile. "Also, I'm pretty sure I got the *pay attention to where you're going* speech at least five thousand times when I was a kid."

"Yeah, but, who didn't? Really?" The guy favored her with a smile—a nice, friendly smile with just enough smolder to be sexy rather than obnoxious. He then glanced to the pavement. "Collateral damage. Allow me." He bent over and began collecting her spilled books. Elizabeth made to help, but he waved her off with a, "Nope. You stay up there, otherwise our heads will knock together and we'll both be down for the count."

"You don't have to do that," she protested. "Really. It's my fault."

"Hey, it takes two to crash." He straightened, her books in his arms. "Come on. I'll walk you to class."

"You don't know where I'm going."

He nodded toward the lecture hall. "I'm going to go out on a limb here and guess...this way?"

"You really don't—"

"It's not every day I run into a damsel." He shifted the books. "Or, in this case, a damsel runs into me. Let me enjoy it."

Elizabeth arched an eyebrow. "Damsel?"

"It's a way to make myself feel more important," he continued smoothly. "Trust me, I can tell just by looking at you that you aren't an actual damsel."

And she could tell a few things of her own. Still, she couldn't deny the guy was charming. Charming and not wearing designer shoes or sporting a new backpack, which might make him one of the common-folk.

Bonus: he wasn't Will.

"Well, good knight, if you are to escort me, I suppose I should know your name."

He grinned. "Sir George is at your service, milady. Though most of the other knights just call me Wickham."

She snorted and fell into step beside him. "Why, did you lose a bet?"

"You wound me," he replied in a tone that clearly indicated she did anything but. "It's my last name. I went to school with one too many Georges at one point in my life. This was the way they kept them all straight. Thing is, I've now trained myself not to respond to my first name, so it's just easier to go by the last."

"Yeah, I guess there aren't a lot of ways to shorten *George.* Suppose I'm lucky." When he looked at her, she went on, "As an Elizabeth, there were tons of variations. Lizzie, Liz, Beth, Libby, Eliza, Betty, and so on."

"I've always loved the name Elizabeth."

"I get the feeling there aren't many female names you haven't loved."

"Ouch!" Wickham threw his head back—and it was a nice head, full of dark hair and situated on an admittedly biteable neck which led to broad shoulders. He had wonderfully expressive eyes too, she noticed, and his mouth seemed curled into a permanent smile. "You wound me *again.*"

She found herself grinning. "Ehh. You look all right to me."

Wickham released a long, put-upon sigh. "Now you accuse me of not being genuine and mock my pain."

"I never said you weren't genuine. I just *implied* you might have a lot of favorites. There are plenty of girls around here that, unlike yours truly, are genuine damsels."

"Yes, but the pretend ones are so much more fun." Wickham repositioned the books with a bounce. "So, *Elizabeth,* where are we off to this fine morning?"

"Calculus," she said. "Room one twenty-seven, I think."

"Calculus this early?" Wickham shuddered and hung a right down the appropriate hall. "You're right—you're no damsel. I should have spotted that right away."

"Well, we'll see if I make it through the semester. It's been a while since my math skills were put to the test." Like since high school, but she decided not to mention that. "So, George Just-Call-Me-Wickham, what about you? What am I keeping you from this morning?"

"I almost don't want to tell you."

"Well, you gotta now."

"You're going to feel really bad. So bad you'll want to make it up to me."

Elizabeth snorted. "I cannot be guilted, good knight. I challenge you to do your worst."

Wickham paused suddenly and hung his head. "Coffee."

"What?"

"You're keeping me from coffee."

Her eyes widened. "I stand corrected."

He raised his head and grinned, his eyes twinkling. "Coffee is what makes the campus go 'round. I usually head out to chug a cup or twelve before my first class."

"A solid game plan."

"Thus far, it hasn't let me down."

They continued navigating the corridors until the air began

to break with chatter and thicken with other students. Apparently, Elizabeth had chosen the entrance that took her along the scenic route. Yet she couldn't say she was disappointed at the moment, her spirits lighter. Flirting with Wickham was a nice palate cleanser, even if he was a walking cliché. Not all clichés warranted avoidance.

"Here we are," Wickham said, drawing to a halt outside Room 127. "Your classroom awaits."

Elizabeth held out her arms. "My books, if you would?"

"A true gentleman would escort you to your seat."

"Then let's be thankful there are no true gentlemen here," she retorted.

Wickham grinned and slid her books into her waiting arms. "I've learned something new about myself today."

"Oh?"

"Yes. Apparently I have a thing for pain. Would you like to grab coffee with me after your class?"

"Coffee. With you."

"I'm going to be at the Meryton Mudhouse all day," he said, then rounded his eyes in an imitation of a puppy dog look. "All alone."

"You don't have classes?"

"Not on Fridays. Fridays are my official *get-the-jump-on-home-work* day. Best way to enjoy the weekend is to not have a deadline looming."

She could definitely see the wisdom in that. "You'll have to teach me your secret."

"You know what they say about great magicians." Wickham smiled broader and edged nearer, bordering on the personal-bubble line without quite stepping over it. "Allow me to buy you a cup of coffee. You know, as a repayment for knocking you on your butt this morning."

"Here I thought the classroom escort had us squared."

"No. This was all for me."

Elizabeth found herself fighting a grin. This was good. A nice non-threatening guy to get her mind off a certain someone else. Odds were her senses would return to her by the time Monday rolled around where Will was concerned, anyway, but in case they didn't, it didn't hurt to have a back-up plan. And while she wasn't up for a relationship, she certainly wasn't going to cross off the possibility of sex.

"I might be tempted to...meander toward Meryton Mudhouse following class," she replied at last.

"Oooh. *Suspense.* I love it." And from the sparkle in Wickham's warm green eyes, he was telling the truth. "I'll leave you to it then."

"See you," she replied, taking a step into the classroom. "Or not."

"Or not," he agreed, then turned and disappeared into a throng of bustling students.

By the time Elizabeth had claimed a seat, she was smiling broadly and earning suspicious looks from her classmates. She couldn't blame their curiosity. After all, no one got that jazzed about calculus.

Except people who had coffee dates to look forward to afterward.

George Wickham was definitely not difficult to pick out in a crowd. It wasn't until Elizabeth met his eyes across the coffee house that she appreciated just how tall he was. He dwarfed the space he had claimed, making everything around him—from the tables and chairs to the bustling baristas—look teeny in comparison. He was also—she had to say—a Grade A Hottie. Massive shoulders gave way to muscular arms that looked like they ought to be registered as official weapons. A firm, broad chest led to an almost too-perfectly tapered waist. He had a strong jaw and prominent chin, and was saved by being too pretty by a nose that had been broken at least once. His deep brown hair was short and neat, and seemingly cut in such a way as to accentuate the angular lines of his face.

He was Will's physical opposite. Well, that wasn't fair. She'd seen firsthand how Will looked without a shirt on and it was definitely nothing to sneeze at, and even she could admit he had a nice face. The difference boiled down to body type, really—Will just had a leaner build than Wickham. Also, he was a few inches shorter, though given Wickham's near giant-like status, that wasn't saying much.

Also, she needed to stop comparing this guy to Will right the hell now.

It occurred to Elizabeth, after Wickham took it upon himself to start waving, that coffee dates were usually better when both parties were at the same table and not separated by the length of the café. A twinge of heat touched her cheeks, but she ignored it and started making her way through the crowd.

"Calculus," Wickham said by way of greeting. "Long time no see!"

"Apparently long enough for you to forget my name," Elizabeth retorted as she claimed her seat. "How goes the homework?"

He cast a mournful eye to the notebook on the table. "Well, it's hard to tell at the moment. The morning's been a little tense. It gets mouthy with me, I get mouthy with it, we both say things we regret, and getting back on track just seems to take longer the more often we fight."

She snorted. "You often anthropomorphize your work?"

"That was an impressive word, that. Really impressive."

"It means to give inanimate objects feelings."

Wickham's eyes went wide. "Shh," he rasped, bracing his hands over the notebook. "It'll hear you."

Elizabeth shook her head, trying to hide a grin. "So, what's the subject?"

"I didn't have any talking points prepared. Should I have?"

"I mean, what are you taking?" She waved at the notebook. "If I'm going to make your homework cry, I'd like to at least know if it deserved it."

"Homework always deserves it," Wickham replied. "And religious studies, actually. This class is on the historicity of Jesus Christ."

Well. That was heavy. Elizabeth blinked. "Are you going into that field?"

"Leaning more toward teaching, myself. Religious studies. It's fascinating."

"That's..." She didn't know what to say.

"A waste of time," Wickham supplied, "an expensive nap, a nice way to end up unemployed?"

Heat flooded her cheeks. "I didn't mean it like that."

"It's okay. Seriously." He shrugged. "I've always been taken with it—religious studies, that is. When I first got here I didn't know what I wanted to be when I grew up, so I started taking classes that appealed to my interests. Seven religious studies courses later, and this *better* be my major or I'm in a lot of trouble."

Elizabeth laughed. "So I guess the look I was giving you..."

"The patented *what the hell are you thinking* look of judgment. I can spot it a mile away."

"I'm not judging you! I think it's great that you know what you want to do."

He raised his coffee mug to his lips. "Do you? Is it calculus? Because that'd be...dull. And full of math."

"You know, you'd think I would, but the thing I wanted to be when I first came to college is very different than it is now."

He arched an eyebrow. "You know you have to give me more than that, don't you?"

"You're awfully demanding."

"And you know how to build suspense. Wait. Is that it? Are you going to write mysteries?" He brightened. "I *love* mysteries!"

Another laugh bubbled off her lips, and she felt her skin going even warmer. "Psychologist," she corrected. "This is up from going into business school. I think my life's ambition once upon a time was to become a CPA. How dull can you get?"

"Not much," Wickham agreed sagely.

"Hey!"

"What? I was *agreeing* with you." He took another sip of coffee. "So when did you have this *aha* moment? Hopefully before you spent too much money on boring accounting classes."

"They could be interesting," she protested.

"Yeah, they could if they weren't about accounting."

"Well, it doesn't matter anyway." She waved a hand. "I'm a freshman this year."

Wickham's eyes bugged. "Get out."

"Afraid it's true."

"What happened? Are you a very mature eighteen or—"

"It's a long story." That she didn't want to get into out of fear of chasing him off. "And are you saying I look old?"

"Yes, because that's exactly the way I meant for you to take that." He shook his head. "Are you saying I should be attracted to teenagers? What does that say about *me*?"

Elizabeth preened, straightening her shoulders. "You are very smooth."

"Kind of you to notice. And even if it is a long story—why you're just getting started—I'd like to hear it."

"I took a break that I thought would be short. It wasn't, so I'm just now getting back."

"That's not what I'd call a long story. How old are you now?"

"That's one of those questions you're not supposed to ask."

"I like to live dangerously."

She chuckled again. "Twenty-four."

"And you got into Meryton?" He blinked, visibly impressed.

"Enrollment exams, scholarship applications, and one painfully large student loan later, yes."

"Why here? There are tons of schools—"

"But there's only one Meryton. And the psych program here is supposed to be the best in the country. They also have a good English department, if I decide to write mysteries on the side."

Wickham nodded absently, staring at her in wonder. "So... you're kind of like a superhero."

"What?"

"You *got in* to Meryton like that? I've heard nightmares about people trying to get accepted and being asked to do pretty much everything, including but not limited to sacrificing a virgin, and still being turned down." He gave himself a shake. "Starting like that...*with* student loans..."

She wiggled, the pleasant warmth morphing slowly into something that was anything but. "I'm not the only finely aged freshman here," she argued. "There's Will Darcy."

Had she not been looking right at him, she might have missed it. As it was, the darkening of Wickham's face was obvious, as was the intense dislike that flashed in his eyes.

He looked over her shoulder and, if possible, stiffened even further. "You're right. *There's* Will Darcy."

Elizabeth frowned and twisted in her seat. Sure enough, Will was standing by the door, looking rumpled in a sexy way that annoyed her for reasons she couldn't say. Maybe she'd hoped that the next time she saw him, he wouldn't appear nearly as lickable as he had that morning. But even the shirt he wore accentuated his lean, muscular physique in ways yesterday's wardrobe hadn't.

He met her eyes over the crowd as though he'd sensed her near. Then his gaze shifted to Wickham, and a shadow fell across his face.

So that dislike was mutual. Noted.

Elizabeth looked at him a moment longer—likely too long to be polite—before turning back to her companion. "You know it's going to be obvious that we're talking about him now, don't you?"

Wickham was still glowering, though at her voice, he at least attempted a smile. "Sorry," he said, waving in Will's direction. "I wasn't expecting to... Well, I wasn't expecting that."

The part of Elizabeth that didn't want to be nosy declared war on the part of her that hungered for information. She'd never considered herself a gossip, but she was human—if there was a story about someone she knew, she wanted to hear it.

"So...you obviously know each other," she blurted before she could help it. "Either that or... Well, I don't have a good analogy here."

This time, the smile that crossed Wickham's face was genuine. "Yes," he replied, though his tone was clipped in such a way that didn't invite questions, "I guess you can say that."

Too bad. Elizabeth was going to ask anyway.

"I take it this story doesn't end with a secret handshake and the pledge to remain best friends forever."

"No," Wickham agreed. "But that's how it starts."

She blinked and waited for him to continue.

He cleared his throat and leaned forward. "How, ah, do *you* know Will?"

"My roomie-slash-bestie is dating his friend."

"Charlie?"

Her eyebrows rose. Wickham knew Charlie too. This was interesting.

"Yes." She paused. "Does Charlie also warrant cross-room stare downs? If so, I need to know. I have a shovel with his name on it if he hurts Jane."

At that, the smile on Wickham's face grew. "You're not one to cross, are you?"

"Just try me."

"No, thank you." He held his hands up. "To put your mind at ease, Charlie's a really good guy. He's possibly the happiest person I've ever met."

"Happiest?"

"Well, it's what he puts out there, being so chipper all the time. I swear, you could run over that guy's dog and he'd apologize for having such a fragile animal. He's like a walking Xanax advertisement."

Elizabeth snorted. "Yeah. I can see that. He's *seemed* like a good guy, but it's good to hear it from someone else."

Wickham nodded. "Understandable. Considering..." He peered over Elizabeth's shoulder, and from the look on his face, more silent eye-wars were occurring behind her. "Well, things."

She leaned back and crossed her arms. "You know you're going to have to tell me more, right?"

Particularly since she was starving for information that would make Will less attractive to her.

"As much as I'd love to go into all the ways Will Darcy is a shitty human being, I don't want to make things awkward for you." He pulled a face. "I hate coming between friends. It'll make it really weird when I ask you out."

"You're going to ask me out?"

He gave her a look that said *duh* and soldiered on. "It'll make things *especially* weird after we've been together long enough to do the merging."

"Merging."

"Of friends. You know, you can't be with a guy who hates your friends, and I want to show you off to all of my friends because none of them would believe a girl like you could go for a guy like me without witchcraft involved."

Elizabeth crossed her arms. "We've known each other two hours and you already have our relationship mapped out?"

Wickham shrugged. "I said I was coming here to work, but thinking about you was so much more fun."

"I can't decide if I'm flattered or creeped out."

"Go for option A. Looks much better on me."

She fought a grin. "Well, seeing as you've decided you're my future boyfriend, I can assure you that Will and I aren't friends."

That technically wasn't a lie. They weren't really anything.

"Oh?"

"I've known him for less than a week. My first impression was he's a condescending jerk." Also not a lie. "Not going to be making him a friendship bracelet anytime soon."

Wickham seemed to consider this, his brow furrowed. Then he released a long sigh, sat back, tossed another look over Elizabeth's shoulder, and nodded.

"I try not to be mad about it," he started. "It's been a long time, but it still…"

It suddenly occurred to her that this might be more than just a petty grudge. The pain on Wickham's face was real and intense, and she suddenly felt like the world's biggest asshole. Pain like that shouldn't be forced to the forefront, especially if it had taken time to…

Well, anything.

"Hey," she said softly. "You don't need to tell me. I shouldn't have pried."

"No," Wickham replied, shaking his head. "No, it's okay. I'm apparently going to have to see him around campus, so I might as well get this off my chest now."

She pressed her lips together and waited.

"We grew up in Derbyshire. Have you heard of it?"

"Not ringing any bells."

"That doesn't surprise me. It's this small town in North Carolina, where all the wealthy cotton planters built their fancy townhouses before the Civil War."

"You're from North Carolina?"

He nodded. "We both are."

"But you..."

"Don't have an accent?" He smiled. "Yeah. Well, I ended up moving away after...after this and I'm very easily suggestible."

"Will doesn't have one, either."

"That's because he worked very hard to get rid of it when we were kids," Wickham said. "He never thought anyone would take him seriously if he sounded like he came from where he came from. And if there's one thing about Will Darcy, it's *image* is *everything.*"

Elizabeth's throat tightened, her mind dragging her back a week to the pre-semester party. Yeah, she could believe that about Will.

"The Darcys are old money," Wickham continued. "The only kind that mattered after the war. They were one of the only families in the area that didn't lose their fortune during the War Between the States. Many planters in that time made deals with the Union army to avoid having their crops burned, and Derbyshire was always home to Union sympathizers. The Emancipation didn't hit Pemberley like it hit other homes, either. Namely because they didn't rely on slave labor."

"Convenient."

"Yeah, well... I think the story goes that Fitzwilliam Darcy the First fell head over heels for a northern girl who happened to be a devout abolitionist. She refused to marry him unless he freed his slaves, thinking he never would because that would've been *insane* at the time." Wickham shrugged. "If the story's to be believed, he did."

"That can't be true."

"I'm not sure if it is or isn't, but it's what I grew up hearing. And there are other stories like that—not quite that radical, but the family claims to have evidence to support it, even if I've never seen it. And in Derbyshire, reputation is what matters. The Darcys' reputation has always been that they were progressive for the time."

"If it's considered progressive not to own people," Elizabeth replied. "Not sure that earns a gold star. Seems a pretty low bar to meet."

Wickham inclined his head. "Yes, well, you grow up in the South, and you learn things a bit different. Not saying it's right—it's not—but for any family to have had as much money as the Darcys *without* slave labor was unheard of. There are even stories that Wilhelmina Darcy—Will's great-great grandmother—volunteered Pemberley as a stop on the Underground Railroad. I think *that's* a load of bull, myself. Seems all the families in the area decided slavery was wrong right around the time that that opinion became popular."

"Pemberley?" she echoed. "You've said that twice now. Am I supposed to know what that is?"

He shook his head, looking a little dazed. "Where I come from, yes. Sorry. Pemberley is what they call the Darcy plantation."

"It...has its own name?"

Wickham smiled. "You haven't traveled in the south much, have you?"

"I haven't traveled much period."

"All the old homes have pretentious names. My family's

home did." The smile turned into a grimace. "At least before the bank foreclosed. Now the property's part of the Derbyshire Hotel and Convention Center. They stopped short of bulldozing it."

"Oh...I'm sorry."

He waved like it was no big deal, but his eyes told a different story. "That was a long time ago, and like I said, Pemberley is pretty much the only one of the old homes that was completely unaffected. It *is* the only area home that's stayed in the same family, aside from Rosings." He released a long breath. "Before we lost the house, Will and I were inseparable. His dad was a great guy. Paid my tuition to Derbyshire Academy—private school—and everything when he knew my dad couldn't afford it. But as we got older..."

Elizabeth stared at him, edging closer. "What?"

But a new look had fallen over Wickham's face—one that made her belly clench. "You know what? I really shouldn't. If you're going to be around him—"

"I won't tell that I know, whatever it is."

"No, it's not that. If your friend's dating his friend... I just don't want to put you in an awkward situation."

She bit back a laugh at this. "My definitions of an awkward situation are not the same as other people's."

Wickham looked at her for a moment, his eyes conflicted. Then his smile resurfaced, and he inclined his head in acknowledentgment. "Fair enough." He paused and glanced across the room again, as though to verify Will couldn't overhear. "Things are different when you're a kid. You notice that your friend has a larger house, a larger room, and gets whatever he wants, and you accept it as a fact of life."

"If you say so."

"I'm not saying I wasn't aware that Will had more money than us—it was just *there*. But his house kind of became my house. On weekends and over summers, I practically *was* a Darcy. And it was great. Will was like the brother I never had." Wickham's face fell. "But as we got older, he became more distant. He stopped inviting me over, stopped sitting with me at school—childish shit that feels like it's really big in the moment. I tried to ask him what the problem was, but he always insisted there wasn't a problem. And for a while, I believed it. He'd just found some new friends, all with parents in the same income bracket, and I had been phased out. Fitzwilliam Senior—Will's dad—still checked up on me and my family every now and then, because he was good people, and he knew how much I wanted the scholarship."

"The scholarship?"

"The Darcy Foundation scholarship. It was important to my family that I come here"—he gestured around the café to indicate the campus—"and it became important to me. But we could never afford it. Fitzwilliam Senior didn't like showing favoritism, but he would often drop harmless hints as to what would look best on an application in terms of extra curriculars and stuff."

"He sounds nice."

"He was the best," Wickham said loyally. "I think he wanted me to come here especially because Will had started struggling at school, which doesn't look good on a transcript, no matter how rich your family is. Turns out Will's friends had gotten him... Well, it started with weed. Harmless stuff that we all experiment with. His grades dropped and he started missing classes. I think he was doing some harder stuff too—I never found out, but the guys he hung out with definitely were, and he bore all the signs."

Elizabeth wrinkled her nose, trying to picture the studious Will Darcy that had offered her his bed the previous night as a substance abuser. The image wouldn't come. "He doesn't seem the type."

"I know," Wickham agreed. "I never would've thought it of him, either. It shocked the hell out of me. But this was also when his mom was getting really sick and I guess I thought it was just his way of coping. I didn't know..." He broke off, a heavy sigh tearing off his lips. "Sorry. It's still hard to believe."

She held her breath, waiting.

"That day, he came over to see me at lunch," Wickham continued after a moment. "It surprised the hell out of me, because for the past two years, he'd pretended I was invisible. He had a book—one I had lent him such a long time before this that I'd forgotten he had it. He said he'd found it while cleaning his room and wanted to get it back to me, which I thought was nice." He barked a bitter laugh. "Yeah. Real nice."

Elizabeth swallowed hard. "What happened?"

"He put the book in my backpack, said something about getting together, then walked back to his buddies." The look on Wickham's face was savage now. His eyes slanted, his cheeks pink—every bit of good humor that had been present earlier having faded. "Turns out I was the butt of a joke. The book had been hollowed out. Inside was half a kilo of cocaine."

Her jaw went slack.

Wickham offered a sage nod. "And about fifteen minutes later, I was *randomly* searched. The best I can figure is he knew they were about to pin him with distribution—they searched him first—and he saw me as a good patsy. Everything went to shit in two seconds flat. I was kicked out of school, out of home, and I was lucky not to go to jail. The only thing I can think is that Fitzwilliam Senior knew what had happened—or at least suspected—and pulled some strings."

"That..." She stared at him, her brain scrambling to catch up with the multitude of information. To learn that Will had been an insufferable rich kid wouldn't have surprised her, but *this* was beyond anything she would have expected from him. It seemed too ludicrous to be true—completely at odds with the picture her mind had drawn of Will.

Except she knew better than most how some people looked one way and acted another. And the pain on Wickham's face was real. He'd worked himself up—his eyes were shining with angry tears, his jaw firm and his hands clenching the table so hard she was surprised when it didn't crack.

"Sorry," Wickham said a moment later, then released a long, tortured breath. "Sorry. I always tell myself I'm over it."

"How could you be, though? That's...damn, that's the worst thing I've ever heard." She turned to catch a peek at Will, who had sequestered himself in the opposite corner of the café and apparently was taking great lengths to not look in their direction. "Has he ever spoken to you about it?"

"What?" Wickham replied bitterly. "Something like, 'Hey, George. You know how I ruined your life? Sorry about that. Misunderstanding.'" He shook his head and wiped at his eyes, his skin flush. "He doesn't have the balls to talk to me."

Elizabeth pursed her lips. "I'm sorry. It's just... At the worst, I never expected something *that* bad."

"Yeah, well, he covers it well." Wickham crossed his arms. "I'd like to think his dad dying might have changed him. Maybe it did. Maybe he's better now. Maybe he's...seen the light or something. But if that were the case, he could go back and at least try to make things right. I don't see that happening."

Elizabeth sat still for a long moment, her mind a tangled mess. God, she didn't know what to think. She wasn't sure she wanted to. That anyone could do anything like this to another human being was beyond her—especially if that person had been a friend. And try as she might, reconciling Wickham's version of Will with the guy she had kinda been crushing on seemed impossible. That Will had been an ass at times, yes, but he'd also been kind and considerate.

Hell, she'd been fooled before. If her father could make her believe things that weren't true for years, then certainly a professionally rich guy like Will could as well.

Plus, there was Wickham, and the hurt on his face was very real. He had no reason to lie to her. The story was too outrageous to be anything but true.

"I'm sorry," he said at length, looking away. "I...damn, I shouldn't have said anything."

"No," Elizabeth said immediately, "I'm glad I know. I'm just... sorry that happened to you."

A bitter smile twisted his lips. "You and me both." He blew out a breath. "But we were having a good time and that topic is kind of a downer."

"You were having a good time?"

"I was. I thought—err, hoped you were, too." He rubbed the back of his neck, the smile becoming sheepish. "'Cause I'm still vying to ask you out."

Elizabeth hesitated, which he noticed right away.

"And on any such date," Wickham continued, "I solemnly swear to never mention Will Darcy again."

"That's—"

"Look, no one likes a woe-is-me jackass."

Her uncertainty began to wane. Elizabeth sighed and reached across the table. "It just surprised me. I've... Well, I have classes with Will. I actually stayed in his room last night."

Wickham turned an interesting shade of red at this news. "Oh god. Shit god *fuck*, I am such a—"

"Alone," Elizabeth said firmly, squeezing his hand. And felt herself relax—apparently, he wasn't adverse to profanity, which meant she didn't have to watch her tongue. "I got caught in the storm over there and he...well, insisted I take his bed, which I thought was so nice. But—"

"Oh, don't get me wrong." Wickham shifted forward. "Will

can be *smooth* when he wants to be. It took me a day and a half to realize that he'd set me up after I was arrested. It just didn't seem like him. But if you and he are—"

"We're not. At all. It's nothing like that." Something in her gut twisted at the words, but she didn't care to examine it too closely. Because she shouldn't be disappointed for herself—there was no world in which she was going to pursue Will, anyway. And if there had been, Wickham's story had Death Stared it to smithereens. "And like I said...I'm glad to know. I'll at least know not to drop my guard around him."

Wickham nodded. "Is that a no, then? On the date?"

"It's not a no. It's a maybe."

"Isn't maybe just another word for no?"

"For some people, it might be," Elizabeth agreed. "For me, it's an 'I've had a really long week and I want to make sure I'm not already behind before I agree to let a cute guy distract me.'"

"Wow. That's a long maybe." Wickham grinned. "Can I at least get your number? I won't send unsolicited dick pics, but I might shoot over a few texts with irresistibly cute emoticons."

Elizabeth considered this for a moment, but her brain was tired of thinking. "Phone," she said, holding out her hand. After he handed it over, she sent herself a text and tossed it back. "There you go."

He nodded appreciatively and glanced at the screen. "That looks like a real number."

She dug her phone out of her pocket. "I don't do fake numbers. If I don't want you to have something of mine, you don't get it. Anyone who has a problem with that gets a date with my pepper spray." She flashed the screen to him so he could see the text she'd sent. "Keep that in mind."

"Aye aye."

"Thank you for...well, walking me to class and inviting me for coffee." Though she'd never gotten around to ordering, which was fine. At the moment, she didn't think her stomach could handle solids or liquids. "And thanks for...trusting me with that information."

"You won't tell anyone."

"Of course not. It's not my place to tell." She shrugged her bag onto her back. "I'll see you around."

"You too, Elizabeth. And thanks." Wickham smiled again. "For listening. I'd forgotten what that felt like."

She didn't know what to say to that. After an awkward moment, she swallowed and managed a weak, "Anytime," before turning toward the door.

12

No matter how hard he tried, Will couldn't get the image of Elizabeth and Wickham out of his head.

In the six weeks that had followed the night that Elizabeth had stayed in his bed, Will had done an admirable job of convincing himself that he didn't care at all who she spent her time with, except that was crap because he did care a lot—he just hated that he did. The fact that Elizabeth had gone from not-so-subtly checking him out to cool politeness had not gone unnoticed.

Mostly, though, he was worried.

And pissed.

And damned if he could do anything about it. Because what, exactly, was his recourse here? He and Elizabeth had shared a few nice moments, but nothing solid enough that he felt comfortable asking her about what he'd seen in the café.

Had he known that Wickham was a student at Meryton... Well, Will wasn't sure what he would have done. And it was only by virtue of not wanting to drag Georgiana down a dark path that he'd managed to keep from launching himself across the coffee shop and succumbing to his baser instincts. Namely, ripping Wickham apart piece by bloody piece.

No, he thought, shaking his head hard. *Not going there. Not now.*

Because if he started thinking those thoughts, his temper would begin to creep up, and his otherwise sensible brain would find itself overrun with baser urges. Wickham was the one man in the world that could provoke him into violence, and as much as he might relish the thought of pummeling the asshole until he was unrecognizable, that would only feel good for a few minutes. The minutes and hours and days and months that followed would be a new kind of hell.

For Georgiana's sake...

Except it wasn't just Georgiana he worried about.

Of all the women on campus, of course—of course—Wickham would set his sights on Elizabeth. And of course she would fall right into him. It was no fault of her own—Wickham had always been proficient at the art of a first impression. Hell, he could woo a nun if he put his mind to it.

Will wanted to believe Elizabeth was smart enough to see through it, but experience had taught him otherwise. After all, *he* hadn't been smart enough until after it was too late.

It wasn't his place to worry about her.

Except he couldn't help himself.

One of the first things he'd done after realizing Wickham was a student was call his lawyer, whose enthusiasm at hearing Will's voice was so palpable he could almost see little golden dollar signs wafting from the phone's speaker. He'd learned that Wickham was in his third year at Meryton. His grades were admirable—honor role admirable—and he'd maintained a clean record. No incidents. No complaints. No nothing. He reported to his probation officer like clockwork and regularly passed each mandatory drug test.

By all accounts, the man had indeed turned over a new leaf.

Except Will knew better. A new man would be honest, even if the truth wasn't pretty. And given the fact that Elizabeth had only spoken to him when forced in the weeks that had passed, the truth was not what she'd learned. Or not a version of it that he was familiar with.

And there was no way of clearing the air without sounding like the jealous mess he was.

This was why getting involved with anyone had been a bad idea. Not that he was even involved, but damn, for a few hours there, he'd thought...

Well, it didn't matter. He'd been wrong.

The weeks that had spanned since the night Elizabeth and Jane had been marooned at Netherfield Heights had not been uneventful. Jane had become something of a regular fixture around the dorm, and though Charlie did everything he could to monopolize her time, Jane could often be seen sequestered in corners with Caroline, who had made good on her promise to nominate Jane for the Realis Society for Women. In fact, Will heard Jane—whenever she was around—speak of little else. She otherwise just watched Charlie blab about any and everything that popped into his head, which took the pressure off everyone else to do the same.

Also, the semester's coursework finally started to get serious. Professor Greenfield had scheduled the first debates and their topics, as well as the designated class periods for group study sessions that need not meet in her room. Will's group—comprised of himself, Randall and the chatty blonde that had cornered him at the Meryton Mudhouse, whose name he'd learned was Penelope—had taken to meeting in a private room of the campus library. And thankfully, after she'd disabused herself of the notion that he was at all interested, his group partner had stopped hitting on him, which made these meetings much less uncomfortable.

On the Friday following their seventh completed week at Meryton, Charlie came bursting into Will's room without so much as a tap on the door.

"Get up!" he cried with his usual enthusiasm. "We're going to be late!"

Will, who was lying in bed, studying the patterns on the ceiling, didn't even look at him. "Hard to be late to something I'm not going to."

"Don't be stupid, of course you're coming." Charlie helped himself to Will's dresser and started pulling out garments at random. "Do you have anything that doesn't suck?"

"What are you doing?"

"You dress like Wilford Brimley. It's tragic."

"Why do you care how I dress?"

"Because if you're going to be seen with me, you need to look like you're not about to apply for an AARP membership."

Will grunted and sat up on his elbows. "I'm not."

"Well, I know that. You have to be, like, at least fifty to—"

"I'm *not* going to be seen with you."

Charlie looked up, frowning. "What? Did I do something?"

"No. I'm just not in the mood."

He snickered. "You know, you sound like my last three girlfriends?"

"I think that says something about you."

Charlie rolled his eyes, waving one of Will's undershirts at him. "Dude. It's Friday night. *Friday.* The weather's good and we're both free. You're not going to mope around here."

"I have class work to do."

"Uh huh. I see you're really hard at work on that *impersonate a dead man* assignment." Charlie snorted at his own joke, then turned back to Will's dresser. "Okay. Here's something that doesn't suck." He pulled free a pair of dark wash jeans. "And what's this? I knew you had some good stuff. Why is it all buried?"

Will didn't answer—partly because he was embarrassed and partly because it was none of Charlie's business. When he'd first announced his intent to return to college, Georgiana had insisted on taking him shopping for clothes the modern student would wear, as opposed to the baggy tees he hid behind, or the occasional suits he had to wear when dealing with the company.

Elizabeth had seen him in one of Georgiana's selections the morning he'd taken her to campus, and the look on her face had been...

Brief. It had been brief. Because of Wickham.

He scowled and flung his head back against the pillow.

"Darcy. *Darcy.* Get your sorry ass up." Charlie threw a selection of clothes at him without awaiting a response. "We're going out."

Will grunted. "No."

"Darcy—"

"Stop calling me that."

"Then get dressed and meet me downstairs. You and me are going to go out and have a damn good time tonight. We haven't done that since the semester began."

"You've been a little preoccupied."

"Well, Jane's hanging out with Elizabeth tonight, so I'm all yours."

"Great. Everyone loves to be the second pick."

"You're awfully close to whining, you know. I might have to record this." And with a grin, Charlie drew his cell phone out of his pocket and held it up. "Why so gwumpy?" he asked, adopting an exaggerated baby voice. "Does Will need to get waid?"

Will rolled his eyes and sat up. "You're pathetic."

"I think Will needs to get waid," Charlie repeated, maneuvering the phone so it mimed nodding. Then he whirled it around and beamed into the screen. "Come on, gang. Let's see if we can find that special someone to put the spring back in Will Darcy's step. Away!"

He bounded into the hallway with a dramatic flourish.

Will sighed, seizing the jeans Charlie had chucked at him off the bed. "One. Two..."

Charlie materialized in the door, beaming. "See you downstairs!" And he was gone again before Will could contradict him.

"I knew this was a bad idea."

"What?"

Elizabeth cupped her mouth and bellowed, "I knew this was a bad idea!"

"What do you mean?" Lydia had yet to stop bouncing in her seat, which by itself was very distracting. The fact that she couldn't seem to bounce in time with the music was almost enough to give a girl a headache. "This place is *boss*!"

Elizabeth frowned. What the hell did that even mean?

"Oh, there's Kitty!" Lydia clapped her hands together. "You'll never guess who asked her out."

"Probably because I can't hear you."

"What?"

Elizabeth sighed, rolled her eyes, and formally gave up on verbal communication. She could be back at the dorm, starting to put together the outline for the presentation she, Lydia, and Mary had to make before their final paper was due. Hell, she could be trying to get into *The Gunslinger* for the umpteenth time. She could be catching up on sleep.

But no. Her mother had called and put her in a mood where she desperately needed to get out. So when Lydia had come asking if she wanted to blow off steam, she'd agreed without fight.

All that to say, she had no one to blame but herself.

The club they'd chosen was also a popular refuge for Meryton students, which somewhat defeated the purpose of a change in scenery.

The table had been abandoned for a while, save for her and Lydia—after everyone downed their first shot, they had hit the dance floor, serenaded by what could only be described as the college-girl mating calls. Even Mary, who often appeared to have her own definition of fun hidden away in a secret dictionary, was enjoying herself, though the vodka martinis had undoubtedly had a hand in it.

Elizabeth felt every bit her age. She didn't have too many years on the others, but the years she did have might as well be decades.

"Lizzie. Lizzie!" Lydia was shaking her arm. "Is that—oh, it is!"

Elizabeth's head snapped up. "What?"

"That's either Charlie Bingley or Jane has some 'splainin' to do."

There had either been a lull in the music or Elizabeth's ears had acclimated to a new decibel level, because she could suddenly hear just fine. Fine enough to know what she'd see when she turned around. She twisted in her seat just as Jane threw her arms around Charlie's neck and greeted him with an enthusiastic kiss, which, hey, go Jane. Only Elizabeth's focus didn't remain on Jane for long, because Charlie hadn't come alone.

It was little comfort that Will looked about as thrilled to be there as she was thrilled to see him.

"Yeah," she said, twisting back around. "That's Charlie."

"And that Darcy guy from our class is with him, looks like."

"That's him."

"Charlie and Darcy are friends?" Lydia asked, wide-eyed.

"Rich boys travel in packs," Elizabeth replied, willing herself to calm.

Yeah, this wouldn't be awkward at all. Elizabeth had spent the past few weeks doing her best to pretend he didn't exist. Childish, perhaps, but ignoring him had seemed the safest way to respond to what she'd learned. That excited-but-wary tingling sensation she'd entertained at Netherfield Heights might have scared the crap out of her, but it had also been kinda-sorta nice, and its swift death during that first coffee date with Wickham had left her hollow, angry, and a little down.

Plus, her body had not yet received the memo from her brain that Will was a douche. While somewhat accustomed to shutting down during their shared class, it refused to listen to her now that he'd caught her off guard. Rather, she felt like her every nerve was drawn to him.

Her body was a goddamned traitor.

Focus. Elizabeth shook her head and forced her thoughts back to the internet search she'd conducted after talking to Wickham. Google had led her to Wickham's mug-shot, along with the charges of possession with intent to distribute. The photo itself didn't do Wickham many favors on first glance. The twist of his mouth and the anger in his eyes were almost incompatible with the guy who had walked her to class, but she couldn't say she blamed him, given the situation. Had a friend set her up, she imagined she'd look ready to commit murder.

"Looks like Darcy brought a date," Lydia said. "Oh, they're coming this way."

Elizabeth scowled and looked over her shoulder. Sure enough, Jane was leading an entourage to their table. Charlie dogged her steps as though afraid of letting too much air get between them while a miserable-looking Will followed. Behind him was another familiar face, and one almost as unwelcome.

"That's Charlie's sister," Elizabeth told Lydia.

"Does she always look like that?"

"Look like what?"

"Like someone smeared shit under her nose?"

Elizabeth barked a surprised laugh, some of the tightness in her chest loosening. "Actually, yes, I think she does."

"Great." Lydia sighed heavily. "Guess we need to get more chairs."

Or Elizabeth could just slip off hers and get the hell out of here. She couldn't explain to anyone why she wanted to avoid Will, no more than she could explain how thoroughly pissed off she was with herself for having ever had any feelings for him. Not only had that gone against her plan, but she'd developed them for the poster child of why the plan was necessary in the first place.

Jane was the only one who might connect the dots to Wickham, as Elizabeth had looped her in. But Jane hadn't seemed to take the story seriously—at least not enough to demand all the details, which had been for the best. Elizabeth *had*, after all, promised to keep mum. She just hadn't had much of a chance to come up with a reason as to why she'd been looking at a guy's old mug shot.

"Elizabeth!" Charlie cried happily, stretching his arms wide and swinging in for a hug. "It's been ages!"

He pulled her completely off her seat in his enthusiasm, which made keeping the smile off her face next to impossible.

"How are you?" Charlie asked after he released her. "Good? I hope you're good. Jane's great, but you know that. Of course you know that. Have you met my sister?"

"I have," Elizabeth replied with a polite nod in Caroline's direction. "How are you?"

The snooty blonde's mouth twitched in response. "Feeling a bit overdressed, actually," she said. "I had no idea this place existed." She nudged Will. "It's...quaint. Don't you think?"

Elizabeth might not have a bajillion dollars, but she was savvy enough to know that *quaint* was rich-people talk for *not good enough.* "Considering it's a converted warehouse, I'm not sure what exactly you were expecting."

Caroline shifted her attention to her, gave her a once over, then favored her with a nasty smile. "Oh, it's you. I remember you. Will's old plaything."

Elizabeth straightened. "His what?"

"My what?" Will said at the same time, jerking his head to Caroline.

"Didn't I see her sneaking out of your bedroom a few weeks back?"

Charlie's smile faded and Jane's eyebrows went up.

The smart thing to do would be to keep quiet, but hell, she couldn't help it. Caroline was trying to embarrass her, and using sex to do it. That violated all kinds of feminist law.

"Sneaking?" Elizabeth replied, crossing her arms. "Implying shame, of course. Does sex make you that uncomfortable?"

Caroline's smile withered—not by much, but by enough to encourage Elizabeth to take an inner victory lap.

Attempting to recover, Caroline offered, "If you had such a good time, why haven't you been back?"

"Why? Still haven't mastered poke-ball?"

"What ball?" Jane asked, her eyes wide and her mouth set somewhere between a grimace and a smile. "What have I missed?"

"A lot, by the sound of things," Charlie said, glancing to Will, who—Elizabeth was somewhat pleased to note—had turned rather red. "If you've been getting laid on a regular basis, why have you been such an ass these last couple months?"

Will brought his hands up, a line of sweat visible along his forehead. "Elizabeth did not spend the night with me. She—I offered her my bedroom so she could get some rest and took the couch. *Nothing* happened."

Elizabeth tilted her head, her irritation dying a little as amusement took over. In lieu of what she'd learned since that night at Netherfield Heights, she'd forgotten how easy it had been to make Will blush.

Funny for a guy who had no qualms sending a friend to prison.

At that thought, she felt her smile dim and her irritation skyrocket.

Thinking of the things she liked about Will was exactly how guys like him got away with the long-con. She couldn't afford to be that stupid.

"You stayed in Will's room?" Jane asked, jerking her back to the present.

"Alone," Will added. "Alone. Completely alone. Without me."

Don't say anything. Don't—

"Yes, don't worry," Elizabeth said. "Will's virtue is still intact."

Good going, Bennet.

He paused, staring at her, his mouth slack. "My what?"

Lydia released a timely giggle.

"Your virtue," Elizabeth replied, smirking. "You seem to be worried about it."

"I'm not worried about my virtue. I'm trying to protect yours."

She crossed her arms and tilted her head. "How gallant of you."

"I just thought you might not want it spread across the whole damn campus that we slept together." The confused look on

Will's face had started to harden. "I didn't realize that made me a bad guy."

A thrill raced down her spine. "Any number of things can make you a bad guy. Assuming my worth depends on my sex life just makes you typical."

Goddammit. Despite everything, she'd forgotten how much fun he was to verbally spar with.

"Who said anything about your worth?" he shot back.

"If you think my reputation needs protecting because it might get out that consenting adults occasionally have S-E-X, then you've answered your own question."

"I never said—"

"Guys!" Charlie forced himself between them, gesturing with the universal *time-out* signal. "Seriously, Will, this is why I never take you anywhere."

It became very clear very fast that Charlie was on thin ice, as Will looked about two seconds away from committing murder.

"If I'm remembering right, coming out tonight was your brilliant idea," he snarled.

"Yeah, well, that was before I knew you'd insult my girlfriend's roommate."

"I didn't insult—"

"Hey!" Elizabeth brought her hands up, willing her pulse to slow. She had to get out of here. "Why don't I make this easy? I have about a stack of reading I could be doing. You guys go right ahead."

A wounded look crossed Jane's face. "Lizzie—"

"It's fine. Better, actually." She grabbed her purse forced a smile, trembling. "You have a good night. Really."

She tore toward the door without awaiting another word, weaving through a sea of sweaty bodies. Her pulse was thumping so hard her ribs rattled—or perhaps that was the music, but she didn't know. She just needed to get to fresh air.

At last, Elizabeth broke through the crowd and fought her way to freedom. The cool night air was kissing her cheeks and she felt she could breathe again.

"Elizabeth!"

Oh jeez.

She inhaled, then whirled around in time to see Will skid to a halt in front of her, panting. He stared at her for a few seconds as he tried to catch his breath, his chest—his annoyingly nice chest—heaving with effort.

She waited for him to say something, stuck in that awful place between dread and anticipation. And in that moment, she wasn't sure what she wanted. If she hoped he'd mention Wickham, since she knew he'd seen them together that day, or...

Or what?

Finally, when she'd become aware of how long they had been staring at each other, Elizabeth squared her shoulders. "Did you want something or did you just follow me out here to gawk?"

That did it. His eyes hardened. "Have I done something to offend you?"

"Yes."

"Can you at least tell me what it is?"

You made me like you.

But she couldn't go with that, so she cast her mind back to the conversation she'd just abandoned, desperate for a hook. And, fortunately, there was one there waiting. "My value is not tied to how much sex I have or haven't had."

There. That was a nice, concise argument she could make without invoking Wickham or Will's past douchery or any of it.

"I never said it was!"

"Right. I just made up that whole *protecting my virtue* bullshit."

"You're the one who brought up virtue at all!"

"Because you were three seconds away from issuing a PSA about the sex we didn't have," Elizabeth replied, her blood starting to heat the way it did before she went on a tangent.

"I'm sorry, did you want me to tell them we fucked all night?" He took a step forward, his nostrils flaring. "All I was doing—"

"I don't care. I don't care what you were doing and I *don't* care what they think we did." Elizabeth gestured at the club behind him. "That's the whole point. I'm not embarrassed by sex. I have it. I have lots of it." Okay, that wasn't true, but she wasn't about to back down now. She was riding this freaking wave. "I *enjoy* sex. Know what I don't enjoy? Misogynists who think they're the good guys, who get their rocks off by trying to protect some outdated ideal of what a virtuous woman is supposed to be. So, there you have it. *Spelled out.*"

Will's jaw seemed to be in a losing fight with gravity. He opened his mouth, closed it, and opened it again. "What do you want me to say?" he asked in a tone that was neither even nor strained, rather some bizarre combination of the two.

"Start by telling me why the hell it mattered to you so much that they know that nothing happened," Elizabeth said. The words were out before she could vet them.

He started back for her, and she released a long breath.

"You want to know?" he demanded hotly. Then he was close —so close the warmth from his skin damn near had hers sizzling. Elizabeth's heart did a funny little jerk that she didn't want to understand, her veins suddenly pumped full of liquid heat. She'd never seen him like this—a pace away from uncontrolled, struggling with a temper that she imagined was the thing of legend.

"I didn't want anyone to think less of you," Will said, his voice low, and shakier than before. "I didn't want anyone thinking you'd gone to bed with me because of who I am."

"Who you are."

"You're smart enough to know what I mean."

Yeah, she was, but she still wanted to hear it.

"No one here is going to care how liberal you are about sex," he continued. "They're going to hear you stayed in my room and then they're going to look at you, then look at me, and make snap judgments."

"That's *not* my problem."

He stared at her, incredulous. "Like I said, you're too smart to mean that."

"I am too smart to think that I should have to play the part of the virgin maiden in order to be taken seriously as a person."

"No one is disagreeing with you. That's just not the world we live in."

"Yes, and standing back and saying nothing is the perfect way to change that."

"Makes just as much sense as yelling at people who are on your side just because they're trying to look out for you."

"I *don't* need you to look out for me!"

"You obviously need someone to!" He gestured toward the club. "Is this really how you think minds are changed?"

Well, no. She hadn't set out to change anyone's mind tonight. She hadn't set out to do much of anything, except appease her friends and try to clear her head.

Then Will had shown up and her brain had gone a little fuzzy. He was a threat to rational thought.

"For the record," he said, "I agree with you."

"You do."

"Yes. A woman's sex life is no one's business but her own." He paused. "But I know what people think about women from your..."

He broke off, looking uncomfortable.

Elizabeth perked her brows. "My what?"

For a moment, she was certain he was going to walk away for real. He didn't. Instead, he pressed closer.

His nearness was making it hard for her to concentrate. There were reasons to not want him so damn close. Reasons she trusted. But when she shivered, it wasn't out of disgust. The fire in his eyes had parts of her lighting up that hadn't so much as flickered in years.

His gaze dropped to her mouth and lingered there for a long beat. When he spoke again, his voice, while measured, sounded deeper.

"I know what people think when women in your income level sleep with men in mine. I didn't want that to happen to you."

"I don't—"

"Care, I know." He raised his eyes to hers. "But I do. Not about what people think of you, but how that might affect... where you go. You get a reputation for having a taste for rich men and that can ruin you here, which can ruin you out there. I don't want that to happen."

Elizabeth studied him, trying to hide how hard she trembled, and knowing she failed miserably.

"You're right." At least her voice wasn't shaking. Bonus. Now she just needed to make her escape. "There is an easy way to avoid getting that kind of reputation. Thanks for your concern."

She turned on her heel, intent on continuing the storm off she'd started inside, but then she felt his hand on her wrist, and the warmth of his skin sent electric sparks through hers. All her logic sensors powered down. He must have felt it too, because his grip on her cemented, and he pulled as she pushed toward him. She wasn't sure entirely how it happened, only that when it did, the section of her brain that was in charge of vetoing bad decisions checked out for the night. Hell, she couldn't even blame the asshole, seeing as she had practically jumped on him.

Then his mouth was on hers, and *goddamn*.

Elizabeth liked kissing as much as the next girl, but she'd never been the type to swoon from a liplock. Until, that was, this moment. Perhaps it was because she knew she shouldn't be doing this, but the second she tasted Will, something inside her shifted in such a way she knew it would never shift back. And she might have been embarrassed at the gusto with which she responded had it not been for the deep moan he rumbled against her mouth as he pulled her flush against him. He tore at her with naked desperation, pulling hot, heavy kisses off her lips. His chest at hers, she felt his heart thrumming against her breast, felt his hands move from her hips to her hair, his fingers massaging her scalp as his tongue slipped inside her mouth. And when she moaned, he answered in kind, which would have brought her to her knees had he not been holding her up.

No man had ever sounded that hungry for her. Ever.

It was a heady feeling, and damn, she wanted more.

In that moment, she wanted whatever he had to give her. Which, judging by the bulge pressing into her belly, was quite a lot.

It couldn't last forever, though god knew she wanted it to, but the need for oxygen eventually became too pronounced to ignore any longer, forcing her to pull her lips from his. The second she drew in air, her brain kicked back into gear, filling her in on all the reasons why this was a bad idea.

Like facing the scale the morning after eating one's weight in ice cream.

Only Will tasted so, so much better.

And was probably about a million times worse for her.

He had his brow pressed to hers, his eyes closed as he gulped lungfuls of air. His hands remained on her, rubbing soothing circles into her skin, making her insides feel funny. Elizabeth had never seen him so...vulnerable.

And she couldn't start noticing things like that now. Not *now*.

If he kissed her again, she might not come back. And that was dangerous, because Will was not someone she needed in her life, no matter how much her vagina protested.

The Lyft driver had amazing timing. At once, the parking lot lit up with the flash of headlights, followed by the rumble of a car engine. A jolt of relief shot through her, chased almost instantly by one of regret. The arrival of the getaway car meant she'd run out of time to justify her behavior. It was back to the real world.

Elizabeth swallowed hard and pulled away.

Will's eyes widened and he tightened his grip on her. *Don't go,* that look said.

Words bubbled up her throat, then, twisting into excuses and dismissals. But with him looking at her like that, like she was tearing a part of him away as she moved, they died unspoken on her tongue. Thankfully, her feet still knew what to do.

Will didn't say anything as she slipped into the car, but he didn't move, either. He was still standing there, watching her, when the vehicle pulled out of the parking lot. And even after she could no longer see him, as the distance between them grew farther, she felt his eyes. His hands and his mouth too. His body pressed against hers. His dick against her belly. The way he'd looked at her.

And she wondered, not for the first time, what the fuck had gotten into her.

13

It took Will a good fifteen minutes to convince his feet to move, and his heart another ten to accept that she wasn't coming back. For a while, though, he'd both looked and felt the fool, standing in the parking lot as people spilled in and out of the club behind him, jumping at every sound that might possibly be that of a red-faced Elizabeth, ordering her driver to bring her back to him.

Except she wasn't coming back.

Will swallowed hard and slid his hands into his pockets, gave the motionless parking lot one last look, then turned and made his way back into the club. He still had her taste in his mouth, still felt warm where she'd been pressed against him. His cock had taken its time in realizing she wasn't coming back, spurred by the echo of her kisses. It didn't seem possible that Elizabeth could have felt and tasted better in reality than she had in his fantasies, but if he'd learned anything over the past few weeks, it was that she defied expectation at every turn.

What would happen when he saw her again? The thought did a funny thing to him, excitement and dread running hand in hand. He'd expected things to change after the night she'd spent at Netherfield Hall, but she'd met Wickham almost immediately after he'd dropped her off.

The second Will had seen them together, he'd closed down. He hadn't wanted to think about it—about them existing in the same spheres of his life. He hadn't reached out to her to talk and had grumped around that she hadn't approached him. Hell, since that night at Netherfield, he hadn't pursued her at all after, hadn't done anything to indicate his interest or intent. He'd assumed that Elizabeth would warm to him on her own, perhaps suggest they do something together, or at the very least, tag along with Jane when she visited Charlie. But this thinking alone had been his mistake with Elizabeth from the beginning —assuming she was like every other girl who had ever been interested in him.

Elizabeth was not every other girl.

Will shook his head and forced his feet to continue until he was back inside, where the air was so thick with the heavy thrum of music that his body seemed to rattle with every beat. He inhaled a breath that tasted of sweat and beer and battled his way toward the table Elizabeth's friends had claimed.

The girls from Longbourn had scattered to the dance floor, having left Charlie at the mercy of his sister, who was whispering furiously into her brother's ear while said brother gazed adoringly at a point across the room. Will turned and saw Jane was on the dance floor, laughing at something one of the other girls—Lily or Megan or whatever—had said. The contrast was rather starling—he'd seen Jane a lot over the past few weeks. At Netherfield, she seemed demure to the point of being rigid. Polite and friendly but not outgoing. Not like she was truly enjoying herself.

Not like now.

Huh.

"Will!" Caroline had spotted him and waved him over.

Will blew out a breath and continued negotiating his way between sweaty couples.

"Where have you been?" Caroline asked when he was near enough to hear her without her yelling. "Is everything okay?"

He frowned, thinking it obvious where he'd been—he'd taken off rather abruptly after Elizabeth's departure. His intentions couldn't have been too difficult to discern.

"Everything's fine," he said, then looked to Charlie, who had yet to acknowledge his presence. "I'm going to head out."

"Why?" Caroline blurted, sitting up a little straighter. "We just got here."

Yeah, well, the club's biggest attraction had sped away about twenty minutes prior. There was little chance in taking his mind off her tonight—not with the taste of her still on his lips.

And he didn't want his mind off her. He didn't want tonight to fade. He didn't want to go back to whatever they'd been doing, and it occurred to him—in a jolt of pure panic—that that was exactly what would happen if he didn't do something.

He needed to go after her.

Will shook his head and met Caroline's imploring gaze. "I just—I need to take care of something." He looked again to Charlie, who hadn't acknowledged his presence at all. "You okay catching an Uber or something to get back?"

Charlie nodded absently but didn't respond.

A mutinous look crossed Caroline's face before she poked out her lower lip in a frown. "We'll miss you."

He ignored her. "Charlie?" Nothing. He waved a hand in front of his friend's face. "Anyone home?"

That seemed to do it. Charlie blinked and shook his head. When he looked at Will, his eyes cleared a bit and a slow, distracted smile drew across his lips. "Oh. Hey."

"I'm heading out," Will said.

"Okay."

"You understand this means that you'll need to find another way home, right?"

Charlie frowned as though trying to figure out a complex equation, then nodded. "That's right. You drove us."

Yeah, though why he had, Will still hadn't figured out. It took forever to get to his car from Netherfield Heights. But Caroline insisted on not paying good money for a cab when they had wheels across campus. She claimed it to be common sense, but Will suspected she didn't want to be seen in any vehicle with a sticker price valued less than a middle-class family's annual salary.

"You'll be all right getting back?"

Charlie frowned. "Sure. Do what you gotta, but I think you're calling it a night a little early. There's still plenty of time to—"

"Charlie, you dragged me out to come see your girlfriend. Under false pretenses."

"I object. My pretenses weren't false. I did and still do think you need to lighten up a bit." He paused. "I didn't happen to mention Jane was here because I didn't know if she would be."

"You did so," Caroline interjected. "You found out she was coming out with friends and made a point of learning where so you could crash the scene."

Charlie froze, blinked, then inclined his head. "Yes, I might have done that."

Will sighed and rolled his eyes. "There's a word for this, you know."

"Romantic?"

"Did she even want to see you tonight?"

"When I asked her what her plans were, she said she was going out with friends. She never said she *didn't* want to see me." Charlie shrugged. "And it sounded like a good idea to me. I like her friends. I like you. I like it when you're less surly, and it's been a long freaking time since that's been the case."

Caroline shook her head. "You are pathetic. Stalking your own girlfriend."

"I am not stalking! There is no stalking! I just... I like being around her and I like being around you." He paused. "Will, really. Not so much you, Caroline. You're kind of a buzzkill."

Will snorted in spite of himself.

"And," Charlie continued, "I maintain what I said earlier. You definitely needed to get out. You've been downright depressing to be around recently. Lydia and Mary are both, um, charming. And Kitty—I think that's her name. She's Lydia's roommate and they're both very outgoing."

"I'm not interested in Lydia or Mary or Kitty."

"Well, good about Mary," Charlie said matter-of-factly. "I think she's gay. But the others—"

"Charles!" Caroline snapped. "Stop throwing women at him."

"The man needs to get laid."

Will rolled his eyes, though his thoughts couldn't help but drag him back to those stolen seconds with Elizabeth outside, and he felt a familiar jolt in a part of his anatomy that he really didn't want waking up right now.

"He deserves better than garbage from Longbourn," Caroline hissed. "And you might not have noticed, but Will has self-respect."

Charlie glared at her. "Jane's at Longbourn."

"And Jane may well be the exception," Caroline replied without missing a beat, though the look in her eyes said plainly that she didn't believe it. "But the others are just..." She waved a hand at the dance floor, where Lydia and Kitty had a man between them and were being downright indecent, and Mary and Jane were bouncing enthusiastically and notably off-beat to the music. "Not to mention that Elizabeth. Screaming at Will for saying he *didn't* sleep with her. What kind of people are they?"

Will flexed his fists, but didn't respond. Caroline was trying to get a rise out of him.

"I've never seen Elizabeth like that before," Charlie said. "She might just be having a bad night."

Caroline shook her head. "She was awful."

Charlie didn't look like he agreed, but he also clearly wasn't up for debating his sister on the issue. Instead, he shifted his attention back to Will. "Point is, there are plenty of people of the female variety that wouldn't mind ending your dry spell. It was worth a shot."

Caroline huffed and crossed her arms, her face contorting into a disapproving scowl.

Will tightened his jaw and shook his head. "Thanks for that. I'm still leaving, though. So as long as you two can get home all right—"

"Of course we can," Charlie said.

"Then good night."

He turned on his heel and threw himself back into the crowd before either of them could get in another word. He knew if he delayed any longer, he'd talk himself out of it, and that was something he couldn't abide. He and Elizabeth needed to discuss what had happened. Now. He needed to let her know that his silence over the past few weeks hadn't been because he wasn't interested, and hope she felt the same way.

With the way she'd kissed him, she had to.

She *had* to.

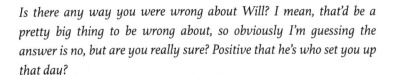

Is there any way you were wrong about Will? I mean, that'd be a pretty big thing to be wrong about, so obviously I'm guessing the answer is no, but are you really sure? Positive that he's who set you up that day?

The damn cursor was blinking. She hated the cursor.

Elizabeth pressed her lips together and moved the mouse to the *send* button for what might have been the fiftieth time since she'd typed up her email to Wickham. And likewise for the fiftieth time, she sighed and moved it away. It felt like she should write more, explain herself and the question, but she didn't want to get into a discussion about how she'd just made out with the guy who had stunted Wickham's education and nearly ruined his whole life.

Because if she started to explain that, she'd have to explain it to herself first, and she wasn't ready for that.

"Ugh." Elizabeth slammed her laptop shut and shot to her feet. Yeah, there was no way she was emailing Wickham. How pathetic would that be?

Hey, sorry, you know how Will Darcy royally fucked you over? Well, surprise surprise, assholes apparently get me off and I'd feel a lot better about it if you'd tell me he didn't do that thing that caused the aforementioned royal fucking of you.

All she wanted to do was assuage her guilt, but there was no doing that. And what the hell did she expect, anyway?

Did I say Will Darcy? God, how embarrassing is that? No, the guy who fucked me over is Bill Parsley. Sorry about the confusion! Have fun having all the sex.

Elizabeth snorted and shook her head, her feet carrying her from one end of the dorm room to the other. Given that Wickham had been flirting with her for a few weeks now via text message, she seriously doubted he'd give his blessing for her to fuck anyone.

Not that she needed it.

A growl clawed at her throat. Not for the first time since getting home, she wondered about texting Wickham for a booty call. Put her no-strings sex policy into action. Something told her he wouldn't turn her down. The trouble was, Elizabeth had also never been a big fan of sleeping with someone just to forget someone else. It wasn't fair to anyone. And how would he feel if he knew she was just with him because she'd lost her mind and kissed his ex-bestie and now couldn't stand still?

Shitty. That's how he'd feel.

And Elizabeth knew she wouldn't be able to go through with it even if she could ignore his feelings. Nice guy though Wickham was, conjuring his face didn't do much for her libido.

The fact of the matter was she didn't want him. At least not now, and not like that.

Elizabeth sighed and swung around to make another trek across the room when her gaze landed on her dresser.

Specifically, the top drawer of her dresser.

And she thought, for the first time in a long time, about the thing she'd put in it.

A giddy rush scored down her spine. She cast a glance to Jane's bed—though why was anyone's guess, seeing as Jane had not mastered the power to Apparate. Given how lively things had been at the club, Elizabeth doubted she'd see her roommate for another couple hours at least. Maybe longer, if Jane decided to embrace her inner sex kitten and finally put poor Charlie out of his misery.

She made a beeline for the dresser without another thought. The top drawer was filled with the usual—socks, panties, bras. But under a clump of winter socks was the one sex toy she'd allowed herself to pack when she'd made the decision to reenroll—a simple dildo. The type that was so realistic in appearance it was a little disarming. It didn't use batteries and had no special functions. She'd never been big on the vibrating sort, rather preferred those that could best imitate an actual penis.

Elizabeth stared at it for a long moment, then closed her hand around it. She disrobed in a hurry, pondered whether or not to remain naked, and ultimately decided it would be kinder to Jane—should her roommate get home early—if she wasn't completely nude. While the thought of being caught masturbating didn't embarrass her too badly, she knew Jane would likely be unable to look her in the eye for a month should that happen.

She decided on one of her favorite sleep-shirts. It was long enough to hit her knees, which gave her a perfect reason to ditch her panties.

Elizabeth pulled back the blankets on her bed and slipped onto the mattress, her right foot buried safely under the covers and the left dangling out. Then, slowly, she hitched the hem of her sleep shirt over her thighs and higher until her pussy was exposed.

And then, at last, she let her thoughts drift to Will. To the way he'd looked at her before pulling her to him, and the sounds he'd made as his mouth had explored hers.

A fresh rush of lust scored down her spine and her sex became heavy. She inhaled and grabbed the dildo, took a moment to admire how cool and fleshy it felt in her hand, then lowered the head to her clit and pressed down.

Pleasure jolted through her body at contact. Elizabeth threw her head back and sighed. God *yes,* it had been a long time. Too long. Maybe that was her problem. Go too long between orgasms and your brain starts finding everyone sexy.

Will's image flooded her mind, then, and she knew that wasn't true. It'd just be a whole lot more convenient if it was. Just thinking about him over her, rubbing his cock against her, dragging the blunt head up and down the seam of her pussy was enough in itself to push her over the edge. But Elizabeth didn't want to come yet—she was looking for much more than a quick fix. A quick fix on a problem like this would be like throwing masking tape at a broken arm.

She needed to get him—get this—out of her system so her system and everything else could go back to normal.

Elizabeth inhaled deeply, running the tip of the dildo across her soaked flesh. She called to mind the feel of Will's lips on hers, the way he seemed to want to pull her into himself. How he'd felt against her, like he was fighting a losing battle with his own rigid control. Her throat tightened and her clit throbbed desperately for attention. With her free hand, Elizabeth pressed down on her needy flesh as she positioned the dildo at the mouth of her sex.

She closed her eyes then and saw him. Will trapping her beneath him, looking at her the way he had tonight, breathing hard and fast like he was about to come apart. A soft cry tore from her lips as she inched the toy inside her, her mind filling in the rest of what wasn't there. It was easy to imagine the heat of Will's body, even the ghost of his kisses along her neck and jawline. That sexy little moan he'd rumbled into her mouth on autoplay, but joined by the sound of her name and a few curses for good measure. Will was always so collected. So poised. With her, though, he'd release the hold he had on his control. He'd fuck her until she couldn't walk straight.

Quite the stallion was mental Will. It was likely a blessing she'd never have the real thing, because this act would be a hard one to beat.

A smile played across her lips at that thought.

And was immediately chased away by three hurried knocks that thundered at her door.

Elizabeth froze, the dildo seated completely inside her now, her body so near the edge of a precipice that backing away was nigh impossible. A tangle of frustration pulsed through her, one so potent she just about decided to remain where she was—a good orgasm should not be interrupted, thank you very much—when he spoke.

"Elizabeth?"

Her heart performed some funky spastic move.

You've got to be kidding me.

"Elizabeth, it's Will. Open up if you're in there."

She remained frozen for a beat, then another, the only sound courtesy of the jackhammering occurring in her chest.

It'd be so easy not to say anything. *Do* anything. But her curiosity began to outvote her horniness—much to her body's dismay—and she found herself easing the toy out of her cunt. A moment later, she rose to her feet on wobbly legs, looked down to ensure her nightshirt covered all the important stuff, and began making her way to the door.

By the time she got there, the lusty haze that had nearly had her at orgasm had faded into a more comfortable, more familiar irritation.

What the hell is he doing here?

"Eliza—"

She threw the door open before he could yell her name again, took a moment to appreciate the surprise that filled his eyes, then spat, "What?"

Will stared at her for a moment as though trying to ascertain whether or not he was truly seeing her. Then he cleared his throat. "We need to talk."

"About what?"

At this, he seemed genuinely stunned. "About...about what happened."

"When?" Yes, she was being ornery, but she was at her wit's end. And she so very badly needed release—needed the pent up energy to find an outlet and give her some relief.

"What do you mean, when? Tonight. Just now."

"Just now, meaning when you interrupted my last ditch effort to make the night not totally suck."

A welcome flicker of irritation rose behind his eyes. "You

know damn well what I'm talking about."

She shrugged. "What's there to talk about, Will? People kiss every day."

"You and I don't."

"We'll call it an anomaly then. A lapse in judgment. Temporary insanity." She flashed a smile. God, he needed to leave. Now. "So there. We're all talked out. Thank you so much for—"

"No."

A note of finality carried in his tone, and a shiver ran down her spine. A shiver ran somewhere else too.

She'd never heard him sound so...

God, why in the world would this turn me on?

Just more proof she was not quite right upstairs.

After a moment, Elizabeth managed to swallow the lump in her throat. "No?"

"No. We need to talk about this."

"No, *you* need to talk about it. I need to get back to my night." She waved at her bed in demonstration, which she realized, a moment too late, had been a mistake.

Her dildo was only partially covered by her blankets and, thanks to the soft lamplight in the room, visibly slick.

Elizabeth felt her stomach drop.

Shit.

The initial urge was to run over and throw it under the bed, but doing that would be about as effective as lobbing it at Will's head. Instead, she turned back to Will with what she hoped was a sufficiently unbothered look.

The second their eyes met, she knew she was out of luck. That strange light that had stormed into his gaze earlier had returned, the fight fading fast in favor of something even more primal. Something that brought to mind how he'd felt pressed against her. He took his time, looking from her to the dildo, then to her again, taking in the state of her undress—slowly. And when he raised his face to hers, what she saw there had her squeezing her thighs together.

And damn, that was not a good sign. Not at all.

"So," she said. Her voice was a pitch lower than usual. "If you'll just leave, I'll—"

"What?" he blurted, his nostrils flaring. "You'll...*what*?"

She was pleased, at least, to hear his tone was also rougher than usual. Meant she wasn't the only one perving out at the moment.

At the same time, knowing that he was turned on did not incentivize her body to pull the emergency brake.

Elizabeth inhaled. "None of your goddamned business, Darcy."

"Did I..." His gaze shifted to the incriminating evidence on her bed and lingered. "...interrupt something?"

At these words, she experienced a much welcome rush of irritation. Her muscles tensed. "What the hell do you think?"

He blanched. "I—"

"I dunno, Will, you seem like a pretty smart guy. I'd have thought you could solve this brain buster all on your own." She gestured toward the bed again, this time with intent. "But in case it wasn't perfectly clear, you interrupted me while I was straight on the way to what would have been a truly terrific orgasm. So thank you so much for that. Now please, don't let the door hit you on the—"

"Why did you answer?"

The question was the perfectly aimed wrench at her otherwise flawless rant. "What?"

"You could've ignored me. You could've just stayed where you were—doing what you were doing." He flushed but didn't waver. "You answered the door for me, Elizabeth."

"And I can't tell you how proud of myself I am for that."

"You knew it was me. Why would you answer then?"

"Because if you look up *glutton for punishment,* the first thing you'll see is my smiling face." She demonstrated said smile. "Now go away."

She swung the door hard—so hard it would have sent a fierce tremble through the building had it made it all the way home. But Will caught it without so much as a blink, his gaze still intent upon hers.

"Answer me one question."

"No."

"Were you thinking about me?" He paused, swallowed, but didn't back down. "About earlier?"

Elizabeth just stared at him, her tongue unwilling to work. And she knew in her silence that she had given him the answer, for the longer he looked at her, the more his eyes changed. His whole face seemed to change, softening from hard lines into something she couldn't quite identify. It wasn't pride or snark, either of which she would have expected, rather a sort of quiet awe.

That look did funny things to her stomach. It also made her intently aware again that she needed to come. If she didn't get to, she might just explode.

So she did the only logical thing she could think of.

She slammed the door. Turned and took three paces toward her bed.

Then he knocked again, and something inside her raised a white flag.

Elizabeth threw the door open and lunged into his arms. Will's mouth came crashing down on hers hard enough to knock her off balance, but he tasted too damn good for it to matter. Every sensation she'd experienced earlier came rushing back with gusto. He hooked his arms under her shoulders and drew her to him, bringing her bare lower half against his body— against where he was hard for her.

Elizabeth trembled, sucking his tongue into her mouth and swallowing one of those glorious moans. Like before, it seemed to echo its way through her, curling her toes and sending a fresh wave of want through a body already overdosing on the stuff. He stroked her tongue with his, his lips hot and insistent as his hands began to wander. First to her face and neck, then down her shoulders. He paused before palming her breasts, though, rather drew his fingers up and down her sides—close enough to feel his intent. He stayed there long enough for her to realize he was waiting on her.

For permission.

Elizabeth pulled her mouth away from his, met his heated eyes, and nodded. "Yes."

Will kissed her again and dipped his hands under the hem of her tee. She thought he'd make a beeline for her breasts, but instead he cupped her ass, squeezed once, then pulled her as close to him as possible, allowing her to feel every thick inch of his erection in all its denim-clad glory.

And yeah. That she hadn't expected.

Elizabeth was a firm believer in the size-doesn't-matter philosophy, having been with men who were exceptionally endowed but clueless where it counted, and others who weren't packing as much but definitely scored marks in the performance category. Will seemed to be a rare breed, because she could feel how large he was, and she was already sold on the thought that he knew what to do with it. Just having him there, the hard length of him, pressed against her damp pussy was enough to have familiar sparks shooting in every direction.

And she needed to have him inside her. Right fucking then.

"Please," Elizabeth whispered, thrusting her hips against his and watching his expression darken. "Please, please, please for the love of *god* tell me you have a condom."

The look on his face would have been funny had she not

been so close to the edge. Will's eyes widened and the heat there began to cool almost immediately.

"I'm sorry," he whispered. "Damn, you have no idea how sorry I am."

A pitiful mewl scratched at her throat, but she refused to let it out. No matter if she felt she could start bawling at any second out of sheer frustration. "You don't bring condoms when you go out?"

"I wasn't planning on any of this tonight."

Elizabeth closed her eyes. Right. Raging hormones aside, this was likely a good thing. A healthy thing. Jumping into bed with Will might seem like an awesome idea now, but in the morning, she'd hate herself enough for letting him feel her up. Toss actual sex into the mix and she might need to transfer to a different college on principle.

Except at the moment, her rational brain had taken a hike, and her primal brain wasn't very good at making her otherwise logical arguments sound convincing.

Especially with Will so close, his cock still rubbing her in all the right places.

He pressed his forehead to hers. "Can I touch you?"

Elizabeth's eyes flew open. "What?"

"Say yes." He fingered the edge of her nightshirt. "Please let me touch you."

She shivered as her rational brain tried to rally and failed. The need in his voice shook her to her core. "Yes," she said.

The word had barely touched the air when Will captured her lips again. It was unfair how skilled he was with that mouth—equally unfair that her primal brain took the bait to flash her suggestions on what he might do with it. Elizabeth whimpered and he answered her with another one of those panty-wetting moans, which made her want to whimper all over again.

When he slipped the hand that had been toying with her nightshirt under the hem, she did.

Loudly.

"Oh fuck," Elizabeth gasped, breaking her mouth from his as his warm hand palmed her pussy. "Oh fuck."

"God, how wet you are."

Will Darcy was a talker during sex? Color her stunned.

And he wasn't lying. The situation had just about gotten out of control. His fiery skin was freaking kindling on an already blazing inferno. She might have been embarrassed if she weren't so damned turned on.

Will rubbed the heel of his palm against her, nearly at the cost of her balance. He pressed a kiss to the corner of her mouth as he spread the swollen lips of her sex. Then—*shit*—he was dragging his finger up and down her slit, edging near her clit but not close enough. He seemed to need this as much as she did.

"You're gorgeous, Elizabeth," he whispered hotly, dipping a finger inside her. They both moaned. "God, that's tight. So tight." He pulled back slowly so she felt every drag against her skin, then pushed back inside. Out and in. Again. And again.

Then he added another finger and she about came undone.

"Will..."

Something that sounded like a growl rumbled through him. *Goddamn.*

"Please." She barely recognized the voice as her own. Her hips had begun moving of their own volition in time with the thrusts of his fingers, crashing back against him every time he tried to pull away. The breaths tearing from Elizabeth's throat had gone from heavy to ragged. She needed more.

Needed him. In this moment, she needed *him.*

Will peppered a series of hot kisses along her throat. "Tell me what you want," he whispered before nipping at her skin. "I'll give you whatever you ask."

"Please..."

"Please what?"

The start of what she knew would be an intense orgasm began to flicker. Elizabeth clutched his shoulders and squeezed.

"My clit."

He pulled back far enough to see her face, a grin spreading over his. A grin that made her tremble harder, made her breath catch. It was a smile unlike any she'd ever seen him wear—one she would have thought out of place on him. Both the quiet, reserved guy she'd gotten to know and the picture that had been developing over the past few weeks. Even when her mind was being its most unforgiving in its depiction of him, it hadn't gone so far as to make him cocky.

But that grin was cocky.

It was also hot as fuck.

Which would be damned annoying if he hadn't earned it.

"This clit?" he said at last as his thumb circled her swollen flesh.

Elizabeth nodded fiercely. "Yes."

"What do you want me to do with it?"

What she wanted involved him dropping to his knees, hiking her leg over his shoulder, and putting that suddenly smart mouth of his to good use.

But that was too much. Too personal. Even more than outright fucking would have been. It was one thing to interlock bodies—it was another thing altogether to put one's mouth south of the border.

"Keep doing that," she said instead, banishing the image. "The circling. That's good."

"Yeah?" Will kissed her forehead, which was lined with sweat. His thumb continued its lap around her clitoris, aided with the hint of light pressure but not much more. "What else?"

"Uhh...really, really good?"

He chuckled, and dammit, even that was sexy.

"No, what else do you want me to do?"

Elizabeth met his eyes and nearly bit her tongue to keep from whimpering. What she really wanted him to do was keep looking at her like that.

Except that had nothing to do with sex and everything to do with Will, and that terrified her.

"Press down."

Will arched an eyebrow.

"On—on my clit. Don't rub. Just press—"

He did and that was it. She came apart. Elizabeth threw her head back, her pussy clenching around his fingers as waves of pure white ecstasy scored through her. One of those glorious orgasms that seemed to have no beginning or end, just hit after hit of *fucking awesome* until the body couldn't stand it anymore. It stole the strength from her legs and left every inch of her absolutely humming and *oh god,* she wanted to do that again. Again and again until she forgot how words worked.

As though from a great distance, she heard him saying her name, heard him telling her things. About her. About how she felt. About what he wanted to do to her.

Seconds, minutes, centuries later, when Elizabeth felt her feet make contact with terra firma again, she found herself resting against Will's chest, her body upright only by the grace of his grip on her.

It was good of him to hold her up, seeing as her legs were still jelly.

The fog surrounding her head started dissipating at once, and the things her rational brain had tried to warn her against were suddenly clear again. Her paradigm shifted back where it needed to be, bringing with it exactly what she'd expected.

The knowledge that this had been a mistake.

Well, to be fair, she'd known that much the entire time. It

just hadn't been all that important while in the heat of the moment.

The larger knowledge that she had crossed her personal Rubicon.

Slowly, Elizabeth raised her head, not wanting to meet Will's gaze but knowing she needed to all the same. No matter how she felt about this now, she owed him the courtesy of acknowledging his presence. After all, she'd gotten a happy from the encounter, which—as she was reminded by his persistent erection—was more than she could say for him.

That hardly seemed fair.

No, it *wasn't* fair. At all.

Will seemed to relax when she looked at him. "That was beautiful," he said in a dopey sincere voice that was at such contrast with the cocky smirk from before she could hardly believe both came from the same guy.

Except she *could* believe it because both things fit.

"Umm..." She swallowed and looked away, not sure what to say now.

Thank you for the orgasm. Now please leave.

By Wickham's account, that much would serve Will right. The thought alone gave Elizabeth a somewhat twisted sense of satisfaction. But that sensation didn't last, namely because she wasn't the sort of person to receive without giving. And it'd be cruel. While she might not always succeed, she usually went to great lengths to ensure she wasn't cruel.

Decision made. Elizabeth met his gaze again before slowly, deliberately, sliding a hand between them and over the outline of his thick cock.

And took definite pleasure in watching his expression dissolve as he released a low moan. The feel of him against her palm was addictive. She wanted to see him. Feel him in her hand. Wanted to watch his face as she pulled on his dick—see if those delicious sounds he made got any better.

She had just trailed her fingers up his zipper when the undeniable sound of a door opening downstairs echoed through the building.

Damn.

Will held his breath. She worried her lower lip between her teeth. They didn't need to wait long to get their answer before the floor below populated with loud voices.

And one of them belonged to her roommate. It was a little louder than she was used to hearing Jane speak—and the words were somewhat slurred—but there was no denying it was her.

It took about five seconds for Jane to announce she was going to bed.

Elizabeth met Will's gaze again. There was resistance there, but he wasn't going to push. Instead, he offered a soft smile and kissed her before she could protest.

"Good night, Elizabeth," he whispered against her lips.

Elizabeth licked her lips, tasting him there, and glanced down to his still-prominent erection. "Try not to scare anyone with that thing."

Will chuckled, making her shiver.

"I'll do my best," he replied. He released her and put some space between their bodies. She hadn't realized how cold the air was. At the door, he paused and turned to her again. "See you Monday."

There was promise in those words.

And it occurred to her as he left—as she listened to him exchange pleasantries with a somewhat stunned Jane in the hall —that she had probably just dug herself into something that she wouldn't be able to escape easily.

"Shit."

14

Will groaned and rolled over for the fifth time in ten minutes.

It was no use. He couldn't stop replaying the way Elizabeth had come apart around his fingers. Hell, he didn't want to stop replaying it. It had been the single most significant sexual encounter he'd ever experienced, which in itself was rather alarming since he wasn't sure where they stood.

Damn, he wasn't sure of anything anymore.

It was times like these Will felt the absence of his parents most profoundly. There wasn't anyone in his world equipped to help him see things from beyond his own perspective. Charlie was the best friend a guy could have, but he reserved his serious moments for special occasions, and didn't have enough of a filter to trust with confidential information. It had taken Will several years to work out that Charlie wasn't callous—he just didn't process things like other people. His brain didn't give off warnings whenever anyone brought up something potentially sensitive, and he'd end up spewing everything he knew on a given subject before it occurred to him to hold his tongue. In fact, the only thing Charlie had ever taken seriously was the whole incident between Georgiana and Wickham.

As a confidant, Georgiana herself wasn't much above Charlie. She was still too young, and though perhaps not as romantic as she'd once been, romantic enough that she'd try to fix via oversimplification. Plus the last thing Will wanted to do right now was trouble her with his problems. Especially since he wasn't sure anymore if he even had a problem.

He certainly hadn't had a problem earlier. Elizabeth attacking his mouth with her own. Her breasts pressed against him. Her pussy around his fingers. Her clit under his thumb. Her eyes glossy and on him—watching him as she trembled and tightened and drenched his hand.

Will groaned into his pillow. He'd stroked himself to orgasm twice since arriving back at Netherfield Heights, but every time his brain dragged him back to Elizabeth's room, his cock twitched with interest. No other woman had ever done this to him—shoved him away before dragging him close. He'd never wanted a woman like this, either, and even acknowledging that was terrifying.

The fact that he didn't know what tonight had meant to her left him unsettled.

Life would have been a thousand times easier if he'd been able to stick to his own damn plan. Go back to school. Get the diploma. Walk into Darcy Media with the degree his father had been so intent he receive, as someone who knew what the hell he was doing, rather than the silver-spooned orphan whose name happened to be on the building. Relationships beyond those with his professors and close friends had not been in the brochure. The kind of relationship he wanted required dedication and time to do right, and those were two things he had in short supply, especially considering he'd started years after he should have.

Also, he'd be a piss poor role model for Georgiana if he couldn't keep his hands to himself.

Will grumbled into his pillow before rolling over again.

There was only one thing he knew for certain at the present—and that was that he couldn't wait for Monday to arrive.

Will came to slowly the next morning, only to find it wasn't morning at all. Well, not early morning. For the first time in longer than he could remember, he'd slept past ten, and every inch of his body felt it. Seemed a cheat, really, to get extra sleep but feel extra tired as a result.

In a concerted effort to distract his mind from thoughts of Elizabeth, Will got busy with his typical routine. A long shower —happy ending included—later, he parked himself at his desk and cracked open one of the books he'd intended to dive in to the night before. There was at least half a day's reading to do before Monday's first class. Trouble was, every time he set to focus on the words, his mind would hijack his concentration and take him back to Elizabeth's room. Remind him of the sounds she'd made. How she smelled. The way she'd looked at him when her pussy had tightened and—

Will growled and slammed the book closed.

This was ridiculous. The whole damn point of going over to Longbourn had been to talk about whatever was happening between them for a slew of reasons, not the least of which his concentration was shot to hell. While he wouldn't trade those stolen moments for anything, the fact that they existed at all had done nothing but dig the hole he'd made for himself a little deeper.

A long sigh rode off his lips. Will slumped over, elbows on his desk, his fingers tunneling through his hair along his scalp. Though midterms had come and gone, he had to start thinking about finals, and somehow felt like he'd lost more knowledge in the time he'd been here than he'd gained.

Yet he couldn't stop thinking about her.

All right, so studying was out of the question for the moment. Maybe that was his fault. His brain typically required at least a modest dose of caffeine before it felt up to the challenge of performing even the most mundane tasks.

Or maybe he was just that pathetic.

His phone began to vibrate, and Will's pulse spiked. It was Elizabeth. It had to be.

But it wasn't. It was his sister.

"Georgie," he answered, plastering on a smile. He didn't know why. It just seemed easier to fake enthusiasm if there was a smile involved.

"Don't call me that," she replied right on cue. "How's my favorite brother doing?"

If only her favorite brother knew how to answer that question...

"Good. Really good."

There was a pause, then a long sigh rattled through the receiver.

"What's wrong, Will?"

"Nothing."

"You know you're lousy at keeping things from me. Wanna try again with honesty this time?"

Will cursed inwardly. "I'm fine. Everything here is fine. How are you doing?"

"You sound like you're reading a script, I hope you know."

"What do you want me to say? Getting back into the swing of all things academic has been a breeze? It's taken a few weeks, but I'm starting to feel more grounded."

That much at least was true. He just happened to be fantastically ungrounded everywhere else.

"Have you met people? Had fun? Done stupid shit—"

He cleared his throat and grinned when she groaned in response. He'd resigned himself to the fact that she wasn't going to censor herself around him a long time ago—it was the only bad habit left over from the Wickham incident, and she had never indicated a desire to cut profanity out of her vocabulary, even when he'd told her those words were not used by respectable ladies. She'd rolled her eyes and given him the finger.

That sounded now like something Elizabeth would do.

"Jesus Christ, Will," Georgiana said, "you need to get a life. How else do you think you're gonna get laid this semester?"

That comment would have earned a genuine spit-take if he'd been drinking anything. "Dammit, Georgie—"

"I told you not to call me that."

"Well, then don't say things like...like what you just said."

"About you getting laid?" She laughed. "Dude, you *need* to get laid. You are wound more tightly than any ten people I know."

"That is not the point."

"I think it is the point. And since the cause of your tragic affliction happens to be yours truly, I think it's my job to make sure you do everything you can to have some freaking fun every now and again."

"You are not the cause of any affliction, tragic or otherwise."

"We both know that's not true."

Will winced and tunneled the fingers of his free hand through his hair. While he knew better than to be surprised, he hated that Georgiana still felt like this. The fallout from what had happened with Wickham had been intense and painful, and once she'd seen how badly it had affected him, she'd had a mental breakdown. The guilt of knowing she'd caused him pain combined with the pain she herself had suffered had shoved her dangerously close to an edge that there was no coming back from. Time and therapy had helped, but the residual guilt had yet to fade completely. According to what her therapist had shared with him, it might never.

That had been another reason he'd agreed to go back to school this year rather than next—to alleviate Georgianna's guilt. She'd sworn on a stack of *Harry Potter* books—her holy scripture—that she would be fine spending her evenings alone, so long as their housekeeper was there during the day. Had he dragged his feet, he feared the progress she *had* made might have been undone.

Georgiana breathed a soft sigh. "I was calling to see how you were doing. I miss you, assface."

Will couldn't help but grin at that. *Assface* was one of Elizabeth's go-to insults, he'd noticed. That Georgiana favored it as well made him oddly...proud. Which he'd never tell her, or else she'd never take his campaign to get her to stop swearing seriously. "I miss you too. Is everything going all right there?"

"Oh, sure. Everything here's peachy keen."

He narrowed his eyes. "You know I'm not the only one who's no good at lying. What's wrong?"

"Nothing."

A blip of panic made his pulse spike. "Georgie, you need to tell me if something—"

"Nothing's wrong, I promise. It's just big and lonely here. And *no*, that's not me hinting to see if you'll drop out and come home," she said before he could speak. "If you do, I'm going to sell your 1977 Jawa collectible on eBay."

Will inhaled sharply. "You wouldn't."

"Just try me."

"That thing is worth nearly twenty thousand dollars."

"Is it really that much? Well, my wardrobe is going to get a complete makeover." She laughed her my-big-brother-is-a-nerd laugh, which was sometimes interchangeable with her how-evil-can-I-be laugh. The answer to that question was *very*.

"Georgiana—"

"Why in god's name is this piece of plastic worth twenty G's?"

"Because it's in the package and has the vinyl cape. They didn't make too many of that one." And it had been damn near impossible to track down. The guy who had parted ways with it hadn't known what it was worth. "Do you... You're holding it right now, aren't you?"

"No," Georgiana replied coyly. "But I am in your room. Bet the key to that case is in your nightstand." A pause. "You know, where most normal guys keep their condoms."

Will experienced a rush of panic that only siblings could truly appreciate. The panic that came with the knowledge that while his sister likely wouldn't do anything to harm his things, he still didn't like the thought of her standing close to them. "Go into my room often?"

"No. Your room's boring."

"Then turn around and walk out."

"As soon as you promise that you're not going to panic about me admitting I'm a bit lonely and throw away your education for me *again*."

"I didn't throw anything away. I'm here, aren't I?"

"And that is where you'll stay, else the Jawa gets it."

"I know you better than that."

"This is how badly I want you to not drop everything and come home. I am willing to risk your wrath. Classes are good. Grades are good. Meds are good. It's just...easy to feel like you're all alone in the universe out here."

"Well, there's nothing stopping you from meeting new people."

"Oh yes there is. The people I'd want to hang out with, at least. A booming metropolis Derbyshire ain't. And our neighbors have *long* memories." Another thick pause filled the line before Georgiana cleared her throat. "All that to say, I miss my big bro."

An ache, large and horrible, manifested in his chest. "I miss you too, Georgie."

"Duh," she replied. "Good news? Thanksgiving break will be here before you know it. And we can drive each other so crazy that you'll practically run screaming back to campus. Well, until Christmas."

Will jerked his head up, fixing his eyes on the calendar mounted to the wall above his desk. She was right, though her observation made the passage of time seem even more significant. Thanksgiving, after all, was a holiday that happened everywhere, not just at Meryton.

Then it would be time for finals, and Christmas. And the whole next semester of classes which might not be shared with Elizabeth.

That thought made his chest ache for an entirely different reason.

"Hey," his sister said, "I better get going, or else I'm never going to get this chapter read."

"What are you reading?"

"*Lord of the Flies.* We have a test next Thursday."

"Liking it?"

"Let's just say it confirms my theory on the male sex."

"Yes. All boys are like Jack and should be avoided at all costs."

Georgiana snorted. "Gee. Subtle."

"I was just agreeing with you."

"Thanks. And thanks for not freaking out. Much."

"Much," Will said, smiling in spite of himself. "You let me know if I need to—"

"I will. Promise. Love you."

"Love you too, Georgie."

"Ugh. Stop calling me that."

She hung up before he could respond.

It took a few minutes for Will to remember what he'd been doing before she called, but less time to remember why he'd had such little success. After several failed attempts to reengage with his reading material, he decided to stop being a hero and get the coffee his brain needed if the half day of studying and coursework he intended to put in today was to be accomplished.

The second he stepped out of his room, though, he wondered just how in need of caffeine he truly was. From the sound of things, Charlie and Caroline were in the middle of one their more spectacular fights. Will hesitated for a moment, waffling between wanting to keep out of this and wanting to not fall asleep on his books. In the end, sensibility won out—given the fact that he'd volunteered to live with a pair of siblings who couldn't be further apart personality wise, he guessed he'd been lucky that there hadn't been a blow up sooner.

Perhaps he and Charlie needed to discuss getting their own place, because Caroline had no shame in dragging him into their arguments—a point she proved the instant their eyes connected.

"Will!" Caroline said. "There you are. Will you tell this moron that he's making a huge mistake?"

Will tossed a glance at Charlie, who looked about as un-Charlie-like as a guy could get. He must really be pissed. "On any given day, Charlie makes around seven huge mistakes," he said, aiming for jovial and knowing the second his voice touched the air that he'd missed the mark. Still, now he was committed. "What's going on?"

"Fuck you," Charlie all but snarled. "Fuck the both of you."

Will's eyes went wide and he brought up his hands. Okay, apparently this one was serious. "Whoa there," he said. "I'm just here for coffee. Feel free to leave me out of whatever's going on here."

"Sorry, Will, but I need you to back me up," Caroline said. "He won't listen to me."

"Because you're full of shit," Charlie replied. "I tend to not listen to people who are full of shit."

Will shook his head and turned to the kitchen. Maybe they wouldn't notice if he sprinted. "Yeah, I'm not touching this. You guys go back to—"

"She's trying to convince me that Jane's after me for my money."

He froze. "What?"

"For the last time, I don't think it's about the money!" Caroline barked an indignant laugh. "The money is a perk, sure, but what she really wants—"

"Oh, this will be rich."

"If you'd just stop and think for a second, you'd see this too!" She waved a hand. "She's all over you one second and completely aloof the next."

"And like I said, if she were after my money, that wouldn't be the best strategy to get it, now would it?"

"You're not listening to me!"

"No, I'm not buying what you're saying. Two different things."

"You're—"

"My girlfriend isn't a criminal mastermind. And if she is, she's not very good at it. She's always busy. Hell, trying to see her now is damn near impossible. We barely get to talk at all."

Caroline crossed her arms. "And yet she manages to email me twice a day about the Realis Society for Women."

Charlie paused. "What?"

"Yes. And they aren't short messages, either. They are dissertation-length odes to the society."

"You have already sponsored her."

"I *know*," Caroline said, waving a hand. "Which is what makes it weird that she keeps on badgering me, but every day, like clockwork, those messages arrive in my inbox. It was cute at first but it's becoming a nuisance. She really wants in, and she knows there was little to no chance she'd qualify without a sponsor from the club president." She paused and arched an eyebrow. "Think about it. It was all she could talk about last night when she wasn't making a fool out of herself with Missy and Kissy or whatever their names are. She barely looked at you at all."

"I introduced her to you because I knew she wanted into Realis. It was *my idea*. She never even brought it up."

"Are you so dense to believe that she didn't know I was your sister? She's wanted into the Realis Society since she was a kid. Do you really think she didn't know *exactly* who you were when you started hitting on her?" Caroline barked a snide laugh. "God, Charlie, open your eyes."

Will held his breath. He'd been too preoccupied with Elizabeth to pay much attention, but he recalled well the distance between Charlie and Jane when he'd reentered the club. Charlie gazing dopily from afar as Jane danced with her friends, seemingly completely oblivious to his presence. While she certainly seemed to enjoy Charlie's company, he couldn't deny that Caroline had a point. The few times Will had had the chance to speak with Jane, the Realis Society had been the topic of conversation.

Some of the ire had faded from Charlie's eyes. He turned to Will. "What do you think?"

Will opened his mouth to again plead ignorance, then hesitated. It was true Charlie could be a manwhore; it was also true that Charlie had a tendency to crash into love rather than fall in it. Never had Will seen his friend so single-minded about a woman—at least not for a period of time stretching beyond a month. The fact was that Charlie was as moony-eyed about Jane as he had been in August and showed no signs of relenting.

If Caroline was right, and Jane was using her relationship with Charlie to gain access to the Realis Society for Women…

Still, it seemed unlikely that Jane didn't care for Charlie at all.

"Will?" Charlie said, his voice sharp. "Do you think Caroline is right?"

"I don't know." The words were out before he could stop them.

"What do you mean you don't know?"

"Just that," Will replied, bringing his hands up. "I like Jane, so don't bite my head off, but Caroline raises a good point."

Caroline shot a triumphant look at her brother.

"In that she may be using me because I have money and influence and access to Caroline," Charlie said. "Yeah, that's not insulting at all."

"I said I don't know," Will said calmly. "But she has been rather single-minded about the Realis Society. I don't think I've heard her talk of anything but that in the last few weeks."

"She's just excited. And what does this have to do with me, anyway?" Charlie turned back to Caroline. "I have no sway over the Realis Society—"

"She knows I wouldn't have nominated her if it weren't for you," Caroline said.

"Why not?"

"Because I likely wouldn't have met her otherwise. We don't exactly have the same taste in…well, anything." Caroline shrugged. "We also don't have any classes together and I certainly don't care for her friends."

At this, Will frowned but didn't object. It wasn't as though

Caroline's opinion of anyone who called Longbourn home was a surprise.

Charlie shook his head. "She would have applied anyway."

"Yes, and then she would have been a name on a list next to other names from other applicants who are all good candidates. Without a personal connection, the odds of getting in are steep." Caroline pursed her lips. "I think Jane is nice. Very nice. But I also think she's smart."

"She is!"

"Yes." Caroline nodded. "She's a very smart, talented, *African American* woman on a predominantly white campus, relying on student loans and scholarships to get her through school, and knowing full well that having the Realis Society on a resume can be a real career boost. So she went after you, and when she realized that there wasn't anything there, she made a calculated decision not to end the relationship because there was still something in it for her. I'm sorry, but you have to open yourself up to this possibility."

For a moment, Will was certain that Charlie would explode. Splotches of red bloomed across his cheeks and stretched down his throat. His eyes, darker now than Will had ever seen them, seemed the size of saucers, and a vein popped out in stark relief across his forehead. His chest rose and fell with hard, raspy breaths that echoed throughout the otherwise quiet common area—a powder keg waiting for flames.

Yet when he spoke, his voice was soft.

"You ever make an accusation like that again, Caroline, and you're out of here."

Caroline went pale. "Out of..."

"*Here.*"

"Netherfield Heights?"

"Try Meryton."

Will held his breath.

"You can't do that," she said, though she didn't look certain. "That's not your decision."

"No, but it's not your decision, either. You're being bankrolled by our father, and that can go away at any time." He smiled unpleasantly. "One little phone call to Dad and it's sayonara, sister."

Will held his breath. This was a low blow, and he knew at once that the words had had their desired effect. It had taken a lot of persuasion to get Charles Bingley Sr. to part ways with his 1950s attitudes about women long enough to tolerate the idea of Caroline attending college. If Charlie called their father and said that Caroline was best suited as the shiny trophy touted out by a rich businessman than academia, she'd be out of Meryton faster than she could scream, "Unfair!"

And Charlie knew it.

And no matter how much Will didn't care for Caroline, that was not right.

The fight had vacated Caroline's eyes, replaced with a different kind of anger—the sort that had the power to wound rather than rile.

Will cleared his throat. "Charlie—"

"No," Caroline barked, the stricken look on her face fading. "Will, thank you, but there's no need. I have done what I can. My brother is perfectly entitled to his own mistakes."

Charlie prowled a step forward, his nostrils flaring. "I—"

"Please excuse me." And without another word, Caroline whirled around and started for the stairs.

Will waited until the telltale sound of her door latching shut echoed down the hall before turning his attention to his friend.

"Really," he said flatly. "You're going to hang her education over her head because she's concerned about your girlfriend?"

For a moment, Will expected Charlie to round on him and

resume screaming. It looked like he wanted to do just that. Yet that moment passed, taking Charlie's anger and tension with it.

"Caroline's a racist snob."

It wasn't a shocking statement, and Will couldn't say he disagreed. Caroline, in fact, might be the very worst kind of racist—at least those who were overt were easy to spot. Subtle racism was harder to fight.

"She doesn't like Jane because Jane's poor," Charlie continued, his voice rising again, but not much. "Jane's poor and she's here on scholarship money and student loans. If that wasn't bad enough, she's black, so obviously she can only be after me for my money and connections, right?"

"You're right. She is a racist snob."

"But you said she might have a point." Charlie whipped his head up, his eyes flashing again. "Earlier, you said she might have a point about Jane."

God, this was why he needed to stay out of relationships. Anyone's relationship.

"I said she might," Will agreed slowly. "I don't know if she does."

"But you think she could."

He paused, considered. "I *like* Jane, Charlie. A lot. We haven't talked much, but when we have, I've found her clever and... sweet." A beat. "But recently, it has seemed like she's been... avoiding you."

Charlie arched an eyebrow. "By coming over here every other day?"

"She's here a lot but she has been..." Will flicked his gaze in the direction of the stairs. "I'm not saying that means anything, but it could mean something."

He waited for the inevitable explosion. It didn't come. What did was worse.

Will watched as it happened—as Charlie fought down the urge to deny the possibility and allowed himself to consider.

It was that moment that Will realized something he should have seen well before now.

Charlie was in love. In *real* love. Not in lust or infatuation, or anything in between. To him, Jane wasn't a college girlfriend— she was the long haul.

And if Jane didn't feel the same way, Charlie wouldn't just be upset—he'd be devastated.

Will inhaled a deep breath, held it, hoped to whatever was out there listening that Caroline had it wrong. With as fully and deeply as Charlie felt, he might not come back from losing Jane.

15

Time had a funny way of behaving when one was anticipating something. For Will, the space between his leaving Longbourn and arriving at the first class on Monday seemed to stretch for months. Even with the distraction that was a mopey Charlie Bingley—something no one should ever have to see—and the increasingly intimidating pile of coursework to tackle, the weekend couldn't have crawled by any slower if someone had slipped it a sedative. Every time Will thought of Elizabeth, his heart did a funny jig and adrenaline tore through him like the Roadrunner on speed.

Then he woke up and it was Monday, and Will didn't quite know what to do with himself. He didn't want to seem overly eager to see her but he also didn't want to ignore her. There was no handbook to refer to and even if he had been the sort of guy who would rely on others for advice of this nature, he couldn't have asked Charlie, anyway.

In the end, he decided to go for calm but pleasant. See if she wanted to grab coffee after class or something so they could discuss what had happened in further detail.

He chose a pair of medium-wash jeans and a long-sleeved

navy tee, then spent a few seconds examining his expression in the mirror to double-check how he looked when going for blasé. It was ridiculous but he didn't care, and once he entered that classroom, all the variables that were in his control would be exhausted.

Will arrived at Professor Greenfield's class with a good twenty minutes to spare, and this last stretch of waiting was, perhaps, even more egregious than two days prior. Professor Greenfield didn't show up to unlock the room until around five till, and Elizabeth was nowhere in sight.

He'd hoped that perhaps she'd spent the weekend in the same state of anxious anticipation that he had. That she'd show up early so they could talk.

She didn't. She showed up right on time, and the second she crossed the threshold, she pinned her gaze on her desk—right next to his—and dove for it. She moved in such a way that let him know she was very aware of him, but she didn't so much as sneeze in his direction.

At first, as that terrible sinking sensation fell past his ribs and somewhere in the vicinity of his stomach, Will tried to reason that she didn't want to interrupt class. It made sense, after all. Elizabeth arrived just in time to retrieve her books and her notes from her book bag before Professor Greenfield launched into their current debate topic—which happened to be condoms in schools. Then she became the picture of a model student, jotting furious notes, gaze fixed determinately on the instructor as conversation bounced from peer to peer.

If it weren't for the concerted effort Elizabeth was making *not* to look at him, Will might have felt invisible. But he thought this might be worse.

Invisible people weren't ignored intentionally, after all.

"Mr. Darcy."

The sound of his name cut through the fog that had settled

in his mind. Will gave his head a shake and jerked his attention to the front of the class. "Yes."

"What were your thoughts on Mendelson's argument?"

Will blinked. *Mendelson.* The name sounded familiar, but for the life of him, he didn't know why. A fact evidently not lost on Professor Greenfield, who looked less than impressed.

"Did you do the reading, Mr. Darcy?"

Yes, he had. He just didn't happen to remember any of it at the moment.

His brain did not take pity on him, and to make the morning worse, his mouth likewise decided to go on strike and failed to respond to his commands to say something.

At length, Professor Greenfield sighed and shook her head. "It's your dime, Mr. Darcy. I get paid whether you learn something or not."

A giggle erupted from the back of the room.

Will's cheeks heated and he managed, somehow, to jerk his head in a nod.

Professor Greenfield shifted her attention to Elizabeth. "What about you, Ms. Bennet? Did you—"

"I think Mendelson's got his head up his ass," Elizabeth offered. "Every piece of information that is available to us at the moment tells us that access to contraceptives prevents unwanted pregnancies and STDs."

"You hand a kid a condom and he's gonna want to have sex," said a guy from the front of the class. "You're practically giving him permission."

Elizabeth arched an eyebrow. "Yes. And we know, from the mountain of data at the ready, that if we don't provide condoms, kids won't have sex. Congratulations. You just solved teen pregnancy."

"There's a difference between sex education and handing out prophylactics!" the kid continued. "Your way is reckless."

"No," Elizabeth replied. "What's *reckless* is ignoring the data that we've gathered for the last few years. If kids want to have sex, they're going to have sex. Not talking about sex or emphasizing an abstinence-only environment gets us nothing but a spike in teen pregnancy and a generation of clueless kids with itchy genitals."

A laugh rumbled through the classroom. The guy she was arguing with flushed but didn't look away from her. "So your answer is to give walking hormones permission to fuck. How is that responsible?"

"Mr. Zelner," Professor Greenfield said. "That sort of language is not needed to express a point."

"Also, since we're debating, you might wanna look up what a straw man is," Elizabeth said.

"Fuck you, you know-it-all cunt."

Will sprang to his feet, an action that went largely unnoticed considering the entire room exploded with noise. At once, everyone was yelling at the guy—none more loudly than Professor Greenfield. From the back of the room, Elizabeth's housemates were making suggestions that were anatomically impossible but rather creative, and though Will couldn't say he thought much of them overall, he couldn't help but swell with pride at their ferocity.

"In case you were wondering," Elizabeth said brightly, her voice somehow carrying over the calamity around her, "that's called an *ad hominem*. Also not a very effective debate tool."

In spite of himself, Will grinned, then wider when she finally met his eyes.

The contact lasted half a second. She tore her gaze from his and some of the humor faded from her face. As though she'd forgotten he was there until that moment.

Something inside him gave a pitiful mewl. His brain, sluggish and reluctant, tried to provide a reason but came up empty.

How could she want to pretend it hadn't happened?

It took a few seconds for the noise around his head to start sounding like words again. By the time he clued back in, Professor Greenfield was yelling at the back of a departing student. Will shot a look to the space the kid had occupied— empty. A coil of satisfaction unfurled, then closed again when he remembered the woman sitting beside him.

"All right," Professor Greenfield said, turning back to the students. "Well, that was certainly...lively. Mendelson is quite divisive, but I have never had anything like that happen in a class before."

Elizabeth wet her lips and shifted in her seat. Will pulled his eyes off her and tried to focus on what the professor was saying.

"I suppose I should have laid some ground rules on day one. Silly me, thinking you're all college students and capable of having adult conversations." Her gaze landed briefly on the desk the student had vacated. "Needless to say, here is the only rule that, if broken, will get your ass kicked out of my class so fast your head will spin. We do *not* attack the speaker, ever. What Mr. Zelner called Ms. Bennet was not only uncalled for—it was uncivil. Debate means that—*debate*. We will not always agree with stances others take, but we must treat each other with respect." She looked at Elizabeth. "On his behalf, I apologize."

Will tried not to follow the professor's gaze and failed.

Elizabeth shrugged. "Not my first misogynist. Won't be my last, either."

"Just because he doesn't agree with you doesn't make him a misogynist," the blonde from Will's debate group—Penelope— said, her tone frosty.

"No, but the fact that his go-to insult was *cunt* sure as hell does."

Penelope rolled her eyes. "Whatever."

Perhaps sensing another blowup was imminent, Professor

Greenfield raised a hand. "All right. I think that's enough for today. We're not getting anywhere. Instead of discussion, I'd like a minimum of five pages on the Mendelson reading by Friday."

"Oh no!" Lydia whined from the back.

"This should be simple as most of you, undoubtedly, have an opinion on the subject of condoms in schools. Provide your response to Mendelson's argument *with* sources. I want no less than three cited." The professor collected her briefcase and heaved a long sigh. "Office hours from one to three this afternoon. Happy Monday."

With that, she made a hasty escape.

The room exploded once more in a flurry of hurried conversation, some excited about what had happened—after all, those sorts of outbursts weren't common at Meryton—and others bemoaning the unexpected assignment. Will sat quietly as Elizabeth gathered her things, not knowing what he was waiting for but waiting all the same. Hoping she'd look at him again, give him some sort of indication what was going on in her head.

She didn't. Once her books were back in her bag, she turned for the door.

And that was it. Something in him snapped. Will cursed and shot to his feet again. He debated leaving his things where they were but decided it would be better to not have to return here and draw more attention to himself. Whatever was happening between him and Elizabeth wasn't anyone's business, and if he took off without his things, it'd be obvious that she was the reason.

Still, it was harder to catch up with someone when shouldering thirty pounds of text books.

Elizabeth usually turned left when leaving Greenfield's class, so Will did the same. The hallways were thankfully empty, being that most classes were still in session. He became intently aware of how much noise he was making, his heavy steps plonking against the ground, his breaths hurried and loud, his pulse racing in his ears. When he rounded the corner and spied her halfway down the corridor, his rational brain clicked off.

"Elizabeth!"

He expected her to ignore him. She didn't. Instead, she stopped dead in her tracks, her shoulders slumping.

"What?" she asked without turning around.

Will picked up his pace. "We need to talk."

"About what?"

"What do you mean, about what?" He drew to a halt beside her, aching as his lungs clamored for oxygen. "About what happened the other night."

Elizabeth turned to face him but still didn't meet his eyes. "Why?"

"Why?"

"Why do we need to talk about it? It happened. The end. There's no need to go over it."

Will blinked at her. "Are you serious?"

"Do I look serious?"

"I dunno. Why don't you try looking *at me* and we'll see?"

That did it. Her brilliant gaze swung upward, sparking with fire he knew she couldn't contain. And though it wasn't exactly what he *wanted* to see when she looked at him, he was glad to see anything at all.

"It happened," she repeated slowly, her cheeks reddening, which intrigued him, since it was clear she was clamoring for control. "But there's no need to talk about it. It's over."

Will stared at her. "You can just do that?"

"Do what?"

"Turn it off. Whatever it is you're feeling."

Elizabeth stepped back, her eyes going wide. "Who says I'm feeling anything?" she demanded.

"Look, I was there too. I know what I saw."

"No, you know what you wanted to see."

"What happened in the parking lot wasn't just me, and we both know that what happened in your room wasn't just me, either."

"You wanna say that a little louder for the people in the cheap seats?"

He looked around to see if they had indeed drawn a crowd, but the hallway remained vacant. Then something occurred to him. "So now that something actually happened, it matters what I say? What happened to not caring what other people think?"

Elizabeth blinked as though confused, then rolled her eyes. "I *don't* care what people think. I just don't think all conversations should be equipped with a megaphone."

Will barked a laugh. "You're unbelievable. You nearly tear my head off for trying to be discreet over something that *didn't* happen and now you're—"

"People are in class!" she spat. "This isn't a parking lot, it's a hallway. Do you need me to draw you a diagram?"

"If you think it'll help me keep up with you."

"There's nothing to *keep up* with. You're a smart guy, Will. I'd think you'd be able to tell the difference between a club and a school."

Will pushed himself forward another step. "Okay. You don't feel anything."

"That's right."

"Can you tell me why you let me... If you feel nothing, why did it happen?"

Elizabeth squirmed a bit, though she didn't drop her gaze from his. As though now maintaining eye contact was a personal challenge. "Because sometimes people do stupid things." She gestured between them. "Case in point."

Will arched an eyebrow, his feet carrying him toward her another step. He was asking for it, he knew, but he didn't have the will to pull himself away at the moment. His blood pumped and his temples throbbed, and he needed her to say it —to own it—once and for all so he stood a chance of moving on.

"So I'm a stupid thing you did."

"I didn't *do* you."

"By virtue of the fact that neither one of us had a condom." Will shook his head, heaving a laugh that he didn't feel. "But maybe that was for the best, if what happened was so stupid." He looked at her a moment longer before giving his head a shake. "Guess we're done here."

Never mind that a piece of himself had broken in a way he didn't think could ever be fixed. It was dumb, *beyond* dumb to feel like this over her. It had been dumb enough to let himself fantasize all weekend when he'd known there was no way she was on nearly the same page as him. He'd done a lot of work to convince himself it was possible, but the truth had always been within reach. He just hadn't wanted to acknowledge it.

Because, dammit, he didn't *want* to be done.

Apparently, neither did she.

"That easy, huh?" Elizabeth said.

Will paused, having been about to turn away from her and put as much space between them as possible. "What?"

"I guess I expected more of a fight from you."

"I'm not the kind of guy who *fights* to stay in a woman's life. If she says she wants me gone, I'm gone."

Elizabeth's looked torn between pleased with this response and annoyed by it, which only served to make him more confused than he had been a moment ago.

Will couldn't help it. He laughed.

Elizabeth blanched. "What?"

"You don't know what you want."

"Excuse me?"

"I chase you and you shove me away. I back off and you yank me back."

She brought her hands up. "I am not yanking. There is no yanking."

"Then what was that about?"

"What?"

"You expected more of a fight from me?" He spread his arms. "That's not who I am. Never has been."

Something flashed across her eyes—confusion followed by defiance.

"Then who are you?" she asked.

Will arched an eyebrow. "Who am I?"

"With all I hear, a girl has to wonder. It's all over the place with you."

"I guess that depends on who you talk to."

"And if I talked to George Wickham?"

There it was. Will released a long breath, struggling to maintain eye contact with her because he knew it was important. Yet on a primal level, he wanted to rip away and roar his frustration.

"Wickham talks to a lot of people," he said, his brain stumbling over itself to find the right, measured words. "While he's not good at keeping friends, he's very good at making them."

"He told me you were friends once. Was that a lie?"

Will felt his temper tip into dangerous territory. His need to know what Wickham was telling people was dwarfed only by his need to ignore the man completely and hope that Wickham lost interest if he saw he couldn't get a rise out of him.

So he decided on a roundabout version of the truth.

"He was a friend once. He's not now."

"Why?" Elizabeth pressed.

"Because he's not." Will broke off, searching. "There are certain lines you never cross. Ever. If you do, then I'm through with you."

"Then I'm sorry for him," Elizabeth said. "Losing your friendship seemed to really cost him."

He barked another laugh.

"What?" Now she sounded pissed. "That's funny?"

"Yes."

"Pretty damn cold, Darcy."

If all she knew about the situation was that he and Wickham had once been friends, he supposed it would seem cold. But he could live with that—until he was certain he could trust her with the truth.

And if that *was* her understanding of the situation... Well, it was a relief. There was little chance she'd hold back if there was anything else.

Hell, with as little crap as Elizabeth took from anyone, Wickham had probably set off her bullshit alarm faster than a politician during election season.

"I don't want to talk about Wickham," he said at last. "I want to talk about what happened the other night. About you and me."

"We already did."

"You called it dumb."

"Yes."

"But it wasn't." He stepped forward, right into her space, and something within him roared with triumph when she didn't back up. Instead, those wonderfully expressive eyes of hers widened before darkening. "It wasn't random, either. You went home from that club and touched yourself. Thinking of me."

Elizabeth didn't respond, nor did she look away, despite the blush scaling up her neck. This was one of the things he admired most about her. She didn't back down. Didn't hide when he might expect her to, or get embarrassed easily.

Instead, she held his gaze, defiant.

"And," he said, pressing closer, "you opened the door and let me in."

"I slammed the door on you first." Her voice wasn't as firm as it had been a moment ago.

"Yes, but then you opened it." His own gaze had fallen to her lips and become trapped there, transfixed. "And it was... Touching you was..."

He didn't know how to finish that. Words escaped him.

She released a ragged breath, and he looked up again just in time to see her focus on his mouth, and he knew it was over.

Will's hands moved of their own accord, capturing Elizabeth's face as she flew to him. That same thrill raced up his spine —the one that had chased him all weekend, haunted him before he found sleep, and drove him to hope a little too much. But this was easy, and they seemed to be good at it.

Elizabeth tugged him down and then his mouth was on hers and everything around him began to fade. He'd had time to wonder if his mind had exaggerated their chemistry. Exaggerated her taste. But no, she tasted amazing. Her lips hot on his, wrestling away kisses that made his mind go loopy. It was unfair that she felt this good, that his body, happily ignoring the weak warnings issued by his mind, responded to her with enthusiasm. And then it didn't matter—nothing mattered—because Elizabeth was pressed against him. Her tongue stroking his tongue, her lips tugging on his, her hands tangling their way through his hair as she rolled her pelvis to meet his thickening cock.

This was *not* the place to do this, but the part of him that cared was quickly losing its steam.

Elizabeth broke the kiss well before he was ready, gasping for air. She stayed still for so long he could practically hear her brain working, even if he couldn't make out what it was saying. Exasperation battled with need and ultimately bowed to want.

She might be the most infuriating woman on the planet, but he wanted her anyway.

He *liked* her anyway.

Hell, as far-gone as he was, he figured he might be falling in love with her. And that was truly terrifying.

Elizabeth opened her eyes and met his without faltering. Will's lungs were working overtime. She studied him long enough to give him a complex, then seized one of his hands and tugged.

He didn't ask where they were going. At the moment, he would follow her anywhere.

Even if *anywhere* happened to be a maintenance closet.

Elizabeth shoved the door closed behind her and shucked off her backpack. He barely had time to do the same before she was on him again, that hot mouth of hers tearing at his. Will tried to hold back a whimper and failed, the last strands of reason vanishing as her tongue teased his lips. The last of his anger gave one last rallying cry before fading altogether.

Apparently taking rational thought away with it. Because the Will he knew had vanished, transformed into some bizarre hybrid creature that had no sense of self control. He'd never been big on public displays of affection, never mind sneaking into some darkened corner to rub against a woman like some hormone-addled teenager. With other girls, Will had been careful to temper his physical reactions as much as possible. Not to just come at them like some horny farm animal. But every stroke of Elizabeth's mouth against his chipped another piece of him away, leaving behind a pulsing cluster of pure animal want. It unnerved him but not enough to stop. To pull back. To *care*.

"God," Will murmured between kisses, unable to keep himself from thrusting his hips against her. His cock hit her center and she whimpered before thrusting back.

Then he felt something else—her hand was between them. On him.

Cupping him.

Pulling down the zipper to his jeans.

Will pulled back to look at her, straining in the dark. He couldn't see her face. "What—"

But then his cock was free and between them, and her hand closed around him with a tender squeeze. Will blinked madly, then let out a long moan.

Elizabeth released a shuddering breath, leaned in and caught his lower lip between her teeth. She squeezed his cock again before developing a steady rhythm. Up and down, base to tip.

He couldn't believe this was happening. He couldn't believe he was letting it.

He threw his head back, jerking his hips.

Fuck.

Fuck.

This had gotten out of control really freaking fast. Not that Elizabeth had fooled herself into thinking she'd ever had it *in* control. Obviously, the very fact that she'd all but dragged Will into a secluded closet to molest him should be an indicator of how very *not* in control she was.

Coming to class had been difficult enough today knowing that she'd have to see him. Knowing that he'd probably want to talk about what had happened, when she'd known that was a bad idea and she needed to go back to the strategy where she pretended he didn't exist. Except she hadn't been able to—she'd lost the power to ignore him sometime over the weekend, likely around the time she'd come all over his fingers. All morning she'd been off and now...

Now she was pulling at his dick as her mouth got even more acquainted with his. This was wrong and stupid and she was only making things worse, but all things being fair, she did owe the guy an orgasm, at least. No matter what kind of skeazoid he was, he had outperformed her dildo ten to one. Returning the favor was just polite.

Also, she was addicted to the sounds he made. Just thinking about those whimpers and moans had ensured she'd been in a state of perpetual horniness all damn weekend. Now, every time she stroked up the length of his cock, a stifled cry would tickle her lips and she'd melt.

Will pulled away again, breathing hard. Yeah, that was a turn on too. Damn him.

"Elizabeth," he murmured. "Your hand. God. Feels so good."

Elizabeth swallowed, running her fingers down his shaft again until she reached the curly hairs at his groin. Then she fisted his cock at the base and dragged her hand upward again.

Will sighed and kissed the corner of her mouth. "Your hand," he said again. "Your mouth…"

Whoa buddy.

Her mouth?

Elizabeth paused in mid-stroke. "Are you seriously asking me to blow you?"

Her eyes had adjusted well enough that she could clearly see him blinking as though to clear his head. "What?" he asked.

"Why is a handjob never good enough? I swear, guys—"

"No," he rasped harshly. "No. I wasn't…I'd never ask for that."

Elizabeth arched an eyebrow. "Never?"

"I wouldn't…*demean* you by asking you to—"

"Oh, so blowjobs are demeaning?" Who the hell was this guy?

"I just don't think—"

"Clearly not," Elizabeth said before sinking to her knees and sucking his cock into her mouth.

"Wha—" Will released a strangled gasp that made the other delicious sounds he'd given her seem like dairy-free froyo pitted against the most decadent item she could order at Cold Stone.

She took his cock further into her mouth until the tip of him was nudging the back of her throat. It had been a long time since she'd wanted to give a guy head—mostly because the men she'd been with had been demanding, which took the fun out of it for her.

Will made this fun.

She drew back slowly, reminding herself to breathe through her nose, tightening her lips and savoring each inch of him as she pulled back. It occurred to her only after she'd released his dick that the thing itself was massive. Perhaps not the largest cock she'd seen, but definitely one of the top three. She'd been so intent on making her point that she hadn't taken the time to appreciate him fully, which was a crying shame after all the mental pictures he'd given her over the weekend.

"Elizabeth—"

She closed her mouth around the tip of his cock and gave a small suck.

"*Shit, shit, shit.*"

A bubble of laughter rose in her throat. What else could she make him say?

Elizabeth tongued the underside of his dick, then rolled her lips over her teeth and pressed down on his cockhead. Not too much pressure, but enough to make those delicious moans of his grow in volume. Any more and she'd worry about being caught, but dammit if that wasn't half the appeal.

How would Will react if the door suddenly opened? If the world saw that, underneath his piles and piles of money, he was just a dude after all?

Then she thought of Wickham seeing her with her mouth around his enemy's prick and experienced a rush of shame. She knew she was being stupid, but she was also enjoying herself and for the moment, she wanted to focus on that.

Forget promises she'd made. Forget things she'd learned. Forget everything and just *enjoy*.

She could go back to being responsible later. She hoped.

Elizabeth wrapped a hand around the base of his erection and squeezed, then began sucking in earnest, dragging her mouth up and down his shaft as his hips jerked and his skin heated. Every time she took him back in, she made sure to lave the head of his cock with her tongue, to squeeze him with her lips. She reached up with her free hand to massage his balls, and at first contact, he damn near buckled at the legs.

"Oh god," Will murmured, tunneling his fingers through her hair. "Elizabeth... I..."

But she didn't want to hear it—she wanted him to come.

Elizabeth drew his cock in as far as it would go once more, until his smooth head was again pressed as far as he could go. Then she began to work her throat around him, and Will went wild.

"Oh fuck. Oh fuck. Oh fuck oh fuck oh fuck." He fisted her hair—not enough to hurt but enough to restrict movement, and hell if that didn't turn her on more. Because, yes, she was a sick, sick girl. Will looked down and despite the darkness, she found his eyes.

And shivered.

"Gonna...gonna..."

He didn't get the words out, but that didn't matter. She knew what he was *gonna,* and she wanted him to.

So she kept swallowing.

And with a final tremble, Will spilled himself down her throat. Elizabeth stayed where she was, holding onto him as his cock pulsed and jerked, working her head back and forth again to milk him for everything he was worth.

Finally, when the spasms subsided, she drew back until just the tip of him remained between her lips, then released him with a wet plop.

A thick, shuddering sigh tore through the confined space. It took a moment to register that his hands were still in her hair, his fingers lightly massaging her scalp.

It was the sensation of those subtle, tender touches that dragged Elizabeth back into the real world. In a few seconds, Will's brain would reconnect and he'd want to talk about what had happened, what it meant, analyze it to freaking death and she didn't think she could stomach that because she could *not* go there.

So she pulled back until her head was free, patted his cock, then bounded to her feet.

Apparently, she'd sent Will suborbital. He didn't blink back to himself until she slid her arms through her backpack straps.

"Where are you going?" he asked hoarsely.

"Somewhere that's gone," Elizabeth replied, fluffing her hair and hoping it didn't look too tangled. "We're even now."

"Even—?"

But she didn't elaborate. There was no point. Instead, she opened the door a sliver and slid back into the hallway. No sooner had she taken three steps than the class across the hall let out, and a steady stream of students piled into the corridor.

Which meant Will would be stuck for at least a few minutes.

Good timing, as it turned out, was everything.

16

Jane, the happiest person on the face of the planet, was crying.

Elizabeth's stomach dropped. She stood in the doorway to their room, staring at her friend and willing the scene in front of her to change. It didn't. Jane was sitting in the middle of her bed, hugging her legs and releasing a gut-wrenching sound that could only mean one thing.

Charlie had dumped her.

But that didn't seem possible. It couldn't *be* possible, because if there was one thing Elizabeth knew, it was the sign of a smitten man. Charlie hadn't been able to peel his eyes off Jane for more than five seconds since they'd met. He couldn't possibly go from that to splitsville in the course of one freaking weekend.

Elizabeth was going to beat him to death with lawn equipment. It was only fair.

As though sensing her presence, Jane looked up, her eyes swollen, tear-tracks wending down her cheeks.

Something twisted in Elizabeth's gut. "I'm going to kill him."

"Liz...Lizzie..."

"I mean it. Charlie Bingley is one dead dude."

Elizabeth had been holding out hope that she was reading the signs wrong. That Charlie wasn't responsible for the mess that was her best friend, that there was something innocuous, even something laughable behind this. But at the sound of Charlie's name, Jane drew in a sharp breath, her eyes watering all over again.

Oh yeah. There was a dead man walking over at Netherfield Heights.

"I-it's fine," Jane said in what had to be the least convincing voice in the history of oral communication. "I-I am fine."

"Yeah. Obviously." Elizabeth stormed forward, dropped off her backpack so it landed in the middle of the floor with a resounding thud. She gazed down at Jane's miserable face, swore, then wrapped her friend into a bear hug. And Jane began to lose it again.

"It's not a big deal," she insisted between sobs. "I should have seen it coming."

I should have too.

The thought surfaced from nowhere, buried under the disbelief of just seconds ago, but so damn true it made her bones ache. Because despite however smitten Charlie had seemed, Elizabeth had learned the hard way that appearances meant shit. Guys who seemed too good to be true always were. Always.

Elizabeth blinked hard and tightened her arms around Jane. "Did he tell you why, at least?"

Jane released a rattling breath and pulled back. "He said he needed...to focus on his studies and that we wanted different things."

"Meaning you wanted to kiss and he wanted to cuddle?"

"I think it's because I didn't sleep with him."

Elizabeth's eyes widened. "Are you shitting me?"

Jane bit her bottom lip. "I know. I know. My nerves just..."

She paused. "I've never done it. Had sex. I was...waiting. For someone I really liked. Or loved."

"Oh, Jane..."

"And I thought that person was Charlie." She sniffed, fresh tears brimming to the surface. "But every time I thought I was getting close, I'd chicken out and run to Caroline so she'd distract me. I think he got tired of that. I know I would have."

Mother. Fucker.

"That sleazoid dumped you for not spreading your legs?" Elizabeth was on her feet in an instant. "Now I really am going to kill him."

"Lizzie, he didn't say—"

"I'm going to kill that fucker dead."

Jane bounded up too, waving her arms. "He never said that. He never even mentioned it. Sex was not a part of the conversation. That's just my insecurity speaking."

"You wouldn't have said that if you didn't think there was some truth to it," Elizabeth fired back. "And if you think there's truth to it, it's because he put that thought in your head."

"No. *I* put the thought in my head. I am in charge of my own thoughts."

"Well, I am in charge of punching Charlie Bingley right in the fucking throat."

Jane released a pitiful cry and launched herself at the door, stretching her arms and widening her legs to block the entrance.

Elizabeth arched an eyebrow. "Please. I could totally take you."

"That's not the point," Jane said. "You're not taking anyone. Charlie didn't do anything wrong by breaking up with me."

"That's for me and my fists of justice to decide."

"No. *No.* You are not going to go over there." Jane stomped her foot—actually *stomped* her foot. "This entire thing is humiliating enough without my badass bestie storming off to defend my honor. Guys break up with girls every day. I just happen to be one of them."

Elizabeth felt the fire under her skin ebb a little, but only just. "Come on. Can I at least break one of his toes?"

"Elizabeth!"

"I'll even take the pinkie."

Jane blinked at her as though trying to decide whether or not she was serious, then gave her head another shake and, amazingly, broke out into a soft smile. "I love you," she said, dropping her arms and straightening her posture. "You know that, right?"

"I do. You'll love me even more after you see my plans for rearranging a certain dickhole's face."

"Lizzie..."

Elizabeth groaned and rolled her head back. "I am so losing my street cred."

"Worse things have happened."

Once she seemed reasonably satisfied that Elizabeth wasn't going to bolt for the door, Jane moved back to her bed. While she had stopped crying, her eyes were lined in that telling way. There wasn't enough foundation or powder in the world to cover that look. And the last thing Jane needed was it getting back to Charlie that she was taking the breakup hard.

The next time anyone saw Jane, she needed to look eat-your-heart-out fabulous.

"What do you want tonight?" Elizabeth asked. "Name it."

"What?"

"Greasy burger, extra bacon? Pasta loaded with all the cheese and noodly goodness a gal can ask for? *All* the ice cream? Whatever you want, I'm buying."

Jane barked a laugh at that—a real laugh. "You're impossible."

"Hey." Elizabeth brought her hands up. "You're denying me

the pleasure of beating your ex-boyfriend to death. You will *not* take away my right to spoil you with post-breakup calories. So name what you want and I'll go get it."

"Greasy burger, extra bacon," she said. "And a double chocolate milkshake."

"Now you're talking. Fries?"

"The biggest size they offer."

Elizabeth beamed and picked up her purse. "One mild heart attack coming up."

"You're the best, Lizzie."

"I do try."

For the next few hours, Elizabeth kept her mind on Jane. No wandering to dangerous places, especially places inhabited by one Will Darcy. But after Jane had stuffed herself into a food coma and drifted off to sleep, Elizabeth's mind revved its engine and dragged her back to the thing she'd successfully avoided thinking about all day.

It seemed no matter what she did, no matter her intentions, she couldn't keep herself from losing control around Will. There was no reason that she could see why she should be drawn to him now—why resisting should be any trouble at all—yet here she was.

What did that say about her?

She swallowed, turning over in bed, pulling the blankets over her shoulders. Whatever was going on with her, it had to end. This thing with Charlie and Jane had driven that point home like nothing else could. Feelings were toxic, especially if they were aimed at someone like Will. The past few days had been an exercise of stupidity on her part. Fooling around with

Will was bad enough—to do so knowing what he was capable of?

But is he?

There was a very real part of her—the part that kept taking control of her mind and body when he was around—that voiced its doubt. Because she *had* to doubt on some level, didn't she? Why else would she have shoved him into that closet today, or opened the door when he'd knocked a second time, knowing full well what would happen if he came into her room?

A part of her doubted. Or rather, hoped.

But goddamn, if he was capable of framing Wickham, he was certainly capable of lying about it, if he ever did more than dance around the issue like he had today. And what exactly did Wickham have to gain by making something like that up?

Besides, lies weren't exactly easy to come up with on the spot. Wickham hadn't had to search or think about anything he'd told her. It had been straightforward—the sort of straightforward that came with the confidence of the truth.

Which meant she was an idiot of the worst kind, knowingly getting involved with someone as powerful and vindictive as Will Darcy. Hell, if she did something he didn't like, she might as well kiss her scholarship goodbye. If something happened that he didn't like, she knew he had the power to make sure she never set foot on Meryton campus again.

This was her future. It was time to stop self-sabotaging.

Mind made up, Elizabeth forced out a deep breath and snuggled deeper into her blankets.

Except her brain wasn't that kind. Almost immediately, she began composing her script. The things she'd say to Will next, including some variation of *so long* and *thanks for the orgasm* and *we're cool, right*? The key was to not get into another argument with him, since arguing for them was foreplay, and the safest recourse was to not go down that line at all. Be civil. Be brief. Be gone.

The more she thought about it, the more adrenaline pumped through her veins. Elizabeth rolled over and eyed the clock on her nightstand. It was barely after midnight and she was wide-awake.

She sat up and eyed Jane, who was curled into a ball, sawing logs.

If she got this over with now, there was every chance she'd be able to get some sleep.

Elizabeth chewed on that for a moment, then cursed and rolled her eyes. She couldn't possibly be thinking about going to Netherfield Heights, could she?

God, she totally was.

Her heart began thudding hard, her hands grew cold and clammy. Going over there was the worst of all bad ideas, but goddammit, the more she thought about it, the more she needed to move. The more tempting the prospect became. Elizabeth swallowed and shook her head, lying back down.

No. That was nuts. There was a time and a place for the conversation she needed to have with Will, and it was most certainly not now.

Except when *would* it be a good time?

He tried to talk to you earlier and you didn't let him.

Yeah, well, that had been dumb. All of it had been dumb. And it was time to stop being dumb.

Elizabeth blinked her eyes open.

Jesus Christ, she was going to do it.

With a heavy sigh, she threw back her blankets and bounded to her feet. She moved as quickly as she could while still not making noise. She wouldn't worry about finding the right wardrobe—it didn't matter for this conversation. Sweats and T-shirt were fine. Hell, the less put together she looked, the better. It'd give Will the right impression.

Once dressed, Elizabeth stopped and checked in with herself.

Yeah, she still wanted to do this. If anything, she was anxious to get it done.

She grabbed her phone, fired off a quick message to Lyft—so not walking across campus at this hour—and left the bedroom.

Twenty minutes later, she was standing outside a very dark Netherfield Heights, her heart in her throat and second thoughts in her mind. Not that she was reconsidering her new resolution—she wasn't, not even slightly. But the idea of marching over in the dead of night didn't seem so brilliant now that she was actually here. It seemed rude and intrusive, and contrary to what others might think, Elizabeth didn't relish the thought of being either of those things.

She licked her lips and considered her options. On one hand, she'd already taken the steps to get her here. On the other...

Her treacherous mind took her back to that damned maintenance closet. To the sensation of Will's dick in her mouth, his hands in her hair, his moans coloring the air as her lips worked up and down him. The way he'd looked at her and said her name.

Fuck.

Elizabeth shuddered and pressed her thighs together. Yeah, she needed to nip this in the bud before her sex-starved lesser half could talk her out of it. She moved forward, shoving her phone into her pocket, doing her best to ignore the hard thumps shaking her ribcage.

The front door was unlocked. She wasn't sure whether or not this was troubling, except that hadn't been a hurdle she'd considered when she'd made the decision to come here tonight, so it definitely worked in her favor. Still, it seemed careless to leave the door to the palace, so to speak, ajar. Or maybe this was just her lucky night.

Elizabeth took in the familiar surroundings. The couch where she'd tried to sleep the night of the endless storms and the staircase that led to Will's dorm room. She hadn't been here but that one time, but she was surprised at how much her brain had preserved, even in the dark.

She licked her lips and started toward the staircase, feeling like a criminal. Her chest ached, her mind conjuring up a variety of scenarios that might take place over the next few minutes. Most involving Will looking at her like she'd gone mad and taking out a restraining order, which would make attending class difficult, but might solve a lot of her problems in the long run.

There was the other scenario, though. One she refused to play out.

Finally, she found herself standing outside Will's door.

17

Elizabeth allowed herself one more instant of doubt before she raised her hand and knocked. Hard.

The response was immediate. He hadn't been asleep, and that thought provided some measure of comfort. She wasn't sure if she could have done this knowing she'd just woken him up.

Then the door opened, and Will was standing there, wearing nothing but a pair of sweats. The lamp on his desk was on and his laptop was set-up, but she barely had time to take in those details before her eyes were drawn back to his marble-like naked chest.

Fuck.

This was so not good.

"Thank god," Will said, and seized her by the wrist.

Elizabeth barely had time to blink before she was pulled against that lickable chest of his and his mouth was on her. Pulling, tugging, and exploring her so thoroughly she could have forgotten her own name. Just like that, all intent vanished from her mind, because damn, the man could kiss. It was unfair, really, that his mouth seemed to know exactly how hers liked to be stroked, his hands knew just where to go to render her a pile of goo. Elizabeth's sexual past wasn't comprised solely of selfish lovers, but no one had touched her the way Will did.

Wait. She had a plan, didn't she? She hadn't come over here for sex. She'd had a reason.

Yeah, well, try again tomorrow.

That was the selfish part of her talking. The part of her that had gotten her into this mess to begin with.

Elizabeth managed to get enough of a grip on herself to break away from his lips, but the next moment, he was kissing a line down her throat and she was gone again.

Will had somehow turned her so her back was to the room without pulling his mouth off her skin. When he drew back, it was with a ragged breath and a heated, burning look behind his eyes that made parts of her she didn't know were sensitive cry out in delight.

"I've been thinking about you all night," he murmured, kicking the door shut. "About today."

Right. *Right.* Elizabeth shook her head, willing her brain to reengage with the rest of her. *Work, damn you.*

"I—well, that's why I came by."

He grinned and nodded, then cupped her cheeks and kissed her again. "I was hoping for this."

"Y-you were?"

"For you to show up here. Just like this." He dropped his hands to the hemline of her T-shirt. "Can I?"

Now. Now was the time to tell him why she was here. He was asking for permission to undress her, dammit. And if he undressed her, she was not going to have the talk. She was going to have the sex. Lots and lots of sex. Something told her Will's room did not lack the condoms hers did.

She hoped it didn't, anyway.

No, no she didn't.

"Elizabeth?" He pulled back just enough to capture her eyes. "Is this okay? Can I..."

But her hands were already moving—intent on batting his away. Somehow they got distracted and ended up whipping her T-shirt off over her head. She had a moment to take in Will's surprised gaze before he was on her again, his mouth pulling hot kisses from hers as he pulled her into his awesome, warm chest. She felt his cock nudging her belly, and a corresponding pool of heat began to flood her panties. Her clit throbbed and her pussy clenched, and she wanted him inside her so badly she nearly forgot that she needed to breathe.

Thankfully, he remembered for her, heaving a lungful of air as their lips broke apart.

Her brain tried to kick on again. It sputtered and failed.

"Love the way your skin feels," Will murmured, dragging a hand down her naked arm. "You are so damn soft."

"You're not."

He chuckled—a sound that so should not have been sexy, but was—and began peppering kisses down her throat again. Goddamn, someone had slipped Will a map of her erogenous zones. Or he just had a lot of practice—a thought that shouldn't have bothered her but did. Even still, when his lips wound over her flesh, her mind went to that blank happy place where thought was discouraged.

Then his lips were moving lower. Over her collarbone, between her breasts. The ball of need that made up her stomach seemed to tighten. Elizabeth watched, mesmerized, as Will took one of her nipples between his lips and sucked. She had never found her breasts to be particularly sensitive in the past— though most guys she'd been with had definitely tried to include them in foreplay. Perhaps that was the reason. Will didn't seem to be trying to do anything except taste her. He ran his tongue over her again and again, making that sound that drove her out of her mind—like she was delicious, or something, when she knew damn well there was nothing special about her nipples.

Will opened his eyes and looked at her as he kissed his way to her other breast.

Fuck.

Every tug of his mouth seemed to have a direct line to her clit, which felt like it had its own heartbeat. By the time Will was done, her breasts were swollen and tender, and she was about ready to claw her away out of her skin.

Will grinned as though sensing this, and goddamn if that didn't turn her on more. Elizabeth released a long, heady moan, reached between them to cup him through his sweats. That cocky look dissolved on a whimper, and he thrust against her palm.

"You're gonna be the death of me," he murmured, walking her back.

When the backs of her knees hit the bed, the gravity of what was about to happen crashed over her all over again. Elizabeth blinked up at him, scrambling to find the thread of why she'd come here again, but gave up without much of a fight when he pushed his sweats down and his cock bobbed free.

"I've got condoms," Will said, hissing when her hand encircled him. "I've got—"

But Elizabeth wasn't listening. She'd drawn him into her mouth and was sucking sweetly. Knowing what she was doing to him—loving the way he abandoned all thought at the simplest touch. Damn, the man made giving head fun.

"Eliza...gotta...stop."

She licked the head of his cock impishly. "Oh?"

"Can..." He seemed to lose his train of thought for a second —coincidentally as she started squeezing the base of his erection—but found it quicker than she would have given him credit for. He reached into the nightstand and drew out a box of condoms.

"Someone's prepared," Elizabeth said dryly, sitting back.

"Not prepared. Well, yes, prepared. More...hopeful." He smiled at her, and that made her uncomfortable, because there was so much more in that smile than she was ready to see.

Hell, she'd come over here to—

Will had knelt before her and was rolling her sweats down her legs. He paused once that was done and took a moment to study her, and despite herself, she wondered what he saw. She was breathing hard, her breasts somewhat pink still from the attention of his mouth. Her hair was all over the place, and she had on only her panties, which she could plainly feel were soaked through.

"You are so beautiful," he murmured, palming one of her breasts. "So beautiful, Elizabeth."

That squirmy, uncomfortable feeling was back, but it didn't last. It didn't have a chance to last—Will lowered his head and tongued her pussy through the thin, sodden fabric of her panties. Elizabeth squeaked—literally squeaked—and jolted.

"Mmm." Will pulled back and aimed a devastating grin at her as he hooked his fingers under the elastic of her underwear. "Wanna come back down here. But I don't think I can stand it. Lift?"

Rationally, she knew what he was saying, but it wouldn't compute. Her body, though, was right on page with him. Her hips rolled and lifted of their own accord, and then cool air hit her cunt as Will stripped the last part of fabric off her body.

Then he was kissing her again. Those awesome kisses that curled her toes and blanked out everything except the need to keep kissing him. Elizabeth found herself moving back, and then she was against the mattress and he was over her. Perched between her legs, his thick cock rubbing against her soaking flesh and it occurred to her that this was really going to happen. She and Will were going to have sex.

So much for planning.

It was she, not he, who reached for the condom box, so she knew it was her decision. She tore open a package with her teeth, watching his eyes flare as she did so, and slipped her hand between them. Her fingers encircled his dick, gave it one, languid pull before she fitted him with the condom. Will stared at her, breathing hard, before shifting so the blunt head of his cock was dancing up and down her slit.

"Elizabeth," he murmured, "look at me."

A long breath rattled off her lips as her gaze locked on his. She hadn't even realized she'd closed her eyes.

He stared at her for a long moment, then lowered his mouth to hers as he thrust his hips forward and began to edge his cock inside her.

Goddamn, why did he have to feel so good?

Elizabeth clamped her teeth on his lower lip and fed him her moan, her body turning to hot wax around him. Will pushed until he could go no deeper, then held against her, breathing hard.

"Oh," he said at last.

Such a simple word. *Oh.*

Then he withdrew his hips, dragging his cock away again, and she would have screamed in outrage had he not plunged back inside. Elizabeth arched her neck, her eyes fixed on the ceiling as Will experimented with a rhythm. The first few pumps were slow and languid, almost nervous, but soon he was moving inside her in earnest.

"So good," he murmured, then began pressing kisses along her collarbone. "Elizabeth, you feel so good."

She willed her eyes closed, her hips rolling. She had never been a passive lover and she wasn't about to start now. No matter if this was wrong or doomed or whatever it was—she'd made her decision and she'd chosen this. If she was going to make mistakes, she was going to make the hell out of them.

Elizabeth pushed at his chest until he sat back, a frown falling across his face.

"Did I do something—"

"Shut up," she said, then took his mouth. He melted into her kiss almost immediately, giving her more of those wonderful little moans of his. She pushed until he was on his back, then cast herself astride his hips and took his cock in hand again.

Will pulled back, blinking hard. "Elizabeth—"

She pressed his blunt head against her clit once, twice, then slid him to where she needed him.

And sank down.

Will sucked in a deep breath, his wide eyes flickering between hers and the place where they were joined. And when she started to move, rolling her hips, working herself up and down his cock, she saw something on his face she hadn't seen on anyone else's. And it scared the shit out of her.

"So good," he said again, steadying his hands on her hips. "You feel so good."

Elizabeth bit back her own reply and leaned forward until her nipples grazed his skin.

His hands kneaded her ass, encouraging her as she began to move again. Her pussy hugging his cock, her legs trembling, and her mouth busy trying to keep from telling him just how much she loved this. Instead, she zeroed in on his lips and busied herself there, taking him in a hard kiss that had them both moaning.

Elizabeth pulled back abruptly and sat up. His cock shifted within her, sending a fresh wave of chills down her sweat-drenched spine.

This was to get him out of her system once and for all. God, that had to be what it was. It didn't matter how fucking good he felt inside her, how it seemed she couldn't be in the same room with him now without succumbing to the need to pounce on him. It didn't matter that his kisses drove her out of her head, or that she was addicted to the way he looked at her when she sucked his cock. It didn't matter now that he knew exactly what to do with his hands—cupping her breasts but not squeezing, massaging—just holding as she worked her pussy up and down his dick, flicking her nipples every few seconds. Just enough to send a zing of pleasure down her back. And when he moved those hands back to her hips—that was good too. It was especially good when he flattened one palm on the small of her back as his other hand moved to where they were joined.

"I want to feel you."

Elizabeth blinked and looked down. Will was staring at her with intent, those eyes sharper than she'd ever seen them.

"I want to feel you come on my cock, Elizabeth," he said, his voice rough. "Give that to me."

She scraped her teeth across her lower lip, but that didn't prevent her from moaning. "Oh shit."

Then his fingers were prying apart her slippery flesh—not enough to jolt her, but enough to let her know his intent. She thought this might be the moment she stopped enjoying herself.

But Will didn't pinch or rub her—he just placed his finger in the spot. The right spot. The spot that ensured she'd feel him when she slid down his cock, and *oh my god*. Elizabeth released a sound that was somewhere between a sigh and a moan, her muscles aching as she began moving faster, harder. Every time her pussy slid over his dick, there was his thumb, waiting for her, brushing against her clit and stoking the fire in her belly. And in seconds she'd given up the fight and was moaning in earnest, her hard breaths coloring the air, mixing with his and offsetting the rhythmic tempo of the bed's springs.

"Elizabeth." His eyes, normally so dark, were on fire. He was breathing hard, sweat beading his brow, his nostrils flared and his eyes on her face. The need blazing there was almost enough to send her over. She didn't think she'd ever seen a man that close to the edge before. "Shit. *Shit.* I can't—"

But whatever he couldn't, she didn't hear. Elizabeth swirled her hips on a down stroke and held, focusing on the sensation of his skin against her clit, his cock buried deep inside her, and that was it. The ball of energy in her belly exploded outward, and a long, hoarse moan tumbled off her lips as pleasure in its full concentration shot through her veins. She was moving again nearly without notice, addicted to the feel of him slipping in and out of her.

Then the earth tumbled and she found herself on her back again, Will over her, bucking wildly into her spasming pussy. He buried his head in her throat and murmured her name. Once, twice, then over and over as he jerked his hips and pounded her toward another orgasm.

Elizabeth felt like she could suffocate on air. She'd never had more than one happy moment with a guy before, ever. But fuck, Will was going to get her there again. Her body was still buzzing on its last high, and his hard thrusts were keeping the flames going.

She forced her legs, which she couldn't entirely feel, to wrap around his waist. When she passed the point of no return— when she knew she was going to come again—Elizabeth raised her head and latched her teeth into his shoulder. And Will fucking lost it. He made some inhuman sound that both terrified and excited her and pumped hard, fast, his cock jerking inside her as she convulsed hard around him. She didn't know how long it lasted. Hell, she might have left her body altogether. At that moment, everything seemed possible.

It wasn't fair. It wasn't fair at all that she'd had the most explosive sex of her life with someone she couldn't see again.

But those thoughts, however logical they were, had no place in her post-coital haze. A few minutes later, Elizabeth became aware of cool air against her otherwise sweaty skin. Of the shift in weight on the bed as Will sat up and disposed of the condom.

"Elizabeth," he said to the room.

She forced an eye open.

"Will you stay?"

"Huh?"

"Tonight. Stay tonight." He turned and looked at her, a soft smile on his face. "I need to..." He nodded toward the bathroom. "I just don't want you to be gone when I get back."

Something awful twisted in her chest and for a horrible second she thought she might cry.

God, she had fucked things up rather spectacularly, hadn't she?

Whether she actually replied or not, she couldn't say. After a moment, though, Will climbed to his feet and padded toward the bathroom. The light in there went on and the door closed. Everything inside her seemed to fall as her brain commanded her limbs to seize the chance to flee.

But that wouldn't be fair to him.

Also, she wasn't sure that she could move at the moment.

When Will stepped out of the bathroom and saw she was still in his bed, his shoulders dropped and a long sigh filled the air.

"I know we need to talk," he said, moving toward her, naked still. "I just...I don't think I can talk...right now."

Good. Because she knew she couldn't.

Elizabeth didn't say anything. She just nodded.

Will gave her a smile, then leaned over and kissed her brow, which seemed oddly chaste given what they had just done.

Then he was in bed with her, his skin against her skin, and the room went quiet again.

Sleep did not find her. Elizabeth lay awake, listening to Will's rhythmic breathing for what felt like years. Eventually, she couldn't ignore her bladder any longer and climbed out of bed. When she came back into the room, her eyes sought the clock on the nightstand, and her gut took what felt like the umpteenth dive that night.

It was chickenshit, leaving him in the middle of the night, but when her mind took her to what awaited her in a few hours, she knew she couldn't do it. The morning after talk or the *we can't do this* conversation she'd come here to have in the first fucking place.

She couldn't do any of it. The way she felt now, the wrath of Will Darcy would be immeasurably better than confronting whatever the fuck had just happened.

Elizabeth dressed in a hurry, amazed but thankful when Will didn't stir. Though she didn't have much to put on, she felt like she might as well have been channeling every high school marching band in the vicinity for as much noise as she made. But either Will naturally slept like the dead or he'd been relaxed beyond the telling of it, because he didn't stir once.

Not even when a part of her wanted him to as she reached for the door handle.

Not even when she closed the door a little harder than she needed.

Nothing.

That sick feeling was back, but Elizabeth refused to dwell. Instead, she expelled a deep breath and started for the stairs. Gray streaks had broken through the night sky. Soon the harsh light of day would descend in all its unforgiving glory. She wanted to be home before that happened.

Elizabeth had almost made it to the front door when she heard her name.

Her stomach sank. It wasn't Will.

"Elizabeth," Caroline Bingley said again. "What on earth are you doing here?"

Elizabeth turned. Caroline was standing in the doorway of the kitchen, wearing something that only women in showbiz and adult films would consider appropriate bed attire, and nursing a cup of coffee.

"Leaving," Elizabeth said, forcing a smile onto her face. "I, ahh, climbed into the wrong bed last night."

Even from a distance, she could tell Caroline had one of those perfectly plucked eyebrows arched.

"Won't happen again," Elizabeth continued, backing up until her spine hit the door. "Have a good night—err, morning."

Then she turned and made a break for freedom, not daring to chance luck again by looking back.

18

When Will opened his eyes, there were scant indicators that anything remarkable had happened. No warm Elizabeth beside him, no running shower, no forgotten pair of panties. Hell, even her side of the bed was cold. Had it not been for the scratch marks on his shoulders he might have ruled it all an elaborate fantasy.

But there *were* scratch marks, and his lower lip was a little swollen from where Elizabeth had bitten it. Not to mention he felt far too relaxed for someone so sleep deprived.

Once he settled on the fact that yes, last night's amazing sex had actually happened, Will found himself in the best mood he'd been in since...well, likely before his parents died. The fact that Elizabeth hadn't been there to share the morning with him was unfortunate but, he decided, not all that surprising. Not nearly as surprising as the way she'd randomly showed up last night. And being that this was Tuesday, there was a very strong chance she had that god-awful early morning class and she'd needed to rush back to Longbourn to get ready.

The fact was, it had happened. Elizabeth had sought him

out, come to him, leapt into his arms and ridden him like a good horse. That had to mean she felt it too.

That had to mean...

Well, perhaps he was better not putting labels on things.

Will glanced at the clock. He had about a half hour to get to campus. If he hoped to be presentable, he needed to drag himself into the shower now. Which he did, though inexpertly as his body kept protesting every time he commanded himself to move. He'd functioned on less sleep before, back when sleep itself hadn't been the precious commodity it was these days.

But last night had been worth it.

And after showering in record time, he was still mostly on schedule. Will threw on clothes, dropped the books he'd need into his backpack, and had almost broken to freedom across the common area when her voice shattered the pleasant calm his thoughts had occupied.

"Will!"

A shot of irritation bolted down his spine. Will froze, plastered on a smile, and turned to nod at Caroline. "Sorry, I can't talk," he said. "Going to be late for my accounting class."

"You will never guess who I ran into this morning."

There went his stomach.

"Elizabeth Bennet," Caroline said, arching an eyebrow. "It was barely dawn and she was here. Would you know anything about that?"

Will paused, the fire beginning to fade. "You saw her before she left?"

"Quite the little criminal, isn't she?"

"Criminal?"

"Well, I can only assume sneaking out the way she did." Caroline arched an eyebrow. "So..."

Will blinked at her, unsure what she wanted him to say. Explain, perhaps? Provide her with an innocuous reason for

Elizabeth to be in a state of disheveled dress and leaving Netherfield Heights at an ungodly hour? But Caroline was not an idiot —she had to know why. Occam's Razor was enough for her to go on.

But then he remembered the night Elizabeth had previously stayed at Netherfield Heights. How Elizabeth had teased him about Caroline having feelings for him. It hadn't been breaking news or anything, but he also hadn't thought there would be cause to worry or explain when he started dating women that weren't her. After all, they had been in each other's lives for years and he'd had girlfriends before.

Maybe she thought being here together would make things...well, different.

"Will?"

He gave his head a shake and rejoined the present. "What?"

Caroline frowned, but forced a smile the next instant. "Elizabeth Bennet. Do you know what she was doing here last night?"

Yes. Me.

"Elizabeth and I..." He paused long enough for the sentence to finish itself without help. Either Caroline was exceptionally slow or a glutton for punishment, because she just looked at him expectantly until he felt compelled to continue. "I like her, Caroline. A lot, actually. She and I have gotten, well, close over the past few days."

The color in Caroline's cheeks had started to pale. Her mouth formed a very thin line. "I see. Well...I'm surprised, Will. She doesn't seem your type."

He shrugged. "My type hasn't exactly been... Well, I don't know if I have a type."

Except he saw that she disagreed right off. *You do,* her eyes seemed to say. *I'm it.*

The thought made his stomach churn. Will plastered on a

smile. "Anyway, I'm going to see where this goes," he said. "With Elizabeth."

"Elizabeth Bennet."

"Yeah. I thought that was who we were talking about."

Caroline stared at him for a few empty seconds, then shook her head and contorted her face into the faux smile he knew so well. "Well," she said at last, "I can't say I saw that coming. Especially after everything we told Charlie."

"What does this have to do with Charlie?"

"Well, we know Jane wasn't interested in Charlie for Charlie, so..."

Will held up a hand. "Whatever happened there is completely separate from Elizabeth and I," he replied. "Elizabeth isn't interested in the Realis Society, or any society that I'm aware of."

"But she's a scholarship student." Caroline said the words the way others might say *child molester*. "Even if she's not after—"

"Caroline, I appreciate your concern, but it's unfounded. Believe me, if Elizabeth was after my money, I'd know by now." And he wouldn't have had to chase her as hard as he had. "I like her. I like her more than...well, more than I thought I could like a person."

Caroline's mouth was now so thin it practically dissolved into her face. "She stayed the night here. I assume you slept together."

Will stiffened, his eyes narrowing.

"I'm just saying, she's not the kind of girl who can be a good influence on Georgiana."

That was too far. Will took only a little satisfaction in the knowledge that Caroline saw she had overstepped. Her eyes went wide and she edged back, her cheeks pinking.

"Georgiana is my concern," Will said softly. "And I think... I think you're wrong. Elizabeth has a healthy attitude toward—"

"You can't be serious!" she blurted, the pink on her face fast-tracking to tomato-red. "Just the other night, she was yelling at you for saying then that you hadn't slept together. *Hadn't*. You were trying to protect her reputation and she threw it back at you. Need I remind you that Georgiana—"

Will held up a hand and, thankfully, Caroline stopped talking before she could dig herself in any deeper.

"Caroline," he said after a moment, his voice tempered, "I repeat: Georgiana is *my* concern."

"I can be concerned too, Will. I love her."

"I know you do. But I don't... Elizabeth is different, but she's not... She's not a bad influence. I think she could be good for Georgiana. God knows I've tried everything else."

Caroline sniffed and rolled her eyes but made no further comment. She didn't have to. After so many years of knowing her, Will could guess at what she wanted to say.

"Anyway," he said, turning, "I better get going. I'm already late."

Caroline mumbled something he couldn't understand, then made a shooing motion. He didn't bother hesitating. There was no need to drag out an already awkward conversation.

He wondered what Elizabeth would make of it. And it occurred to him that he could ask. After last night...

Well, nothing was certain, but he had a good feeling.

He couldn't wait to see her again.

～

There was little to no hope Elizabeth would manage the walk of shame without Jane being any the wiser, but still she winced as she crossed the threshold to their room and met her friend's eyes.

Jane had clearly been waiting. She sat on her already-made

bed, her backpack ready and beside her. Her arms were crossed and she arched one flawless eyebrow. "Oh, *hi*, Elizabeth. So you *do* live here?"

For someone who had been crying her eyes out just hours before, Jane looked much too chipper. Something Elizabeth would have relished had it not been at her expense. As it was, she could only muster a grunt that might have been *hello* in another life.

"You're not going to tell me, are you?"

"Nope," Elizabeth said, flopping onto her bed. Which might as well have been a slab of concrete.

Will's bed had been warm and bouncy. And she could have awoken there this morning.

But then she would have had to talk to him, and given how swimmingly that plan had gone last night...

Ugh. She so sucked.

"Was it at least good?" Jane asked.

"Was what good?"

"S-E-X. I'm assuming you didn't ninja-sneak out of here to get homework done, on account of all your things were still here."

She inhaled a deep breath, once more feeling like the world's biggest moron. "I really didn't...*mean* for any of this to happen. And that might be the dumbest thing that has ever been said in the history of forever."

Jane was quiet for a moment, then sighed. "I've got maybe a half hour before I have to be on campus. If you need to talk—"

"I don't."

"Are you sure?"

Elizabeth closed her eyes, willing herself to calm before she had some kind of cardiac episode. "There's a guy I've been... Well, I don't know what. And I couldn't sleep last night, thinking about you and Charlie, and I decided I needed to tell him that whatever our thing was was over."

"Lizzie, just because Charlie and I—"

"No, I need to get my act together. What happened with you and Charlie was a big ole reminder of why I don't want to get involved with anyone." She paused, winced. "And I'm sorry. I know that's my making your breakup about me and that's lame and not cool, but I was doing some major wallowing and decided that the best way to end this thing was to do it last night before my hormones talked me out of it."

"And what happened?"

Elizabeth groaned and dragged her pillow over her face. "My hormones talked me out of it," she said against the pillowcase.

There was a lengthy pause. "Do you like this guy?"

"Let's just say my feelings about him are very mixed." In that she couldn't convince her body not to do stupid things when she was around him, and that confused the hell out of her. Elizabeth was perfectly rational and in control of herself in all areas aside from those that concerned Will Darcy.

"Well," Jane said thoughtfully, "maybe that's for the best, then?"

Elizabeth hesitated before dragging the pillow off her face so she could favor Jane with a skeptical look.

Jane offered a small smile. "What happened with me and Charlie shouldn't affect your relationships."

"I don't *want* a relationship, though. I really, really don't." She forced herself to sit up. "And I really don't want one with someone like... Well, anyone I can't get a good read on. Because if someone as freakin' open as Charlie Bingley can turn out to be a jerk, then why even bother?"

A frown pulled on Jane's lips. She released another deep breath, then rose solemnly to her feet. "I'm not giving up," she said as she slung her bag over her shoulder. "Charlie...caught me off guard. But I don't regret what happened with him. If nothing else, the experience showed me what I want."

Elizabeth smiled weakly. "That's something."

"I think so." Jane squared her shoulders. "I am t-minus fourteen hours into this breakup, so who knows where I'll land on it tonight. But if I let Charlie sour my view on all relationships... Well, he doesn't deserve that much of my headspace."

"Definitely not."

"And," she continued, "he doesn't deserve credit for making you swear off men, either."

"He didn't. He just reinforced it."

"Well, maybe don't consider that ship sailed just yet. That you left here with your mind set on ending something and you ended up..." Jane gestured, going a little pink. "This guy must be something else. I know you."

Elizabeth snorted and shook her head. "Either that or I just really needed to get laid."

Jane barked a startled giggle at that. "And on that note, I'm gonna assume you're okay and see if I can grab a coffee before class." She started for the door, then paused, her hand on the knob. "Oh. Before you got back, Caroline called."

Elizabeth's stomach knotted. "What? What'd she want?"

"To tell me that the final acceptance and rejection letters for the Realis Society were going out today, and to warn me ahead of time that the news wasn't good."

"Oh, Jane—"

Jane held up a hand, plastering on a smile. "It's okay," she said in that it's-really-not-but-I'll-fake-it-till-I-make-it tone. "I think it's for the best. There are a lot of Society events and things that would have had me over at Netherfield. And even if that wasn't the case, I think... I don't know if I could be around Caroline and not ask about Charlie and I don't want to be *that girl,* you know?"

"But still, this sucks." And it sucked doubly so that it came on the heels of a breakup. Elizabeth bolted to her feet and crossed the room to drag Jane into a hug. "I'm sorry."

"It's okay."

"I can't believe you let me whine about having had awesome sex like it was a big problem or something."

Jane pulled back, grinning. "I didn't know the *awesome* part."

"Oi. Me and my mouth."

"Wanna repeat tonight? You, me, plus our weight in calories?"

"Uh, I don't think I can tonight." Jane pulled a face. "Not only am I still full from that last gallon of ice-cream, but I said I'd meet some classmates for a dinner-slash-study session. Since I lost last night, I really need to hit the books to keep from falling behind. Especially for the class that Charlie was helping me with. I'm probably going to camp it out in one of those private rooms at the library."

"Ah, maybe we'll catch up there. I'm meeting Lydia and Mary at the library after my last class today so we can get caught up on the group project." But if Jane didn't plan on being in the dorm tonight, that meant Elizabeth might be able to focus on her other work after that meeting. "So no on calorie-laden goodness, but if you find yourself in need of a caffeine boost, I'll likely head to the Mudhouse before the library between two and three."

"You just want to make sure I'm not in pieces about Charlie."

"That plus coffee."

Jane grinned and shifted her backpack. "I'll probably swing by. For coffee. Which I really need to leave *now* to get if I want to be on time."

"Of course."

Jane opened the door and had almost disappeared on the

other side before pausing and sliding it open again. "And Lizzie? Might hop in the shower before you head to class."

Elizabeth snickered at the door and shook her head. Like that wasn't already going to be her first stop. She needed to wash last night the hell off her.

The thought made her stomach knot all over again.

She had to end it with Will. *Had to.* This entire thing had gotten so far out of control she didn't recognize herself anymore. The person she'd been just a few short weeks ago had morphed into someone who was all too happy to throw her convictions out the window in exchange for physical pleasure.

But it wasn't just that—maybe the sex thing alone was something she could reconcile. But there were feelings. Feelings that prevented her from doing the right thing, the smart thing. Feelings that kept latching onto him and pulling him back when she thought the end might be in sight. He'd as much as said so yesterday before she'd sucked him off, and he'd been right.

She liked arguing with him. Talking to him. Seeing him get ruffled. Liked the way his eyes flashed with challenge. Liked the way he didn't hold back.

But he was a guy she could never trust, relationship embargo or no. Will's genuine self was someone who would frame a friend—even if this was years in the past, it spoke to a level of deceit that she'd sworn she'd never tolerate. That she'd let herself overlook that at all over the past couple days made her feel like shit.

Even so, they should have an honest conversation. One in which she clearly broke things off. He deserved at least that much.

They just needed to have it on neutral territory.

Public territory.

Where there were no closets around.

Will spent the morning being forcibly reminded that he was not the type of person who could function on little sleep. He also spent the morning reliving the better parts of the night before, which only added to his inability to focus. Still, even though he could only claim to be around halfway present for his classes, he managed to solider on, motivated by the promise of coffee at the first opportunity.

That was another thing. If he was going to stay up to all hours, he needed a handy IV of caffeine. As it was, Caroline's lecture had set him back several minutes, which had made him late to campus and ultimately resulted in getting his morning hit of coffee hours behind schedule.

As he entered the Meryton Mudhouse, he immediately caught sight of Elizabeth, nestled in a corner booth. The table was scattered with books and her laptop and at least three cups of coffee. Will's spirits picked up almost at once and he found himself moving toward her before he realized she wasn't alone.

Of course she'd be with Jane. Just yesterday, Charlie had announced that he'd gone through with the breakup, which meant Elizabeth was likely in full supportive-friend mode. Jane didn't look bad, per se, but she was definitely a far cry from the normal, smiling version of herself.

Will didn't realize he'd stopped to stare until the guy behind him in line gave him a hearty shove.

"Dude. Dude! You're up."

Will blinked and shook his head. He turned to nod his thanks and flicked his gaze back in Elizabeth's direction before he could help himself.

Their eyes met and a pleasant shiver shot down his spine. He flashed her a smile, but she looked away, as though embarrassed. His smile faded, but he refused to lose spirit. They obviously had talking to do, and he needed coffee before he did any more thinking for the day.

After he had his steaming cup in hand, though, Will didn't know what to do. Well, he knew what he wanted to do—join Elizabeth, see if he could get an idea as to how she was doing now. What was going on in her head. If she was as preoccupied with thoughts of the night before as he was. And, most importantly, when they could do it again, preferably after coming to some sort of understanding about their relationship.

With that thought, he swallowed the lump that had climbed into his throat and began negotiating his way between tables toward her.

"Hi Will," Jane said kindly as he approached. "How are you?"

"Well, thanks." He nodded, thought for a moment, then decided it would be more awkward if he didn't address the elephant in the room. "I...umm...I was sorry to hear about—"

Jane spared him and held up a hand. "It's nice of you to say so, but you don't have to. I know it's weird when you run into a friend's ex."

Will cut a look at Elizabeth, who was steadfastly not looking at him.

"It is," he said at last. "Are you... How are you doing?"

Jane smiled—a perfectly lovely smile that made her eyes brighten. "I'm well," she said, and he believed her. She was the type of person he couldn't help but believe.

And she was good. Jane was a good person, of that he had no doubt. He also didn't doubt that she had cared for Charlie in her own way, but that smile paired with the warm sincerity of her words went a long way in assuaging the doubt he had entertained ever since he and Caroline had confronted Charlie about their concerns.

Well, not that he'd had much hand in the confronting part. He'd sort of stood there and watched it happen, chiming in when appropriate. Still, he knew that Charlie would never have ended things with Jane on Caroline's testimony alone. So yes, Will felt culpable.

Though Elizabeth had done a phenomenal job of distracting him from this.

"Say hi to Caroline for me," Jane said, edging around the table. "I gotta run."

Will didn't know what he expected once he and Elizabeth were alone. A coy smile, perhaps, or a warmer greeting. An invitation to sit and join her for coffee. Basic eye contact. Whatever it was, he didn't get it. Instead, he ended up standing there like an idiot, watching as she packed her computer and the last of her books into her bag. She had just turned her attention to the trash on the table when he couldn't stand the silence another beat.

"How are you?"

Yeah, that was lame.

Elizabeth, for her part, didn't even look up. "Late," she said, fastening the straps on her laptop bag.

"Elizabeth—"

"Really, Will, I'm late." She slid her phone out of her pocket and checked the time. "I was supposed to meet Lydia in the library about ten minutes ago for the Ethics presentation next week."

"Look, I just wanted—"

"I need to go."

"Fine. Can I come by later? I really think we should talk."

For a horrible moment, he thought she was going to blow him off. The thought seemed to cross her mind at least, from the long look she gave the door. But then she turned to him, something tender flashing in her eyes.

"Yeah," she said at last. "We can talk. We should. You're right."

Excitement and relief burst through him. So accustomed to fighting her it took a moment for Will to find his footing. "Umm, do you wanna grab dinner, or—"

"Sure. I guess. Yes. We can. With food." She broke her gaze from his, cheeks going pink. "I'll be back at the dorm around six."

"Then I'll come by a quarter after, maybe? Or does that not give you enough time?"

"No, that should be fine." Elizabeth looked at him again, hiking her bag higher on her shoulder. "So... I need to go."

"Of course." Will hopped aside. "Tonight, then."

"Tonight," she agreed, and bolted out the door without a backward glance.

Leaving Will grinning like a fool after her.

19

Elizabeth couldn't concentrate, because, *of course* she couldn't concentrate. She'd already read the same paragraph seven times and the eighth time didn't seem likely to be the charm.

Her mind kept dragging her back to the Meryton Mudhouse. To Will's face. To the script of what she had to tell him when he came by tonight.

Somewhere deep down, he'd had to expect this, right? After all, she'd told him she was off relationships. Granted, that had been before the sex, but the conversation itself had been a memorable one, and she knew she'd never given any indication that she'd changed her mind.

Except, again, for the sex...but sex didn't equal a relationship. If nothing else, Will had to know that. It was one of the cornerstones of guydom.

Hell, maybe she had it all wrong and Will just wanted to tell her that he was through, though he wouldn't be adverse to one for the road.

Attempt to read number nine.

This was ridiculous. She'd snapped at Lydia and all but

commanded her to leave the premises on the pretense that she was too chatty to get anything done.

Thirty minutes and the same damn paragraph later...

"Oh my god!"

Elizabeth started and looked up. "Wickham," she said, closing her book.

"I can't believe it!" he continued, slapping a dramatic hand against his chest. "Could it be that I am in the presence—breathing the same air—as the elusive Elizabeth Bennet?"

Warmth tickled her cheeks. She blinked and looked away, licking her lips. "What are you doing here?"

"Glad you asked." He welcomed himself to the seat across from her. "I've heard the most amazing rumor you could imagine."

Elizabeth met his gaze again and arched her eyebrows in invitation.

"It turns out," Wickham continued in a stage whisper, "that you can actually take these"—he waved at the textbook —"keepers of knowledge back to your dorm room *without* taking out another student loan. Something free on campus? I had to see it with my own eyes. Lo and behold, I find two miracles in one day."

She snorted at that. "Miracles? Really?"

"You don't think unfettered access to generations of knowledge is a miracle?"

"Well, when you say it like that..."

"And," Wickham continued theatrically, "when you throw in a genuine Elizabeth Bennet sighting, you can't help but think that perhaps we aren't alone in the universe."

"How thick are you planning to lay it?"

"Just thick enough to be cute without being obnoxious. How am I doing?"

Elizabeth made a see-saw motion with her hand, and Wickham clasped his chest again, his head lolling back.

"All right," she said, laughing in spite of herself. "You've officially crossed into obnoxious territory."

Wickham peeked an eye open, a lazy grin spreading across his face. "Well, the important thing is I tried." He righted himself and folded his hands primly on the table. "Madam, I have a bone to pick with you."

"Madam? Really?"

"Too much?"

"The use of French or this whole conversation?"

"Now you're just being mean."

"Yeah, but you like it."

Wickham's grin widened and he waggled a finger at her. "You're not wrong there. Okay, so what is up with this?"

"This what?"

"This you not calling me thing."

Elizabeth tilted her head, the weight that had made itself at home on her chest lifting for the first time all day. "And here I could have sworn I gave you *my* phone number. We've texted and everything."

"Yeah, but you're a twenty-first century girl. I kinda thought you'd want to do the asking."

"Oh really?"

"Don't pretend you haven't seen me lurking outside Prentiss Hall hoping to bump into you again."

"I haven't."

"Then you haven't been looking." Wickham glanced down, at once looking almost shy. "The truth is I think you're pretty awesome and entirely out of my league. And I thought I might have scared you off with all the...Will talk the day we met."

Elizabeth didn't have much of a poker face, so she could only hope she looked composed. "I didn't know what to think, really. I mean, I couldn't believe it. Just with...he's so..."

Wickham nodded wisely. "Nice?"

"Well, yes."

"Yeah, I don't get it either." He made a face. "Seriously. It's like a Jekyll and Hyde thing. Or a...humans and Cylons thing." He paused. "Tell me you got that."

Elizabeth smirked and quoted, "'So say we all.'"

He released a long whimper. "Smoking hot, smart as hell, and a nerd. I knew you would be trouble."

"Thanks. I think." She released a long breath. "Actually, I didn't mind at all, you opening up about Will. I'd rather have found out that way than another way."

Hell, the feelings she had for Will were bad enough knowing what she did. If she'd let herself go with the flow, who knows what might have happened?

Wickham flashed her a grin, which faded almost as fast, as though he was remembering something. His gaze went sideways and fixed on a point over Elizabeth's shoulder. It didn't last, whatever it was—in a blink, he had snapped back to himself and scrubbed a hand down his face.

"It'd be easier if I knew how he does it," he said after a moment. "I don't know. Sometimes, part of me thinks I imagine all of it. Or maybe I was wrong or remembered something that didn't happen. I think I've landed on the idea that Will believes he genuinely is a good guy so much so that he can be when he wants to be. And hey, maybe he regrets what happened. It was a long time ago and things have changed dramatically for him. But...I'd just like an apology, you know?"

And this is the guy you chose to lose your shit over, Bennet. Strong work. "I take it he hasn't."

"Are you kidding? The guy won't even talk to me." Wickham sighed heavily and shook his head. "When you come from a family like the Darcys, it's easy to crack under pressure. I understand that. And it's easier still to pin shit on poor kids. After all, who's going to believe them when they're against a team of lawyers that could get Mussolini acquitted? If that was what it was...if he just said something..."

She pressed her lips together to keep herself from doing something stupid, like screaming or throwing her book across the floor. Every bad thing she'd thought about herself since she'd stumbled out of Netherfield Heights came soaring back with a vengeance, only now Wickham was leading the charge.

Will might regret everything—regret the drugs, regret lying, regret sending Wickham up a creek. That narrative fit the Will she'd come to know. Except she wasn't sure she knew Will at all, or if she knew some phantom version of himself he brought out whenever he wanted to play the hero. Wickham had hit the nail on the head—Will could be a nice guy. Nice in an aloof, superior kind of way that drove her nuts but also, apparently, really worked for her when it wasn't pissing her off. And from the first night on campus, she also knew he could be combative, insulting, rude and sexist, but tell that to her dumbass body.

Having these thoughts at all was indicative of the colossal mistake she'd made last night. And truly, what the hell had she been thinking? Show up at a guy's dorm in the middle of the night and be surprised when he took her presence for a booty call? And yeah, she could have pulled back and said no at any time, but she hadn't.

If he hadn't kissed her, she wouldn't be in this mess.

"Elizabeth?"

She blinked slowly and turned back to Wickham, who was studying her intently. "Sorry," she said. "I drifted off there."

He nodded. "Everything okay?"

"Just a lot on my mind."

His face fell. "I did it again, didn't I? Bringing up Will? I made things weird."

"No. Well, he's not... It doesn't matter."

Wickham leaned forward. "Is there...something going on between you two?"

"No!"

That came out a bit too eagerly and carried far enough down the row of tables to earn Elizabeth a reproving *shh* from the librarian.

Wickham didn't look convinced.

Gee, go figure.

"It's okay. He's a charming guy. When he wants to be. And he has a *lot* of money—"

"I don't care about money."

Wickham spread his hands. "Wouldn't blame you either way."

"But I don't. And Will and I are not involved."

"But you kinda go funny when I mention him."

She shrugged, hoping like hell she looked nonchalant. "You know why I know him. My best friend was dating his best friend. They broke up yesterday. I share exactly one class with Will, but I doubt I'll have to see him again after the semester wraps up." Especially after tonight.

"Well," Wickham said, leaning forward, "I might as well bite the bullet. Here's the thing, Calculus. I like you a lot and I'd like to see if maybe we could... I dunno, meet somewhere intentionally, perhaps at a predetermined time for an activity of some sort. Say for food. And maybe some form of entertainment to follow."

Elizabeth tilted her head. "Are you setting up a really complex math problem or asking me on a date?"

"Can't it be both?"

She pressed her lips together and considered. The healthiest, safest bet would be to say no. The last thing she needed was to add more to the tire-fire that was her life at the moment.

But he wasn't Will. He was the anti-Will, and the fact that he did little for her in the engine-revving department made him feel nice and safe. Hearts couldn't be broken over guys who you weren't invested in. And try as she might, she just couldn't muster a twinge of anything for Wickham.

Which was sad, because he might be good fuck-buddy material, if nothing else.

Maybe that was her problem. She'd never given her no-strings-sex thing a fair shot. She'd kept looking at guys like Will who appealed to her on levels beyond the physical—no matter how much her brain scolded her for it. Wickham was nice to look at and quick-witted, even if he laid it on a bit thick.

"Your silence does not bode well for me," Wickham said, drawing her back to herself. "If I overstepped—"

"No. I mean, no you didn't overstep. Not *no* on the date." Elizabeth offered him a small smile. "I'd, umm, I think that would be nice."

"Yeah?"

"Hell yeah. I'm all for dinner and a movie. Just what I need. Plus, you know, mildly attractive company."

Wickham's face split into a wide grin. "You know you had me dangling there."

"What can I say? It's more fun when they squirm."

"Evil."

Elizabeth shrugged, then caught sight of the clock hanging on the wall over Wickham's shoulder. "Crap," she said, and sprang to her feet. "I better motor."

"When do you want—"

"Just text. Or call. Probably won't be open until the weekend." Because of homework and exhaustion, courtesy of all the sleep she hadn't gotten the night before. Elizabeth shook her head—and the thought—away as she shoved her book into her backpack. "Maybe Friday?"

"Maybe Friday sounds great!" Wickham said.

She shot him another grin and made her way around the table. "To me too," she said. "See you then."

"I'll be the one with bells on!"

She chuckled, hoisted one of the straps of her backpack over her shoulder, and dived into the maze of bookcases.

So she hadn't gotten any actual studying done, but she couldn't help but feel the trip to the library hadn't been a waste. Confusing thoughts and wayward emotions aside, going out with Wickham was just what the doctor ordered. It gave her something to look forward to at the end of the week—an *eyes on the prize* kind of thing to help her avoid the massive amounts of awkward that would undoubtedly dog her for the next few days.

The biggest hurdle standing between her and her weekend date was due at the dorm by a quarter after six. She was one dinner away from being done with this whole mess.

Elizabeth turned the corner at an aisle of books, readjusting her backpack over her shoulder, and had almost cleared the checkout desk when a voice broke through the mantra running through her head.

"I kinda hate you. The Realis Society is super hard to get in to. I tried last year and fell flat on my face."

Elizabeth paused on instinct. The voice had come from behind an aisle of books—whispered and not meant for her ears. The smart thing to do would be to move on. She needed to get back, anyway, if she hoped to have any time to mentally prepare for the conversation she had to have.

But she couldn't convince her feet to budge.

"Pretty sure it was just luck," another girl said. "The competition this year was fierce. You wouldn't believe what some applicants did to get in."

"What?" the owner of the first voice asked breathily.

"Well, this one girl started dating the president's brother."

"Charlie Bingley?" A giggle. "That boy is fine. And also kind of a whore. He dated my roommate two semesters ago. She dumped his ass after he hit on a waitress while she was in the bathroom."

"Well," the other voice replied, "apparently, he was really into this girl. Seriously into her. Like, talking about bringing her home for the holidays so she could meet his *family*, but it turns out she was just using him to get into Realis. Probably didn't hurt that he's super rich, either."

"Aww, poor Charlie. Even whores have feelings." A pause as they shared a snicker. "How did he find out?"

"I don't think he did. From what I heard, Caroline had Will Darcy step in."

Elizabeth went numb and hot at the same time. She reached out to the bookcase for support, willing herself not to make a noise. Which, granted, was hard when every nerve in her body was suddenly screaming.

"Oh, *Will Darcy*." The name was repeated with such emphasis that the air practically pulsed. "God, that man. To be that fucking hot and that rich. There should be a law against it."

"Pretty sure that was why Caroline tagged him in," came the reply. "Nothing talks like experience. Can you imagine how many sluts throw themselves at him each day? Well...whatever he said thankfully brought Charlie to his senses. He dumped that bitch in an instant."

"Eh. Gotta say, having trouble finding sympathy. The way he played my friend, maybe he deserved to be played himself."

The girls' conversation quickly devolved from there, and Elizabeth stopped listening. Couldn't have kept on if she tried, she was shaking too damn hard.

Goddammit.

She'd known. She'd known for weeks since Wickham had first told her—she'd *known* what Will was capable of. She'd been warned and she hadn't listened. Or worse—she had listened but hadn't taken it seriously. Not seriously enough, anyway. It had been too fucking inconvenient for her hormones to hear that the guy who did it for them had seriously screwed over his own friend, and why the hell would she be any different? No, once she'd stopped ignoring him, she'd all but thrown herself at him. Over and over again.

Worse, she'd made excuses for herself. A part of her had known. Of course it had. This was the way things went and fuck anyone who claimed otherwise.

How could I have been so stupid? So goddamned *stupid?*

Elizabeth stopped just outside the library entrance, barely having registered she'd moved at all. Sweat lined her forehead and dribbled down her cheeks. She heaved hard, lumbering breaths. Her fingers tingled and her legs wanted to call it a day and quit.

But she couldn't. Because Will was coming over.

The asshole would be at her dorm soon.

And she'd be there to make sure he heard, in no uncertain terms, just how done she was with him.

20

The rage didn't dissipate. It grew. By the time the knock came, Elizabeth was shaking so hard she thought she might drill a hole in the floor. That was never good—for her or anyone in her path. It had been a long time since she'd lost control of herself beyond just having a smart mouth and a hot temper. When the situation in her head went to DEFCON 1, it typically meant heads were going to roll.

And yet, knowing she was a danger to herself and others, she opened the door anyway.

Calm down. Calm the fuck down.

There he was, bright and eager, a smile affixed to his face. But Will Darcy was nothing if not an observer of his environment. He took in her expression and the hopeful gleam in his eyes faded. "Everything all right?"

If she gritted her teeth any harder they'd shatter in her mouth. But in the span between his knocking on the door and her opening it, she'd managed to regain enough self-control to not immediately leap to manslaughter charges, which was a big bonus.

"I need to talk to you," she said, doing her best to keep her voice controlled. Steady. Not yell-y.

"I know. I need to talk to you too." Will looked at her expectantly, and after debating whether or not this was the sort of argument she wanted to have in a hallway, Elizabeth opened the door wide and gestured for him to come inside.

Though that might have been a mistake. The last time they'd been alone in a room together, she'd experienced hands down the best sex she'd ever had. And that hurt to think about because it just drove home, again, what a monumental idiot she'd been.

Breathe, Bennet. Count to ten.

"Do you...want to do this now or over dinner?"

"Now." Because she wasn't having any fucking dinner with him.

He nodded, either ignoring the edge to her voice or not hearing it. "Okay," he said, swallowing and closing the door behind him. "If you don't mind, I'd like to go first."

Well, wasn't that typical.

But since time would hopefully help her calm down, Elizabeth didn't bother to protest. She didn't bother to say anything, either. Just turned to look at him—because she had to at least do that much—and gave him a curt nod.

"Umm." Will offered another smile and tore his hand through his hair. "Why don't you sit down?" He nodded at her bed.

Elizabeth didn't follow his gaze but she did arch an eyebrow.

The smile faltered a bit. "Or not."

No. She was an adult. She could sit down on a bed in a room with him. Sure.

So with that in mind, she parked her ass on the mattress, crossed her arms, and met his eyes.

Will blinked at her for a few seconds, looking uncertain, then shook his head and blew out a deep breath. "All right, so here it goes." He met her eyes again. "The last thing I wanted when I came back to school was to be distracted. I had a plan once. A good plan, one that involved graduating early while I worked my way up the ranks at Darcy Media. I was going to graduate at twenty-one and spend the next few years of my life proving to the shareholders that I wasn't some dumb kid who'd been handed the keys to the chocolate factory. I *love* the company my father built. I want to do right by it. It was always important to him and my mother that I get my education—and it was important to me too. But after they died, everything got put on hold."

Elizabeth wet her lips, the anger that had taken residence under her skin having faded in favor of curiosity.

What the hell was he going on about?

"I say all this so you know just how much I didn't want to feel this way," Will continued. "Especially after the last few years. I was supposed to come here and finally get my life back on track. And then you happened."

"I happened?"

"Yeah. I wasn't asking for it and I sure as hell wasn't looking for it. And I don't think you were either, but..." He trailed off, looked away, drew in a deep breath and turned back to her. "I know we haven't talked about whatever...whatever's been happening here." He gestured between them. "And I know we... clash. We don't really make sense at all. You're smart as hell and you speak your mind, even when you shouldn't. And your friends are...interesting. I guess what I'm trying to say is you're not the sort of person I'd have thought I'd...feel this way about."

Oh. Well didn't that just sweep her off her feet?

"But I can't focus at all and it's because I'm thinking of you. And I don't want to wonder about this anymore." Will met her gaze again, and this time when he smiled, it was with the air of someone who had just crawled to safety from under a big boulder. "I guess what I'm trying to say is I think I'm falling in love with you and that seems to be the sort of thing you tell a person. I also know you said a while back you didn't want a relationship so I'm about twenty steps ahead of myself, but there's either telling or not, and...I think it's better to be honest. I know we haven't defined whatever *we* are, but I'd like to. Hell, I *need* to so I can get back to doing what I came here to do. So..."

For the first time in Elizabeth's memory, she didn't have words. Not one. Her heart had done a weird little leapy thing when he'd mentioned *love,* because that particular word happened to be very heavy. But the rest... Her mind was blank.

No, that wasn't quite right.

She was thinking things. A lot of things. Things that were so jumbled together they didn't make sense, fueled by a sudden, intense rush of feeling. Make that plural. The anger from before roared back to life with a vengeance, only this time it wasn't the Hulk. It was whatever made the Hulk piss itself and cry in the corner. It seemed impossible that a person could get near this, let alone experience it, without exploding on impact.

Honest? It's better to be honest?

Fuck him. *Fuck him.*

"Elizabeth?"

She pressed her lips together and slowly rose to her feet.

Then she met his eyes—his concerned but still somehow hopeful eyes—and spat, "Fuck you, Darcy. And get the fuck out of my room."

She tore for the door and nearly yanked it off its hinges, then gestured for him to leave, doing her best to keep from looking at him. She didn't think she could stomach it, seeing him standing in her room not two steps away from the place he'd given her that first habit-forming orgasm. The place she'd officially thrown all sense out the window and gone against logic. Against her own sense of right and wrong. If she looked at him, the rage beast in her chest might just gouge out his eyeballs.

But he didn't move. He stood there, breathing hard, not moving, and she had no choice but to look. What she saw made her want to cry.

Hurt and confusion and, yes, some anger, comprised the lines of his face.

His stupid fucking face.

"Is that all you're going to say?" he demanded at last. "After everything I just told you?"

"I'm sorry. Were you expecting me to swoon? I repeat, fuck you, Darcy."

"Elizabeth, talk to me."

She slammed the door shut again, the rage beast scratching under her skin, willing to be released. "And tell you what?"

Will stared at her incredulously. "Maybe what I did to deserve this?"

"What did you expect to happen?" she snapped. "That I'd *thank* you for making me a part of your fucked up life when it was clearly the last thing you wanted? That I'd ignore what you said—or didn't have the balls to say—about my friends? That I'd overlook the fact that you just said you *know* this isn't what I want, but it's what you want, so fuck me, right?"

"I didn't—"

"And when someone tells you that you're not the sort of person they would normally go for, how exactly is that a compliment?" She crossed her arms. "Really. Tell me. I want to know. I mean, it's not a line I haven't heard, but I've never understood why people think it's a good thing to tell someone. Especially if the point you're trying to make is that you think you love them? 'You're not up to my normal standards, but I'll make an exception just this once'?"

"That's not what I said!"

"Really? Did you *hear* yourself, because that was *exactly* what you said."

"No, no. You're taking this all wrong—"

"I'm taking it as you said it." Her jaw tightened, raw, unkempt energy streaking through her body like a livewire. "So thanks, Will. Thanks for deigning to slum it with me for a few days, but I think it's time we both headed back to the real world."

She twisted around and made to open the door again, but Will grabbed her arm and whirled her back to face him.

"I deserve an explanation," he said.

"You deserve a kick to the balls," she replied, wrenching out of his grasp. "Anyone ever tell you it's not a good idea to grab someone like that?"

He brought his hands up, his eyes going wide. "Sorry. Sorry. You're right, I shouldn't have—"

But she had already turned back to the door.

"So what was it?" Will asked before she could open it. "What was any of it to you?"

Don't cry now, Bennet. Don't you dare.

"It was sex," she said, her voice wobbling as she forced herself to face him again. "That was all it was. I never pretended that I wanted anything else, and that was because I didn't. I didn't even want to want sex, but it happened and every time I thought I was going to be smart and put an end to it, I got swept away."

Will swallowed, but his expression became harder. "So you never wanted anything else with me?"

"No."

"All this time? You can just do that. Be intimate with someone you don't have feelings for."

"I told you all this weeks ago! You just said—"

"I thought—"

"You thought you could get me to change my mind because

I've made things inconvenient for you? I told you what I was about, Darcy. I was crystal clear. I didn't ask for your feelings and I don't want them." She took a deep breath to calm herself. Then another. In a cooler tone, she continued, "Had I known you felt anything like *that*, I would've nipped it in the bud. Hell, I *should* have never let it start to begin with but—"

"Why?"

"I just told you why."

He shook his head. "Not that. But...you seem to..." Another swallow. "It's not just that you don't have feelings for me. You... don't like me at all, do you?"

A pang struck her dead center. "There were times I did."

"But you slept with me despite this? How?"

That pang hit again, harder this time and triggering Elizabeth's innate defense mechanisms. "Well, you see, when a man is aroused, his penis becomes hard and—"

"I know *how*."

"Then don't ask stupid questions."

"Why would you ever *want* to have sex with someone you don't like?"

"And welcome to the hell that has been my world." She shifted her gaze away, crossing her arms again. "Like I said, I didn't mean for you to get all...attached. When I came over last night? I couldn't sleep because I knew things had gotten out of hand and I wanted to stop them—then, before it got any messier. But you opened the door and then there was kissing and my good sense went out the window."

"You came over there last night to...put an end to it."

She nodded, aimed her gaze south when looking at him proved difficult.

There was pain in his eyes. Pain and anger and loathing. Things that she'd put there.

In that moment, she hated herself. That she'd brought any of that to another human being made her feel like something someone would scrape off the bottom of their shoe. Not even gum. Mystery goob.

"And I'm willing to admit I did a lousy job," she said a moment later. "So this, some of this—hell, maybe all of it—is on me. The sex stuff, at least. I could have said no. *Should* have. I should've ended it when I meant to, or hell, not even started. Whatever else, Will, I didn't mean for you to catch feelings for me. And I know this...sucks. I hate that I did that to you. I didn't mean to. What you're feeling now... I'm genuinely sorry for that."

Will was still a moment before he gave her a short nod. And she thought that might be the end of it. There didn't seem to be anything else to say.

She was about to turn back to the door when his voice hit the air again.

"Why?"

The smart thing to do would be to pretend she hadn't heard.

Except she had heard.

And she had unfinished business too. She meant to ream him for what he'd done to Jane before he'd gone and made with the love talk that would probably go down as one of the worst declarations ever.

Just thinking about Jane—about what she'd overheard—had her temper climbing back up toward the danger zone.

"Why what?"

"What did I do," he asked again, and she heard him take a step forward, "to make you feel like this? About me?"

And there it was. A gift-wrapped opportunity to tear him a new asshole.

Still, her voice remained calm as she turned and met his eyes. "You told Charlie that Jane was after his money and connections."

Will blinked. "What?"

"Jane. You know, my best friend. My roommate. You decided to tell him that Jane was using him to get into that Realis place. You told him to break her heart because, why? She's not good enough? She's too poor? She's *black*? Why?"

His eyes went wide. "Wait, no. I was asked my opinion and I gave it. I never told Charlie to dump her but he clearly wasn't getting what he wanted out of the relationship—"

"You mean she hadn't boinked him."

"I mean she didn't seem to want anything to do with him!" Will all but screamed. "Charlie was already thinking up names for the children. Toward the end, it seemed she couldn't stay in the same room with him."

"That's bullshit."

"You wouldn't know, would you? You weren't there, apart from that one night. *I* was." He huffed and shook his head. "Charlie's a guy who falls fast and deep, but I've never seen him fall for someone like he did Jane. So yeah, I paid attention. I watched them both. That night at the club? She seemed happy at first but spent the rest of the night ignoring him."

"She was nervous!"

"Then maybe she should have told him so. From where I was standing, she seemed to like him just fine, but not once did she seem to be as nuts for him as he was for her."

"You are so full of shit it's practically coming out of your ears."

"I—"

"And what about George Wickham?"

The color seemed to drain from Will's face and she felt a thrill of victory.

"What about," he said through clenched teeth, "George Wickham?"

"I mean what about what you did to him."

"What *I* did?"

She nodded, encouraged. "You mean you don't remember ruining his life? Too much of an everyday type thing for you?"

"I ruined his life." He stared at her a moment longer, then barked a laugh and tore his hand through his hair. "I ruined *his* life. He told you that."

Another nod, this one fueled by renegade nerve. "He told me everything. The drugs. The book you put them in. How you set him up so you wouldn't get caught."

Will was staring at her like he'd never seen her before. "He told you all this."

"Yes."

"When?"

"Weeks ago."

"So all this time..." He breathed hard, his nostrils flared, his chest rising and falling in a hard cadence. "He told you this and you still slept with me."

"Hey, my body doesn't always know what's good for it. Case in point." She shrugged, her pulse beginning to race, though she didn't know why. Maybe it was the adrenaline talking. Knowing that finally everything was out and she could go back to her world with Will Darcy finally consigned to the *past mistake* bin rather than the *present* one. "But I'm hoping to get back on the straight and narrow now. Starting Friday."

It was clear he didn't want to know, but he asked anyway. "What's Friday?"

"A date. Wickham and I—"

But the words stopped before they could come out. Will went from living statue to his own version of the Hulk in two seconds flat, his face contorted with enough rage and pain that Elizabeth felt she could choke on air.

Right then, she wanted to say something—anything—but she also didn't because, fuck him.

Except...

In the end, it was easier just to open the door.

Something told her Will wouldn't stop her this time.

And he didn't. Instead, he firmed his jaw, gave her a tight nod, and walked out.

21

Leaving without saying anything might have been stupid, but in the moment, Will hadn't been flush with options. The room had seemed drained of air. He wasn't sure he took a breath at all until he'd stepped back outside.

Of course, then, his mind had exploded with things he needed to say. Or rather shout, preferably while shaking something. But the moment had passed, and before he knew it, he found himself storming through the door to Netherfield Heights and nearly claiming Caroline as a casualty in the process.

Fortunately for him, Caroline didn't seem to notice. "Will," she said, grabbing his arm. "I've told Charlie, but we're having a Realis Society meeting here tonight, so if you could spare us the study, I... Will?"

"Yes, fine. Whatever." He didn't so much as spare her a glance as he tugged himself free. "I'll be in my room all night."

"Is everything all right?" Caroline called after him, but he didn't pause. He was a man on a mission.

To get stinking fucking drunk.

So he bulldozed his way to the kitchen, skipped right over the cheap stuff Charlie had on reserve and went straight to the bottles that, if sold, could fund a scholarship student's entire semester.

He didn't know if price made the booze taste any better, but that was the theory he'd work with. In the end, it all boiled down to the fact that this was an occasion for alcohol. Lots of it.

Anything to numb the open pulsing, painful wound that was his heart right now.

When he came back into the common area, Caroline gave him a wide berth, doing her best to look busy. Which was fine. He didn't want to talk and she would be too preoccupied with her society meeting to try and play therapist.

There was no one who could make him feel better at the moment.

Thanks for deigning to slum it with me for a few days, but I think it's time we both headed back to the real world.

Yeah. Time to get good and sloshed, but he had the where-withal to wait until he was behind his door to pop the bottle of —well, whatever—open and take a hard swig. It burned all the way down, but in that pleasant, albeit punishing way that had him swallowing another gulp the next second.

The place in his chest still throbbed.

Will didn't know what was worse—the fact that he'd believed something that wasn't true, that Elizabeth believed something that wasn't true, or that he felt now there was a chance he hadn't known her at all. Not really.

People had sex without feelings all the time. He knew this. He'd done it, though once had been enough for him to understand he needed a connection. He'd been content, if not happy, thinking that whatever was going on between him and Elizabeth was surprising to them both, but there had always been the assumption that she...

That she felt something.

Well, that was the problem, wasn't it? She'd felt things.

Many, from the sound of it. She'd believed him capable of something horrible and she'd still gone to bed with him.

Will stopped, leaned against his bedroom door, his mind at once assaulted with a collage of memories from the night before. Elizabeth smiling at him. Elizabeth closing her mouth around his cock. Elizabeth rolling the condom over his shaft. Elizabeth sinking onto him.

All that—every moment—had been stolen. Meant for someone else. She hadn't even wanted to have sex, but they'd ended up in bed. His bed, the one made up with sheets that likely still smelled of her.

None of it had been real. Not what he'd felt last night or the hope he'd awoken with this morning. While he'd been fantasizing about the nonexistent future, she'd been making plans with another man.

Will took another hearty swig and looked up. The room felt haunted now; everywhere he looked, he saw her ghost. She was standing where he was, sopping wet and looking at him with wide eyes. She was on the bed, eyeing him hungrily as he stepped into the room with only a towel wrapped around his waist. She was whipping off her shirt and falling into his arms.

God, he'd been such a fool.

But for her... Will didn't think he'd stood a chance. Not from the moment she'd dressed him down at the inaugural party thrown at Greggii House. No one had ever spoken to him like that, and it had been invigorating. Hell, no one ever challenged him, here or elsewhere. Talking with her was a sport all in itself, and as exasperated as she'd left him, he'd also...

Well, he'd liked her.

He'd liked her so much he'd concocted a fantasy. And the entire time, she'd believed him capable of...

Well, he didn't know what. With Wickham, it could be pretty much anything.

Fucking Wickham. That part of his life was supposed to be over. After everything Georgiana had been through—after the hell that was the past few years and rearranging his world to get back on the path he'd neglected—he thought he'd earned a break.

But of course it was Wickham. Anything that Will touched—anything good in his life—Wickham found a way to poison.

Will tightened his jaw, his gaze falling on the laptop at his desk. He might not be able to defend himself regarding the action he'd taken with Jane, but if nothing else, Elizabeth needed to know the truth about the guy she was going out with this Friday.

And he needed a way to exorcise the sudden cacophony of words screaming in his head. An endless parade of things he should have said when he'd been in her room. Because beyond the hurt was something else—something he hadn't felt since the day Georgiana had made that phone call.

The flame inside him flickered at the memory, pulsing toward familiar territory. It had been a long while since he'd let himself get angry, but hell, anger was better than heartache. Anger didn't make him feel pathetic.

Anger gave him direction.

Decision made, Will plopped into his desk chair and powered up his computer. He performed a quick search of the campus database and pulled up Elizabeth's email address. Right there next to her student ID photo and her declared major. And for a second, the anger dulled, summoning back that awful pang from before. It struck him so hard he was surprised when it didn't knock him out of his seat.

Her brown hair hung around her shoulders, sexy-messy in a way that defied logic. Her eyes were full of mirth. Her beautiful mouth was quirked in a saucy smirk, somehow managing to look confident and not cocky. She had the same look on her face that had drawn him to her from the beginning—the kind that said she knew something he didn't, but she would be glad to share it if asked. The more people in on the joke, the better, the photo seemed to say. No one was a stranger to Elizabeth.

Not even those who should be.

Wickham's face rose to the surface of his mind again, and the pang bowed out in favor of anger once more. Expelling a deep breath, Will pulled up his email program and, after a few false starts, decided the best way to get this out was to shut off his filter, lest he'd be writing and deleting the same line for the rest of the night.

And what the hell did he care about how he sounded? Elizabeth had made her opinion of him perfectly clear.

All he had to gain from this was the satisfaction of the last word. Those things he'd thought of saying only after he was away from her. He'd use them all.

And he would not hold back.

22

"Oh my god, are you okay?" Jane asked, dropping her backpack, her face stricken. "What happened?"

Elizabeth shook her head, willing herself not to burst into tears. She'd been doing all right, she'd thought. Better than she would have expected, considering the conversation with Will had gone about as well as your average train wreck.

"Nothing," Elizabeth said at last. "I'm just tired."

"Bull. Something happened." Jane rushed over to her bed and pulled her into a hug. "Talk to me."

"I don't want to bore you with—"

"Lizzie." She pulled back, her eyes narrowing. "You have two choices. Tell me freely or I'll yodel at full volume until you do."

Elizabeth stared at her for a moment. "Yodel?"

"Very, very poorly."

"Is there such a thing as good yodeling?"

"No." Jane sat back, crossing her arms. "Or maybe I'll just guess. Was it Will?"

There was that pang again. "Huh? W-why would it be Will?"

"Because you're not as stealthy as you think when you're

talking about a guy you had amazing sex with. That was not the toughest mystery to crack."

"Will and I haven't seen each other in weeks!"

"Except that class you guys have together and the way you both disappeared after running into each other at the club." Jane arched an eyebrow. "Are you forgetting that I ran into him in the hall as he was leaving that night? You guys were fooling around."

"We were n—okay, yes, we were fooling around. I didn't realize it was that obvious."

Jane snorted. "I'm a virgin, not an infant. You looked really...*relaxed* when I got home."

Elizabeth let out a burst of laughter before covering her mouth. "Fair enough. I should not have doubted your sex-radar."

"Indeed." Jane nodded, looking immensely pleased with herself before the concern returned to her eyes. "So, what happened? Did you guys fight?"

That was putting it mildly. She chewed the inside of her cheek for a moment in a bid for time, then released a long sigh and glanced down. "I suck."

"What happened?"

"This whole thing with Will has been a disaster," she said. That awful, chest-crushing sensation returned with a vengeance. Elizabeth inhaled deeply but her lungs burned as though denied oxygen. "I don't even know how it happened."

Jane offered a soft, Jane-like smile that made Elizabeth feel better and worse at the same time. "You guys have chemistry. Everyone can see it."

"I don't want chemistry with him. You know what he did to Wickham."

Jane pursed her lips. "I know what Wickham said he did to him, based on what you told me. But do we know if that's even true?"

"What reason would Wickham have to lie?"

"Well, he likes you, doesn't he? I'd say turning his main competition into a super villain is a good way to come out ahead, don't you?"

"I told him Will wasn't competition," Elizabeth said.

"Yes, and I'm sure you were very convincing."

"He didn't even know I knew Will when we first met." Though he'd found out pretty fast. "I told him what I'd thought about him and it wasn't flattering."

There was a long pause, and the skepticism in Jane's eyes didn't go away. Which, naturally, made Elizabeth feel even more like shit and she didn't care to investigate why.

"I don't know," Jane said at last. "I mentioned Wickham to Caroline once and—"

"You what?"

"Just once. It was right after you told me."

A half-sigh, half-groan tore through Elizabeth's lips and her body went slack. "Jane—"

"I just wanted to see if she knew anything. Obviously, the Bingleys have been close to Will's family for years, so if there had been anything there, she'd know."

"Yes, and she's head over ass in love with Will, so you're not exactly going to get an objective opinion."

"Perhaps. She didn't say much and I didn't push for more. I know Wickham asked you to keep that under your hat."

"Yeah," Elizabeth muttered dryly. "Can't imagine why."

"But Caroline said—"

"I don't care what Caroline said. Caroline is not my idea of a character witness. Hell, if she thinks Wickham's a creep then that's pretty much an endorsement for the rest of society."

Jane expelled a deep breath. "Just because she's not the nicest person doesn't mean she's wrong all the time."

"Yeah, but it doesn't give her the best odds from where I'm

sitting." Elizabeth shook her head, turned and made a beeline for her bed. "It doesn't matter anyway. The thing with Will is over. There shouldn't have been a thing in the first place."

"I'm sorry."

"I'm not. I think I'm going to sleep for about seventeen years."

"For what it's worth, I'm sorry you guys...broke up."

"We weren't together."

"Well, you were *something*. And you're not now."

"This, by the way, is why I swore off relationships."

"Yeah..." Jane pressed her lips together. "How's that going for you?"

This time when she laughed, she kept laughing until she cried.

There were two different types of hangovers—the traditional kind following a night of drunken debauchery and the emotional kind that followed a night of full on, snot-nosed ugly crying. While neither hangover was Elizabeth's idea of a good time, it occurred to her, as she rolled over and the room seemed to roll with her, that she preferred the former. At least traditional hangovers had the added benefit of alcohol. There was nothing fun about waking up feeling like three-day-old road-kill, then remembering why.

She figured she was going to regret this, but Elizabeth decided, when the alarm clock blared at its usual six-thirty, that she didn't have it in her to haul ass to class.

Hell, she didn't think she could people at all today.

To her astonishment, Jane didn't seem surprised. Elizabeth listened as her roommate climbed out of bed at the normal time and went through the motions of getting ready for the day's first class, all the while playing dead and hoping Jane didn't come to examine her too closely.

"I'm glad you're staying in today," Jane said before she opened the door. Apparently Elizabeth's possum act hadn't fooled anyone. She was really off her game. "I know you'll be kicking yourself later, but trust me, the best thing you can do for yourself is give your head a break."

Elizabeth was still a moment, then rolled over and dragged a pillow over said head. "Mmmffpphbt."

"Love you too," Jane replied. She was gone the next moment, and the room again fell silent.

Elizabeth didn't move, though she couldn't say that her face pressed flat to the surface of a dorm room mattress while the pillow sat on top of her head was a position she'd recommend for sleep. Her limbs just refused to cooperate.

When she awoke a few hours later, foggy headed and breath tasting like something had died in her mouth, she found her pillow at the foot of her bed and the blankets kicked to the floor.

And though she felt she'd slept more than she ever had in her life, her body refused to reward her with energy. At least, the throbbing in her skull had somewhat subsided.

A glance at the clock told her it was nearly noon. Elizabeth groaned and dug her forehead into the mattress. Her body responded to the lure of even more sleep like a wagon-abandoning addict might a shiny brick of cocaine, but she forced herself to ignore the pull and gave her head a shake.

No. She would not spend the entire day in bed. Sixteen plus hours of sleep had been enough.

Instead, she sat up. It took herculean effort and her body whined with every move, but dammit, she managed to get vertical. The room went sideways for a moment as her equilibrium put up the last of its fight, but she steadied herself and waited.

Then she eyed her laptop.

Clear over on her desk.

"Fuck."

Elizabeth pressed her lips together. She wasn't quite ready to get out of bed, but the guilt demons had already begun their assault on her gut for having skipped classes today. The best way to satiate their demands was to check in with her professors, send apologies where needed, and see what she could do to make up her absence.

A struggle and a few minutes later, she had her laptop seated on her pillow and was squinting at her inbox.

That was until the name *Fitzwilliam Darcy* solidified as the sender of an unread message.

Elizabeth's spine went ramrod straight, the last of her emotional hangover blinking out of existence.

Will had emailed her. Holy shit.

Elizabeth shook her head, dragging her finger over the built-in mouse until the cursor hovered over the subject line.

Re: Matters needing clarification

Shit, she was going to throw something, wasn't she?

For a long moment, Elizabeth debated moving that sucker straight to her trash and being done with it. Well, she debated debating it. There was no way she could actually go through with it. An awful curiosity compounded with fear and excitement.

Fuck it.

She clicked the message open, expecting to be greeted by a few curt lines.

Instead, a wall of text flooded her screen. Her stomach fell. Again she considered getting rid of the email—or the laptop itself. Maybe she'd open her window and throw it onto the sidewalk before her overly curious mind could delve in. The visual was so tempting that she felt her body jolt, but destroying a costly computer seemed like something she'd fast regret.

And in the battle of knowing versus not knowing, Elizabeth always chose to know.

Heart in her throat, she began to read.

Hi Elizabeth,

Don't worry. I'm not groveling. You made yourself perfectly clear. I just wish I'd heard it sooner.

That said, I do think I have a right to be heard. You did a lot of talking and accused me of some pretty awful things. I thought, apparently foolishly, that you might give anything George Wickham said the same scrutiny you give everything else. But as I've told you before, he's good at making friends. He knows how to sell his story. On the other hand, I have nothing but the truth to back me up—but the truth is, I believe, rather powerful, no matter how it's presented, and I can only hope that given what I tell you (and the attachments to this email) you won't let Wickham close enough to do to you what he did to my sister.

Also, I'll likely hit "send" before I can think better of this so there's every chance this will come to bite me in the ass, but I ask you to do me the small courtesy of not broadcasting this email, its contents, or anything relating to my sister anywhere. She has worked hard to get well and doesn't deserve to have her life upended again because I was stupid enough to fall in love with the wrong woman.

Wickham and I were friends a lifetime ago. Very close friends. I've known him longer than I've known anyone. My hometown is one of those that moved very reluctantly into the twentieth century, never mind the twenty-first. If you combine every stereotype you've ever heard about the Deep South, you might have an idea of the environment.

When I was about five, there was a gambling scandal. George Sr., Wickham's father, had taken out second and third mortgages, maxing out lines of credit, but he never got ahead of it and the property foreclosed. I've included a link to an archived article from the Derbyshire Daily Herald that goes into this in more detail.

Until that point, Wickham and I had been inseparable. Actually, we remained inseparable for several years to follow. He was like a brother to me. My father made sure that Wickham would not be punished for his own father's failures. Education has always been a virtue championed by my family. Wickham went to Derbyshire Junior Academy and Derbyshire Academy due to my father's generosity.

It wasn't until our eleventh year in school that I noticed things had changed. He became someone else. He had always been funny, but suddenly the things he was saying were personal. For instance, I paid for my first car myself through the money earned working summers for my father. Wickham was offered the same opportunity but declined. That was until after I had purchased my car. He was insistent that my father had paid for it, which would have been my father's prerogative in any case but it simply wasn't true. He told me that I had everything handed to me, and while I don't deny I had an extremely privileged childhood, we had always done whatever we could to make him feel like part of the family. He had his own room at our home, complete with things my father purchased him that his father couldn't. Yet every day that passed, Wickham seemed to become more resentful, and eventually I stopped sitting with him at lunch and making plans for the weekends. It was around this time Charlie and I became friends. He was a freshman when I was a senior. The little brother I'd never had.

Wickham responded by stealing my car and wrapping it around a telephone pole outside the Lambton Inn in town. Please see the second link at the bottom of this email. At this time, I ceased all contact with Wickham and sent over anything of his (bought by my family or not) that had been left at Pemberley—that's the Darcy estate where I grew up.

Wickham would go on to steal three more cars, two belonging to my father (see links 3, 4, and 5), which resulted in a DUI charge and three months' probation (link 6). My father never once pressed charges for theft.

During my senior year, Wickham practically ignored me, and I was grateful for it. However, one day, near graduation, I overheard him while in the library making arrangements with one of his new friends to sell cocaine to the students at Derbyshire Junior Academy, where my sister was about to enter the sixth grade. Drugs have always been a problem in our community, particularly at our school, and I will not pretend otherwise. I had suspected he might be doing something like that but I honestly hadn't cared until he set his sights on kids.

So yes, I narked. Wickham was searched and the drugs were found in his bag. He was arrested and expelled.

Wickham admitted everything almost immediately upon being questioned and seemed to have, as they say, his own come to Jesus moment. He also agreed to a lesser charge in exchange for entering a rehab program and giving presentations at my sister's school and other regional public schools on the dangers of drugs. To confirm this, I dug through my old email account and located the newsletter that was issued to the parents following the agreement. Please see the attachment.

I didn't see Wickham for a while after that, and that was fine by me. You are aware, of course, of what happened to my family following graduation. First, my mother died, and my father needed my help with the company. He was in no state to assume that responsibility solo, and though he was the best man I've ever known, he was also a man with enemies who would exploit my mother's death to their own financial advantage.

My father made me promise that I would return to complete my education after I turned twenty. I had every intention of doing just that, as I'm sure, my father had every intention of living. It was my third week of my first semester when I received the call that he was sick. I didn't know just how sick until I got home. I spent the next fourteen months escorting him to and from various doctors and tests, as well as caring for my sister, Georgiana, who was at that point in the eighth grade and experiencing troubles of her own that I was not equipped to deal with. My lengthy absences and preoccupation with our father left Georgiana more or less alone, and this is something I will never forgive myself for. Because while I wasn't there, George Wickham was.

At this, Elizabeth had to tear her eyes away—her eyes that were stinging and blurry. She hadn't stopped to check any of the links or the attachments, but she didn't need to. The fact that they existed told her enough.

Told her more than enough.

Told her she'd been worse than the world's biggest asshole. And god, she didn't want to read anymore. The scrollbar told her she'd made it just past the halfway point. Her gut told her things were about to get worse.

Georgiana didn't tell me about Wickham. Honestly, at that point, I had forgotten he existed. She made excuses for her absences from Pemberley and it was more convenient for me to believe her at the time than to dig deeper. I'd like to say I suspected something was wrong but the truth is, I was too exhausted from caring for my father to notice much of anything. And as our father deteriorated, anything that would have ordinarily struck me as odd or unlike her was easy to justify as stress and grief, because that was how I felt.

Three weeks after the funeral. That was when she first came to me and the first time I really saw her. She was a mess, and admitted that she had been experimenting with drugs to dull the pain of losing her mother and Dad's illness. I did not handle that well, and that is another thing that is on me to regret. Georgiana reached out to me in a time of need and I pushed her away. I was not in a place to be the brother she needed, but that is no excuse. She has always been the best of us, and I couldn't fathom how someone with her potential could be so reckless. My solution was to ship her off to a rehab facility and consider the matter dealt with.

Wickham followed her. I still don't know what his end-game was. If it was revenge on me or our family, or if he thought he could get Georgiana pregnant and force her into marriage—maybe it was all of the above.

I don't know why she didn't tell me then that Wickham had been her dealer, but I can only assume it was because she thought she was in love with him. The affection he showed her when I was too self-absorbed to give her what she needed earned her loyalty. That was why she left with him when he checked her out of rehab. He had convinced her that he loved her and I didn't. That she was too broken for me to love her anymore and he was all she had.

That wasn't the only thing he convinced her to do. He pressured her for several days to sleep with him—claiming it was better with someone who loved her and would take care of her. I only have Georgiana's account of this, but I trust it. She told him no at first, but he kept pushing for it and eventually, she relented.

She called me afterward from the motel bathroom in tears. I won't go into more detail here—it's hard enough to think about, let alone write. I hadn't even known she'd been checked out of the voluntary rehab, let alone that she and Wickham had any sort of relationship. I got to her as fast as I could. How I left Wickham alive, I'm still not sure. But I did.

It will come as no shock to you that small towns talk, and there's nothing they love more than a story of a rich girl who hit rock bottom. Wickham threatened to go public with some version of story if I didn't pay him. He believed he was entitled to the scholarship my father had established for students of the Derbyshire Academy, or a sum equal to it. At this point, I just wanted him out of our lives. Permanently. Even if he made good on *his threat and lied about everything, the end result would be Georgiana being victimized again. The insult of him asking for money after what he did to my sister didn't really register. However, I did have conditions, which he met. The first being that he was never to see Georgiana again or try to contact her in any way. He agreed. The second was that he would provide a handwritten account of what he had done to her that I would keep in the event he decided he wanted more money down the line and thought to come asking with the same old threat. While I don't want the world to know what happened to Georgiana, she and I agreed it was better to have leverage over Wickham than leave ourselves vulnerable. He doesn't have much family pride left, but enough to be threatened by the last of their legacy being exposed. See attachment #2.*

I am happy to say that my sister has been sober for nearly four years, but the road to recovery has been a difficult one. She is in therapy and attends online meetings for survivors of sexual assault, though I had to talk her into that. It was only when I was absolutely certain she was in a good place that I could consider coming back to school. She, herself, will be graduating Derbyshire Academy in the spring.

I don't know what Wickham hoped to gain by telling you whatever it was that had you convinced I had done something to him. I just hope that you are careful when you are around him.

Regarding the issue with Charlie and Jane—yes, I did tell Charlie that she might be with him for the wrong reasons. I didn't do this to hurt anyone, rather to save my friend from being hurt by a girl he had fallen in love with. Jane is a perfectly nice person and for a while, I thought she might be just what Charlie needed. But the more time they spent together, the less she seemed interested in Charlie. I started noticing this shortly after the night you and Jane spent at Netherfield. When Jane would visit, she would spend a few minutes at most with Charlie before seeking out Caroline. I didn't think anything of this at first, but the more it happened, the more it stood out.

And as much as I like Jane, I didn't get the sense that she was as attached to him as he was to her. I would hope that you would understand the need to protect your friends from heartache. Charlie deserves someone who loves as hard and irrationally as he does, who doesn't make excuses to not be with him when all he wants to do is make her happy. He deserves someone who isn't with him because of who he is or how much money he has or how much influence he has over campus politics.

I didn't tell Charlie to break it off with Jane. I just pointed out what was obvious to me. Given what I saw, I don't regret this at all. I was asked my opinion and gave it.

I hope this message helps clarify things from my point of view. Again, I'm not going to bother you anymore—you made your feelings perfectly clear. I'm just sorry I misread you. But it's better to know now than find out later. You just wanted to fuck. That's fine. But that you wanted to do it thinking whatever it was you think about me just boggles my mind.

I guess I'm just old fashioned.

— WILL

23

The email was a cancer on her computer.

Elizabeth spent the next hour checking, double, and triple checking each link and resource Will had provided while building his case.

These had been easy enough to find—some in the same newspaper report she'd looked up after Wickham had told her his story. Had she done any deeper digging, she would have found these articles.

The ultimate nail in Wickham's coffin was the handwritten letter. In it, he'd detailed everything he'd done to Georgiana Darcy in a bloodless, dispassionate manner that made him seem something less than human. Part of her wanted to believe that Will was capable of fabricating something like this just to fuck with her, but she knew that wasn't right.

She'd been a giant asshole.

And Wickham was a bona fide sociopath.

With whom she had a date on Friday.

That thought alone was almost enough to convince Elizabeth to seize her phone and fire off a cancellation. Hell, that would have been the smart thing to do—quick and easy. And she wanted quick and easy. She wanted to never have to see, speak to, or think of George Wickham again.

At the same time, she needed to tell him what she really thought of him to his face. Make sure he knew he wasn't fooling anyone.

Except he had. And that was the kicker. He had fooled her. Completely one-hundred percent, can't-get-around this fooled her.

What was worse, she'd been an easy mark.

A sour taste invaded Elizabeth's mouth. She had been many things over her brief life, some good and some very not. But gullible had never once been on that list. Sure, she was known for making snap decisions without looking back, but her intuition had rarely steered her the wrong way. Wickham had completely blindsided her and she'd let him because that had been easier, more comfortable than...

God, she hated herself.

Jane returned to the dorm a little after four that afternoon, a pint of mint chocolate chip and a plastic spoon in hand.

"Thought you could use a pick-me-up," she said by way of greeting.

"Bless you," Elizabeth replied. She'd been too overwrought to eat today, but ice cream was one of those things that the stomach learned to accept, even and especially when the soul felt ill.

Jane handed it over, the smile on her face fading into a frown. "What's wrong?"

Elizabeth already had the top of her treat pried off and was stabbing the cold surface with her spoon. Harshly at first, then with more patience as she realized a broken spoon would do her no favors. "What makes you think something's wrong?"

"Don't take this the wrong way, but you look worse than you did before I left."

She looked up at that, deadpanning, "How can I possibly take that the wrong way?"

"What happened?"

The surface of the mint chocolate chip finally gave way to the spoon's endless prodding. Elizabeth stuck a healthy bite into her mouth, then did the whole body shiver that came with eating something so cold it made her teeth hurt. Jane must have found this at the very back of the freezer.

"Lizzie, talk to me."

"Will emailed me."

Jane expelled a deep breath. "Oh boy."

"Yeah. That sums it up nicely."

"Was it... Do you want to talk about it?"

Elizabeth considered this a moment, then braved another bite. It was still on the too-cold side, but not so much that she couldn't taste the minty goodness. "No," she said at last. "But kind of."

"All right." Jane backed slowly to her bed. "I'll just be over here if—"

"I was wrong."

There were no more humbling three words in the English language, Elizabeth was sure. And hearing them aloud, having said them, feeling them, both calmed and intensified that sick sensation in her gut. On one hand, it was nice to admit as much to herself—there was some liberation in that much alone.

On the other hand, being wrong was the pits.

Jane seemed to know this, for she didn't immediately demand an explanation. Another reason she was pretty much the best person on the planet who had already won friend of the year.

Whose relationship had been torpedoed by misunderstanding and one mean rich girl. Of everything Elizabeth wanted to share with Jane, this was the most pressing, and likewise the hardest to swallow. But she wasn't sure how Jane would react if she'd known that Charlie had broken up with her because he'd been convinced she didn't care for him, or only cared for him insofar as where his connections could get her. Because that by itself was rather awful, especially considering Charlie hadn't opted to talk with her about these things before cutting it off.

Jane had already been heartbroken by Charlie once. She didn't need to go through that again.

"I have a date with George Wickham on Friday," Elizabeth said at last, her stomach turning. Maybe this was a problem ice cream couldn't solve after all. She placed the pint on her desk. "Did I tell you that earlier?"

Jane hesitated, then shook her head. "Do you think that's a good idea? You don't seem to be in date mood."

A bitter laugh squeezed Elizabeth's throat. "It's a brilliant idea. Haven't you heard? I'm just full of them. I know everything."

"Lizzie, whatever he said...you have to know it was coming from a place of hurt."

"Yeah." She swallowed. "I'm going out with Wickham on Friday because I want to tell him to his face that he's a... Well, I'll come up with a suitable insult by then. My brain's a little fried."

Jane looked downright worried now. She took a step forward. "Look, it's okay. We all make mistakes. Look at me. I pushed away probably the greatest guy in the world because I was afraid of sex."

Elizabeth looked up. "Did...did he know?"

"No." She barked a short laugh. "That would have been easy, right? Tell the guy I'm mad about that I'm a little nervous about being alone with him because yes, I am the last virgin standing." Jane hissed a long sigh, fixed her gaze on the wall behind Elizabeth's head. "I've actually been thinking about that a lot today.

About the Realis situation and Caroline and..." Another long beat, then Jane gave her head a shake and plastered on a smile. "But that's not important. What did Will's email say?"

Elizabeth pressed her lips together. "He said many some-things and most of them amount to I'm an asshole."

"I think you're probably oversimplifying."

"I'm not. In this case, I am an asshole." She shook her head. "I can't tell you what the email said. I'm sorry."

There was no response. When she met Jane's eyes again, she found them wide.

"What?" she asked, wiggling.

"You're not going to tell me?"

"I can't. There are things in there that aren't my things to spread around." Plus Will had asked her to not tell anyone, and there hadn't been an asterisks and a BFF clause. Though he might have left her angry and confused, he had also confided something intensely personal and she didn't want to betray that.

"Wow."

Elizabeth narrowed her eyes. "Wow what?"

"I think you might actually like him."

"What? Who?"

Jane gestured emphatically. "Will."

Elizabeth swallowed but didn't reply.

"Wickham asked you to not tell anyone about the drug thing, and you told me. Hell, you told Mary too. I'd be surprised if Lydia and Kitty don't know."

"Yes. What a wonderful choice that ended up being."

At least Jane had the good sense to look somewhat abashed. "I admit I was careless with that information...but don't you kind of think that was exactly what Wickham wanted?"

"What do you mean?"

Though now that Jane said it, Elizabeth could see the clear path. Wickham shows up for college, finds the guy he got to bankroll his education is on campus and gets people to dislike him because of some made-up history pieced together by just enough truth to pass the smell test.

"That asswipe," she muttered, shaking her head. "Literally no words for how much I am going to enjoy mopping the floor with his ass."

"Uhh...Lizzie?"

She glanced up. "Don't worry. It'll be a figurative mop." Maybe. She really couldn't stand to be arrested for assault, no matter how cathartic pummeling his pretty-boy face would feel at the moment.

Jane sighed. "Just be careful."

"I'm always careful." Elizabeth reached for the ice cream pint again. It had melted a little, and the next spoonful came without a fight.

"I don't think you've had a careful day in your life."

"Probably not. But there's no time like the present to give it a try."

"And...maybe don't give up on Will so quickly?"

Elizabeth swallowed a mouthful of minty goodness and arched an eyebrow. "Huh?"

"I don't know what all happened there," Jane said, bringing up her hands. "I don't know if I want to know. But I do think you like him."

"I—"

"Just think about it." She glanced down. "Will was always decent to me when I was over there. I admit, he can be a little...intense, and he's said some things that are downright rude... But I think... I don't know, Lizzie. But maybe just don't write him off so fast."

It was lovely sentiment—really it was. She wondered how Jane would react if she knew that Will had been one of the voices behind Charlie's decision to break things off. For a moment, she was tempted to tell her just that—get it all out there so that Jane would stop seeing the good in everyone for five seconds and realize that some people were just dicks.

But if Jane had been avoiding Charlie out of her intimacy fears all the while blabbering to Caroline about how much she wanted in the Realis Society...

Well, Elizabeth didn't want to take Will's side or sympathize with Will's side or even acknowledge that his side existed. But she could see it.

"I need to move," she said, kicking her legs over the edge of the mattress. "I need to shower like something awful, email my professors, eat something with protein and start scripting how thoroughly I'm going to dump Wickham's ass on Friday."

Jane nodded but didn't reply. "Let me know if you need anything."

"I need many things, but I don't think you can help."

"I'll try."

"I know you will and I love you for it."

Elizabeth sought out some clean clothes, grabbed a towel, and made her way to the hall.

The first step toward feeling human again was a shower. And if she got lucky, she'd have a game plan in place by the time she emerged.

Friday night arrived after days of hellish classes. Elizabeth ended up skipping her Ethics course for the rest of the week— she couldn't handle seeing Will just yet. Thankfully, Professor Greenfield was good enough to buy her excuse of sickness and send her the reading, as well as a reminder that her class presentation was coming up.

Just more to worry about, but she couldn't afford to pause. Not with the Wickham confrontation still on the horizon.

Wickham, who had been texting her like mad all week. She'd replied here and there, confirming her address and the day and time, but not taking the bait for any of his flirty messages. Anything she sent him was curt and to the point. Either he didn't notice or noticed and didn't care.

As the countdown narrowed to Wickham's arrival, Elizabeth worried that Jane might linger to watch the fireworks, but thankfully, her roommate announced that she had a study group at the library and would be there for a few hours.

This only served to remind Elizabeth of the mountain of work that she had waiting for her. The assignments she needed to make up, the reading she had to do, and making sure the presentation was ready.

Except she couldn't seem to stop ruminating over Will's email. She hadn't been able to reread it since the day it hit her inbox, hoping her shame would fade with time. But that was a tall order—she didn't know if she'd ever forgive herself for being such a blind idiot.

Finally, at a quarter till seven, a knock sounded at the door.

Elizabeth stilled, closed the book she'd been trying to read, and rose to her feet. She paused long enough to give her hair a good fluff and admire the outfit she'd chosen for Operation Castration. A sleek black skirt with a matching camisole—minus a bra, thank you—and a pair of heels. Not big heels, she wasn't into those—just enough to give her an extra inch or so.

Yes, she did look particularly fabulous, if she dared say so herself.

And when she opened the door and Wickham's eyes immediately roved her body, she knew her mirror wasn't lying.

"Wow," he said, rubbing his jaw and grinning like men did when they thought they were going to get lucky. "You look...

smoking hot. Is that too forward? You know what? I don't care. *Smoking hot.*"

Elizabeth smiled, hitching her purse higher on her shoulder. "Thanks."

He met her eyes, nodding. "So...everything all right?"

"Why wouldn't it be?"

"Well, when a girl seems about as excited to go on a date with you as she would for a root canal, you think things."

"And we wouldn't want you to strain yourself."

He blinked at her, confused, then apparently decided she was poking fun at him and grinned again. "Right. So...are you ready to go?"

"Oh. I am. But not with you."

It took a second for him to process that. Then he gave another chuckle. "Just proves you have good taste. I wouldn't go anywhere with me, either."

"Too bad you're stuck with you. I get the option of leaving at least."

Wickham stared at her a moment longer, the smile at last fading. "What's going on? Are you—"

"Disgusted with myself for being had by a guy who redefines the word *asshole*? Yeah. I am." Elizabeth took a step forward, right into his personal space, and shut the door behind her. She saw anger flash across those eyes, combined with confusion and a healthy amount of pure want that made her skin crawl. "You know what the kicker is? Woe-is-me bullshit has never been my thing. But you know how to work it."

Any trace of a smile had completely abandoned Wickham's face. The look he was giving her now was, she assumed, courtesy of the man behind the curtain.

"So you and Will have been getting extra cozy?"

"This isn't about Will," Elizabeth replied. "Though you'd love it to be."

"I knew it," he muttered, breaking away from her. "I knew there was something going on there."

"Oh please—"

"Don't *oh please* me. The second he walked into the Meryton Mudhouse that day, I knew it. You had that look. The same, sick look everyone gets over Will fucking Darcy." Wickham shook his head. "What is it? The money? It has to be that. And what, you think you're different? You have any idea how many sluts throw themselves at him just to be used up and—"

"Is lying compulsory for you? I mean, do you realize you're doing it?"

"So you believe Will?"

"No, jackass." She reached into her purse, never taking her eyes off the human turd, and withdrew a printed copy of the PDF Will had sent her containing Wickham's account of what he had done to Georgiana Darcy. "As it turns out, I *do* believe you. Just not the you that you want me to believe."

It was a bittersweet victory, watching Wickham pale as he realized what she had. What she'd seen. He snatched the sheet away and held it up, his throat working. After a long moment, he lowered it, his jaw hard and his eyes cold. "You can't prove this is me. That I really wrote this."

"Well, as much fun as it would be hiring a handwriting specialist, I don't need to prove shit," she replied. "All I need to do is make about five hundred copies of this bad boy and post it all over campus. Sure, you can deny, deny, deny, but them's your words. And while a few loyal friends might stand by you, I'm gonna guess most of them won't."

"You wouldn't dare." But from the look on his face, she could see he wasn't certain. He waved the sheet, crinkling it. "You know as well as I do that Darcy doesn't want this out."

"Yeah. I thought of that, and I think I have a solution via

some top-notch tech that can help mask the identities of the victims. It's called a marker."

"I'd tell. You go public with this and I'll let everyone know just what a little fucking cocktease slut Darcy's sister really is."

Elizabeth felt something inside her go cold. "You do that, and I'd cut off your balls and shove them down your throat."

At last his face twisted into something truly ugly, the sheen of white chased away by blotchy red. He seized her by the shoulders and thrust her against the wall hard enough that her spine whined in pain. "You just try, you fucking cunt," he growled, his breath hot on her face. "Just fucking try."

A rush of fear shot through her veins, but she forced herself to swallow it. He would not see her blink, dammit. "Okay," she replied coolly, right before smashing her knee into his family jewels.

The pressure at her shoulders vanished as Wickham doubled over, sucking in deep, heaving breaths that rattled through the air like an audible bruise. The now wrinkled sheet containing his confession tumbled from his fingers as they rushed to cup his testicles. Elizabeth caught it easily and stuffed it back in her purse.

"Whoops," she said. "That didn't *quite* cut them off, but hey, if at first you don't succeed..."

Wickham growled—yes folks, he growled—and reached for her with one of those meaty paws of his. Elizabeth kicked him away, turned around to close and lock up her dorm. Then she delicately stepped over the lump that was Wickham and began making her way down the hall.

"You..." he half moaned, half screamed. "You... fucking...*cunt.*"

Elizabeth turned, rolling her eyes. "Yeah, you said that already. How stunningly original."

"Crazy bitch. You're a crazy motherfucking bitch."

She snorted. "You come near me, near Jane—hell, anyone in Longbourn, and I will make your life a living hell. You keep spreading lies about Will? Go near him at all? You'll see just what this crazy bitch is capable of."

Then she turned and strolled down the hall, serenaded by a slew of half-coherent insults interspersed here and there with a pitiful moan.

24

Will stopped refreshing his inbox eventually. By Friday, he resigned himself to the reality that if Elizabeth planned to respond, she would have done so by now. And honestly, he hadn't really expected to hear from her. Hell, he'd be marginally lucky if she hadn't deleted the email upon seeing it was from him just on principle.

But he didn't think that was the case. Elizabeth might be a hothead, but she was too damn curious to ignore something like that.

For the millionth time, he found himself guessing at her reaction. And for the millionth time, he found himself wishing he'd never set eyes, hand, or mouth on her to spare him the empty feeling now consuming his chest and throat and entire goddamn existence.

He had forced himself not to reread the email after hitting *send*, but just barely. The brief read through he'd given it before making the decision not to delete it and forget the whole thing had been painful enough. The mind had a way of pulling the worst experiences from the past without struggle, so that when a certain time period was revisited, it came with more than just a memory. The ghost of that helplessness, that despair, that pure rage had resurfaced. Just looking at the words made him burn.

And it was all he could do to keep from sending her an email to see if she had decided to go through with her date or not. To see if she believed him. If she was sorry at all for the things she'd said.

Or if Wickham was touching her now the way Will had just a few days ago.

The true test would come next week when they had class together again. Elizabeth hadn't shown up this week and he'd been relieved. His group presentation was now behind him, and he'd spent much too much time worrying about being in front of the class with her eyes on him as he argued for school uniforms. He didn't think he could stand that so soon after the blowup. He needed the weekend to process and compartmentalize.

He needed to get his fucking life back together.

Will sighed and leaned back in his desk chair, scrubbing a hand down his face. He flicked a gaze to his phone, hoping for a notification light that would indicate an email or a text or—

Stop.

He gave his head a shake and turned his attention back to the blinking cursor awaiting his command on the document screen. With Elizabeth officially out of his life, he was determined to reapply his focus on schoolwork, which meant—in his world—getting a healthy start on the term paper due for his ethics course.

God, the semester was almost over, but not quite. He still had a few weeks of sitting next to Elizabeth to contend with. Of listening to her talk. Watching her present. Breathing her air.

Perhaps education was overrated.

Will dropped his face into his hands and released a long groan. This was ridiculous.

The air broke with the vibration of his phone. He jerked his head up and looked down, heart suddenly in his throat.

It was her. It had to be. She was going to tell him—

Georgiana: Hey big bro

Will swallowed, poisoned with disappointment. Never before had he had that reaction to seeing his sister's name appear on his phone.

And the fact that he had made his insides burn with sudden fury because *Georgiana* was the one person in his life that actually mattered, and she rarely reached out unless she was struggling with something. The second he'd seen her name he should have been on high alert, not dejected.

Yes, it was good that things had gone the way they had with Elizabeth. Anyone who could incite that reaction was not someone he needed in his life.

He picked up the phone and fired back.

Will: Everything OK?

Georgiana: That's a weird way to say hello

Will: You only text when you're feeling off

Georgiana: I'm fine

Will: How about the truth?

Georgiana: Seriously, Will. Lighten up.

Will: Helps if you're honest with me

There was a prolonged beat, and for a moment he thought he might have chased her off for the night. But a few seconds later, the little ellipses at the bottom of the screen started moving again.

Georgiana: Normal stuff

That was anticlimactic.

Will: Details are your friend

Another pause. Then the ellipses returned.

Georgiana: It's getting to be that time of year is all

Shit. He hadn't even thought about that. Though it was

wholly fruitless, Will found himself glancing at the calendar he had pinned to the corkboard above his desk. Sure enough, they were nearing the anniversary of Georgiana's flight from rehab. Made Thanksgiving an awkward time of year at the Darcy dinner table, but she'd been getting better steadily over the past few holidays.

Will: You know I'll be home soon

Georgiana: Yeah. And I'm checking into group tonight to see if anyone's around.

Will: Do you need me to come home now?

Georgiana: Again, this is why I don't tell you things. You always overreact.

Will: You not telling me things causes me to overreact. Ever think of that?

Georgiana: You will not confuse me with your logic. How are things there?

Will stared at the screen for a moment. Loaded question, that, and there wasn't much he could tell her. Modern though their family may be, the last thing she needed was to hear he was hung up on a girl who had seen him as little more than a vehicle for sexual gratification.

Especially now that Elizabeth might be out with Wickham.

Will squeezed the phone so hard it shot out of hand and onto the desk. Dammit. He had to stop thinking about her. Had to.

Will: Nothing exciting happening

Georgiana: Lies!

The response came so quick he didn't know what to do with himself. Then, tentatively, he began typing a response.

Will: Explain?

Georgiana: Caroline says you have a girlfriend

A growl tickled the back of Will's throat. He took a moment to return to the fantasy in which he strangled Caroline with her hair. The woman was nothing if not persistent—an admirable quality wasted on an unadmirable person.

Will: You won't be surprised to learn that Caroline is full of shit

Georgiana: OMG NOW I KNOW THERE'S SOMEONE WHO IS SHE?

Will blinked at the screen, bemused.

Will: ??

Georgiana: Come ON! You never say anything like that to me. Even though I've been well-versed in the art of profanity for many moons

Will: There is no one. Goodnight

Georgiana: Will has a girlfriend, Will has a girlfriend. I'm chanting this. You can't hear it, but that's the effect I'm going for.

Will: Goodnight

Georgiana: You suck, you know that? BTW, Caroline hates this girl. I know, shock. But you might be careful about letting them talk.

Will: Just how much has Caroline told you?

Georgiana: Enough to know she hates this girl, wants you to bone her (her=Caroline) and thinks your GF isn't good enough because she doesn't come from money

Will: Please never refer to me boning anyone ever again

Georgiana: No promises, though I don't need the word picture of you + Caroline

Will: You're the one who said it

Georgiana: I know. I am my own worst enemy. But it sounds like this chick is awesome. I hope you guys are big with the PDA when Caroline's around. That'll learn her

Will: 'That'll learn her'? Who talks like this?

Georgiana: Oh go back to macking on your girlfriend or whatever you're doing. I'm cool

Will: I can tell when you're lying

Georgiana: Then you need to get that superpower checked because I am Fine with a capital F (as you can see). Later, bro

Will fired off another goodnight, but didn't get anything back. He wasn't surprised. Once Georgiana announced her intention to stop talking, it was impossible to get that door open again.

And though he worried about her—always would—hearing from her had done something for him. It had reminded him why he was here.

And why it was a good thing that his relationship with Elizabeth had fizzled out before it began. In the long run, this hurt would transform into the best thing that could have happened to him, because it would have gotten him back on track where he needed to be.

Will inhaled deeply, eyeing the mountain of coursework that he could be doing. Then his gaze wandered to the Google Chrome icon on his desktop screen. A dangerous impulse buried itself in his gut, and before he could talk himself out of it, he seized the mouse and clicked the browser open.

"This is a bad idea, Will," he muttered, pulling up his seldom-used Facebook account.

Yes, it was a bad idea. But it was one of those bad ideas tied to a compulsion so strong he felt he might physically ache if he didn't give in. So, being the masochist he was, Will went to the search bar and typed in Elizabeth's name. He paused, then hit the enter key, and there she was. Right at the top of the list.

Courtesy of *mutual friend* Charlie Bingley.

Charlie was Elizabeth's Facebook friend. Will didn't know why this surprised him, but it did. Or perhaps it was another nail in the coffin that was their nonexistent relationship. She'd connected with Charlie over social media, but not him. She hadn't mentioned it once.

Will swallowed hard and forced his gaze to her profile picture itself.

And he couldn't keep from smiling.

Elizabeth stood in front of a mirror in a bathroom, he presumed, her phone stretched in front of her, her hip cocked at an exaggerated, almost painful angle, and her head craned so far back it looked like it was trying to escape her body. She had the goofiest look on her face—eyes wide, cheeks puffed out, nostrils flared. Honestly, she couldn't look more unattractive if she tried, but he knew her well enough to know that was the point.

So confident was he that, when he clicked her picture and it opened into a new window, he wasn't surprised to see the text that accompanied it.

Fine. I cave, world. You win. Here's my inaugural selfie. #NailedIt

Will barked an actual laugh at that, then that pang came back and chased the smile from his face.

The profile picture hadn't been updated in more than three years. He thought that might mean she wasn't active on Facebook—active enough to friend Charlie, granted—but maybe she just hopped on once in a blue moon the way he did.

He went to her page. Just to check. Because apparently he had a sickness.

Except there wasn't much there to see. She was among the Facebook users smart enough to make their profile private. Aside from some photos she'd been tagged in—most notably by Lydia and Kitty—her page was closed to him. The photos themselves didn't yield any more information, either. Most were of Lydia and Kitty, with an occasional blurry Elizabeth in the background.

The pang struck him again, hard enough to make his bones vibrate. And though it seemed to last forever, it didn't—a few seconds had it calming, though it morphed quickly into something almost as ugly.

What the hell was he doing, stalking Elizabeth's page? Was he really this pathetic?

Will gave his head a shake and moved to x-out of the browser when another, impossibly worse idea occurred to him.

And like before, he couldn't help himself. He didn't even pretend to try. Instead, he went back to his main feed, to the search bar, and typed in the name George Wickham.

The asshole's face was there. Will released a steady breath and flexed his hand into a fist, then relaxed again. He hesitated, hating himself, and clicked on the name despite the very urgent voice in his head screaming at him not to.

Unlike Elizabeth's page, Wickham's didn't have the same privacy settings, for the first thing that popped up was a status posted not fifteen minutes earlier.

Elizabeth Bennet is one nasty bitch, boys. Into some REAL SICK SHIT. Fuck but she does love the D.

At first, Will could only stare.

Then a pulse of anger pounded through him. Adrenaline spiked and his temples began to throb.

If that wasn't enough, there were comments. Already the thread looked to be rather popular. Now completely ignoring the piercing wail of his better angels, Will couldn't click fast enough.

The thread consisted of Wickham's friends chiming in on psychotic, dick-starved women and asking for details on the "sick shit" Elizabeth was into. Details Wickham was all too happy to provide.

After the shock wore off, Will sat back in his chair, staring blankly at the computer screen, his breaths coming easier.

He couldn't believe it. Except, no, he could, because that was who Wickham was. This was all he was. A guy who lashed out when cornered—who did whatever he could to bring pain to others. And in his view, women were easy to humiliate. Say anything about them sexually and the job was done.

This, at the very least, did settle one question mark in Will's mind. And despite the fury pulsing through him, he couldn't deny there was a modicum of relief as well.

Wickham lashed out when wounded. Which meant Elizabeth had wounded him.

Which meant she believed him—believed Will.

And that victory, small as it was, was a sweet one.

Elizabeth had known Will would keep his word, but she couldn't deny being disappointed that he didn't so much as look at her that first class they had following his email. And maybe if she hadn't been such a chicken-shit, she could have done something about it. But she was a chicken-shit—a big one—and being that this was new territory for her, she wasn't sure how to go about addressing it. If there was even a way to do it.

Hell, if there was anything to salvage there at all.

At first she'd thought to give him the time he needed, somewhat convinced that after a couple weeks, he would end the silent treatment and ask if they could talk. So she turned up for class, listened to the other groups' presentations, took her notes and made arrangements with Lydia and Mary to work on theirs, all waiting for Will to catch her eye or indicate he wanted a word with her. But that time never came, and it became apparent to her that if any part of their relationship was worth salvaging, it would be up to her to make the first move. Will had proven to be a man of his word; he'd said he wouldn't talk to her again and he was determined to not be called a liar.

But Elizabeth couldn't let it rest at that. Just couldn't. The more time that lapsed between receiving that email and kneeing Wickham in the balls, the more she found herself desperate to talk to Will. To apologize, at the very least, for some of the things she'd said.

Or, you know, all of them.

Except Elizabeth was becoming increasingly convinced that Will wouldn't be interested in anything she had to say. Particularly with the way he'd signed off. How he had been flummoxed that she could have slept with him while thinking the worst about him, and—though he hadn't said it directly—what that meant for the sort of person she was.

This would alternatively piss her off and make her feel like shit, and neither was something she cared to experience longer than necessary. She would tell herself she'd been nothing but forthright with him from the get-go, but then wonder if that was actually true or if she'd done a good job of convincing herself. Then she would swell with indignation that anyone would judge her by her sex-life while, at the same time, asking herself that very question. It wasn't like it was a new one.

So Elizabeth decided to do the decent thing—leave him alone.

Which was how she found herself going through the motions in ways she hadn't since well before the dissolution of her parents' marriage. The hysterical calls from her mother had gone from every day to infrequent and were now almost nonexistent, which any other version of herself would have seen as a massive win. For Elizabeth, the lack of crisis only made the rest of her life look tame.

And kinda dull.

Which was a horrible thought, but without fires to put out, Elizabeth's world fell into a quiet she honestly hadn't thought possible. She buried herself in schoolwork, telling herself she should be grateful for the lack of distractions. Random annoyances were bound to happen. The project she was working on for her ethics course required a lot of QT with Lydia and Mary, which left her with little time to do anything but work.

And obsess over the fact that since it was a presentation, Will would have no excuse but to look at her, something he'd gold medaled in avoiding since the email.

When the day of the presentation arrived, Elizabeth ended up doing most of the talking by virtue of the fact that she was prepared—unlike Lydia—and not shy, unlike Mary. At least, she wasn't shy normally. Though she told herself not to so much as sniff in his direction, Elizabeth couldn't keep her eyes from connecting with Will's every few seconds, it seemed. And each time they locked gazes, she felt a pulse of heat zip through her body—a mini-endorphin boost that she found herself starting to crave.

"Reducing the frequency of abortion is a noble cause, but time and again, we have seen pro-life proponents dismiss and even vehemently campaign against the best ways to keep abortion rates low," Elizabeth was saying. "That is, easy access to affordable birth control and comprehensive sex education. What do pro-life advocates want? Abstinence-only education. More specifically, and I promise this is a phrase you'll find if you troll any internet comment section on the topic, for women to keep their legs closed."

At that, someone snickered from the back of the class. "And we know that'd be a real problem for you."

Elizabeth paused. She hadn't caught the speaker, but something told her it was the same guy—Zelner or whoever—who had previously been booted from Professor Greenfield's class. Still, she was determined to keep her head high and continue, interruptions be damned.

"If you have a rebuttal for Miss Bennet's argument," Professor Greenfield said, her face contorted with irritation, "or anything else her group presents, you're more than welcome to share with us your side when it's your turn to present. Do I make myself clear?"

The answer came in a silence so pronounced Elizabeth was certain she could have heard a mouse fart.

When she was satisfied, Professor Greenfield leaned back in her seat and gave a stiff nod. "You may continue, Miss Bennet."

Elizabeth swallowed hard, flicked her gaze to Will, then away again as soon as their eyes connected.

"As I was saying," she continued, "abstinence-only education has faced the same test time and time again. And time and time again, it's failed that test. In their comprehensive study, Kathrin Stanger-Hall and David Hall draw a concise correlation between the lack of comprehensive sex education and the increase in teen pregnancy. If the ultimate goal of the pro-life movement is to eliminate abortion across the board, they are ignoring the one thing guaranteed to help prevent unwanted babies from being conceived in the first place. Yet it isn't enough for these groups and their supporters to see a decrease in abortion—women continued to be policed, judged, and punished for their sexual decisions in ways our male counterparts cannot begin to fathom. The usage of birth control—"

"Just admit it," came the same voice, startling her out of her talk. "You decided to use this assignment to justify the fact that you're a whore."

At that, Elizabeth felt herself go both red hot and bitter cold. "I'm sorry?"

Professor Greenfield released an exasperated sigh and rose to her feet. "All right, Mr. Zelner, I've had it. Out of my class."

Something had seized Elizabeth by the insides and shook hard. Behind her, Lydia had melted into what sounded like feverish giggles, which was pretty much the largest contribution she'd made to this project, so that was something. Mary was stone silent.

It took three full sweeps of the classroom before her gaze landed on the familiar, smirking face of the douche from a few weeks back. Elizabeth had managed to ignore him in the subsequent class periods—hadn't hurt that she'd been preoccupied with thoughts of Will—but now...

Now she was just pissed.

"Seriously, dude," she said with a sigh. "Who pissed in your Cheerios?"

"I just think it's funny, is all."

"And I just want you out of my class," Professor Greenfield snapped. "Seriously, Mr. Zelner, what—"

"Wickham's told everyone how nasty you were," the assface continued. "Not to mention easy and clingy. So I just thought it might be of interest to the class that Elizabeth Sluts-Around is using her homework to justify—"

"That is enough!" Professor Greenfield's voice rang throughout the room. "Mr. Zelner, I'm not sure if you're just in my class for kicks or if you truly don't give a flying crap about your semester grade. But I'd like to remind you—all of you— that this isn't high school and you're not required to be here. I don't give a good goddamn how much money your parents have donated to the school or which campus halls bear your surname. Unprovoked verbal attacks are never okay in my classroom and they are certainly not okay during a presentation. Mr. Zelner, please show yourself out. If you're fortunate, I'll let you skate by the semester with an Incomplete, but I'd be very careful with your next steps if I were you."

For a moment, Elizabeth would have sworn the woman breathed fire. The words were almost enough to make her forget that her skin was melting off.

Because it wasn't what Zelner had said about her that had her unnerved. It was what he'd said about Wickham.

Wickham's told everyone how nasty you were. Not to mention easy and clingy.

Of course. Elizabeth bit the inside of her cheek to keep from screaming. She barely noticed as Zelner rose from his seat, gathered his things and stalked out. A dull buzzing filled her ears.

Fuck, she was so stupid. Of course Wickham had said something. *Of course he had.*

Then her eyes went to Will, whose face was turned in the direction of Zelner's desk, his skin red with what she recognized as anger.

And something within her—something she hadn't known existed—abruptly shattered.

Despite his many attempts to push her from his mind, Will had found that not thinking about Elizabeth or the email or anything tangentially related to either was futile. Rather, his mind had turned into a station programmed solely with Elizabeth and the greatest hits of their non-relationship.

Today was the first day he'd allowed himself to look at Elizabeth, and he hadn't missed the way her eyes seemed drawn to his, either.

He also hadn't missed the horror on her face when Zelner had mentioned Wickham. Horror and disgust and yes, some guilt. Her mouth had fallen open and her eyes had gone saucer-like. Her skin, which he'd only seen color when she was angry or aroused, had bloomed bright red. And she'd suddenly found looking at him a challenge.

Granted, the urge to talk to her had been there all along. Itching beneath the surface, desperate for recognition. The first time he'd seen her after sending the email he'd had to bite his tongue to keep from asking about it. About her. About anything. Time had made this more bearable, but not as quickly or as effectively as he'd hoped. And today had walked back all that wonderful progress because he'd wanted to grab her and tell her Zelner was an ass who hero-worshiped Wickham for reasons no sane person could explain. That much Will had gathered almost instantly in his now nightly habit of lurking on his former friend's Facebook page. Wickham had launched an all-out cyber attack against Elizabeth with lavishly embellished posts that had quickly escalated from graphic details of all the sex they'd had to essentially painting her as a crazy stalker who was one bad turn away from leaving him a boiled rabbit. Zelner was a frequent guest star in the comment section, and he'd made his opinion of Elizabeth more than clear. Wickham had acted as he always had once he realized he had a captive audience and the stories had become more and more outrageous.

Will had been under the assumption that Elizabeth knew this was going on mainly because it seemed everyone knew about it. Hell, he couldn't go anywhere on campus without hearing some sordid reference to it, often coded in the slew of inside jokes that had been birthed in the mile-long comments section. He'd thought that Elizabeth, being Elizabeth, had decided to ignore the talk in her brash, unapologetic way and go on with her life.

Today had effectively destroyed that thought, and he'd wanted—like he couldn't remember wanting anything else—to go to her and tell her it was all right. The people who knew her knew it wasn't true and the rest of campus could go to hell.

Instead, he'd walked away the second Professor Greenfield dismissed the class. He'd given Elizabeth his word he wouldn't bother her again and he intended to keep it. If she wanted to talk to him, she would. He knew her well enough to know that.

In the meantime, he'd have to content himself with reporting Wickham's posts as abusive. And sending screenshots to the administration so they knew what was going on. No matter what had happened with him and Elizabeth, she didn't deserve Wickham's smear campaign.

But beyond reporting Wickham, this had to end. Will was sick of being sick over this. What had happened couldn't be undone, and no amount of wishing would compel her to end the silence between them. And even if it did, what good would that serve? He'd come here to get his goddamned education and instead had spent his first semester acting like a teenager who just discovered the joys of masturbation. That he wasn't outright flunking any of his classes was a miracle, either of the divine or financial variety.

Will dropped his book bag onto his desk chair and fished his phone out of his pocket. If nothing else, speaking with Georgiana would provide him with a much-needed break from the torture that was his head. And thankfully, very soon, he'd be through with the semester from Hell and everything associated with it.

Will collapsed back on his bed as he tapped Georgiana's number. The phone rang once, twice, and just as he began to compose the message he'd leave her when it went to voicemail, she answered.

"Hey Will," came the weak greeting, followed by a snivel.

Will went ramrod straight. "What's wrong?"

"What? What makes you think something's wrong?"

"Well, the fact that something's wrong, for starters. Why are you crying?"

"I'm not crying."

"Georgie, this is me you're talking to. I am not other people. What's wrong?"

There was nothing for a moment, then a grumble sounded

through the line.

"What was that?" Will asked.

"I said I knew I shouldn't have answered. You're going to flip your lid and it's nothing."

Will's throat tightened. "It's not nothing. It's never nothing."

"It's just a part of the process, okay? Today happens to be a bad day. I get to have bad days."

"I think your definition of *bad day* needs to be worked on."

Georgiana was quiet a moment longer. When she started speaking again, her voice was low, soft, but rough in that telling way that Will knew all too well and hated, because there was nothing he could do to remove the pain.

"I had a panic attack," she said. "I watched...something I shouldn't have watched and it reminded... It triggered something of—"

"What did you watch?"

"Does it matter?"

Will held his breath, then released it on a long sigh. No, he supposed it didn't...except he'd want to make sure there were no copies of whatever it was within a ten mile radius of Pemberley. Perhaps he should look into parental locks for access to media. Was that even a thing anymore?

Fuck. This parenting by proxy thing sucked.

"Georgiana," he said again, doing his best to curb his temper, "I can't help you if you don't talk to me."

"This isn't something you can help with. I just gotta go through it on my own."

"That's bullshit and you know it."

A long sigh sounded on her end. "Look, I know this is hard for you to accept, but there really isn't anything you can do. It's one of those things we talked about before you left, okay? You told me you knew and understood I wasn't going to be one hundred percent every day."

"And you told me you'd call on those days so we could talk," he replied. "What did you watch?"

"It's not important."

"If it triggered you, it damn sure is."

Another brief silence. He heard her swallow.

"It's a Netflix show," she said at last. "I was sort've bingeing it. A girl in group said it was weirdly cathartic for her and the counselor was on the fence about recommending it and I wanted to get my own idea, so—"

"So you knew this could trigger you and you watched it anyway?"

"I knew parts of it could. There was another part I..." Georgiana trailed off, then drew in a deep breath. "I think if I'd seen it at any other time, I'd've been okay. Just the subject matter and this time of year and it's a whole mess of crazy inside the head of one Georgiana Darcy."

Will closed his eyes. This settled things nicely. "I'm coming home."

"What? No! Will, you—"

"If I leave here within an hour, I can be there by morning."

"Fitzwilliam Darcy, don't you dare!"

"It's cute when you try to tell me what to do."

"Please, Will." Her voice had grown thick, and he knew she was one good shove away from sobbing. "Please don't do this. Not again. You promised me you'd—"

"And you promised me you'd let me know when stuff like this happens," he replied. "Look, I was already thinking about cutting home early. This just made the decision for me."

"No! This is dumb. Look, I feel fine. I—"

"I had one class project and that's behind me. All I have left are finals, and three of those are papers that will be a lot easier to focus on if I'm not down the hall from Charlie."

Georgiana sniffed. "And the ones that aren't papers?"

"I'll work something out."

"Will—"

"Georgiana, it's good to be the king. Trust me, it'll all work out."

There was another pause, then she barked a laugh. "That's not fair," she complained. "Quoting Mel Brooks on me. Cheater."

"I play dirty when it matters." Will heaved out a breath and ran a hand through his hair. Each second that passed, he liked this new plan more and more. He felt he could breathe easier just knowing he'd be away from campus—from the mess he'd made of his life.

From Elizabeth.

"Cheating's never okay," Georgiana said. "And if you use me as an excuse to not get your degree, I swear I'm going to run away from home."

"I'm not using you as an excuse for that."

"But you are using me as an excuse?"

He hesitated. "Let's just say I could do with some home-time myself right about now. I need to get my mind off some things."

That seemed to pique her interest. "Oh?" Georgiana said, her tone careful. "Some *things?*"

"Yeah. That's right."

"You break up with your girlfriend?"

Will scowled, pulled away to glare at the phone, then pressed it again to his ear. "I never had a girlfriend."

"What about what Caroline said?"

"Caroline was wrong. Big shock."

"Yeah, I didn't buy it then and I still don't. I know you. If you're having trouble focusing, there was definitely a woman involved."

"Now I'm having trouble focusing?"

"I'm glad you admit it. Admitting it's the first step to recovery."

Annoyed as he was, Will felt his mouth twitch. If nothing else, learning that he had problems of his own seemed to have put Georgiana in a good mood. "When have I ever been distracted by a woman?"

"Never. But you're also usually never distracted. So what's her name?"

Will's throat tightened. "It's not important."

"I think that's for me to decide. Spill."

He waited a moment, considering, then blew out a long breath. "Tell you what," he said, "once I get home, I'll tell you whatever you want to know."

"I'm going to hold you to that, you know. You show up and I'm gonna follow you around until you tell me everything."

"Don't you think I know that?"

"And you still want to come home?" Georgiana let out a low whistle. "All right. Yeah. Get your butt here. I need some deets."

Will grinned in spite of himself. If there was going to be a silver lining regarding what had happened with Elizabeth, he was glad it involved Georgiana.

She was the only person in the world who could help convince his heart that the pain had been worth it.

26

The second he rounded the bend and Pemberley came into view, Will knew he'd done the right thing. The tension he'd carried with him from Meryton College seemed to evaporate.

There truly was no place like home.

He parked in the vast gravel circle drive that his father had sworn would be paved one day, but that day had never come. Cement didn't have character, his mother had argued, and it didn't look period appropriate. Will could appreciate that—appreciate the way he knew the gravel would crunch under his feet, the familiar clanking of tiny rocks hitting the air. He figured he could be anywhere, blindfolded, and know the Pemberley drive just from the sound.

Here, the outside world didn't exist. Nothing existed, especially not women who may or may not have shattered his heart.

Will heaved a sigh and threw his book bag over his shoulder. He hadn't bothered packing clothes or toiletries—he had more than enough of those at home. The only things he needed were the books, notes, and assignments that he was expected to keep up with in absentia. Even the weight of all the work ahead of him couldn't diminish the warmth of returning to the one place in the world he truly belonged.

It didn't hurt that the second he opened the door, Georgiana plowed him over with the force of her hug.

"You assface!"

Will blinked at the mop of strawberry-blonde currently plastered against him, then chuckled and wrapped his arms around her. "Missed you too."

Georgiana drew away almost immediately, her sparkling blue eyes—their mother's eyes—sharpened into daggers. "I can't believe you actually did this. Do you have any idea how dumb you are?"

"I have a feeling you'll let me know."

"Seriously, Will. I—"

Will held up a hand, silencing her. "We talked about this before I left. Plus there was the text message campaign and the never ending phone calls while I was on the road which, by the way, weren't at all distracting, thank you."

Georgiana crossed her arms and sniffed. "It's not my fault you didn't turn around."

"No, it's not," he said, his tone serious. "I know you have Colleen here during the day, but that's not the same as a full-time older brother."

"Will, I'm not a kid anymore."

"That might be the dumbest thing I've heard you say, but okay."

She rolled her eyes at him.

"Believe me," Will said, his voice dropping. "This is not a referendum on what I believe you can or can't handle. I wanted to come home as I believe I have now assured you for the seven hundredth time."

"Right," she replied, arching an eyebrow as her pinched expression melted into something worse. The only thing more dangerous than a pissed off Georgiana was a conniving Georgiana. "Because *Fitzwilliam's in looooove.*"

Though he'd known to expect it, Will couldn't help the way his gut twisted. "It doesn't matter. It's over. There really was nothing to begin with."

"Yeah, that'll work."

"Georgie—"

She rolled her eyes. "You know how this is gonna go, right? You withhold information from me and I'll hide your homework."

Will threw her a narrowed look. "You'll jeopardize my education because you're angry with me for coming home early and jeopardizing my education. A teenager's logic, through and through."

"Come on! She must be something special if she has your knickers in a wad."

"My what?"

She shrugged. "It's British for underwear."

"I know it's... That's not the point. When did you start talking like that?"

"Umm, binge-watching *Dr. Who*, duh." Georgiana rocked on her heels, grinning like an imp. "Will, your coming back early was contingent upon my learning about your girlfriend."

"Funny enough. I thought it was contingent upon me having a key and my name on the property title."

"You prom—"

Will held up a hand, unable to keep his lips from kicking up in a grin. God, he'd missed her. "I know," he said, then nodded at the sweeping stairway that took up the right side of the entry hall. "Let a guy at least get to his room and change before you start grilling him."

Georgiana furrowed her brow, suspicious. "You're not weaseling out of telling me all about her."

"I wouldn't dream of it."

Namely because he'd already resigned himself to telling her about Elizabeth. At least the parts that mattered.

A half hour later, freshly changed and showered, Will meandered into the grandiose front parlor—the same his mother had forbidden him and Georgiana from setting foot in as children. Too many family heirlooms, breakables, and pretty furniture to risk chocolate-stained fingers and childlike clumsiness. He found Georgiana on the antique settee by the fireplace—it had become her spot after the Wickham ordeal, particularly if she wanted to talk or read or nap. He'd once suggested bringing a television in here—Georgiana was something of a video-game junkie—but she'd refused. As much as possible, she wanted the house to remain as it had been before their parents had died. He didn't know if she'd ever outgrow that.

He didn't know if he wanted her to.

Will parked himself in the Leesburg armchair beside her, then leaned forward, resting his forearms on his knees. "You may begin your interrogation."

Georgiana looked up and grinned. And that grin made everything worth it.

"What's her name?" she asked.

"Elizabeth."

"Is she pretty?"

Will swallowed, his mind suddenly overrun with images of Elizabeth. Her smile, her brilliant brown eyes, the way she looked when she was heated, when she was passionate, when she was under him. Over him. On her knees in front of him.

He shifted. Those were not thoughts to think when with his sister. "Yes," he said at last. "Very pretty."

"Boring. Describe."

Will blinked. "Huh?"

"Tall and blonde? Short and redhead? Big boobs and hips? Paint me a word picture. I want to see this girl."

Seemed about right, when all he wanted to do was forget her. Still, Will had made a promise, and promises weren't something he'd go back on for reasons as petty as personal comfort. And he supposed if he told her enough she'd get off his case and he could enjoy the rest of his sabbatical Elizabeth-free.

"She's about your height," he started. "Long hair, brown. Brown and very thick." He'd tunneled his fingers into that thick hair, felt it slide across his skin. He'd never had a strong position on women's hair before he'd met Elizabeth. Hell, he hadn't even known he'd had a type, though now he wasn't sure what exactly that type was. Fierce and argumentative. Intelligent and quippy. Brutal and honest. Funny and charming.

"You would like her," he told Georgiana, managing a small smile. "She's fearless."

Georgiana straightened at that. "Oh?"

"And she wasted no time putting me in my place, from the first night we met to... Well, how we ended things."

"So things have officially ended. This isn't a temporary—"

"No," Will said shortly. "I thought it was something more than it was. She made it very clear that she... Well, she felt differently."

Some of the merriment faded from Georgiana's eyes. She reached over and clapped him on the shoulder. "I'm sorry."

"So am I, but I suppose these things happen."

"Yes, to people who aren't you. I've never seen you hung up on a girl before."

"I can't say I like the way it feels very much, so don't get used to it." Will hesitated. "She thought things about me that weren't...nice."

Georgiana scowled. "Bitch."

"Watch it."

"You're the nicest guy in the world. She—"

"Georgie, I love you, but how long did it take *you* to think that?"

Georgiana opened her mouth to protest, then closed it. "Okay," she said slowly. "Point taken. But in my defense, I was a fucked up kid with—"

"Language."

She stuck her tongue out at him. "Fuck that."

Will heaved a long-suffering sigh and bit back a grin when Georgiana giggled. "Elizabeth had her reasons for believing the things she did about me. Suffice to say, whatever it was is over now."

The scowl returned to his sister's face. "Just like that?"

"You might be getting the short version."

"But...you didn't try to talk to her?"

He snorted. "Believe me."

"But... Will, come on. If this girl has you all twisted up... It's just so not like you to walk away from something. Or someone."

"It's not that simple here."

"Why not?"

He didn't mean to say it, truly. Of all the things he'd anticipated talking with Georgiana about, the one topic he'd been determined to keep off limits was George Wickham. But by the same token, Georgiana wasn't a wilting flower, no matter how much Will wanted to treat her like one. It had been his own failings and inattentiveness that had led her to Wickham in the first place. So when he heard himself say, "Because of George Wickham," he found himself caught somewhere between courage and reservation.

Georgiana inhaled sharply and fell quiet for a long moment, during which the ticking of the clock on the marble mantelpiece became damn near deafening. At length, she wet her lips and straightened her shoulders. "Okay."

"Yeah? I don't have to go on."

"I know. But now you know you gotta, otherwise I'll be thinking crazier things than usual and we really can't have that." A strained, watery smile stretched across her lips. "For starters, Wickham's at Meryton?"

"Apparently he's interested in his education."

Georgiana rolled her eyes. "Yeah. That seems likely. I can't believe you didn't tell me this sooner."

Will arched an eyebrow. "How do you think that would've gone? You'd have spent a lot of time worrying and calling me every five seconds, and it wasn't like I wasn't distracted enough."

She seemed to consider this. "You're not wrong, but still. It's the principle of the thing." She swallowed and straightened again, as though the topic demanded better posture than usual. "Has he been awful?"

"Wouldn't be Wickham if he wasn't." Will offered a flat grin. "We haven't talked. I've seen him around campus here and there, but he makes a point of avoiding me and I can't say that hurts my feelings." He paused again, his thoughts going to Elizabeth, to the way she'd looked that night in her dorm. Her eyes filled with righteous heat, her mouth a firm, unmovable line. And then as she'd spat back every awful thing Wickham had filled her head with, the fact that she'd believed it...

"Will?" Georgiana seized his shoulder and squeezed. "What did he do?"

Will swallowed. "It's not so much what he did as what he said. To Elizabeth."

The pressure at his shoulder abated. Georgiana released a harsh exhale as her hand collapsed into her lap. "Is she okay?" she asked after a beat. "He didn't...hurt her, did he?"

"No." At least he didn't think so, and god he hoped not. He'd never forgive himself if he'd abandoned Elizabeth before Wickham had done something else unforgivable. "He told her some botched story about me, though. I don't know how he found out that I...that she meant anything to me, but he did, and he took it upon himself to rewrite history with me playing the bad guy. I don't remember his version of things—she yelled them at me the last time we talked—but there was enough truth in his lies to make it believable, apparently."

"Please tell me you told her the truth."

Will released a long breath. "I did. I told her everything. About me and you. Everything. And I am sorry for that—it wasn't mine to tell, but I did it anyway. I wasn't thinking clearly at the time, and I didn't let myself stop to reconsider. I was angry and hurt and she—"

"Stop making excuses. I'm glad you told her."

"You are?"

"Duh." She gave his shoulder a playful shrug that did more to convince him than words ever could. "In a perfect world, Wickham would be castrated. But this is not a perfect world, so unless he pisses off someone with a short temper and a very sharp knife, that's not going to happen. Which means other people out there can fall for his bullshit. I don't wish that on anyone." She rubbed her arms as though chilled. "But I'm guessing since the big reveal didn't result in you guys riding off into the sunset that she didn't believe you."

At that, his spirits lightened somewhat. "Actually, I'm fairly certain she did believe me."

Georgiana frowned. "So what's the problem?"

"Telling her the truth didn't magically change her opinion about me." Will pressed his lips together. "Actually, I'm not sure. We haven't spoken since I sent it."

"Sent what?"

"The email."

Georgiana blinked. "You sent her an email."

"To clear the air about Wickham, yes." And a few other

things that weren't worth getting in to at the moment. Will had reached an inner stalemate on the subject of Jane and he wasn't interested in shifting gears. "But even then, it doesn't matter. She wanted something completely different than what I wanted, and—"

"You told her about Wickham in an email. As in, not face-to-face."

"She'd made it pretty damn clear she didn't want to see me again."

Georgiana rolled her head back with a long groan. "God love you, Will, but you are such a fucking tool."

"Language!"

"Yeah, fuck that. I've earned a few eff-bombs."

"I think you've used them all."

She smirked. "Fuck that too. But seriously, *an email*? This isn't the kind of stuff you dump on a person in an email."

"Trust me when I say that it was more productive than trying to have a conversation with her. You don't explain things to Elizabeth. You argue with her. I wouldn't have gotten a word in."

"So essentially you took the wussy way out and gave yourself a handy excuse."

Will huffed a short laugh. "You don't know her."

"And you didn't try." Georgiana crossed her arms. "So she didn't reply to your email, I take it?"

"No."

"Go figure. How long was it?"

About the length of your average bible, give or take a few verses. But he wasn't about to tell her that. "As long as it needed to be."

"So for all we know, she hasn't made it to the end yet."

"Georgie—"

"And you haven't talked to her at all since sending it?"

"I told her I wouldn't. I told her I'd respect her wishes and leave her alone."

Georgiana released a long, full body sigh. "Fucking tool."

"Well, what would you have me do? Stalk her? Hound her into getting a restraining order? She told me in no uncertain terms how she felt—"

"Because Wickham lied about you and you're too much of a wuss to defend yourself in person. Yeah, bro, got that memo."

Will fisted his hands, his jaw tightening to the point of discomfort as he reminded himself that, yes, he truly did love his sister. Even during times like these, when she refused to consider viewpoints outside of her own. That much was a Darcy trait, anyway, and he wouldn't get far in pointing it out. "I did what I thought was right," he said at last, even and measured. "If she wanted to talk to me afterward, I would have listened."

"And I'm sure she knows that because you're a very clear, concise communicator who leaves no room for doubt," Georgiana agreed soberly. "I'll also bet that finding out that you'd been had by an assface like George Wickham isn't at all embarrassing and she doesn't think you think she's an idiot for falling for his bullshit."

At that, Will's chest tightened. That much hadn't occurred to him, but then, why should it? Elizabeth was a smart woman, and she knew he felt that way because, well, he'd told her. He had no reason to think she'd be ashamed now—enlightened, perhaps, but not ashamed.

Except he might not have sent that email when he was in his right mind, and since he hadn't been brave enough to revisit what he'd written, he couldn't say that it reflected his best self. In fact, he distinctly remembered wanting, *relishing* the idea of cutting her with his words, because dammit, she'd cut him with hers.

And smart though Elizabeth was, she was also proud. If she

learned that her judgment about Wickham had been so far off the mark...

Yeah, now he could see it.

"Trust me, Will," Georgiana said after a moment. "I know of what I speak."

Will dug his fingers into his palms and forced himself to relax. "Damn."

"Yeah."

"I screwed up."

"In a big ole way."

Will tossed his sister a glare. "You don't have to sound so pleased."

"That finally it's not me who made a colossal mistake? No, I think I do."

"I'm glad my heartbreak can at least serve some good."

"Hey, bright side of life, and all that jazz." Georgiana threw an arm around him and squeezed him into a hug. "And you can always make this better. After Christmas? How about you do some of that *mano a mano* communicating I hear it's all the rage these days."

The thought alone was enough to have Will's stomach in knots, but also delivered a shot of what could only be called hope. It was a sick, familiar feeling with a sick, familiar conclusion, but perhaps he was crazy, because it didn't sound like a horrible plan.

Maybe that was the travel fatigue talking.

"We'll see," he said, non-committal. That wouldn't be enough to convince Georgiana to drop the subject altogether, but he knew her well enough to know she'd recognize that he was done talking about it now. "What do you want to do for dinner, hmm? Order in or fix something here?"

"Umm," she said slowly, "you're here so you're making me breakfast for dinner. And I might add, duh."

Will grinned, thankful that some things didn't change. "Yes, ma'am."

All things aside, it was good to be home.

Figured. Fucking figured.

Elizabeth squeezed her eyes shut and counted to ten.

"You still there?" her father's voice came after a few seconds.

"Yeah, I'm still here." She blew out a long breath, gave her head a shake, and leaned forward in her desk chair. A few waves of the mouse and her final paper vanished in favor of Google. "I'm checking right now."

"Checking what?"

"My bank account. I'm joint on Mom's. It was easier. I should be able to see if any weird purchases have been made."

Her father sighed. "Thank god. I knew I could count on you, Lizzie."

She bit the inside of her cheek to keep herself from saying something she'd regret, but dammit, her fuse these days was even shorter than usual. Ever since her stupid presentation.

Ever since Will had stopped showing up for class.

But that was another matter altogether and she wouldn't think of it now while Mom was having one of her clockwork crises.

"So...she's in Florida. Or was as of four days ago." That was news to her. Elizabeth swallowed a lump of growing dread. Or tried to. It got stuck on the way down. "There's a charge for a room at a casino hotel. In St. Augustine."

Her father sighed.

"There's been activity as recently as three hours ago," Elizabeth said, scrolling through the list of transactions. "Looks like... wait a minute."

"What?"

"She bought a drink." That was not good news. "Or at least, this says Derby's Fine Wines and Spirits."

Her father released a long moan. "I knew it," he muttered. "I knew it. The second it went to voicemail, I knew something was wrong."

"I don't see why you called her in the first place," Elizabeth said shortly. It was easier to focus on her irritation with her father now that mother-induced anxiety was on the climb. She clicked open Google in another browser and typed in *Derby's Fine Wines and Spirits*. A handful of results populated the page, and yes, there were a few locations in St. Augustine. So maybe Mom hadn't left that area just yet.

"Your mother has a tendency to have...episodes on our anniversary. You know that."

"Yes, Dad. It was actually me, not an imposter, who was with her last year when she dyed her hair hot pink and maxed out her cards at Forever 21."

There was a pause. "I don't think that tone is necessary. I'm just worried about your mother."

"Yeah," Elizabeth shot back, feeling decidedly less than charitable. She was so sick of men getting their way with everything. From Wickham to Zelner to Will—even though Will didn't technically deserve to be lumped in with them, she could have done without the sloppy mess of feelings he'd left for her to sort out. "Thanks for taking the time from your busy schedule to let me know I have an errand to run."

"Lizzie, that's not fair—"

"Neither's life, so I'm told. But hey, I'll go deal with it. You can go back to your real life now."

She hung up before her father could fire anything back, and before her guilt could jump in and tell her how unfair that had been. Because fuck it. Fuck him and all men.

Elizabeth gave her head a shake and opened her email client. First things first—she needed to get her paper off to the professor, as well as an explanation as to why she wouldn't be turning it in in person.

Except apparently technology was conspiring against her. She tried several times to attach the final document to her email and kept receiving an error message. Elizabeth grabbed her phone again, preparing to fire off a text to Jane when she saw she had missed a text from the Meryton administration. A reminder that the campus server would be down for maintenance starting at seven and would not be up again until sometime past four in the morning.

She glanced at the clock on her phone. It was 7:03. Her father had called just in time.

Great.

Elizabeth chewed on her lower lip, her mind tripping over itself to come up with a solution. The next second she was on her feet, hastily shoving spare articles of clothing into a duffle bag she managed to rescue from the abyss that was the space under her bed. By the time she had packed everything up, she had a plan of action in place.

Twenty minutes and three sweeps of her room later, Elizabeth was outside Kitty and Lydia's dorm, banging on the door and doing her best not to snarl at the giggles rupturing from the other side.

Just once she'd like to have one of their problems.

"Oh, hey, Lizzie," Lydia said in her perpetually bubbly voice. "What's up?"

"I have to leave town for a few days," Elizabeth replied, shoving a flashdrive into Lydia's hands. "My term paper is on this. Can you please get it to Professor Greenfield?"

Lydia blinked at the flashdrive as though she'd never seen one before, the laughter fading from her eyes. "What?"

"My mom's in trouble." Maybe. "Can you please turn this in? The school system is down or I'd email it myself and I don't need to have this hanging over me while I make travel plans."

Lydia nodded, her expression falling serious in ways Elizabeth hadn't known it could. And then she experienced a jab of guilt for the mean thought—one that didn't do much to improve her already crappy mood.

"Is it serious?" Lydia asked, pocketing the flashdrive. "Is there something we can do to help?"

"No. I mean, I don't know, but thank you. I just...need to go find her." Elizabeth offered a soft smile. "Thank you, Lydia. I appreciate it."

"Of course."

Elizabeth was quiet for a still beat, then found herself propelled forward and into a tackle-hug Lydia clearly hadn't anticipated, but returned all the same. And dammit if that didn't make her cry.

"It's okay," Lydia said, patting her back awkwardly. "Everything will be okay."

On the Lyft ride to the airport, Elizabeth sent Jane a series of text messages explaining what had happened and asking her to check in with Lydia over the next couple days to make sure that paper got turned in. She then decided to spare her battery, as she wasn't sure what the next few hours were going to look like, and the packing frenzy she'd gone into meant her charger could be pretty much anywhere.

At the very least, she decided as she stormed up to the counter of the first airline that she saw, the next few days would give her little reason to think about Will Darcy. And given the state her mind had been in as of late, that was quite the silver lining.

27

Usually Elizabeth could sleep on airplanes just fine, but frustration, worry, and dread were a lethal combination, and could turn anyone into an insomniac. It wasn't until she was behind the wheel of her rental, Orlando in her rearview mirror and the morning sun crowning over the horizon that the universe decided to throw her a lifeline.

Her mother called.

Elizabeth pulled onto the shoulder of the freeway and answered, doing her best to keep her voice from shaking. "H-hello?"

"Lizzie, how are you?"

"Mom? Are you okay?"

A pause. "Why wouldn't I be okay?"

She exhaled a long breath. "Where are you?"

"I'm in bed at the moment. I just discovered I had several missing calls from you and your father. Is everything all right?"

Elizabeth was still for a long moment. Then she laughed. A harsh, ugly laugh that soon devolved into a series of ugly cackles.

"Lizzie, what in the world...?"

Tears were streaming down her cheeks and her body felt about ready to call it a day and crash. Cars zoomed past her on the freeway and she'd managed to rack up several hundred dollars on the credit card she'd been so diligently trying to pay off. And she couldn't stop laughing.

"Lizzie, you're scaring me."

"I'm in Florida."

"What?"

God, she must be losing it if her mother was the rational one between them. The thought tickled her insides and made her dissolve into laughter all over again.

"I'm in Florida," she said again once she got a hold of herself, wiping at her eyes and doing her best to keep her voice from trembling. "I flew in last night and I'm on my way to St. Augustine."

"I'm in St. Augustine!"

"I know. I saw the hotel charge. That's why I'm on my way."

"Elizabeth, what in the world has gotten into you?"

"Dad called last night. Said you...you weren't picking up when he tried to call you."

She blew a raspberry into the phone. Her *mother* blew a raspberry. "And just why would I want to talk to that man?"

"Mom, you know what yesterday was, right?"

"Of course I know what yesterday was. And pardon me if I think it's a bit strange to take a call from your ex-husband on the anniversary of a marriage that no longer exists. Is that the new trendy thing to do these days?"

Elizabeth expelled a deep breath, curling her free hand around the steering wheel, the part of her that had found the situation worth giggling over having run headfirst into annoyance. At least this was an emotion she was familiar with.

"He couldn't reach you. Then I tried and I couldn't reach you, either."

"So naturally, the logical thing to do was hop the first plane to Florida."

"I was worried. And I saw this was the last place you'd been, so..." She wasn't sure how to finish that so she didn't try, because the more she talked, the more her sleep-deprivation kicked in and the less sane her plan sounded. The most she knew about tracking someone down came from crime procedurals and detective movies, and smart money was on the bet that real life was a bit more complicated than that.

"Lizzie?" The concerned-mom tone was back, which only furthered her aggravation.

"What are you doing in Florida?" she asked.

"Well, I thought I'd take a vacation."

"Without telling anyone."

"Who was there to tell?"

"Me, for starters. And Dad."

Her mother scoffed. "I do not need my ex-husband's permission to go on vacation. And you? Every time I called, you yelled at me."

"Well, every time you called, it was because you'd flown off the handle!"

"And forgive me if that made me a little gun-shy. I didn't think you'd want to hear from me at all."

There it was. Right in the heart—the thing she'd known was coming. The cherry on top of the shit sundae that had become her life. She'd been an absolute moron where Wickham was concerned, a complete asshole where Will was concerned, and a terrible daughter to boot.

Elizabeth blinked, horrified to discover she was near tears.

"Lizzie?"

That did it. Elizabeth choked out a sob and slumped on the steering wheel, hard shudders wracking through her body. Fuck, everything hurt. Her arms, her lungs, her feet. Her side was still tender from the kid who had rammed into her while she'd been trekking through the airport and she was going on a full day without sleep. It seemed impossible that she had been in her dorm room just a few hours ago.

"Lizzie! Pull over right now."

"I...I am pulled over."

"Good." It was a tone she hadn't heard her mother use in the better part of ten years. "Now, calm down. I'm going to have Benito text you our location, all right?"

"B-Benito?"

"My lover, of course."

Elizabeth froze, then shuddered. There should be a law forbidding one's parents from using that word.

"Take your time and I'll see you when you get here," her mother concluded.

"Okay."

To her dismay, it took more than a few minutes to get herself under control once the conversation ended. Every time Elizabeth would begin to calm, she'd catch a glimpse of her reflection in the rearview mirror. Eventually, though, the hysterical bubble that had ballooned within her and she was left in the suffocating quiet of her rental car, face hot and wet, body worn out, and heartsick.

The smart thing to do would be turn around and get on a plane. Except the thought made her want to curl into a ball and hibernate for the next six months. And it wasn't as though she had much of a reason to head back with the semester nearing a close and the winter holidays on the horizon. Very few people would remain on campus over Christmas and suddenly, the thought of being among them—especially with Wickham's rumors about her still floating around—made her want to heave the contents of her stomach. Which she was pretty sure was nothing but water and airline peanuts at this point.

Plus, she needed to vet this Benito guy. Make sure he was the real deal before her mother got her heart broken all over again.

And no one fucked with her mother, goddammit.

So Elizabeth waited until her phone dinged with a message from an unknown number, listing the address of a beachside resort in St. Augustine. She asked Google for directions, and the affable robotic voice had her on the road again in seconds.

She vowed to have her shit together by the time she arrived.

The woman waving at her couldn't possibly be her mother.

Elizabeth blew out a long breath, staring at a face she hadn't seen smile in years. Then she cut her gaze quick to the rearview mirror again and almost recoiled in horror. Some girls could bounce back from a hard ugly-cry, but she was not among them. Elizabeth gave her head a shake—not that that helped matters —dragged a hand through the tangled mess that was her hair, and forced her aching muscles to move.

"Lizzie!" Her mother had developed the ability to teleport since they'd been apart, for her feet had barely touched the pavement before she found herself tackled by Lynette Bennet, the Pod Person. "I was so worried about you."

"I'm okay, Mom," she said, the words automatic rather than sincere.

"You didn't sound okay on the phone."

"Well, I wasn't okay then, but all's good now."

Her mother pulled back, lips pursed into a firm line of disapproval.

"So..." Elizabeth backed up a space and cut her gaze to the massive hotel. "Benito?"

A dopey, lovesick smile stretched across her mother's face.

"Oh, Lizzie, he's just marvelous. He owns this hotel, you know. And five more in Orlando and Daytona Beach."

"And you guys..."

"He's my lover."

Elizabeth wrinkled her nose and groaned. "Mom, don't say *lover.*"

Her mother giggled and clasped her hands together in her best schoolgirl imitation. "Well, what else should I call him? I'm a bit old to have a *boyfriend,* don't you think? And *male companion* just sounds so formal."

"So how long have you and Benito been..."

"Fornicating?"

"No!" She scrunched up her face and waved her hands as though this would help keep the mental image away. It didn't, and her imagination's portrayal of Benito wasn't exactly flattering. "I was going to say *seeing* each other."

An innocent blink. "Naked?"

"Mom!"

The cackle she earned gave her the horrible impression that her mother was doing this on purpose.

"I was on vacation with my dear friend, Yvonne Rogers. You know Yvonne, don't you?"

"Only since forever. When did you go on vacation with her?"

"Week before last."

"Over...Thanksgiving?"

"Well..." Her mother sniffed, looking a bit more like the Mom Elizabeth knew. "It wasn't like my *daughter* was going to see to me over the holiday, was it?"

"Mom, I told you that there was no point in going home. We weren't getting a long break and I had a ton of stuff to do to get ready for finals. And I did call. *You* decided not to pick up."

"Well, I was on vacation, wasn't I?" Her mother went back to beaming. "Anyway, there was an incident with one of the slot machines. I demanded to speak with the man in charge—Benito. Well, one thing led to another, and I ended up staying the night with him. I tell you, Lizzie, it was the best sex I've ever had."

Elizabeth felt herself go hot in the face. It was damn hard to remain sex-positive when the sex part involved someone who had given birth to her. "Umm, congrats?"

All she received was a shrug. "I can't lie. Your father was such a selfish lover. Everything was all about him. With Benito, I have never been so *in touch* with my body."

"You realize that you're paying my therapy bills, right?"

Her mother rolled her eyes. "Goodness, Elizabeth. When did you become such a prude?"

"I'm not a prude. I am, however, human, and don't yet have the mental bandwidth to look at this objectively."

"Well, get with the program. I had Benito reserve a room for you. The penthouse, actually." She beamed. "That was *his* idea. I think he's trying to impress me, the silly man. Why don't you take your things to your room and have a nice, hot shower. When you're ready, let me know and we can talk."

Any other time, the prospect of talking to Mom would have required a preemptive Advil and perhaps a Xanax. But this was not any other time—this was a bizarre parallel dimension in which Lynette Bennet was the calm voice of reason and Elizabeth was the one teetering on the edge of a nervous breakdown. She wasn't sure how she felt about that, but she was too damn tired to argue and a shower sounded like heaven. So she nodded, collected her duffle bag, and followed her mother into the hotel.

After her shower, Elizabeth thought it best to take a catnap before facing her mother. Running on fumes had never been a good look on her, and if her car breakdown was any indication, she needed to take a timeout from her head.

The catnap turned into an all day affair. When she awoke for good, the sun had dipped and cast the room into shadows. It took a few moments for Elizabeth's brain to come back online. She sat in the foggy confusion that inevitably followed a hard sleep, trying to remember where she was and why. And when the dots connected again, she immediately wished they hadn't.

Ugh. This was such a mess. She sighed and rolled her head, then decided to bite the bullet and see how many voicemails her mother had left over the last few hours, demanding where she was.

Zero.

That was...weird. And again filled her with the sense that she'd entered the Twilight Zone. She even checked that her phone was connected—it was. She had a message from Lydia confirming that the final paper had been successfully submitted to the professor, and another from Jane expressing her concern and wishing her a good holiday.

The world had indeed continued to spin. She was the only anomaly here.

Elizabeth fought to her feet, her limbs weighted with a different kind of exhaustion now as she forced herself to dress and run a brush through her hair. A glimpse in the mirror revealed she looked mostly human.

When she returned to her phone, she had a new text message from her mother.

You alive in there?

She shook her head and typed out a quick response. *Just woke up.*

The three dots indicating the other person was typing ballooned up almost immediately.

Mom: Good. I assumed you'd pass out for a while. Want to grab dinner?

Elizabeth: Do I get to meet Benito?

Mom: Sadly no. He is entertaining some business friends tonight. Plus, I thought it would be best if it was just you and me.

"Who are you?" she muttered to the screen, but gratitude blossomed in her gut and some part of her relaxed. She definitely wasn't up to meeting new people just yet.

Elizabeth: Have anything in particular in mind?

Mom: Meet me at the hotel restaurant in 10.

The thought of food had Elizabeth's stomach immediately excited. She hadn't eaten since the plane and she was pretty sure that didn't count. Time to refuel.

Her mother was waiting for her when she arrived, smiling patiently. "You look so much better," she said. "Did you sleep well?"

The comment—like pretty much everything else that had happened in the last day—caught Elizabeth off guard. She wasn't wearing makeup and had thrown on a baggy long-sleeved tee and a pair of leggings. The Lynette Bennet of old would have refused to be seen with her in public.

But since these incidents were coming faster, she decided it was better to adapt than overanalyze. Otherwise she'd be a blinking idiot all night.

"Umm, yes," she replied at length. "Hard, at least. I have a nap hangover."

Mom laughed and waved to the seating hostess.

The expediency of service and the way the staffers kept deferring and cooing over her mother forced Elizabeth to accept that this Benito guy likely wasn't a hallucination, though she hadn't ruled out the possibility that she was languishing in a psych ward after having had a mental breakdown.

As though sensing her thoughts, her mother turned to her

with a smile that highlighted the reasons her father had married her in the first place. Lynette Bennet had been a beautiful woman in her youth. She was beautiful still, Elizabeth realized a little belatedly, once the mom-goggles were forced aside.

"Would you stop that?" Mom asked, smiling still.

"What?"

"Looking at me like I'm an alien."

"Are you?"

She lifted a shoulder. "I feel like it. The past few days have been marvelous in ways I didn't think possible anymore."

"Because of...Benito."

"Well, yes. He's a big part of it. A *huge* part of it, if you catch my meaning."

Elizabeth groaned and dropped her face into her hands. "I wish you'd stop saying things like that."

"I'm a woman in her prime, Lizzie, and I haven't had decent sex since before you were born. I think I'm entitled to brag a little." Her mother arranged her napkin in her lap. "Let me put one mystery to bed. Right after you started school, maybe the second or third week, your aunt and uncle convinced me to change doctors."

Elizabeth blinked. "They did?"

"Yes. Dr. Henderson was...well, an ass. He didn't listen to me, just threw whatever medication was most convenient for the symptoms I described and showed me out." She pursed her lips. "For years I thought it was me. That the medication wasn't working because of something I did. I took it and I felt bad. I didn't take it and I felt bad. And every time I had an issue I wanted to discuss, Dr. Henderson waved me off and increased my dosage."

Guilt clenched her stomach. Dr. Henderson had been her decision—granted, a decision based on a quick internet search and cemented on the fact that, unlike others in the area, he'd been taking new patients at the time. Elizabeth swallowed. "I'm sorry—"

"No, Lizzie, don't be sorry. You did the best you could."

That only made her feel worse. "I could've done better."

"How?" her mother replied, blinking, her expression earnest. "You were a child."

"I was eighteen."

"That's what I said. Your world had just collapsed on you as well. Your father was no help. He was off living his new life. You saw that I needed help and tried to give it, best you could." She took another drink of wine. "My new doctor has been a miracle worker. Got me off the crap Henderson was giving me and actually listened. I tell you, Lizzie, even though the new medication takes a few weeks to have an effect of any kind, I felt immediately better just being *acknowledged.*"

"And Dr. Henderson didn't acknowledge you."

"I think he thought I was making it up." Mom rolled her eyes. "In the beginning, I saw Dr. Shumaker—that's my new doctor—twice a week for twelve weeks. Your aunt and uncle helped pay for it. I didn't want them to, but they insisted. After that, we moved to weekly visits and a couple calls. This is actually the longest I've gone without checking in with her, but we're going to resume visits after the New Year."

Elizabeth pressed her lips together, and despite her attempts to keep them at bay, she felt the familiar sting of tears behind her eyes. But dammit, she wouldn't cry. Her mother was better—for the first time since the divorce, she was *herself.* This was all that mattered.

"The best thing you could have done for me was leave when you did," her mother continued. "It felt like abandonment at the time, but...your leaving *forced* me to start living on my own for the first time. That first week, I was a mess, but it was exactly what I needed. I needed to learn how to live without depending on others, and I don't think I would have been open to that if I hadn't been so desperate without you to lean on. When your aunt came to see me and suggested changing doctors, I was willing to do just about anything. And that was best decision I've made in a long, long time. And things are good now. Really good. I will admit, Benito helps, but he's not the reason. He's just a perk." Her mother blinked, her eyes going a little glassy. "I am glad you came down, Lizzie. I've missed you."

Elizabeth swallowed. "I've missed you too." And those words hit her like a ton of bricks, because she *had* missed her. A lot. This version of her mother whom she'd forgotten existed. Hell, the woman had always been her own kind of crazy, but the past few years had taken them out of sitcom territory and into a fresh hell. That her mother had any other setting but batshit had almost faded from her memory.

But there was this version, or something like it—the woman who had played with her growing up, cornered her into tickle fights, let her lick the cookie dough off the spoon. The person her mother had been before she'd had her breakdown. Before things had gotten so bad a simple phone call had the power to zap Elizabeth's energy.

"Now," Mom said after the waiter had placed their salads in front of them, "you tell me what's going on with you. I've let you stall enough."

Elizabeth felt her cheeks go hot. "It's nothing."

"Lizzie..."

"Really. It's...dumb. My problems aren't problems."

"If they are causing you trouble, then they are problems."

"Compared to what you've been through?"

"Honey, take it from someone who knows...comparing yourself to others is going to get you nowhere fast." Her mother took a bite, then waved her fork in the air. "Homelessness."

"What?"

"Homelessness is a big problem. Much larger than anything I went through, right? I always had a roof over my head, no matter how bad things got. But does that make my problems less real?"

"All right. Point made."

"So." Her mother leaned forward, resting her elbows on the table. "Tell me."

So she did. She started with the party she and Jane had attended before the start of semester, and once the words were out, a nuclear blast couldn't have stopped them. And hard as it was, she found a part of herself felt lighter as she unloaded. Reciting the story from the beginning was freeing in ways she wouldn't have imagined, and by the time she wound down to the call she had received from her father, she felt lighter than she had in weeks.

The only part she omitted was the specifics of Will's email. That wasn't her secret to share.

"Hmm." Her mother pursed her lips together, considering. "If I'd known your life would be this interesting, I would have had you followed by one of those reality television camera crews."

In spite of herself, Elizabeth barked a laugh. "Thanks. Any other pearls of wisdom?"

"That Wickham person should have his penis cut off." She made a face and shook her head. "I can see now why you leapt at the opportunity to track me down. By the way, I'm paying off your credit card."

Elizabeth blinked. "Huh?"

"And your first full year at Meryton."

"Mom—"

She held up a hand. "I won eight hundred thousand dollars. I will do with it as I see fit."

"You...*what*?"

"I told you this."

"You did *not* tell me this."

Her mother blinked, frowning. "I'm sure I told you. That was how I met Benito."

"You said there was a slot machine incident."

"Well, yes. *That* was the incident."

"The incident is you won *eight hundred thousand dollars*?" The words sounded so damn bizarre—the concept alone too monstrous to consider. It would have been more believable had her mother announced that she was actually from Neptune and her people were coming to collect her any day now.

Good god, when did my life become an actual soap opera?

"I wanted the money in cash," her mother continued conversationally. "Apparently casinos don't provide cash payouts over certain amounts. And Benito came down to talk to me. That's how we met. And now I'm using that money to do any number of things, including paying for your college and wiping the balance off your credit card."

Elizabeth didn't know how to respond to this. Her brain was still trying to reconcile with the jackpot shock. Leaping ahead to tuition and credit cards required concentration. "You didn't even want me to go to college."

"I didn't want you to leave me. It was selfish and wrong. You *need* your education. And to be self-sufficient. Exiting college with debt is no way to do that."

"Mom, Meryton isn't cheap."

"I know. But I can afford it. I can also afford to pay back my sister, and *lawd* I am looking forward to that. You know how she can hang things over you for years." She smiled and straightened, then started rummaging in her purse. "I was going to wait until after dessert to give you this," she said, pulling out a thick envelope, "but now seems appropriate."

"What are you—"

"I'd love it if you could stay with me and Benito this Christmas, honey," she said, slipping the envelope across the table, "but I'm afraid he's taking me to Madrid to meet his family."

"...His family?"

Mom nodded. "We're getting married in the spring. Isn't that wonderful?"

God, she was going to have whiplash. "Isn't that *fast*?"

"When you get to be our age, my dear, nothing seems too fast. And when you know, you know."

"Mom—"

Her mother cut her off with a wave. "I know this seems reckless. And maybe it is. But I promise you, Lizzie, I am thinking clearly. I see things very differently these days."

"But how can you get married?" Elizabeth blurted. "After... after what Dad did... What happens if Benito does the same thing?"

"If Benito and I don't work out, we don't work out."

"Just...just like that?"

Her mother shrugged. "Well, I certainly hope we do. I *believe* we will, otherwise I wouldn't marry him." A pause. "Lizzie...you need to understand something about me and your father."

Elizabeth inhaled a deep breath, bracing herself. She didn't know how many more bombshells she could take.

"I knew he was going to leave."

The world went crooked. This was so fundamentally against everything she knew, her immediate response shot well beyond shock and landed firmly in Camp Anger. "No," she replied, heated, "you didn't."

"Sweetheart," her mother replied, tone patient, "I knew he was going to leave *for years.*"

"But... No. No, that's not right. I know it wasn't perfect, but you were so happy. And he left and it..." Elizabeth's vision went blurry again. "How could you seem so happy and not be?"

There was nothing for a moment. "I pretended for me, and he pretended for you. But pretend can't last. I did love your father very much, and losing him and our pretend happy life was very hard. But *pretend* is all it ever was."

This was a bit large to unpack. Elizabeth didn't think she could get to the other side all at once, and her brain hadn't recharged enough to give it a try. "And you're okay with...with *chancing* that again."

"It's different with Benito."

"How?"

"Because he knows me. In just a few days, he knows me better than your father ever did. I am my *real* self with him."

"But it could still end."

"Yes. That's a risk I'm willing to take."

"I don't understand that." Especially when she, Elizabeth, wasn't okay with risking it at all. And hell, might as well put that out there. "The thought of going through any of that terrifies me. So much so I decided that it wasn't worth it. I've dated here and there, but only safe guys. Guys I wasn't all that invested in. I knew what I was doing, too. It wasn't subconscious. It was a very deliberate choice. To avoid... Well, to avoid."

Her mother shook her head and patted Elizabeth's hand again. "You're smart enough to know that's not a way to live."

"It was a way to survive. For me."

"But does it make you happy?"

Elizabeth opened her mouth, but she knew her answer was a lie. The past few months avoiding her feelings for Will hadn't brought her much beyond confusion, self-hatred, frustration and a few other things. She'd been so desperate not to want him that she'd allowed herself to believe a story that was incompatible with the guy she knew because it was more convenient for her if it was true. Well, not entirely convenient, because she'd still all but thrown herself at him, but she'd done so while thinking the worst of him and herself as a result.

And no, it had made her the opposite of happy.

Thankfully, her mother didn't push her for a response. Instead, she drew back. "*I* am happy," she said. "For the first time in years. And that's what I want for you, darling. Whatever it looks like. Whatever gets you there."

Elizabeth was quiet for a moment longer. At last, she offered a watery smile. If nothing else, she could be happy for her mother. "Good. Though Benito better be warned I am a force to be reckoned with if he hurts you."

"Oh, believe me, he knows. If nothing else, your hopping on a plane to hunt me down convinced him not to underestimate you." Her mother grinned. "I appreciate and love you so much, Lizzie. Never doubt it. And I think after the months you've had, you should treat yourself for Christmas."

She lowered her gaze to the envelope between them and nudged it closer.

Elizabeth had nearly forgotten it was there. "What's this?"

"Your Christmas present."

"Mom—"

"Retroactive from the past few years, plus interest."

"I don't think that's how Christmas works."

"Darling, I'm marrying a multi-billionaire. Yes, billion with a *b*. Christmas officially works the way I say it does." Her mother sat back, her grin even wider. "You need a break. Why don't you take some time on the way back? There are some fascinating historical sites around here. Have you ever wanted to tour Civil War battlegrounds? There are dozens in this area."

"Yeah. That sounds Christmassy."

"Well, I know Derbyshire is gorgeous this time of year and it's not too far from your school. Even if you don't want to tour anything, Benito has told me they have a lot of holiday-themed events in that area."

Derbyshire. The name sounded familiar, but she couldn't place it in the moment. "I don't know."

"Some of these tourist places have wonderful holiday cele-brations planned," Mom continued. "Take some time for you. That's what I want you to get me for Christmas."

Elizabeth arched an eyebrow.

"The knowledge that my daughter is taking care of herself," her mother clarified. "Please don't argue with me. I can always just put this into our joint account before I remove myself as a signer."

"You're removing yourself as a signer?"

"Yes. Likely sometime next week, before we leave."

"Hey, if you won all this money, why didn't I see it when I signed into the online banking?"

Mom batted her eyes girlishly. "I told you, Benito and I met because I wanted the payout in cash."

"And—"

"I had to sign some tax forms, but in the end..." She lifted a shoulder. "It's in his safe until I open a new account. And what-ever's left in the old one is yours as well."

"Mom—"

"Lizzie, I am not taking no for an answer."

Elizabeth was quiet a long moment, fingers tapping the envelope as she attempted to estimate just how much cash she'd find in there once she was in a place to count. Certainly more than she'd ever had before, and that knowledge both made her nerves come to life and filled her with guilt. Walking away with this in her purse seemed criminal.

"Elizabeth."

She looked up.

"Take the money and run," her mother said. "I want you to."

"I..." Elizabeth swallowed. At her best, her mother had always been open and generous. And mule-stubborn. She *wouldn't* take no for an answer.

There was no use in trying.

Elizabeth blew out a breath, relaxing her shoulders. "Okay," she said.

"Okay? You're not going to argue?"

"No, but if you want to give me the speech you have prepared, I don't mind."

"You knew I had a speech prepared?"

Elizabeth shrugged. "It's something I would do."

"And you are nothing if not my daughter."

An odd sense of serenity encompassed her, warming her from the inside. Elizabeth studied her mother for a long moment, overwhelmed with something she couldn't name.

"Yes," she agreed finally. "Yes, I am."

"You're where?"

Elizabeth flopped back on the bed, gripping her phone tightly to avoid dropping it. "Some place called Derbyshire." A place that still sounded way too familiar to her brain, but she'd somewhat given up on finding out why. "It's gorgeous here. The streets downtown are actual cobblestone. Hand to god. I might never leave."

"But how did you get to Derbyshire?"

"By car."

"Lizzie..." Jane sighed. "You can be so difficult at times. You know that?"

"I've been told," she replied dryly, rolling onto her stomach. "My mother—"

"Is she all right?"

"Did I not tell you?"

"This is literally the first I've heard from you in seventy-two hours. Last I knew, you'd landed and were in line to rent a car."

Elizabeth winced. "Oh."

"Yes, *oh*. So your mother's all right?"

All right wasn't quite the term she'd use. Downright giddy, maybe. Lucid for the first time in Elizabeth's adult life—quite possibly. And her favorite parent at the moment.

"Lizzie?"

"I don't even know where to start. I guess with...my mom's getting married."

"She's what?"

"And she won eight hundred thousand dollars at a casino."

A beat. "Huh?"

"And she's...happy."

She could practically see Jane's scowl. "Well, let's start with the money. Eight *hundred* thousand dollars?"

Elizabeth grinned and launched into the story, which sounded even less plausible coming out of her mouth. She kept waiting to spy evidence of a camera crew, but since she'd made it out of Florida without being asked to sign a talent release form, she had no choice but to believe everything was true.

Plus, she'd met Benito. And she'd Googled the hell out of him. He was the real deal—self-made real estate mogul with a fat wallet and a dopey-ass smile that spread across his face every time he looked at her mother. He'd tried to buy Elizabeth a car before she'd left St. Augustine, insisting it was his pleasure now that they were practically family. But that had been the line—money from her mother she already felt a little guilty for accepting. Extravagant gifts from a virtual stranger were a completely different beast, regardless of the fact that said stranger was on the fast track to becoming her stepfather.

By the time she finished relaying this to Jane, her throat was scratchy and her mouth was dry. And there was nothing but silence on the other end of the line.

"Jane?"

A breath.

"Jane? Can you hear me?"

"Lizzie..." Another breath. "Your life is...weird."

She couldn't help it—she burst out laughing. "Noticed that too, huh?"

"Kinda hard to miss," Jane agreed. "So, where is this Derbyshire place?"

"Pretty close to Meryton, actually. The entire town's done up for Christmas. Seriously, garland around lampposts—they actually have lampposts—and ribbons and everything. The whole place is a Hallmark holiday special come to life. Except it's in the mid fifties and I doubt we'll have a white Christmas."

"Are you at a hotel?"

"A bed and breakfast called Hunsford House." Elizabeth shifted her attention to the clock on the nightstand. Nearly ten, but it felt later, and after the day she'd spent sightseeing, she was somewhat bushed. The Collinses, who owned Hunsford House, served their guests breakfast promptly at eight o'clock in the morning. "Not the nicest place in Derbyshire, but it's cute. And they had an opening. Apparently the whole town is completely booked through Christmas."

"Really? What's there to do there?"

"Lots of little shops and there are a ton of antebellum townhomes to tour."

"Oh, riveting," Jane replied dryly.

"I know what you're thinking, but the tours I went on today weren't as pro-slavery as I expected," Elizabeth said. "One of the guides actually kicked off the tour by telling us that Derbyshire houses were essentially monuments the wealthy whites used to show off how wealthy they were, but they were built with the blood and sweat of enslaved people. And another tour guide corrected this guy who asked how the servants were cared for. Said specifically that they were slaves, not servants. It was...enlightening."

"So...you're surrounded by guilty white people."

"A lot of them, yes."

Jane snorted. "That actually might be worth checking out some time. I tried to tour an old place like that with my folks when we were vacationing in Louisiana when I was a teenager. The others in the group kept giving us the side-eye, like we were on display too."

"Well, I'm not saying you won't get that here. It *is* North Carolina."

"Sure. We can't expect too much progress."

"But they do seem to be making strides to be woke." Elizabeth smirked. "The people are nice enough. Those I've met, at least. And the Collinses are friendly. Well, the wife is. The guy is a little on the weird side. He's obsessed with a house called Rosings."

"That's a house?"

"Apparently. And it's owned by the whitest, richest lady in town."

"Hard pass."

"Yeah," Elizabeth agreed. "It's not a tour home, but he mentioned possibly getting a special invite there at least three times when I was checking in."

"So what are your plans for tomorrow?"

"Eat, shop, hit some tour homes and maybe see about scoring tickets to *A Christmas Carol*. The town puts on a production in the square each year and apparently it's all the craze. How about you?"

"Obsessively hit *refresh* on Blackboard until my final grades post. Then and only then will I know whether or not this Christmas will be a merry one."

Elizabeth bit the inside of her cheek. Before she'd left St. Augustine, she'd made the conscious decision to abstain from anything related to her academic life, which meant no checking email and no stalking Blackboard for updates on her semester grades, which she was confident would be good, if not outstanding. Her focus might not have been where it needed to be the last few months, but she'd always been a good student, even when she found it difficult to commit herself to whatever she was studying.

She'd begun to wonder if leaping right from taking care of her mother and into schoolwork had been setting herself up to fail. But if she hadn't made the decision to enroll in Meryton when she had, she might never have met Jane, and that would have been a true travesty.

She'd also not know the name Will Darcy. And at the moment, she wasn't sure whether or not she wanted to.

"I need a break," she said at last.

"I agree. I just don't know how any break could be enjoyable if you don't know how you did."

"I know me," Elizabeth replied dryly. "If I log on to see my grades, I'll decide to start obsessing over next semester classes. Maybe jump start on the reading. Which isn't the worst idea in the world, granted...but I think I deserve to not think for just a little while. So I'm not going to tempt myself by logging on."

"More power to you."

Elizabeth hesitated, debated whether or not she wanted to know, then bit the bullet and asked. "Anything...eventful happen after I left?"

"No. Lydia turned in your paper, I made sure."

"And...other people? How are they?"

"The only other people that you know are me and Mary. Mary's going to her girlfriend's for Christmas and my dad's picking me up tomorrow."

There was no good way to ask if Will had turned up without drawing attention to herself, and she somewhat doubted Jane would have noticed that regardless. And it seemed unlikely that he'd return to campus before the Christmas break, but part of her couldn't help but wonder. The rest of her was tired of going in circles where Will was concerned. There had been mistakes, some hers—many hers—but some his, as well. And no matter how much she wanted to right some of those wrongs, the healthy thing to do was look forward.

"Lizzie?"

Elizabeth shook her head and eyed the clock again. "I think I'm gonna hit the hay."

"Before eleven? That doesn't seem like you."

"This trip has reminded me of how very much I love sleep. And how real beds feel."

"Fair point. It's gonna be difficult coming back but I am looking forward to being in my own room at home." Jane yawned. "Love you, Lizzie. If I don't talk to you before Christmas, please have a good holiday. And let me know if you want to come play the role of my adopted sister. My folks would be happy to have you."

"I think I'll be fine, but thank you. And Merry Christmas yourself."

Ten minutes later, teeth brushed and jammies on, Elizabeth slid between the sheets of her rather comfortable rented bed. Hunsford House might not be the best rated B&B on TripAdvisor, but the room was cozy, if Spartan, and the house was within walking distance of pretty much everything.

The room was hers until the day before Christmas Eve. Then Elizabeth would have to find new accommodations, if she didn't decide to spend the actual holiday on the road.

Her thoughts before drifting off to sleep drifted back to Will, bringing with them the stab of something unfinished that she couldn't outrun. And she wondered for the millionth time if he still thought about her at all, and what she might do to keep from worrying over things she couldn't change.

Or could, but didn't have the guts to approach.

Because wherever he was, he was almost certainly not thinking of her.

"Good morning, Ms. Bennet."

Elizabeth greeted her host with a sleepy smile and a wave as she stepped off the staircase. Like the day before, the sunroom, which connected the owner's quarters to the main hall, was set up for breakfast. "Morning."

"And how did you sleep?"

The answer was fitfully, but she had no one to blame for that but herself. Without more distractions, like her mother, Jane or schoolwork, Elizabeth had had no reason to not think about Will Darcy.

And once that floodgate opened, she couldn't close it.

"The bed is very comfortable," she answered at last, because at least that much was the truth. "Thanks."

Charlotte Collins offered a warm smile, placing a tray of biscuits on the table. "Like yesterday, the coffee is over on the side table. It's just you and me today. Liam is getting things ready for the pageant this evening."

Elizabeth nodded and made her way to the carafe. That was right—her other host was a minister. He was on the young side and had an air about him that stank of failed car salesmen.

"He wanted me to pass along his apologies," Charlotte continued. "He doesn't think he'll be able to get you into Rosings. Which really is a shame, if you've enjoyed the other homes in the area."

"I have," Elizabeth said, eyes glued to the stream of life-essence pouring into her coffee mug. "Though none of this has been what I expected."

"How so?"

"I dunno. I think of old southern houses and a sort of *Gone with the Wind* picture comes to mind." She paused as she nursed the first drink, reveling in the sensation of her veins warming. "The period of the Civil War has always fascinated me. Before and after. The first place my dad ever took me was to Gettysburg." It was actually one of the few good memories she had of childhood concerning both her parents. "Between that and my mom watching *North and South* over and over... I guess I had this picture in my head of what this place would be like when my mom mentioned it."

"*North and South*?"

"You know. Patrick Swayze. Incredibly bad acting. Steamy love scenes." Elizabeth waggled her eyebrows. "I tell you, I got more of my sex-ed from watching Orry Main and Madeline LaMotte get it on than I did from school."

Charlotte just blinked, though her cheeks had turned a little pink.

"I'm being totally inappropriate, aren't I?"

"Well, let's just say we're lucky Liam isn't home." A small, somewhat conniving grin crossed her face. "He gets embarrassed easily."

Elizabeth shrugged and took her place at the table. "Well, thank him for trying to get into Rosings for me, but it's probably just as well that I don't go. The stuff I read about it online last night pretty much convinced me I'd knock something over the second I walked inside." She hesitated. "And it's kinda..."

"Overwhelming?" Charlotte offered.

"Well...yes and no. The houses are pretty but...repetitive. And I am not sophisticated enough to know or appreciate antique furniture. It just seems like every house has the same stuff. And I'm not as interested in that. The stories are fascinating and...kinda horrible too." She hesitated to see if Charlotte would question what she meant by that, but she didn't, and that might be for the best. Elizabeth didn't need to piss off the person providing her room and board tonight. That seemed more like a last day kind of thing. "Anyway, I guess it's more that the people who designed these houses meant for them to be in the family for years, not turned into museums. That's why I was at all interested in Rosings, because it *has* been in that family since it was built. I was looking forward to seeing how it's changed over the years. But from what I read online—"

"It's another museum," Charlotte said, nodding. "I thought the same thing when I moved here. Liam had just bought this house and wanted to restore it, and was determined that it meet Mrs. De Bourgh's standards."

"That's the woman who owns it, right?"

"Right. She's from one of the oldest families in the area, which makes her Derbyshire royalty. She's also one of the wealthiest women in the country. Liam worships her." Charlotte's eyes widened. "I need to watch what I say. That could be taken the wrong way."

Elizabeth bit the inside of her cheek to keep from grinning —or saying something that might make her host uncomfortable. But she had determined from her limited interactions with Liam Collins that he was one of those people who assumed wealth was contagious. Or thought he might end up the beneficiary if he climbed far enough up a rich person's ass. His erratic, sometimes flamboyant personality and behavior was at such odds with the woman currently filling her orange juice. How they had ended up married was beyond her. Though Elizabeth had wondered if perhaps Charlotte was Liam's beard. Twenty-first century or not, it had to be hard living as a gay man in a small southern town, especially if he wanted to continue preaching. Though what would be in it for Charlotte, she didn't know. And she wasn't nosy enough to dig to see if that theory held water.

"There is a home just outside of town that's still owned by

the family," Charlotte continued a moment later. "And it's absolutely nothing like Rosings. I might be able to get you in if you're interested. The housekeeper is a good friend from my women's bible study class."

"Oh?" Elizabeth popped a strip of bacon in her mouth. "So this house has more than just indoor plumbing?"

Charlotte smirked. "Yes. They even have Wi-Fi, I hear."

"And the historical society hasn't fined them?"

"With the money the family has, I imagine they can keep up with the fines."

Elizabeth laughed aloud, caught off guard. "Damn."

"Would you like me to see if you can swing by?"

"It wouldn't be weird? Random person coming by a private house out of the blue?"

Charlotte shook her head and batted a hand. "It happens all the time, actually. They don't always say yes, but if Colleen is there and has a free moment, she's happy to show people around. So long as she has advanced notice and someone to vouch for whoever's going into the house."

"And you feel comfortable vouching for me?"

"Of course." There was that smirk again. "Typically because whoever I send there has paid with a credit card to stay here. If something goes missing, I have some ways to make their lives difficult."

Elizabeth arched her eyebrows. "And since I'm paying cash?"

The woman's eyes positively sparkled with mischief. In another life, another world, Charlotte might have just been her best friend.

"I'll just have to get inventive," she said.

29

To see this house was to enter a painting or a reel from an old film. It had taken every bit of Elizabeth's control to keep the car from colliding into one of the many live oak trees that lined the winding country road outside Derbyshire. The homes inside the town limits were all gorgeous pieces of architecture, but seeing a mansion standing against a backdrop of greenery had caught her completely off guard. She could only imagine what this place looked like in the spring.

Charlotte hadn't been wrong when she'd said it was impossible to miss. The home was eggshell white, completely encircled by large columns and centered among a variety of scattered, smaller but no less beautiful dependencies. The road curved ahead and gave way to a gravel drive that looped around the a marble fountain situated in the middle of the lawn. A smattering of oaks adorned the grounds in an organized yet somehow still chaotic pattern that she was certain had been intentional by the original builder.

The whole setting looked untouched by time, and the sound of her car engine seemed at odds with the otherwise peaceful tranquility of the environment. It was a dumb thought, she knew, yet even with an invitation—and Charlotte had sworn that her friend was delighted to show her the house—she couldn't shake the sensation that she was intruding.

But that didn't stop her from putting the car in park and climbing out. Elizabeth inhaled deeply, craning her neck as the shadow of the massive house threatened to swallow her whole. She scaled her gaze up the Corinthian columns, which were wrapped with elegant strings of garland and lights, and tried to imagine the scene this must present at night. Elizabeth blinked and turned her attention ahead again, the steps along the gravel walkway hitting her ears as loud and obnoxious. When she looked back to her rental, she was struck again at how out of place it looked. A large anachronism dumped unceremoniously on an otherwise pristine portrait of antebellum architecture.

The porch was a full wraparound, painted sky blue. The wood creaked pleasantly under her feet—just enough to let her know it was well used. Elizabeth straightened her shoulders as she drew to a halt outside the front door, which was flanked by a set of pocket windows. Two miniature designer Christmas trees had been placed in front of them, preventing her from stealing a glance of what was inside.

This family, whoever they were, really did Christmas.

Then the door opened, nearly startling Elizabeth out of her skin. She jumped, forcing out an awkward laugh. "Sorry," she said. "I usually don't gasp my hellos."

The woman on the other side of the door had a warm look about her, which went a long way in putting Elizabeth at ease. Her eyes were soft, her face sun-kissed and pretty. If she had to guess, Elizabeth would put the woman in her early fifties. "Just as well," she replied by way of greeting, "I usually let guests ring the bell before opening the door. But I thought you might be out here for a while if I waited for you to announce yourself." The woman stepped aside and gestured for Elizabeth to enter. "I'm not wrong to assume you're the young woman staying with the Collinses?"

"Yes. I'm Elizabeth."

"And I'm Colleen Reynolds," the woman replied, tucking a lock of faded brown hair behind her ear. "Welcome."

Elizabeth offered a smile and stepped inside, doing her best to keep from gawking at the entry hall. It ran the length of the house. This, she'd learned from other tour homes, was common for the period—allowing airflow in a time prior to central cooling systems. Unlike other homes, this hall didn't tuck away the staircase. It was a grand affair situated against the far right wall, past two open doorways, and spanned what appeared to be miles to the second floor. And there were at least two floors above that.

"I love that look," Colleen said, closing the heavy door with enviable ease.

Elizabeth blinked and forced her gaze back to her host. "What look?"

"The look you're giving the house right now. Tells me Charlotte was right to send you my way." She spread her arms, smiling warmer still. "Well, without further ado, I'd like to be the first to welcome you to Pemberley."

Pemberley?

"I'm sorry," Elizabeth said, struggling to keep her smile in place. Her heart had taken off and was racing at breakneck speeds as her thoughts spiraled. "What's this house called?"

"Pemberley," Colleen replied, lowering her arms. "Didn't Charlotte tell you?"

"I, ahh. No. She didn't." Elizabeth was certain she would have remembered that. "It's...ahh..."

Colleen's smile had all but faded. She took a step forward, concern edging into those kind eyes of hers. "Is something wrong, dear?"

"No." No, because this couldn't be Will's house. It couldn't be. Her luck might not be anything worth writing home about, but it wasn't absolute shit. It wasn't possible that she'd unwittingly stumbled into the home of the guy she'd spent the past few days *not* thinking about.

She didn't even know if *Pemberley* was the right name. She'd only heard the Darcy home referenced a few times.

Shit. Shit shit shit shit shit.

"Miss?"

Elizabeth gave her head another shake, well aware she looked like an idiot but unable to help herself. "Sorry," she said and forced a hard laugh. "I... Pemberley just sounded familiar to me. It caught me off guard."

"Oh." Colleen's smile was back. "Well, that's not all that surprising. The Darcys—"

"The Darcys?"

"Yes—*those* Darcys, of Darcy Media Group. Their ancestral home has graced the cover of several publications, including *People* and *Time Magazine*. They—"

"I've got to go," Elizabeth blurted and turned on her heel. *Shit, fuck, damn.* "I'm sorry, this was a mistake."

"What's wrong?"

Well, for starters, everything. "I just realized..." What, exactly? That she'd banged the owner of the house she was standing in, accused him of being a drug peddler, and forced him to air the family's dirty laundry in an effort to clear his name? That she'd been bound and determined to find reasons to hate him, except for when she was shoving him into closets and sucking him off? That he'd told her he loved her and she'd thrown that back in his face?

Elizabeth felt her eyes begin to well and realized, to her horror, she was on the verge of losing it.

"Miss Bennet?" Colleen said, closing a warm hand around Elizabeth's shoulder. "Are you...?"

She jumped and plastered on a wide smile so fake it hurt. "I just realized that I go to school with the owner," she said. "It threw me and now I feel really weird."

A nice, abridged version of the truth.

"Oh!" Colleen was all smiles again. "You know Fitzwilliam?"

"I know Will." And she was terrified he might round the corner at any minute. What would he think to see her standing in his house? Well, he'd think she was psychotic. Or a stalker. Or a psychotic stalker. "So you see, it's best if I leave."

A blink. "I don't quite follow your logic."

Well, no, she wouldn't. Elizabeth rubbed her lips together. "I just think it might be weird. For Will. If he knew someone that he...sees every day was in his house just randomly."

"I assure you, Fitzwilliam is fine with my allowing guests into Pemberley, so long as Charlotte or another friend vouches for them and his sister isn't on the premises. Just a precaution. I doubt he'd mind it if you met her."

Oh shit. *His sister.* This kept getting better and better. "But he knows me and I just think it's...different than someone he doesn't know."

Colleen arched a cool brow. "I can promise you, there aren't many people Fitzwilliam has outright barred from the house. It certainly wouldn't matter to him if you were a classmate. In fact, he would be much more bothered if he learned someone he knew *didn't* feel welcome in his home."

Fuck, she hadn't thought of that. Obviously Colleen would tell Will she'd been here. There was no getting out of this. It was either stay here and pretend like nothing was wrong or run back to Hunsford House and have Will concoct a bunch of reasons as to why she might have shown up at his doorstep after the messy explosion of their non-relationship. Staying wasn't the best option, either, but if Will did happen to return home, she'd at least have the opportunity to explain that she actually *wasn't* a crazy stalker weirdo and had tried to leave the second she'd realized where she was.

"All right," Elizabeth said at last, her pulse thundering. "Is... is Will here?"

"He went into Raleigh today to visit the office," Colleen replied. "And his sister is with friends. I don't expect either of them back for hours."

So it was a matter of what story Colleen Reynolds would tell Will—that Elizabeth bolted or that she, after a rocky start, managed to collect her panicking ass and act like an adult.

Option B it was.

"Sorry, I was just...thrown by this being a classmate's house. But if I'm not going to be intruding on him, I'd love the tour. Thank you."

The effect was immediate. Colleen flashed a brilliant smile and gestured toward the room on the right. "We'll begin here, in what was formerly the gentlemen's parlor. If you've toured enough of these old homes, you know that, while entertaining, men would sequester themselves away to smoke cigars, drink brandy, and talk politics."

"Yes," Elizabeth said, taking a quick look around. Aside from a few scattered antique pieces, the room looked nothing like the others she'd toured. It was fully decorated for the holidays, for one thing—a huge Christmas tree stood proud against one of the floor-to-ceiling windows, decked out with ribbons and garland and a buttload of carefully chosen blue and silver ornaments. There was a piece of holly or greenery everywhere she looked, but not in such a way that it seemed overwhelming or tasteless. Even the painting above the fireplace was holiday-themed—a winter landscape, complete with a sleigh and a laughing family.

The other homes she'd toured had been subtly seasonal. This was excessive.

Elizabeth shook her head and tore her attention from the décor. Beneath the Christmas explosion was a sleek desk in the far corner. In the middle of the room was an elegant coffee table crafted from a dark wood—she didn't know her woods well enough to guess which kind—and flanked by what she knew was an antique fainting couch and another period-settee. Pretty to look at, but not what she'd call comfortable. A long, narrow table ran along the wall by the door, hosting two regal looking lamps and a small selection of old books. It was a marriage of old and new. Just the kind of thing she'd wanted to see.

Why did it have to be *his* house?"

"You'll notice the ceilings. They were quite high back in the day to help promote air circulation," Colleen was saying. "Seventeen feet here on the bottom floor. That crown molding is original to the house, hand carved and fashioned out of horsehair plaster. The Cornelius and Baker chandelier depicts the four seasons. The fireplace has the original marble—"

"Is this Will's office?" The question came from nowhere, but Elizabeth had turned her attention back to the desk, picturing him spending his nights there. Possibly checking email. Seeing things about her that Wickham had published online, maybe even believing them.

Colleen paused in the middle of her speech. "He does some work down here, yes," she said, doing her best to recover. "He has another office upstairs. I am sorry to tell you the upstairs rooms are not part of the tour."

"No, of course not." Elizabeth pressed her lips together and waited for the speech to continue, though her mind was not at all engaged with following what was being said. Instead, she caught herself throwing hurried glances to the front, jumping at every sound, and certain that Will was seconds away from rushing inside and demanding to know what she was doing here.

Colleen led her from the former men's parlor to the ladies parlor—"Where the women of the day would play music and do their needlework while the men talked business"—and glossed over the current uses for the room, which appeared to be where all the formal family pieces were stored in pristine condition. She led her across the hall to a fully modern kitchen that even Martha Stewart would shit herself over, then to the formal dining room that looked like something plucked from one of those fancy Masterpiece Theatre productions. Directly across from the staircase was a room that had exploded with even more Christmas, but unlike the first room, this one appeared downright cozy.

Another Christmas tree was positioned, not in front of the window, but tucked in the corner against the inside wall. The elegant ornaments that had comprised the other tree's decorations were nowhere to be found. Rather, this tree was weighted down with novelty ornaments—everything from a pink elephant to a Death Star model. A Santa straddling a Coke bottle looked ready to declare war on another that was riding a Pepsi. The lights were a bizarre marriage of vintage and modern, and the floor surrounding the tree was dominated with packages—some exquisitely wrapped and others a cry for help.

"This is the living area," Colleen said as though it wasn't perfectly obvious. "The informal living area. I'm sorry, I meant to close this off before you arrived."

Elizabeth shook her head, looking now to the massive flat-screen mounted to the wall above the elaborate marble fireplace, and the cushy midnight blue couch and sofa combination. There was also a recliner that could easily fit four people, and a foosball table at the other end of the room against the window. Best of all, opposite the television and behind the sofas, massive mahogany bookshelves had been carved into the wall. And the shelves were stuffed and stacked and overflowing.

"This is amazing," she breathed. "Why would you close this off?"

Colleen sniffed. "It's not suitable for guests."

A phone began to ring somewhere within the house, stealing whatever Elizabeth had been about to say right off her tongue. Which, honestly, was likely for the best.

"Excuse me," Colleen said. "I'll try to be quick."

The next thing Elizabeth knew, she'd been left alone in the center hall, haunting the doorway of what she would forever refer to as her dream room from this moment forward. She turned her attention back to the tree with its funky garland and unique collection of ornaments, and the pang that accompanied her every thought of Will struck her square in the chest.

Elizabeth blinked hard, her eyes stinging. The smart thing to do right now would be to use Colleen's absence to escape this mess before she got herself in any deeper. The longer she hung around, the higher the likelihood of Will returning home—business trip or not—and that was a conversation she didn't want to have.

She'd done enough damage where he was concerned.

Elizabeth heaved a sigh and wiped her eyes, forcing herself away from the room of awesome.

Just in time to see the heavy front door swing open.

30

Will was seeing things. He had to be, because there was no explanation on this or any other planet as to why Elizabeth Bennet would be standing in the entry hall of Pemberley.

Yet for a hallucination, it did a remarkable job of imitating the real thing.

"Oh god," she said, then covered her mouth.

He blinked, struggling to find words. The most he could come up with was her name. "Elizabeth."

"Oh god." She wrung her hands, the action so un-Elizabeth like that he nearly convinced himself that he *was* seeing things. "I... I'm so sorry. I didn't mean to... To be here."

Will nodded as though he understood. He didn't. "Oh."

"I mean, I meant to be here but I didn't know *here* was your house. Which I know sounds ridiculous but it's true. It just happened."

"You just...happened to walk into my house."

"No. I mean yes. I mean no. I mean... I'm staying in Derbyshire. At a bed and breakfast. And Charlotte said she could get me in here." Elizabeth paused, her eyes going wide. Eyes that he noticed, for the first time, were bright with something he could have sworn were tears. "But I didn't know *here* was *you*. I mean this house. I mean Pemberley. I've been hitting some of the touristy places and she said... Well, she thought I'd like it. And I do. It's beautiful. But I didn't know it was your house. And I tried to leave the second I did."

Will nodded again, no more enlightened. His mind was still trying to reconcile the fact that she was here at all. It wasn't unusual for locals to send tourists to Pemberley, and Colleen Reynolds did her best to accommodate each request. The house-keeper had been with the family since before he was born and considered the home as much hers as theirs. She relished any opportunity to show the place off.

"What are you doing in Derbyshire?" he asked, lacking anything else to say.

"Sightseeing."

"Why?"

At that, Elizabeth arched an eyebrow, and the look was so refreshingly *her* that any lingering doubts that she was truly standing in front of him abruptly vanished. "Because that's typically what one does on vacation."

"Why Derbyshire?"

"Why not?"

Because this was the one place she hadn't been able to touch him, dammit. His refuge from the memory of things that hadn't been real to begin with.

"It's nearly Christmas," he said.

"I know."

"Why aren't you with family?"

Elizabeth cocked her hip. "How is that any of your business?"

"You're standing inside my home. That makes it my business."

"I told you, I'm here by accident. I wouldn't have come if I'd known it was your house."

"You didn't know it was my house."

"That's right."

That Charlotte Collins could have referred someone without mentioning the name of the home or the owners was a little difficult to believe, but Will decided not to push the issue. "So for Christmas, you've decided to tour other people's houses."

"How I spend my break is none of your concern."

"Again, it is when you wind up here." Will dragged a hand through his hair. His brain had not yet fully come online, stalled somewhere between acceptance and fantasy. And without warning, he became overly aware of the fact that the last time he'd spoken to Elizabeth, it had been to tell her he loved her.

Right before she'd thrown those words back into his face.

Right before he'd stormed out.

Right before he'd unloaded the melodrama that was his recent past into an email she'd never responded to.

When he met her eyes again, he found them round and full of the same misgivings. As though she'd only just arrived at the same conclusion and had no better idea of how to move forward than he did.

But she was nothing if not brave. He watched as she swallowed, the long column of her utterly kissable neck as flawless as he remembered. His mouth went dry.

"I am sorry," she said. "I know it's...weird that I'm here."

Will couldn't help it—he barked a laugh.

"And I tried to leave after I realized this was your house, but Colleen started asking questions and I didn't know exactly how to tell her that I'm probably the last person you'd want in here." Elizabeth pressed her lips together and crossed her arms as though closing in on herself. "There's no good way to say 'I banged your boss and generally made an ass out of myself' to someone you've just met."

Will forced his feet a step closer. "You made an ass out of yourself?"

"You should remember. You were there."

"Yeah, but it's nice to hear you say it."

She made a face at him, but it lacked the acidity he'd grown so accustomed to over the last few months. And while her eyes were certainly guarded, there was something else there too—or there was something missing. She'd never looked at him the way she was looking at him now.

Perhaps he was foolish to hope, to even entertain the thought, but dammit, he did.

Will edged forward another step. The sound of a phone hanging up carried from wherever Colleen had disappeared off to, but he wasn't ready for her to come back in and spoil this. He wanted to keep Elizabeth's eyes on him just a moment longer.

She swallowed again, rubbing her arms. "I... I should get going."

"Have you finished your tour?"

"I don't know." She paused, then nodded to the room that had, in another life, functioned solely as a library. "This is as far as I got."

"Probably the least antebellum room in the house."

"I love the tree. It's so...eclectic."

Will's mouth twitched. "Yeah?"

She nodded, her eyes catching the reflection of the Christmas tree lights. "It tells a story," she said. "Ornaments like these."

He shifted closer still and peeked around the corner to see what she was seeing. "It's my favorite too," he said, his voice low. "It's the one Georgiana and I decorate ourselves. Colleen tends to all the others."

As though summoned, the woman appeared, looking harried and flustered. She started when she saw him, her normally pallid complexion going rosy. "Oh, Fitzwilliam. I didn't expect you home for a few hours still."

"Yes, well, I found it difficult to focus and everyone was already mentally on their holiday break, so it seemed best to come home." He nodded at her. "Everything all right?"

"Yes," she answered quickly. Then winced. "No. That was my son. He and his girlfriend were in a car accident. It's nothing serious, but—"

"Go."

"He assured me he was fine, but—"

"Colleen, if you don't leave right now I'm going to fire you."

From the corner of his eye, he saw Elizabeth's lips twitch.

"Well, if you're sure." Colleen looked to Elizabeth. "Apologies for cutting the tour short, but Fitzwilliam can answer any questions you may have." She paused. "And you two know each other, right?"

"Thank you, yes," Elizabeth said. "You should go."

Colleen waffled a moment longer, then nodded and started for the door. "I'll be back in a couple hours," she called over her shoulder.

"No you won't," Will called back, turning in time to see her pick her jacket off the coat-rack. "Not unless you want to spend Christmas job hunting."

Colleen just snorted. The next moment, she was gone, the resounding thud of the heavy door stamping the air like a large exclamation point.

He looked back to Elizabeth. Thankfully, she looked about as uncomfortable as he felt. It wasn't right that he suffer in solitude, especially since she was the one who had shown up unannounced.

She looked even better than the image preserved in his memory.

"I should go," Elizabeth said, tucking a lock of hair behind her ear with visibly trembling fingers. "I've already intruded enough. Thank you for not freaking out."

Will took a step forward. "About what?"

"Your ex hookup showing up at your house uninvited."

The lock of hair she'd adjusted came loose again. It took every ounce of his control not to reach out and touch it. Touch her. Standing so close to her after so long was intoxicating, such that all the excuses he'd spent the past few weeks piecing together collapsed without ceremony. No matter what had happened, no matter how hard he'd tried, he couldn't turn off the way he felt about her. Those feelings were illogical and surreal.

"You were never just a hookup," he said at last, his voice gravelly even to his ears. "Not to me."

Elizabeth met his eyes, and the wealth of what he saw there was enough to turn a skeptic into a proselytizer. "I know."

This was dangerous. *She* was dangerous. He needed to keep that in mind.

He needed to create distance before she sucked him back in.

Will cleared his throat and gave his head a shake, forcing himself to take a step back. "But that's what I was to you, right?" he said. "A hookup."

The effect was immediate—whatever softness had been in Elizabeth's face evaporated. She straightened her spine. "Yeah. That's all it was."

"I was convenient."

"Very." Elizabeth paused, wrinkling her nose. "Actually, no. You were the definition of inconvenient."

"Oh?"

"Yes. Imagine being attracted to someone who otherwise repels you on every conceivable level. It's not fun."

Will arched an eyebrow and, against his better judgment, recovered that step he'd put between them. "What about being attracted to someone whose biggest accomplishment is in the art of mixed signals?"

"My signals were so not mixed."

"No? You hate me one moment then pull me into a supply closet the next."

"I hated you throughout."

He just looked at her.

Elizabeth shrugged. "I can hate with a dick in my mouth."

"For future reference, that is not the best way to communicate repulsion." Another step. Any closer and his chest would be against hers, the weight of her familiar breasts pressed where he wanted them. He inhaled and got a lungful of her scent—sweet and familiar and all Elizabeth. It was all he could do to keep from whimpering. "Neither is showing up at my dorm and screwing my brains out."

"What little you have, you mean."

He nodded. "That's right."

Elizabeth released a shaky breath, her gaze dipping to his mouth long enough for his cock to take notice.

"Too bad you're a stuck-up asshole," she said.

"You're one to talk."

Her eyes softened without warning and the air between them went electric. "I missed you."

"I missed you more." Will didn't give himself time to think—his body was in action, overriding his brain in desperation to touch her. He seized her by the hips at the same time her hands found his cheeks, and then, *yes,* her lips were on his and every cell in his body cried out in sweet relief.

The reasons against this were plenty and he was sure he'd

revisit them later, but sweet Jesus, he couldn't be bothered to care at the moment. Not with Elizabeth sighing into him, her tongue exploring his mouth like he was the goddamned elixir of life. There was something frenzied in the way her lips moved, as though she was worried he'd come to his senses. But sense had flown out the window. Whatever had happened before didn't matter now. Nothing mattered but this. The taste of her in his mouth again, the feel of her body pressed to his, the needy sounds she made had him diving right off the wagon.

She tasted so good. Just as he remembered and better. Her kiss was all tongue and teeth, hot and frantic, punctuated with passion he was certain was wholly Elizabeth. But there was something else, too—those small whimpery moans she fed him sounded just this side of desperate. That could make him believe what she'd said in the way words never could.

She had missed him.

Fuck. He was a goner.

Elizabeth pulled back with a hard gasp, and for a horrible instant, his happy thoughts stuttered, flooded with the certainty that she was about to shove him away and make for the door. But she didn't. Rather, she looked at him for a long beat, her eyes searching his, her breaths crashing hard against his lips.

"Will—"

He kissed her again before she could say anything else, and she melted into him, wrapping her arms around his neck and pushing her hips forward until his swelling cock was pressed against her. Another of those sultry whimpers tumbled through her throat, and suddenly he couldn't get close enough.

Thankfully, she seemed to be on the same page. Elizabeth scaled a hand under the cotton of his long-sleeved tee and danced her fingers over his stomach, leaving a burning trail in their wake. And her mouth kept battling his, teasing, tasting and tugging until he came undone.

Real. This is real.

Will pulled away again when oxygen became a concern, panting and pressing his forehead to hers. "You're not gonna run away, are you?"

"No."

"You want this?"

"Uh huh."

He slipped a hand up her side until he had one of her soft breasts cradled against his palm. Strange how his body remembered her given the small amount of time they'd actually had together, but everything about her felt familiar.

"I'm serious," he whispered, rubbing his thumb over her nipple. "I don't want you regretting—"

"I'll regret it more if we don't."

"You mean it?"

Elizabeth nodded before pressing her mouth to his again, and whatever lingering strands of resistance he had in him melted. Her fingers abandoned the exploration of his stomach, which made him groan in frustration until he felt her palm rubbing along the hard length of his cock, and every nerve in his body blazed with fire. He remembered that hand—the way she'd held him, stroked him. Over the last few weeks, he'd managed to convince himself that the memory was better than the real thing—because sex couldn't be that good with someone who didn't like him. Who had no reason to want to make him feel these things. Pleasure was not a reward for disdain, so it had to be imagined.

Yeah, he'd been an idiot. Rationalizing things that couldn't be rationalized. Because no matter what had happened between them, he wasn't creative enough to invent the way she felt and tasted or the things she did to him without even trying.

He forced the hand at her breast to move, then ducked under the hem of her shirt and felt her warm flesh burning against his palm. But it wasn't enough, and apparently she agreed for the next second, Elizabeth had pulled back and jerked her shirt over her head. He took a moment to appreciate the sight of her in the center hall of his home, her rosy nipples peeking through the strappy lace of her bra before he was on her again, dragging hot kisses off her mouth as he explored her warm flesh as he'd thought he never would again.

Did the rest of her taste as good as he remembered? He needed to know. Will broke his lips from hers and began kissing a path down her throat as his fingers toyed with the straps of her bra.

"Fuck..."

He pressed a kiss to her collarbone and grinned. He'd missed that mouth of hers. He'd missed everything. "I intend to," he murmured, reaching behind her to pop the clasp. And then the bra was gone and her breasts were bare against his hands, erect nipples pressing into his palms.

"Will..."

He dipped his head and teased one nipple with his tongue, relishing the hard shudder that coursed through her body before sucking her into his mouth. Elizabeth hissed, raking her fingers through his hair and clutching him tight, as though he wanted to go anywhere else. He sucked and swirled, licked and teased before kissing a path to her other breast and doing it all over again.

"Will—"

"Mmm?" he hummed around her flesh.

"You...you think...I could get the rest of that tour now?"

That lent him pause. He flicked his gaze up to hers, uncertain until he saw the heat in her eyes.

"Tour?" he asked.

Elizabeth nodded shakily. "I was told the upstairs was off limits, but since you're here..."

He blinked and straightened before favoring her with a smile that felt downright goofy. "You mean you don't want to get fucked against the wall down here?"

She trembled, her eyes darkening. "Maybe later."

The words sent a thrill up his spine. "More than happy to oblige." Will pulled her back to him, swallowing whatever retort she had ready with another kiss. He gripped her hips and began walking backward, dragging her with him as he made his way blindly to the stairs.

"Is that a yes?" Elizabeth asked against his lips before ripping his shirt over his head.

"Mmm?" He unbuttoned her jeans and drew down the zipper.

"You'll show me the upstairs?" A shoe went flying across the room.

"I'll show you whatever you want."

"Promises." She whipped off his belt and tossed it over her shoulder. Something crashed to the floor but he couldn't be bothered to care. He was too busy kicking off his own shoes so he could help her push down his pants.

"I keep my promises," Will said against her lips. "All of them."

How he made it upstairs, he didn't know. One second he was tugging down her jeans and the next, he had her in his room, naked across his mattress.

Fuck, there had never been a prettier sight. Elizabeth lying spread before him, her nipples hard and her pussy wet and best of all, her eyes full and alert and on him like she was as astounded to find herself here as he was to have her. Not even in his most optimistic fantasies had Will imagined this. But she was here and open and not hating him, and so beautiful he almost wanted to cry.

"There's so much I wanna do to you," he murmured, barely

aware he was speaking at all. He zeroed his gaze in on her wet, swollen pussy and found himself suddenly parched with the need to taste her there. He'd gotten a hint before, a quick one, but the *later* he'd told himself at the time had never come.

"Later," Elizabeth said, as though reading his thoughts. She sat up, linked her ankles behind his hips and pulled him forward. "I need you inside me now."

His dick throbbed its agreement. Will bit back a growl, which faded into a moan when she wrapped her fingers around his shaft. He'd forgotten how warm her hand was, how she intuitively seemed to know just how he liked to be squeezed or how she stroked him at the perfect rhythm. He'd forgotten how much he loved watching her as she touched him, and the way she was looking at him now...

Will inhaled and reached for his nightstand drawer, muttering a quick prayer that he did have condoms in there and that they hadn't expired. He hadn't had much occasion to bring past girlfriends here, typically erring on the side of caution, especially with a teenager in the house. But it had happened a time or two, and...

Hallelujah. There was a box in there. And it hadn't gone bad.

Elizabeth giggled. He looked up to find her grinning impishly at him.

"What?" he asked, fighting off a smile.

"You look so relieved."

Will laughed and fished out a condom. "Wasn't sure I had these nearby."

"I'm pretty sure they're a prerequisite for any single guy's bedroom."

"I don't entertain in here often."

Elizabeth leaned back on her elbows, an action that all but demanded he trail his gaze down her body. He figured he could spend the next few centuries looking at her and not get his fill.

"I guess being filthy rich means you have your own penthouse somewhere?" she asked, drawing his attention back to her face. "So your dates get the full billionaire bachelor experience?"

Will blinked, then shook his head as he tore open the foil packet and began rolling on the condom. He didn't get very far before Elizabeth batted his hand away, took hold of his cock again, and slipped the latex over his shaft with a long stroke.

"Mmm?" she purred a moment later.

"Huh?" He stole a kiss off her lips before she could respond, gripping his cock by the base and placing it where he wanted to be. And *goddamn,* even through the condom, he could feel her heat.

"I was fishing for info on your legions of female admirers."

"I have legions of female admirers?"

She looked up at him, her eyes hooded. "The Caroline Bingleys of the world?"

Will stared at her for a moment. "This would be the first and hopefully the last time that name has been mentioned while holding my dick."

Again, Elizabeth laughed. "That's good to know."

"And there aren't legions of admirers." He paused. "None that I've paid attention to, anyway."

"Oh?"

Will shook his head, tugging her forward so her hips were hanging off the edge of the mattress and he was cradled between her legs. He nudged the tip of his cock against the slick flesh of her labia, entranced by the sight. "The only woman I've wanted is here," he murmured before dipping a hand to spread her open. "So pretty."

"Will..."

He ran his thumb over her clit, smirking when she gasped and arched into him, then slipped two fingers along the seam of her opening. "Gotta make sure," he said before pressing one digit inside. And god, she sucked him right in. She was tighter than he remembered, if that was possible. Tight and silky and so hot he wanted to cry.

"Shit." He added another finger, this time not bothering to hold back his moan. "You feel amazing."

"I'll feel a lot better in a moment." Elizabeth rolled her head back, panting. "Please. I don't need foreplay. Just fuck me."

Will released a long, trembling breath, his gaze glued to the sight of his fingers, shiny with her juices, pumping in and out of her. But he couldn't take it long—he could barely take it now. Later, he promised himself, he'd explore her the way he'd wanted to. With his hands and mouth and he'd feel her come apart on his tongue. But she was right and he'd teased them both long enough.

Elizabeth mewled when he pulled his fingers away, but the sound turned into a whimper of relief almost immediately. The blunt head of his cock parted her folds, and then he was sinking inside her, and it was like coming home or back from the dead or both. Will swallowed her moan with a hard, needy kiss and didn't release her until he was buried to the root.

He'd taken this about as slow as he thought he could. But now that he was inside her, that her pussy walls were squeezing him to oblivion—now that he knew that it really was real, the chains restraining him snapped and wicked need tore through him with all the subtlety of a hurricane.

"This might be bumpy," he warned her. It was only fair.

Elizabeth bared her teeth at him. "Bring it."

He grinned, pulled back, then slammed back inside.

After all, he was not one to deny a lady.

The sharp gasp that tore from her lips was music to his ears. Will braced his hands on the mattress on either side of her to steady himself. Her arms were again around his neck, leveraging her to him as he swirled his hips and answered his body's call for a bruising rhythm. Elizabeth threw her head back and his mouth followed, sucking desperately at her creamy skin as the air thickened with the heady smack of their bodies coming together.

It hadn't been in his head. None of it had. Not the sounds she made or the sweet scent of her sweat or the look in her eyes. Even the way she smiled at him seemed familiar. The silky feel of her pussy around his cock, squeezing him so tightly every time he thrust himself home, as though desperate to lock him inside. She was perfection, and as much as he hated her for it, he loved her all the more.

Fuck. He loved her. He'd never had a chance of stopping.

"Perfect," he whispered and kissed her. Elizabeth moaned and slid her hands over his shoulders until his face was cupped between them. Beads of sweat raced down his back, his skin burning, his lips on fire. The bed whined and their flesh slapped and he was going to come much sooner than he wanted to, but he didn't think he could hold on. Not with her squeezing him like that. Not with her looking at him like that. Not with her kissing him like that. His balls tightened and the base of his spine tingled.

"I need you to come," Will whispered against her lips. He pressed a hand to her belly, then slipped down until his thumb was just over her clit. "Please."

Elizabeth smiled one of those smiles that undid him, clenching her pussy even tighter around his dick in a way made him want to weep. Instead, Will growled, looking between them —at the sight of him pumping in and out of her, and tensed.

"I mean it. I need to feel you come around my cock," he told her, pressing down on her clit.

She gasped and bucked. "Oh shit."

"I know you're close. Tell me how to get you there."

"Just…keep talking."

Will bit back a grin and nipped at her ear. "You like it when I talk to you while we're fucking?"

"Oh…" She shivered, and damn, that felt good. "Apparently," she agreed, the word breathy.

"What do you wanna hear?" He pushed in so hard he nearly went cross-eyed. "That your pussy feels amazing? That I can't wait to bury my face between your legs? That I've gotten off to imagining how you taste?" He tapped her clit again, his words riding off on a gasp when she tightened around him. "Oh yeah, you do like that."

"Will…"

"I can't hold off much longer." He drew a circle around her clit with his forefinger, then pressed down again. The way she'd told him to in her dorm a million years ago. "Elizabeth…"

And that was it. She threw her head back, her body spasming and her pussy clamping down around him so hard he could have sworn he saw stars. Will panted and pressed his mouth to hers in one last kiss before his control snapped. Euphoria shot through him like a bullet, his hips crashing against hers as he emptied himself inside the condom. His skin burned, hot pinpricks dancing along his arm and down his back. He gave one last thrust before his legs trembled and threatened to go out on him. Will wrapped his arms around her and let her drag him back until he was lying half on top of her on the mattress, cradled in the welcoming heat of her thighs. She pressed kisses along his brow and down his cheek, and when she found his lips again, she was smiling.

The noise around his head began to fade. Will blinked at her and his heart gave a lurch.

"You're really here."

Elizabeth nodded.

"You're not going anywhere?"

"Not unless you want me to."

He shook his head. "Stay," he said, the word half a prayer, half a plea. "Stay."

She smiled and a tear skated down her cheek. There was a lot yet to discuss, he knew, but at the moment none of it mattered. All that mattered was that she was here, and she wasn't going anywhere.

"Okay."

31

By the time Will awoke, the sun had begun its descent, casting long shadows into the room. His head felt oddly light and the pressure that had set up camp in his temples the day he'd drafted that email had nearly faded. It took a few seconds through the pleasant post-nap fatigue for his mind to fully kick-on, but when it did, a burst of adrenaline kicked in and forced him into action.

Will sat up and looked over his shoulder.

It hadn't been a dream. Or a hallucination. Or if it had been, he was still in the middle of it. Elizabeth lay curled on her side beside him, naked and, from the looks of things, in the middle of a really nice dream. Her mouth was curved just enough to give the illusion she was smiling. Ribbons of thick brown hair spilled across his pillows, mussed in the best possible way. The sheet he now remembered pulling over their bodies had slipped during their nap, exposing the artful curve and rosy nipple of her right breast.

Will swallowed and blinked.

She was really here. Elizabeth Bennet naked, in his bed. In his home.

He released a ragged breath and tore a hand through his hair. Obviously, they had a lot to talk about. Or that they should talk about, unless this entire thing had been an aberration and she intended to scamper the second she awoke. Hell, maybe she hadn't meant to fall asleep in the first place. She'd left in a hurry the last time they'd fallen into bed together, after all. There had been no morning after, no pillow talk—nothing until the explosion that had followed that evening.

At once he didn't want her to wake up. He wanted to freeze this moment before he had the chance to pick it apart or find out just how right he was. Because no matter what, he hadn't been able to stop loving Elizabeth—not when he'd written that email or any of the days following. No matter what he'd told himself, no matter how much it bothered him that she'd been that open and intimate with someone she hadn't cared for. Her hotheadedness was one of the things he loved most about her. She hated being wrong almost as much as he did and fought tooth and nail when she believed she was right. She was fiercely loyal to those she cared for and didn't give a damn about his bank account—or anyone's, for that matter. None of that had stopped being true when she'd broken his heart.

Will was in the middle of debating whether or not it was better to postpone the inevitable awkward wake-up or start getting dressed so at least he'd have one layer of armor between himself and Elizabeth, when she made a soft noise and opened her eyes. And caught him staring at her rather unrepentantly.

He forced a smile, heat rising to his cheeks. "Hi."

The world seemed to hold its breath for the next second.

"Hi," she replied, then to his astonishment, turned a fetching shade of pink and buried her head in the pillow.

"Elizabeth?"

She responded with a sound he supposed might have been a word, but was too muffled to discern.

"What was that?" Will's grin turned genuine. He leaned closer, his pulse racing as he drew a lock of hair over her creamy shoulder.

She turned to peek at him, her face still pressed to the pillow. "I said *what*?"

"Did you? In what language, precisely?"

"Shut up."

"No, I don't think so. You're blushing."

She gaped at him and covered her cheeks with her hands. "I am not. Stop looking at me."

"That's impossible." Will scooted nearer, an electric shock buzzing through his veins when he encountered the bare skin of her legs. She seemed to start too, which only encouraged his bravado. "This is the first time I've seen you act shy."

"I am not shy," she said, still hiding from him.

"Yes, I can't imagine where I must have gotten that idea."

Elizabeth sighed and lowered her hands, revealing a face that was now almost beet-red. "Well, the next time you're on vacation touring places, let me know how you react when you accidentally screw the owner. I'll take notes."

Will swallowed. "Accidentally? Like you fell over something?"

At that, she released a snort of laughter and dragged the sheet over her head. "Yes," she agreed. "I tripped and fell on your dick. Repeatedly."

"If it makes you feel any better," Will said, "I really didn't mind."

"I can see that," came Elizabeth's dry reply. The next second, he felt her hand close around his swelling cock. "You really *rose* to the occasion."

He tried to laugh but then she squeezed him and the sound came out a moan. "Ahhh... That was terrible."

"The pun or the dick stroking?"

"The pun. I am more than fine with the latter."

"Really? I wouldn't want to be more of an inconvenience." Elizabeth peeked her head out from under the sheet and gave him a wicked grin, her eyes dancing in ways he'd never seen before. In ways that made his chest ache with how much he loved her.

Will leaned in and kissed her before he could do something stupid, like tell her how he felt. When she sighed and opened her mouth for him, the last of his worries melted away.

And maybe it didn't matter if they didn't discuss the things they weren't discussing. Maybe he shouldn't stop to check the gift horse's teeth because some things were just obvious. Whatever else, Elizabeth felt differently about him now and he figured he knew why.

He'd be happy with that for now. As long as it kept her here.

The thought jumpstarted his mind. "Stay," he said.

"Stay?" she echoed, grinning.

He nodded. "When do you check out of the Collins' place?"

"Tonight was supposed to be my last night. I was going to head back to campus."

Will frowned. "What about Christmas?"

"What about it?"

"I just... I thought you'd be with family."

Elizabeth lifted a shoulder, her smile dimming a bit but not disappearing altogether. "Christmas has never been a big thing in my family," she said. "My mom's going out of the country and my dad... Well, it's a big mess and that's really not worth getting into."

He nodded, ran a hand up her arm. "And Jane? I'd imagine she'd have you over in a heartbeat."

"She would, but her family doesn't know me and I don't

want to crash their holiday cheer." She was quiet a moment, struggled to bring her grin back to where it had been a moment ago. "I'm fine."

And though he could have seen it coming a mile away, somehow Will was still surprised when he heard himself blurt the words. "Stay with me."

"What?"

"Have Christmas here. With me." He paused. "And my sister."

"Will—"

"Don't think. Just say yes."

She gave him a look. "Likelihood of that happening, one to ten."

Will grinned. "A guy can hope, can't he?"

"Like I said...my family has never been one that the holidays were all that important for. We didn't have a ton of money so my folks couldn't afford to do the big shebang, especially when they were paying for me to go to private school there for a while. Our Christmas tree was always of the Charlie Brown variety."

He pressed a kiss to her brow.

"But," Elizabeth continued softly, "I've seen enough movies to know that Christmas is a big deal for other families. And if the missing Macy's department downstairs is any indication, the Darcys do Christmas in a big ole way. I really don't want to intrude on that."

"It's not intruding if you're invited. Which you just were."

She worried her lower lip between her teeth. He followed the movement with his eyes, which just made his mouth crave hers again.

"You're not just inviting me because you feel sorry for me about spending Christmas alone, are you?"

"I'm inviting you because I want you here. Stay," he said, leaning close.

"Will..."

"Stay." He sealed the space between them and did his best not to whimper when she softened under his kiss. It was meant to be soft and reassuring, but when Elizabeth wrapped her hand around his cock again, he lost all illusion of control over his baser hormones and rolled her under him.

"You're dangerous, Miss Bennet," he murmured against her lips.

"You have no idea."

"I think I have some." Will pressed a kiss to the corner of her mouth.

She grinned and parted her legs to accommodate him, and the next thing he knew, his prick was cradled between her pussy lips and every inch of him was on fire.

"Fuck, you feel good."

"You really need to say that word more often."

Will arched an eyebrow.

"Fuck," she replied. "It's sexy as hell."

"That's...weird."

Elizabeth giggled, her cheeks flushed. "I think it's because I haven't heard you say it much, except when I've had my mouth on you. It makes me think you're losing control. Which, again, sexy as hell."

"I've been conditioned to not swear in front of women. With you, I have no control."

"And I happen to find that sexy."

"You're...unlike any woman I've ever known."

"Good." She linked her arms around his neck and drew him down for a kiss, and there was hunger behind the strokes of her mouth. The thought that she might want him as badly as he did her was enough to unmake him completely.

Elizabeth reached between them again to seize his cock, and then he was parting her slick flesh and beginning to sink inside her when the lusty fog thinned long enough for him to realize she felt a little *too* good.

"Fuck."

"Uh huh," Elizabeth said against his mouth.

"No, I mean, condom." Will shuddered and gave his head a shake to clear it. That had been close. "Let me—"

The sound of a heavy door opening from downstairs cut him off, and his pulse quickened for an entirely different reason. He froze, hand outstretched toward the box on his nightstand.

A beat. Then another. And—

"Will!"

The undeniable wail of Georgiana Darcy.

"Shit," Will swore, rolling off Elizabeth and bounding to his feet. He spun around the room for a moment, trying to gather his bearings, but the world seemed lopsided and he couldn't quite keep his balance. "Shit, shit, shit."

Elizabeth drew up to a sitting position and wrapped her arms around her legs. Though her face was flushed and tense, he saw her eyes were dancing with amusement. "Going to hazard a guess..."

"My sister," he said as his gaze landed on his dresser. Yes, that was where he kept the clothes. "I'll...be back." Will paused and looked at her. "Don't go anywhere. Please."

Elizabeth favored him with a soft smile and raised her hands. "If anyone asks, I'll say you rendered my legs useless."

"Good to know." He raced over to the dresser and dragged out the first article of clothing that wouldn't scandalize his sister —the pajama bottoms that she had given him last year for Christmas. Flannel, navy blue, and decorated with floating Rudolf heads.

"Will *Darcy!*" Georgiana bellowed. "Don't make me come up there."

Will swore again after dressing, started for the door, then

decided—just on the off-chance that he'd been lulled into a false sense of security and Elizabeth *was* an incredibly vivid hallucination—that he might as well get the most out of it. He doubled back to the bed, captured her face between his hands and took her mouth in a fierce but all too brief kiss. "I'll be back."

Her eyes had this heated quality that made him wish more than ever that he'd been an only child. "Promises."

Will forced himself away and hurried out of the room just as Georgiana began to shout again. He paused at the top of the stairs, prepared to chastise her for very good reasons, but felt his stomach drop when his gaze connected with hers.

Nothing good ever happened when Georgiana Darcy looked *that* smug.

"Oh, *there* you are," she chirped happily, one hand behind her back, the other on her hip. "What took you?"

He blinked at her, his mind racing. "I was...sleeping."

"Sleeping."

"Yes."

"In the middle of the day."

"It's called a nap, Georgie. Look into it."

She just beamed and arched an eyebrow, drawing his attention for the first time to the stairs. Where his pants were strewn and a pair of jeans had been kicked off. There was a boot on the step third from the top, and another five steps below it.

"Colleen has really gotten sloppy," Georgiana said, rocking on her heels. "Look at this mess."

"I was doing laundry," Will blurted, because that was incredibly plausible, considering that the only time he'd done his own laundry in this house had been, well, never.

Georgiana nodded as though this wasn't the most ludicrous thing she'd ever heard. "Laundry. Going *up* the stairs."

"Things fall out of laundry baskets all the time."

"Yes, and rather than pick up after yourself, you decided the stress of washing your own clothes was too much for you and a nap was in order?"

At this point, he was only fighting for the sake of pride and they both knew it. Will lifted his chin in defiance. "Yes."

"Uh huh." Georgiana lifted the arm that had been behind her back, revealing a scrappy lace bra that looked way too familiar. "I honestly didn't see white as being your color."

Will opened his mouth, closed it, and opened it again. "I—"

"You. Are. So. Busted." Georgiana tossed the bra over her shoulder and tore up the stairs.

"Georgiana, don't—"

She cackled. "Yeah, that's happening."

Will wasn't sure why, but his feet chose that moment to stop listening to his brain. He stood there like an idiot as his sister stampeded her way past him; she was halfway down the hall before the numbness melted and his legs kicked back online.

If Georgiana scared Elizabeth away...

The thought made his head begin to pound. Will thundered after her, willing his heart not to leap to freedom when a shriek pierced the air, followed by the never-good sound of Georgiana's laughter.

He skidded to a halt outside his bedroom and found Elizabeth where he'd left her, only she'd drawn one of the oversized pillows to her chest in an effort to conceal her nudity.

"Hi," Georgiana said with a little wave, "Laundry, I presume?"

Elizabeth looked to Will, her eyes shining with something between mortification and stupor. Had the circumstances been different, he would have enjoyed that quite a bit.

"It's not what it looks like," she said, then winced because Elizabeth was many things, but a fool was not one of them—he saw plainly she knew how dumb that had sounded. But bless her, she decided to stick to it. "I...uhh... There was a clothing malfunction and your brother was nice enough to let me rest in here while he...did laundry."

Georgiana rolled her eyes and looked at Will over her shoulder. "Oh my god, you're perfect for each other."

Great, now his face had gone hot. He was going to throttle her. "Georgie, will you just—"

"You're Elizabeth, aren't you?"

Maybe he had died and gone to Hell. This seemed like the sort of thing that might happen in Hell.

Elizabeth blinked at Georgiana before shifting her gaze to Will, and the question he saw there cemented that his little sister was going to be grounded for the next eternity.

"I am," she said after a long moment, surprise evident in her voice.

Georgiana nodded and flashed another killer smile. "Awesome. Super stoked to meet you. I'll let you guys get dressed." She turned to Will. "Bought some sugar cookies. And by some, I mean *all* the sugar cookies. Plus some snickerdoodles because I am only human. Plan is to watch *Elf* and eat all my Christmas feelings."

At that, Will softened, mortification taking a backstage to the part of him that was the perpetually concerned older brother. "All good?"

"The best." Georgiana winked at him. "I'll save you and your girlfriend at least one snickerdoodle apiece if you want to join me."

And without anything further, she turned and promptly flounced from the room.

Will stared after her for a moment. When he felt it was safe, he looked to Elizabeth and didn't release the breath he'd been holding until he saw the warmth in her eyes.

"So," he said, drawing out the word. "That was my sister, Georgiana."

Elizabeth burst out laughing, and the sound made him feel invincible.

32

Mortifying introductions aside, it took Elizabeth about ten minutes to fall head over heels for Georgiana Darcy. The girl was the physical embodiment of charm and sass.

She was also a cutthroat gamer.

"And suck it," Georgiana said with a wide grin as she mowed down another poor red avatar. "That flag is mine."

"Glad someone's on our team," Elizabeth replied, then winced. Another wipe out. "This used to be so easy for me."

Georgiana straightened her shoulders. "I am used to carrying the team. Just keep 'em busy and I'll do the rest."

From his seat by the window, Will gave a small chuckle. He had been mostly silent since coming downstairs and fumbling through the awkward conversation with his sister—whose enjoyment of his embarrassment couldn't have been more obvious if she'd taken out advertisements. When Georgiana had asked Elizabeth if she wanted to kill things on X-Box, Elizabeth had jumped at the opportunity to cut the tension.

Plus, it had been a good long while since she'd held a controller.

"I am a lean, mean, shooting machine," Georgiana muttered. "Just try to get by me, motherfucker."

Elizabeth barked a laugh.

"Language," Will snapped, though there was no venom in his voice.

"Lighten up, dude," Georgiana replied.

"Yeah, *dude*," Elizabeth agreed, dragging her gaze from the television long enough to favor him with a wink. He grinned at her—a soft grin, but one full of promise.

And it hit her again that this was real. For the first hour or so after waking up in Will's bed, Elizabeth had been waiting for the fever dream to end, because everything that had happened since arriving in Derbyshire seemed like something out of a fairytale. Granted, an X-rated fairytale, but right up there in terms of believability.

That she had stumbled into Will's town. Into Will's house. Into Will's arms. That he hadn't screamed at her and kicked her out the second he'd seen her standing in his space. That he still wanted her after everything she'd put him through.

That he wanted her to stay for the holidays.

Elizabeth swallowed and forced her attention back to the television just in time to greet yet another kill-screen.

"I suck," she said.

"Yes," Georgiana agreed rapidly, then whooped as she successfully took down another opponent.

Elizabeth laughed again and shook her head. "Thanks. Don't sugarcoat it."

"Sugarcoating's for pansies. No pansies in this house." Georgiana began pounding the keys with a fury. The next second, it was over, and she'd dropped the controller into her lap to thrust her fists into the air. "Yes! I am the Capture the Flag champion!"

"Glad one of us is." Elizabeth set her own controller aside and flexed her stiff fingers. "It has been *way* too long."

"Hey, I'm just glad you can point in the right direction," Georgiana replied. "Will's useless at this."

"You say that like it's a bad thing," Will replied.

"Wow. Nothing gets by you." She shook her head and rolled her eyes before turning back to Elizabeth. "You're a little rusty, but some practice and we'd make a hell of a team."

"Language," Will intoned.

"Bite me," she shot back, keeping her gaze on Elizabeth. "So, what was your poison back when you were gaming?"

"Golden-Eye," she replied. "A game at which I would *excel* at kicking your ass."

Georgiana wrinkled her nose. "Isn't that an old N-64 thing?"

"If by *old N-64*, you mean the defining system of my child-hood, yes." Elizabeth gestured to her controller. "I never got used to the dual navigation thing. Another reason why I suck at this."

"Why an N-64? I'm pretty sure that was old even when you were a kid."

"I can't tell if I'm flattered or insulted."

Georgiana shrugged. "It's a gift."

Will snickered but didn't say anything.

"The N-64 was all my family could afford, to answer your question," Elizabeth said. "And yes, by the time I got my hands on one, they were old. But that didn't stop me from totally owning every game I played. And if you ever get your hands on an old system, I will wipe the floor with you."

Georgiana's eyes twinkled. She turned to Will. "Can I get an N-64?"

He huffed and waved at the X-Box sitting under the televi-sion. "I just bought you that monstrosity."

"I know and you're awesome, but I want to see if I can whip your girlfriend's ass on more than one console."

Elizabeth pressed her lips together, her heart doing a funny jig at the g-word. She held her breath as long as she could before shifting her gaze to Will, and didn't know whether to be relieved or dismayed when she saw he was equally conflicted.

There was little chance Georgiana didn't realize the bomb she had set up—the girl was whip-smart and a little too insightful for her own good. Still, when she turned back to Elizabeth, her expression was all innocence. It was almost enough to be convincing. Almost.

"I complain," she said, "but Will's actually really good to me."

"Can I get that in writing?" Will asked.

"This thing?" She ignored him and nodded at the console. "Early Christmas present. Best one I've ever gotten."

"You get your Christmas presents early? Lucky."

Georgiana gave her a wide grin. "I can sweet talk big brother into just about anything. Isn't that right?"

Will shook his head, snickering. "I'm essentially a prisoner in my own home."

Elizabeth poked her tongue out at him. "Poor baby."

"Yes," Georgiana agreed dryly. "It truly is the hard knock life."

"As it turns out, Georgie, I'm in need of that particular superpower." Will leaned forward, resting his arms on his knees. "See if you can sweet talk Elizabeth into staying for Christmas."

At that, Elizabeth's stomach dropped. "Wait—"

"You mean you're thinking about *not?*" Georgiana asked, whipping up her head and poking out her bottom lip. "Is this because I caught you two naked?"

Will slid a hand over his mouth, presumably to hide his smirk. It didn't work.

Elizabeth blinked and shook her head, feeling railroaded. She opened her mouth, closed it, and opened it again before giving up and leveling a glare at Will. "Was that really necessary?"

"You never gave me an answer. Figured it was time to call in the big guns."

Georgiana preened and flexed her biceps.

"I told you," Elizabeth said, "Christmas has never been a big deal in my family."

"Best reason to do Christmas Darcy style right there," Georgiana said. "'Cause we know how to deck halls and fa la la la la like the best of them."

"I don't want to impose."

"Kinda hard to do that when you got an invite," the teenager shot back.

"That's what your brother said."

"Weird. It's almost like we're related or something." Georgiana gave a dramatic sigh and batted her eyes. "Seriously. Stay. I know so few cool people. Actually, make that no cool people—"

"And yes, in case you're wondering, that does smart," Will intoned dully.

"Good. It's supposed to." She gave a huff and tossed her red-gold hair over her shoulder. "We have this huge house and none of the staff takes us seriously when we invite them and their families over for holidays. If you leave, you're abandoning a helpless teenager to that walking snore"—she nodded at her brother—"and the *Bingleys*."

Elizabeth straightened her spine. "The Bingleys are coming for Christmas?"

"Their folks are off visiting Louisa and her husband this year so they chose to make merry with us instead," Will explained. "Louisa's Charlie's older sister."

"And Charlie's great, don't get me wrong." Georgiana wrinkled her nose and shuddered. "But Caroline? I'm pretty sure if you leave me alone with her, you'll be in violation of the Geneva Conventions."

The part of Elizabeth that had been teetering toward accepting the invitation wobbled firmly back. Introducing the Bingleys to this situation made everything seem more real. Add to the fact that she and Will hadn't spoken about anything of substance and the whole thing went from awkward to uncomfortable.

"Caroline doesn't particularly like me," Elizabeth said. "Or... like me at all."

"Duh. Caroline is allergic to people who aren't total assholes or dipshits."

"Language," Will said.

Georgiana flipped him off, keeping her gaze on Elizabeth. "Plus she's wanted to bone my brother since grade school. So if she's a snot, it's probably because she wishes she was you."

Will went scarlet red and puffed out his cheeks. "No, please," he muttered, "don't hold anything back."

"Which means, obviously, that you need to stay because *that's* a guaranteed way to make sure Caroline has a crappy holiday." Georgiana clapped. "Best Christmas ever!"

Elizabeth stared at the girl for a long moment, grinning. "You're like the sister I always wanted."

"Would you like to keep her?" Will offered. "She's free to a good home."

Georgiana blew a raspberry at him.

Elizabeth drew her lower lip between her teeth, forcing her brain to the subject it had been avoiding since Will had brought up the possibility of staying for the holiday in the first place. In truth, the thought of leaving made her stomach knot. There was still so much they needed to talk about, and she knew she wouldn't be able to move on until she'd given him the apology he deserved, among other things.

Plus... God help her, she liked him. A lot. Now that she wasn't trying so hard to keep her distance—now that she wasn't assigning his every look and word a motive—the guy that she'd been so desperate to ignore at the start of the semester had proven to be...

Well, she didn't know what. Except he did things to her mind and body that had never been done before. And despite having all the reason in the world to not only show her the door but also take out a restraining order, he had been...nice. Nice and more than nice.

For the first time in her life, she understood how people fell in love so easily.

And that thought was terrifying.

"Please," Will said, his voice a notch lower than it had been before.

She blinked and shook her head to clear it.

"Please stay."

Elizabeth wet her lips. "You really want me to?"

"Yes." He cleared his throat and looked away. "Georgie really likes you."

His sister snickered. "Nice cover."

"And... We should...talk."

"Ugh, no. Serious stuff comes after the holiday festivities and not a moment before." Georgiana nodded as though the matter were settled. "We are on a mission to make with the merry, people."

Elizabeth swallowed. "Okay."

"Okay?" Will's eyes lit up.

"Okay. I'd... I'd love to have Christmas with you guys."

The smile that lit Will's face could have provided enough warmth to power a solar system.

And though the prospect was no less terrifying than it had

been moments ago, the urge to flee was smothered by something more powerful.

For the first time in her life, Elizabeth wished she'd been born a romantic. Because it would be so lovely to believe that this feeling was not only real, but had the power to last.

Will met Elizabeth at the head of the car outside Hunsford House and took her hand before she could bolt down the sidewalk. Not that she looked like a flight risk, but nothing that had happened today had been predictable. Least of all the feel of her fingers curling around his as she pressed her familiar, warm body into his side and let him guide her up the porch steps to the front door.

They hadn't spoken since leaving the house, and while the air between them remained thick, the silence in the car had been companionable rather than awkward. And the way she looked at him now had him dancing on the edge of euphoria. Perhaps in the morning he would believe, truly, that she was here. In the meantime it was all he could do to keep from staring.

The door opened to reveal a relieved Charlotte Collins. "Elizabeth," she said, placing a hand over her chest, "we were starting to worry about you."

"Sorry," Elizabeth replied with a wince. "I...uhh...was preoccupied."

Charlotte pressed her lips together and nodded before turning her attention to him. "Mr. Darcy. Is there something wrong?" She blanched. "Something didn't happen at the house, did it?"

"Sorry," Elizabeth said again. "And no, nothing went wrong. Will and I actually know each other."

She looked to their linked hands. "I can see that."

"Yes, well…" Elizabeth shifted her gaze to him. Not once had he seen her look so uncertain, and he found he was both enchanted and disturbed by the change.

Will squeezed her hand. "Elizabeth is going to stay with me and Georgiana over the holiday," he told Charlotte. "I came to help her gather her things and settle her bill."

"No," Elizabeth said firmly, pulling her hand from his. "Well, yes, I am staying with you but you're not paying for my room here."

"I—"

"Do you really want to fight me on this? Think very carefully.

Will grinned. That was the Elizabeth he knew. "I would lose, wouldn't I?"

"Big."

"Well, we don't want that." He turned back to Charlotte, still grinning. "Just to help her collect her things, then."

Charlotte narrowed her eyes, seemingly undecided if she should be amused or annoyed. In the end, she settled somewhere in the middle. "All right. Please be quiet, though. My husband just went to bed. Early service in the morning."

"Of course," Will said, inclining his head, and tugged Elizabeth into the home without waiting another moment.

There was very little to pack up. A small duffle full of clothes and a few sacks of things it appeared she'd bought on the road. They worked quickly to gather everything, and in less than ten minutes were again outside of Hunsford House and placing things in the back of Elizabeth's rental.

"I'll be right back," Elizabeth said, and turned to head back to the front porch, where Charlotte waited.

Will stood by the car and watched as she handed over the key, then leaned in and took the woman in an impromptu hug. He wasn't necessarily trying to eavesdrop, but he couldn't keep himself from hearing Elizabeth's soft murmur of, "Thank you so much for sending me there today."

Warmth spread through his veins. Will did his best not to grin like an idiot but found he didn't much care if he was caught. If someone had told him twenty-four hours ago that this was what the day would bring, he would never have believed it.

Charlotte replied with something indiscernible and earned a small laugh for her effort. Then Elizabeth was coming back to him, her cheeks flush and her eyes all for him.

Will released a deep breath. "Everything taken care of?"

"Yes. I'm all yours."

There was that idiot grin again.

"I mean, yours and Georgiana's." Elizabeth smoothed her hands down her sides. "I—"

"I very much hope you'll be all mine when we get back."

"Oh?"

Will nodded and edged a step forward. "I'm so glad you're here. That you're staying." He hesitated, but decided the hell with it, and cupped her cheek. "Thank you."

A thick beat pulsed between them. She searched his eyes, smiled and pressed herself upward to brush a soft kiss across his lips. She didn't say anything when she pulled away—she didn't have to. He felt her response deep in his bones, and for the moment, that was all he needed.

The rest could wait.

33

There was something about showering in someone else's home that was unspeakably intimate—beyond even sex. And though Elizabeth had borrowed Will's shower once before, that had been prior to their falling into bed together, and it hadn't been at his private home.

Naked in his bed was one thing. Naked in the place where he cleaned himself felt...different. Made all of this seem like it could be real.

She hadn't asked where she would be sleeping after Will had ushered her inside. Since choosing to stay here for Christmas, it seemed the nerve she had relied on her entire life had decided to leave her hanging. But with so much still left unsaid, and apparently neither one of them willing to broach the subject, she wasn't sure where she stood.

Still, she knew where she wanted to go and it seemed reasonable to start there. Elizabeth gave her reflection one last pass to make sure she didn't look too frightening. She hadn't bothered with makeup at all on this trip, having bolted for the airport after receiving the initial phone call with nothing more than a few things shoved in a bag. She could survive without makeup. Clothing, not so much.

Elizabeth leaned in to search for flaws. Her eyes were not yet baggy, but definitely on the way there. She never slept well in unfamiliar beds, no matter how comfortable the mattress in question, and the past few days had taken their toll. At the same time, though, she was more relaxed than she had been in months. Getting away from campus had been a lifesaver. If she'd continued at the pace she'd been going, she would have eventually crashed and burned.

Hell, maybe she had. Maybe she'd fallen into a coma and everything that had happened since she'd gotten off the airplane was the fabrication of a mind trying to repair itself. It still struck her as thoroughly unreal that she was here, in Will's house, wrapped in a towel and standing naked in his bathroom, just a few feet away from the man himself. Just last week, she'd been certain their paths would never cross again, and if they did, he would pretend not to notice.

Elizabeth swallowed and rocked back on her feet, her gut clenching. The longer they avoided discussing Wickham and the email and everything, the worse it would be. She needed to do the grownup thing and tackle the obstacle headfirst.

And that was exactly what she intended to do. She switched off the light and opened the bathroom door.

The second she met Will's eyes, her resolve to discuss anything went out the window.

He was standing near the bed in the same state she'd left him in—naked save for the towel he'd wrapped around himself before offering her a turn in the shower. It was such a simple thing, but it told her everything she needed to know on its own. He hadn't dressed because he hadn't known if that was what she wanted. He also hadn't presumed anything. He was letting her make all the choices.

Elizabeth released a long sigh, her nipples hardening. She had so resented how much fun he was to look at not that long ago, and done everything she could to ignore him on every physical level. But that was then and she had permission now. She dragged her gaze down the hard lines of his chest, which was firm and broad without being bulky. He had the definition of a guy who worked out, toned abs and well-muscled arms to match, which would have been annoying had she not known him as she did now. Guys who looked like him were typically jerks.

He challenged the pretenses she'd established, and that terrified her.

Elizabeth dropped her attention to the front of his towel, which was beginning to tent. She bit the inside of her cheek to keep from grinning, but even then, she couldn't do much to help herself.

"Tell me that's a yes."

She forced her gaze back to his. "What's a yes?"

"You're staying in here tonight. With me."

"I'm kind of a blanket hog. You might want me in another room."

"I want you," he echoed, dropping his gaze to her breasts and lower still until every inch of her skin was tingling with anticipation.

"Oh."

"You sound surprised."

"I'm not. Or I am. Or… I'm still trying to get used to this."

He smiled at that, and some of the *Will* she was growing to love shone through. "To what?"

"All of this." She gestured to the room. "Today feels unreal."

"To me too."

"And… I know we need to—"

"I'd rather not tonight."

Elizabeth's mouth went dry. "No?"

Will shook his head. "Just a little more time before we have to ruin it."

"Do you think we will? Ruin it?"

"God, I hope not." He broke away then and dragged a hand through his hair. "I want you to stay with me in this room. But I want to touch you too. I want...to feel you. And if that's not what you want, I will find you another room. The invitation to spend the holidays with me and my sister doesn't come with strings. So if you—"

Elizabeth dropped her towel. Sometimes actions were better than words.

Will held his breath a moment, his eyes raking over her body again. And this time he didn't bother to conceal the hunger there and she was glad, because it set her aflame in ways she truly hadn't known existed. His gaze lingered on her breasts a second before trailing lower, encouraging her to press her thighs together. Her clit gave a throb and hunger coiled in her stomach. In her hands. She wanted to touch him too. All over. In all the ways she hadn't let herself before.

"Thank god," Will muttered, and then his feet ate the space separating them until he had her face in his hands and had pulled her mouth to his in a sweet kiss—one that tasted of all the things she'd been craving.

Elizabeth flung her arms around his neck, grinning as his own towel fell to the floor. Then his hard cock was pressed against her stomach, hot and ready and damn, she wanted it in her mouth. Wanted to give him a new memory to replace the angry blowjob she'd given him in the maintenance closet. But she couldn't pull her lips away from his long enough to convince her mouth there was a good reason to go south, and her brain refused to accept that she would remain upright if she let a hand drift between them so she could feel just how hard he was for herself.

She had just managed to slide her right arm down his chest when he caught her hand in his.

"Elizabeth."

She gave a short mewl and forced her eyes open. God, he was close, his eyes boring into hers in ways that should have made her nervous. No one had ever looked at her the way Will did. Ever. The knowledge left her feeling breathless and a little dizzy, but starved for him as she'd never been for anyone.

"There's something I've wanted to do to you for a long time," he said. "Will you let me now?"

She swallowed, nodded. "Okay."

The corner of his mouth ticked upward. "Wanna know what it is first?"

"Will I like it?"

"I *really* hope so, or I've lost my touch."

It was completely irrational and not at all like her, but for some reason, those words made her tense with jealousy. Fleeting but potent all the same. Elizabeth clutched at his forearms and nodded again. "Then show me."

Will took her mouth again, pulling her flush against his body before slowly turning so her back was to the bed. He walked her back until her ass met the edge of the mattress, gave her a parting kiss, then encouraged her to lay down.

"Fuck," he murmured, dragging his gaze from her face to her breasts. "You are gorgeous."

Elizabeth offered a soft smile. "So are you."

He arched an eyebrow and met her eyes again. "Oh yeah?"

"Uh huh."

"How long have you thought that?"

"Pretty much since the first moment I saw you."

"You hid it well."

"I have a natural distrust of pretty things," she replied conversationally, as though she was accustomed to discussing things while spread out naked on a bed, her legs spread, every inch of her body on display. "Particularly pretty men."

"And when the man in question just happens to say something particularly stupid, I assume..."

"It's doomed."

"No exceptions?"

Her smile widened. "Oh, I don't know," she replied. "I could be convinced."

"Allow me to grovel, then."

Will leaned over her to brush a soft kiss against one of her nipples, keeping his gaze on hers the entire time. She watched as those magic lips of his caressed the tip of her breast before venturing to the other.

"I could spend hours doing just this," he whispered. "I *want* to."

She shivered. "I think I'd let you."

"I know you would." He skimmed a hand up her side until her breast was cradled against his warm palm and rubbed his thumb over her nipple. "But not now. I've waited too long to do this."

Then he began peppering kisses between her breasts, over her abdomen. He took a detour around her belly button, laughing when she giggled and jerked, and then he was shifting so his knees were on the floor and her legs were over his shoulders.

"Mmm." Will grasped her hips and pulled her forward until her ass was hanging off the side of the bed.

"Will!"

"I've got you," he whispered, scooting closer. "Won't let you fall."

Elizabeth gave a hard laugh and fisted the comforter for leverage. "Who's worried?"

"Not you. You're not afraid of anything."

"That's right."

"Mhmm." He slipped a hand around her thigh and slowly pulled apart the lips of her labia. A moan sounded at his throat. "Perfect. Everywhere, you're perfect."

"I don't think—"

"So *don't think*. Just let me tell you how perfect you are."

Elizabeth bit her lip to keep in her retort, because the truth was far less flattering. The fact was she had very nearly ruined this. Hell, that she *hadn't* remained a mystery, one she was too much a goddamned coward to try and solve, especially now. That Will could say that word, even think it in relation to her defied logic. It was too much to ask that he still want her—that he still love her, or feel even an inkling of whatever he'd felt before was asking for the impossible.

Yet he was with her, spreading her open and running his fingertips over her slick, sensitive flesh.

Then she felt the tip of his tongue circle her clit and all those less than pleasant thoughts blinked away for a few brilliant seconds. She gasped, her skin suddenly on fire. "Oh god."

Will murmured something unintelligible in response and drew his tongue around her again. "You taste good," he whispered before drawing a line between her clit to her opening then back again. "Worth the wait."

"Will—"

"Shh. Just tell me if something doesn't work for you, okay? Teach me how you like to be eaten."

Shit. Elizabeth squeezed her eyes shut and gave up fighting. Sure, she might not deserve this, but she wasn't going to turn it down. "Oh fuck. What you're doing...good."

"Mhmm?"

"I like the way you stroke my clit. That's good."

He rumbled another sound of approval and encircled her again, giving her enough contact to titillate without crossing the rather sensitive boundary into discomfort. The lovers in her past had treated her clit more or less like a Rubik's Cube, giving it so much attention it took her out of the moment. From the very first time they had come together, Will had allowed her to set the pace, nudging her, teasing her, caressing her without making her feel like the last question on a particularly difficult calculus exam.

Another hint that he had done this a lot, which made her jolt with more unexplained jealousy. It was not sensible to feel territorial over him, yet she couldn't help herself. She wanted Will to be all hers.

"Is there anywhere else you want my tongue?" he asked.

"It's all...all good."

"Do you like this?" He edged a finger inside her, and at her answering whimper, added another. "Damn. I could spend hours doing this too."

"You're making...ahh...quite the to-do list."

He chuckled. "I think my list is just you. Elizabeth on the bed. On the floor. In the shower. Against the wall. Riding my face—"

"Will!"

"Watching as she lets me finger-fuck her." He found a steady tempo, and when she peeked an eye open, she found him staring at the sight of her pussy welcoming his fingers again and again with something that was almost as much hunger as it was torment. "No one could blame me," he said a moment later, flicking his gaze up to meet hers. "This is the prettiest thing I've ever seen."

"Will... I want. Your mouth."

"Good. It wants you too." He lowered his head again and this time, the laps his tongue took weren't tentative, rather emboldened.

Elizabeth fell back against the mattress again. "Oh shit. Just that. Do that. Fuck, do whatever you want."

"Don't give me that kind of power unless you mean it."

"I mean it."

Elizabeth managed to open her eyes long enough to appreciate the devilish grin he aimed her way, then his mouth descended again and he had her clit pulled between his lips. A long howl clawed its way out of her throat and she tightened her thighs around his head. Will growled his approval, sucking at her harder still. Hard tremors seized her arms and legs, pressure bundling and pulsing until she was certain she would detonate. Will left her clit with a kiss and began lapping along her soaked folds until his tongue had replaced the fingers thrusting in and out of her. He licked and sucked and made yummy noises that alone might have gotten her where she needed to go.

"Wa... Will..."

He drew a wet fingertip around her clit and her goddamn cells blazed in response. "Right here," he murmured before his mouth was back where she wanted it, pulling at that bundle of nerves as his fingers slipped back inside her. Then he flattened his tongue against her and pressed down, and it was all over. White hot euphoria came crashing down. Elizabeth bucked and gasped, her skin so hot she was sure it would melt right off. And Will didn't let up. His tongue resumed the swirly patterns around her clit until her legs began to tremble all over again. Will drew his fingers out of her to grasp her by the hips and lift her pussy to his mouth.

"Oh shit oh shit oh shit oh shit."

She stole one final peek of him to find his eyes trained on hers, intense and hungry, and she tumbled over the edge all over again, her mind blanking as her body gave itself over.

When she next became aware of herself, she was lying on her back, completely on the bed now, and Will was beside her, gently caressing her brow.

Elizabeth blinked at him. Every inch of her was tingling. "Hi."

He grinned and pressed a kiss to her temple. "Hello to you too."

"Was I gone long?"

"You went somewhere?"

"Yeah. I think it was an out of body experience."

Will grinned again, this time all male satisfaction. "Oh yeah?"

"Uh huh." She reached up and ran her thumb over his lips. "I have a new appreciation for your mouth."

"I've always had a soft spot for yours," he replied. Then he was kissing her again and all the sensors that had waved a white flag were rallying back to their stations. Elizabeth whimpered and tunneled her fingers through his hair, spreading her legs in welcome. He fed her a groan and rolled so he was cradled in the valley of her thighs, his hard cock sliding along the folds of her pussy.

"I wanna feel you come again," he whispered.

"I dunno if I have it in me."

"You're about to."

Elizabeth rolled her eyes and smacked his shoulder. "You kinda wore me out."

"Mhmm." Will reached between to position himself at her opening. "That a no?"

"No. That's a *you're gonna have to work for it.*'" She shrugged and arched her hips so the thick head slipped inside her. *God yes.* "I know it's not fair after those other orgasms, but I can't really feel my legs and that's your fault."

"Worth it." Will took her mouth again as he began to ease inside her, spreading her, filling her.

Until he stopped and jerked back.

Her eyes flew open. "What—"

"Fuck, I'm sorry." Will was shaking his head, his expression almost pained. "Condom. Nearly forgot. *Again*. Would have. I—"

Elizabeth lifted her head and kissed him. "It's okay. Skip it."

"You're sure?"

"I have that hormone implant to prevent pregnancy. I *was* on the pill, but my schedule became so harried I kept taking it at odd times." She worried her lower lip between her teeth, hesitated, but decided he deserved to know. "My boyfriend at the time had a bona fide latex allergy, so I decided to make things easy and got the hormone implant. We broke up three weeks later. Until you, I hadn't been with anyone else." A pause. "And you're the only person I've been with at all this year."

Will searched her eyes for a moment, and she could only hope he heard everything she wasn't saying.

"How long ago was this?" he asked.

"A few months before semester started."

"Did you love him?"

"No." That had ultimately been what had broken them up. He'd said the words and she'd realized she didn't know if she ever could.

"Good," Will said. "I... I've never had sex without a condom. Not once."

"Will?"

He expelled a deep breath.

"I want to feel your skin. Just you. Nothing else. That's what'll get me there right now."

He released a ragged breath and closed his mouth over hers. The next thing she knew, he was pushing inside her again.

Redefining her world again.

"God, you feel so good," Will murmured at her ear once he was buried to the hilt. "So goddamn good. My Elizabeth."

"Your Elizabeth," she replied, clenching her pussy around him.

Will shuddered and kissed her again as he began to move. And she felt it then as she had that afternoon—that certainty that she was exactly where she was supposed to be. That somehow, despite everything, she'd gotten this much right.

In that moment she found perfection.

And she never wanted to let go.

34

When Will awoke the next day, his arm around Elizabeth's waist, her naked back pulled flush against his bare chest, he understood two things with perfect clarity. The first being he was in love with her, which, while not necessarily a new revelation, meant more to him now than it had before.

The second was they had run out of excuses to avoid talking. Yesterday could be forgiven for the shock of finding her at Pemberley and subsequent determination to keep her from leaving. Last night had been something out of a dream—one he hadn't wanted to disturb with the shadow of reality.

It didn't take long for Elizabeth to stir. And when she blinked her eyes open, Will held, watching as she pieced together where she was and who she was with. He sighed when a sleepy smile crossed her face.

"You awake?" she asked softly.

"Yeah."

"How long?"

"Long enough to enjoy watching you wake up. Not so long that it was creepy."

Elizabeth snickered and rolled onto her back, her bright, vivid eyes meeting his. "I don't think that's for you to decide."

"I'm perfectly impartial."

"Uh huh."

He stole a kiss off her lips, then frowned. "Sorry. Morning breath."

"Yeah, but it's okay. My morning breath cancels out yours. That's how it works."

"Well, in that case." He kissed her again, taking his time and enjoying the way she softened against him. It would be easy, too easy, to roll her over and let his body assume control again. His cock was certainly on board with that idea, straining for the silken heat of her pussy, but he managed to get his head in the game and pull away.

No. They needed to talk. Really.

Elizabeth studied him for a moment with glassy eyes, panting. And apparently, she was on the same page. "We need to talk about things, don't we?"

"It's the responsible thing to do."

"But sex is so much more fun."

"I can't argue," Will replied, forcing himself to sit up. "But the sooner we talk, the sooner we can get back to this."

"You raise a good point."

If Elizabeth was optimistic about returning to his bed, then whatever they had to say to each other couldn't be bad. Not that he had any reason to believe it was.

Except that talking meant dredging up the past and he didn't much want to look in that direction.

"I'll put the coffee on if you want to get dressed," he said.

"*Want* is such a strong word." Elizabeth wrinkled her nose. "I should probably grab another shower, though."

"Me too."

A pause. "Want to take one together? Save some water?"

Will's lips twitched. "For the good of the environment?"

"Of course. And you did mention last night that it was on your to-do list."

He couldn't help himself. He grinned. "You're stalling."

"And angling for shower sex. Is it working?"

Will all but flew to his feet and seized her by the wrist. "This is the last distraction," he told her as he dragged her into the bathroom. "After this—"

"Coffee," Elizabeth said, twisting on the shower.

"Coffee," he agreed, hiking her into his arms as a spray of water hit his back.

"And breakfast." She took his cock into her small, perfect hand and pressed the head against her clit before slipping him down to where he wanted to be.

"Most important meal of the day," Will agreed. His words ended on a sigh as he slid into her pussy. "Shower. Coffee. Breakfast."

"Then talk." The words came out a moan.

"Uh huh," he agreed before nipping at her breast. "Then we'll talk."

By the time they tumbled out of the shower, the water had gone cold.

It was the best start to a day Will had ever experienced.

Elizabeth hadn't had many conversations that were anticipated by both parties. She'd rehearsed conversations she'd wanted to have and ended up having meaningful talks she hadn't planned, but finding the right balance when both people knew they needed to talk was just awkward. The air itself felt charged, almost sentient.

But one of them had to be the one to broach the subject, and since she had quite literally landed on his doorstep and was invading his space—no matter how much he seemed to like having his space invaded—it only seemed fair that she be the one to bite the bullet.

She waited until Will settled on the opposite end of the porch swing, coffee in hand, before forcing her throat to work.

"My parents separated right after I graduated high school."

Will paused, his mug halfway to his lips. "I knew your folks weren't together anymore."

"Well, yes, that's the short version. The not-so-short version involves my father essentially dumping on me and my mom that he'd been unhappy in the relationship for years and had wanted out, but felt he owed it to me to give me a normal childhood."

Will snorted, and her affection for him went up a couple dozen notches. "What's normal?"

"Right? Such a dick move." Elizabeth shivered, crossing her arms. "Thing is, I was... I *am* very close to my dad. I take after him, which scares me stupid sometimes. He and I seemed to have a secret language. He was always reading, attending lectures, broadening his horizons—things like that. My mom couldn't have possibly cared less. And the really shitty part is I used to be in on the joke with him—we'd roll our eyes whenever she'd start in on something that annoyed us. But I thought that was what it was—a joke. At the end of the day, I thought he loved her like I do. That my parents really were opposites who had and continued to attract. Then after I've graduated, he comes clean, says he wants out, and my mom is just...devastated."

Will set his coffee aside and shifted to look more directly at her. He didn't say anything, just drew her hair over her shoulder, comforting her with touch.

"What Dad didn't expect was this to be a bombshell announcement, which remains one of the dumber things he's ever told me. He didn't realize he was upending my life as much as hers." Elizabeth pressed her lips together. "My mom had a massive nervous breakdown. She was... She needed help for a long time. I put college on hold. Well, I tried to go at first but she called me every five minutes and eventually got herself hospitalized, so I dropped out and made her my priority. I realized last year that if I didn't make my education a priority now I never would, and I'd already put my life on hold for too damn long. I felt like a shit, but I needed to do what was right for me."

"That's not what I would call being a shit."

"Well, thank you." She raised her coffee mug to her mouth and took a healthy sip. "Last week, right before break, was my parents' wedding anniversary. My dad called to let me know he couldn't get a hold of Mom. He knows that... She's had episodes around this time of year, and this year was going to be really bad because he's probably going to tie the knot with his girlfriend sometime soon. So he called her to make sure she was okay." Elizabeth shook her head, her gut clenching. "Normally something I do, but I was too wrapped up in my own problems for the date to sink in. Anyway, to make a long story short, I hopped a plane to Florida when I couldn't reach her, either. I'm on her account and saw that her debit card had been used there recently."

"You...just dropped everything and went to Florida."

"In my defense, I was running on negative sleep reserves, stressed to the max about finals and distracted—" Elizabeth bit her tongue to keep the truth from spilling out, but one look in Will's direction convinced her to put everything on the table. They were trying this for real, weren't they? This honesty thing? "I was distracted because you suddenly were just...gone."

Will's eyebrows winged upward. "That distracted you?"

"Boy howdy."

"I..." He frowned. "I want to say I'm sorry—"

"But you're human and I kinda had it coming."

"That's not what I mean—"

"But it's fair. I was... God, Will, I was so freaking dumb. And that kills me because I am not a dumb person."

"Elizabeth—"

She held up a hand, forcing a smile. "We'll get there. Let me get through this first."

He tightened his jaw but nodded.

"Anyway, I got to Florida and realized that I am not an ace detective." She shook her head, a somewhat hysterical laugh bubbling off her lips. "And wonder of wonders, my mother decided that was the time to call, right about the time I had a freaking meltdown on the freeway. Long story short, she's off on an exotic vacation, now engaged to this multibillionaire who owns a bunch of casinos—Benito Delgado."

Will blinked. "Your mother's marrying Benito Delgado."

"Yeah. She apparently won his heart after refusing to accept a check when she hit a jackpot." Elizabeth laughed again, this time with more feeling. "The short story is, when I decided to go to college for real, Mom realized I meant business and actually got some help. She's been seeing a therapist and is on medication. I'm happy for her, but I also... It just seems like I resented her for so long, giving up years of my life to support her, and the one thing that pushed her to get better was me not being there anymore."

The chair creaked as Will slid closer to her, wrapped his arm around her. His now-familiar scent hit her nostrils, awakening parts of her body she honestly hadn't thought worked properly until he'd come into her life. It wasn't that she'd had bad sex—well, she had, but she'd also had really good sex. With Will, though... She didn't know how to describe it, except it felt different.

It felt like more than sex. And though she'd tried to deny it, it had since the beginning.

He kissed her brow. "I think, more than anything, that shows you how much she needed you. That without you she had no choice but to do the work herself."

"Yeah, and if I'd gone off the first time? Maybe she would've been happy these last few years."

"Maybe, but probably not." Will shrugged when she looked at him. "All you can do is guess. *My* guess would be that the help you gave her during those years is what enabled her to make that decision. If she hadn't had that..."

Elizabeth's eyes stung. She sniffed and tried to blink away her tears, but that did no good. "I really didn't mean to go all sob story on you," she said. "But that's a part of why I ended up in Derbyshire. Mom and I reconnected and she told me to take some time for myself before I went back to campus. She gave me money—a lot of money, actually, and... Well, I just started slowly making my way back to Meryton. She's the one who pointed me at Derbyshire, and...the name sounded familiar. Now for obvious reasons. It was in your email."

At that, Will tensed. It was the first time either one of them had mentioned it.

"I can't say I didn't come here because of you, but I wasn't thinking about it. I booked with Hunsford House because they had an opening and I was planning on doing the bulk of my drive back to campus on Christmas. Figured there wouldn't be much traffic."

"And what were you going to do when you got there?" Will asked. "Spring semester doesn't start until mid-January."

"Probably ruminate over my life choices to an unhealthy degree." Elizabeth swallowed, her eyes growing heavy again. There was little to no chance she was going to get through this next bit without crying. "I am so sorry, Will."

"Elizabeth—

"Sorry doesn't really cut it, actually. I was such an idiot and that just kills me."

"I was an idiot too. I don't think you have the market cornered on regret."

"Yeah, but Wickham? I get snowed by a guy like that?"

Will sighed and ran a hand through his hair. "He can be...charming."

Yeah. Like a car salesmen. It was a miracle she hadn't walked away with untold gallons of snake oil to unload. Elizabeth shook her head again. "And I thought I was so smart."

"You are. Elizabeth, I think you're the smartest person I know."

"But—"

"Being smart doesn't make you immune. I am not humoring you when I say Wickham's charming. His being charming is how he gets to be out there with other people rather than behind bars somewhere."

"Where he belongs."

"He had me fooled for years. And Georgiana." He paused. "Georgiana is the other smartest person I know. And no one has punished her more for what happened than she has. She believed the wrong person. So did you."

"And took it out on you," Elizabeth said.

"As much as I'd like to think I was perfect, I was an ass to you too." When she looked at him, she found his gaze focused on a spot on the pavement. "My assuming I could change what you wanted just because I wanted you to want something else."

Did? Elizabeth swallowed but didn't comment. She wasn't ready to know the answer to that question.

"The parts of you that I enjoy the most are also the parts that I'm...not used to, with the women I've been with," he continued. "You're so open and passionate. You don't shrink from a fight and you don't seem to care what people think. That intimidated the hell out of me. It still does. And I treated that like it needed to be fixed."

"I could use some restraining from time to time."

Will shook his head. "No. You don't need to change who you are to make other people comfortable." He cleared his throat. "And what I said about you sleeping with me even though—"

"Will, it's not necessary—"

"You're passionate. And you are not shy about sex." He paused, smirking. "Unless you've been busted by my sister."

Elizabeth snickered and nudged his shoulder with hers. "Don't think you can talk."

"I almost think it was worth it just to watch you go that shade of red."

"That's a one-time thing, my friend."

"I'm not going to ask you to prove it." Will kissed her temple again, his lips lingering this time. "I've seen what happens when you grow up repressed," he continued a moment later. "While my parents weren't bible thumpers, they did shy around topics like this. And god knows I did after they were gone. I wasn't about to give Georgie the birds and the bees talk, so I ignored the fact that she was a girl until it was too late. But in my head, sex was always that thing you did and never talked about. And you only did with people you at least liked. Or at least...didn't hate."

"Parts of me liked you a lot," Elizabeth offered. Another pause. "I never hated you. Not really. That was part of the problem."

"But you didn't like me."

"When I first met you, I thought you were a trust-fund baby who'd never heard the word *no*, or had the right type of legal team to make sure anyone who told you *no* disappeared." She exhaled. "You're hot and you have a ton of money. In my book that means you can't be a good person."

"You think I'm hot?"

"I think you know you're hot."

"It's nice to hear it, either way." Will favored her with a grin before his face turned serious again. "I'm glad you're here. However it is you got here."

Elizabeth pressed her lips together, shivered. "You mean it?"

"Oh yes." Heat flared behind his eyes before he lowered his gaze to her mouth. "Best Christmas gift I could ever have asked for is you...being here."

"You're just a glutton for punishment."

"Maybe. But if you're doling out the punishment, I'll take it." He dipped his head and caught her in a kiss before she could blink. It was soft and sweet, but full of promise of things yet to come.

It was then it struck her how deep she was in this—whatever this was between them. Elizabeth released a low, steady breath, fear racing with excitement and other things she wasn't quite ready to name. Will Darcy was someone she thought she could love, given enough time, and that was terrifying. Because love gave people power to hurt, to crush, destroy, and until right then, she hadn't been sure she believed in it anymore.

But damn, he made her want to believe that what she'd found here could last in the real world. Yet everything that had happened since she'd stepped out of her rental car on Pemberley's drive felt like something out of a storybook. This kind of thing simply didn't happen to real people, and it certainly didn't happen to her. How could anything here be sustainable?

It wasn't just Will, either. It was his home, his sister, everything she'd learned since she'd been here. Squeaky clean and easy, and impossible to trust.

But she wanted to.

And that scared her more than anything.

35

She fit. Into every damn thing. Such that he was beginning to dread the inevitable day when she told him she had to leave. If he had his way, she'd stay right up until the start of the new semester.

Elizabeth *belonged* here. In his bed, his home, his life.

On Christmas Eve, Will and Georgiana typically exchanged Christmas presents and did the whole "leave cookies for Santa" routine as had been started by their mother. Invariably, they got each other a set of Christmas pajamas—another tradition their mother had implemented—and concluded the evening with a fireside reading of *T'was the Night Before Christmas.*

Never before had anyone else been present for this. It was a Will and Georgie thing, a way to keep their parents' spirit alive, especially during a time when it was easier to feel their absence. Will had worried briefly that Georgiana would object to anyone joining in their private celebration, but his sister had insisted that Elizabeth take part.

She'd also made sure that Elizabeth had something to unwrap, though her Christmas jammies were a far cry from the traditional flannel awfulness they usually exchanged.

Will's sister had bought his girlfriend a bona fide Santa teddy. White fluffy lining, sheer red fabric, and a black bow keeping the brassier together. Oh, and a matching thong.

Elizabeth, thankfully, had burst out laughing and tackled Georgiana in a bear hug. Which was fortunate, because he might have otherwise had to kill her.

That night, however, Will couldn't say he begrudged his sister one little bit. When he walked into his bedroom to find Elizabeth in nothing but a scrap of red satin, he'd pretty much set the new mark for best Christmas ever.

"Fuck," he said, stopping short of the threshold. "You look..."

There weren't enough words in the English language to describe how she looked. The hem of the nightie—if it could even be called a nightie—barely kissed the top of Elizabeth's thighs, leaving him no choice but to admire the smooth skin of her legs. Her breasts were supported by a built-in brassiere which did little to keep her rosy nipples from staring at him through the thin fabric. His eyes drew southward, past those soft, perfect globes and to the valley between her legs.

She wore panties, though they were even thinner than the teddy—the teddy that was lined with white rabbit fur along the bottom hem and across the neckline. Panties that, like the brassiere, accentuated rather than supported. Her pussy was at the mercy of his hungry eyes, and Will found himself torn between tackling her to the bed or standing like an open-mouthed dolt who couldn't keep from staring. In the end, the latter won out. She was a wet dream come to life and all he could do was look at her. Stand and look at her, achingly aware of the painful hardening of his cock and the way he couldn't seem to move his jaw from where it had landed on the floor.

"I was feeling particularly festive tonight," she said, grinning. "And since I didn't get you a present, I thought..."

"You are my present."

"That's the general idea." Elizabeth took a step forward, her dark eyes going darker in a way that betrayed her own arousal, and Will had to force his feet to keep from moving, because knowing that she was turned on was its own special aphrodisiac.

"There's something I want to do," she said, hooking a finger into the waistband of his jeans to pull him forward, and he gave up the fight without even trying. Hell, he damn near stumbled in his urgency.

"Looking like that, you can do whatever you like."

"When I did this the first time, it was to win." She coaxed his shirt over his head before dropping her hands to his chest, making his skin sizzle. "I want to do it now because I... I like you. A lot. And I like making you feel good."

A half moan peeled from Will's lips. "I... I don't know what to say to that."

"Say nothing." She turned her fingers to his belt and had it ripped free within seconds. Then she was jerking down his fly, freeing his cock. He hadn't bothered with boxers today and he'd never been gladder than he was at that moment. Will let his head roll back, surrendering as she fisted him and began to pump.

That was until she drew her hand away and shoved his jeans the rest of the way down his legs and he remembered that he still had undressing to do.

"Shoes," Elizabeth said as he toed the first one off. "Now jeans."

He stepped out of the puddle they'd made at his feet, now left only in his socks, which didn't feel nearly as ridiculous as it should.

"Bed."

He nodded and forced himself to move. When he sat on the edge of the mattress, Elizabeth shook her head and gestured to the headboard. "Lay back."

Will swallowed but obeyed. The next second, he felt her pulling his socks off his feet. She paused to pinch his big toe and run her fingers up the arch of his foot, giggling when he jerked.

"Oh, dangerous move. I now know your weak spots."

He lifted his head to admire the wicked smirk on her face. "That's the last one. You had all the others."

"Then you're conquered."

"Officially yours."

"Mmm." Elizabeth climbed onto the bed and moved to straddle his legs, bits of rabbit fur skimming along his skin and sending a wave of goosebumps in their wake. "And here you have a flag." She wrapped her fingers around his cock again, squeezing. "But I think it's on my side."

"Definitely," Will agreed on a moan.

"I think you'll find I am a benevolent queen," she said, leaning forward until those perfect lips of hers were just a hair away from his cockhead. "Very generous."

"Elizabeth..."

"I told you I wanted to do this for the right reasons. I do." She grinned up at him again, then drew a line from the base of his shaft to the tip with her tongue. "Not to win."

"I'm already yours so you've won anyway."

"Bonus." Elizabeth lowered her mouth again, this time pressing a hot kiss against the base. Then another a bit higher. And another. And another until those wonderful lips of hers were again caressing the crown of his cock. "Don't blink. I want you to watch."

Yeah, he wasn't going to last long. At the moment, he wasn't sure he gave a damn. And when her mouth closed around him, that magic tongue of hers doing its magic thing, he was sure he didn't.

Despite his best intentions, Will did close his eyes. It was instinct when wanting to savor something. But he also remembered himself quickly and forced them back open again to find her giving him a particularly impish look, all the more impressive since her mouth was around him.

"Good boy," she said, then brushed a tender kiss to the head of his cock. And before he could respond, her mouth was on him again, and he watched. Watched as she licked around his crown and sucked him in, as that magnificent mouth descended inch over inch, then drew back again.

She had lit a match to every nerve in his body, the sensation both unbearable and habit-forming. Will understood he was, in many ways, atypical of what people assumed of a wealthy twenty-something in this age, which he chalked up largely to his upbringing. Sex was to be enjoyed but not necessarily indulged like this—where he had permission to ogle the sight of his cock disappearing into the heaven she called a mouth as pleasure mounted. And her eyes remained on him the entire time.

Will hissed as her lips tightened around him, the suction of her mouth becoming more intense, taking him deeper and deeper until he felt himself brushing the back of her throat. He bucked without meaning to and was fumbling with an apology when she murmured and began swallowing around him.

"Fuck!" he gasped, hands flailing, unsure where to land. He threaded his fingers through her hair, massaging in an effort to keep from holding her in place. Elizabeth made a sound of encouragement, drew back so that a couple inches of his shiny prick were visible, then sucked down on him again.

"Oh... Elizabeth..." He wasn't going to last and he wanted to last. As much as he relished the idea of spending down her throat, he wanted to be inside her again. Wanted to feel her come around him, because as heavenly as her mouth was, her pussy was even better.

"S-stop."

Elizabeth arched an eyebrow, again managing to look much too critical with her mouth full of him.

"Need...*you.*"

She drew back until her lips were at his tip. "Thought that's what I was doing."

"Need your..." He shook his head, wrestling with propriety—which decided to make him feel self-aware at the oddest times—then shrugged it off. "I need to feel your cunt."

"That's a naughty word."

"You like it when I use naughty words."

"I do." She pressed a kiss to the head of his cock, and he thought for a moment she was going to deny him, but she started making her way up his body instead. The drag of the sleek fabric against his flesh made him burn with awareness. He itched to tear the garment off her, but there was something about admiring her nipples through the satin curtain that halted his fingers.

Will released a ragged breath as she settled on his hips, his cock pressed against the wet strip of silk separating him from her pussy. He scaled his hands up her sides until he had a breast cradled against each palm. "You're my favorite present," he said, running his thumbs over her pebbled nipples. "Fuck, the way you feel..."

"Mhmm." She wrapped her hand around his cock and began to stroke. "You want me like this? On top?"

He nodded. Yeah, if there was anything better than watching her suck on him, it was this. He dropped a hand to delve beneath the hem of the teddy. "You like these?" he asked, fingering the skimpy strands that held her thong in place.

"Sorry to bust your bubble, but I am not a thong person. I'm wearing this on account of it being your present."

"Part of my present is unwrapping then, right?"

She nodded.

"Then you won't mind if I..." He fisted the material and tugged. It was by virtue of the fact that the material had been more or less designed not to last that the fabric snapped as cleanly as it did. Once she was bare to him, he nudged her forward until the wet seam of her pussy was pressed against his cock and he could feel her heat.

"You're very lucky," Elizabeth said, somewhat breathless. "That could have gone badly. Nothing turns me off faster than a wedgie."

He barked a laugh and tugged her down for a kiss before he did something stupid, like tell her he loved her again. The words were there, pressing at his lips and desperate for freedom, but he forced them back for another time.

He wouldn't rush in again. Refused to. With as perfect as the past couple days had been, he didn't want to complicate them now with declarations she might not want.

This time, he was doing things right.

Her kisses were hot and eager. She fed him back his own hunger with an urgency that had every cell in his body blazing, and only with a whimper pulled away to sit up again. Breathing hard, Elizabeth fisted the material of her teddy. "Do you mind if I ditch this?"

Will answered by tugging it over her head. "I was wrong," he decided, hands going back to her breasts.

"About what?"

"Whether or not your nipples looked better behind that satin or like this." He gave them a playful tug. "Like this."

"For the record," Elizabeth said, lifting her hips and running the tip of his cock between her labia, "if a girl offers to wear that stuff for you, it means she likes you. A lot."

"Oh yeah?" he breathed, watching her tease her clit with his cockhead. Then she shifted and he was pressed at the hot mouth of her pussy.

"Yes," she agreed with a moan, and sank down until he was buried to the hilt. "Oh, shit, Will. Every damn time."

"I know." And he did. Sex had never been this good. He hadn't thought it could be.

A ragged breath rode from Elizabeth's lips. She held him inside her for a long second, then began to move. Slowly at first. Rise and fall. Rise and fall. She steadied her hands on his chest, fingers curling.

"You're perfect," he breathed, grasping her hips. "Perfect, Elizabeth."

She shook her head, strands of brown whipping across her face.

"Perfect for me."

"Will—"

"Yes."

He didn't know what he was agreeing to and he didn't care. His senses departed, leaving him stranded in the moment, watching as her eyes grew darker, hotter, as her cheeks turned red. The swing of her breasts every time her pussy took him back in. She looked like a goddess, wanton and gorgeous and for the moment, his. Will dug his fingers into her hips, determined to drink in every second. The way she whimpered and sighed, the shape her lips made when he struck her just right. The intoxicating sight of his cock, slick with her juices, pushing in and out of her cunt as she took him inside again and again. The illicit smack of their bodies coming together as the bed springs whined and their breaths tangled. The way her flesh molded around him, hot and silky and so tight he could hardly think.

"Fuck, you're beautiful." The words left him in an explosion. "Elizabeth."

"Please touch me."

Will lifted himself until he was upright, and they shared a moan. He wanted to feel those breasts against his chest, but not before teasing them with his lips. Elizabeth wove her fingers through his hair, her nails scaling his scalp.

"Will..."

He nodded, nipping at her breast, then dragged his lips up her sweat-laced skin until they were a whisper from hers. "Like this?" he asked, and edged a hand between them.

Elizabeth nodded, her eyes going somewhat wild. "Like—"

He tapped her clit on her downstroke and moaned when she shuddered.

"That," she agreed. "Will. That's it."

"Faster now."

She nodded in agreement and seized his shoulders. Then she was bouncing on him in earnest, every thrust accented with a throaty grunt that drove him wild. He kissed a line up and down her neck, her jaw, tugged at her earlobe with his teeth, and every time she took his cock inside, he was there, pressing against her clit, massaging her slippery flesh, and willing her to topple because *fuck him* he couldn't last much longer. His balls ached and his spine tensed, but he gritted his teeth and willed restraint, needing to feel her first.

Then, thank *god,* she was coming. Her pussy tightened and her body tensed and she threw her head back, a raw, sexy cry tearing at her throat. Will threw his arms around her as she shuddered, pushed her back onto the mattress so she was under him, still whimpering, and began pounding into her, chasing his own release now. Wanting to milk every damn second.

"Fuh...fuck, Will..."

Shit, she was still coming, spasming wildly around his cock. He shuddered and groaned and thrust harder still, until he couldn't hold on any longer. He buried his face in her neck and groaned as he spilled himself inside her, ecstasy blistering a path through his body so for a second, he became a full-fledged believer in spontaneous combustion.

Seconds, minutes, decades later, Will became aware of the sensation of small, whispery kisses fluttering across his brow. He forced his eyes open, found Elizabeth grinning at him, about as gorgeous as he'd ever seen her. Face flushed, eyes warm, her sweat-drenched hair plastered to her skin.

I love you.

The words were unspoken but tangible, and they became more so by the second.

Before break was through, he'd tell her. He could only hope she understood what that meant for him. That when he said the words, he had forever on the brain.

"What are you thinking?" Elizabeth asked, grin still in place.

He dropped a kiss on her lips. "Something along the lines of *best Christmas ever.*"

She threw her head back and laughed, the sound giddy. And that last piece cemented for him.

Yeah, this had better be forever. He wasn't sure he would survive losing her again.

36

The best thing about Christmas that morning was the part that happened before she managed to crawl out of Will's bed, namely because it had involved a naked Will and a tickle fight that neither one of them had really lost. Elizabeth had eventually shoved him off so she could take a shower—a shower she had to somewhat limp toward, given the tenderness between her legs. And yeah, seeing Will's satisfied smirk at her condition had done all kinds of things to her—things that made her care less about limping and more about skipping breakfast.

Sadly, that much was not an option, but it did lead to the second best thing about Christmas that morning.

That was the mixture of shock, horror, and outrage that made up Caroline Bingley's face when Elizabeth joined them at the breakfast table.

"What is she doing here?"

"Elizabeth!" Charlie Bingley, the perpetual opposite of Caroline in every way, bounded to his feet and threw his arms around her. "What in the world brings you to Pemberley?"

"I...uhh..." Elizabeth looked over Charlie's shoulder to meet

Will's eyes. She quirked an eyebrow. "You didn't tell them I was here?"

Will hid his smile behind a hand. "I wanted to," he said. "But I lost the coin toss."

Georgiana straightened her shoulders, beaming. "And, obviously, my way is always superior."

Charlie pulled back and practically dragged her to the vacant seat. "We were taking bets on who was going to join us. I was seriously worried it was going to be Anne de Bourgh."

"Anne who?"

"Snooty McSnooterson," Georgiana said, rolling her eyes. "Since you were staying with the Collinses, I'm sure you got to hear all about Rosings, right?"

Elizabeth snickered as she took her seat beside Will, who promptly passed her a serving dish full of scrambled eggs. "Yeah, Charlotte's husband is...well, I gather a fan."

"If by fan you mean lives with his head crammed up her old lady ass," Georgiana agreed.

Elizabeth snickered again, shoveling a healthy portion onto her plate.

If possible, Caroline went even stiffer, though she tried to smile. *Tried* being the operative word. Her lips were pulled so tight it looked like her face was ready to crack. "I see Elizabeth has already left quite an impression on Pemberley."

"Yes," Will said, exchanging the eggs for a platter full of bacon and sausage. "Georgiana's behavior hasn't been this refined since I bribed her to play nice at Louisa's wedding."

"Anyway," Charlie said loudly, giving his sister an uncertain look, "Catherine de Bourgh, who owns Rosings, has been trying to set up Will with her daughter since... How long's it been, man?"

"Well, I think the first time I heard her mention it, I was in my He-Man phase, so..."

"That narrows down precisely squat," Georgiana said before stuffing a biscuit into her mouth. She turned to Elizabeth, cheeks bulging. "How you can stand to let him bone you in his Fortress of Geekitude, I dunno, but mad props."

Caroline spat out a mouthful of orange juice, her face going bright red.

"Georgie," Will said, turning a little rouge himself, but his eyes were dancing, "remember what we were talking about before breakfast?"

"I distinctly remember making zero promises." Georgiana looked back to Elizabeth. "Anyway, since they're taking forever to get to the point of an already boring story: Old Lady Rosings has been hot for Will to marry Anne because, I dunno, *old blood* stuff, you know." She shuddered. "And before you walk-of-shamed your way to breakfast, Anne was the favorite as to who was joining our happy family for Christmas. Thankfully, big bro has better taste than that snoozefest."

"Georgie," Will said, "Anne's a perfectly nice person."

"With a witch for a mom."

"Well—"

"You two are terrible," Charlie said with a laugh. He shook his head and looked back to Elizabeth. "This can go on for a long time, just to warn you."

"Oh, I've already seen some pretty spectacular throwdowns," she said, smiling her thanks at Will as he handed her the breakfast potatoes. "They might want to invest in a sign or something for the front door—Beware of Sniping Siblings or something."

Georgiana nodded. "It is only fair to warn people."

Caroline, having just finished mopping up the last of her spilled orange juice, looked up and set her narrowed eyes on Elizabeth. "What are you doing here?" The question wasn't so much asked as it was snapped. Her cheeks were stained pink and her hair, which Elizabeth had never seen looking anything but flawless, had lost whatever shaped it had been pulled into. Stray strands stood up in every which direction.

She tried not to enjoy the scene too much, she really did, but Elizabeth couldn't seem to convince her mouth that smiling probably wasn't the best thing to do at the moment. "I was staying at Hunsford House and Will asked me to spend Christmas here."

"What are you doing in *Derbyshire?*"

Charlie stared at his sister. "What is your problem?"

Georgiana snorted and rolled her eyes.

"I was making my way back to campus from St. Augustine," Elizabeth said coolly. "Derbyshire happened to be on the way."

"And I invited her to stay," Will said, his tone firmer than it had been all morning.

"I thought you two broke up."

Charlie blinked, looking from Will to Caroline to Will again. "Wait...you and Elizabeth were dating?"

Elizabeth managed to keep from squirming, but only just.

"Yes," Caroline stated when neither of them volunteered an answer. "But Elizabeth, weren't you seeing someone else before break? I could have sworn I saw something about you and George Wickham."

Every inch of Elizabeth went rigid, her heart giving a wild spasm. *Oh fuck you.*

But she didn't have time to respond. The sound of breaking glass shattered the air and Georgiana, pale as a ghost, leapt to her feet. Elizabeth didn't realize she had jumped too, until she had her arms around the girl.

"I'm fine," Georgiana said, clammy and trembling, but she didn't try to pull away. Her gaze followed the fallen shards of her glass. "I'm fine."

"Caroline," Charlie hissed. "What the fuck is your problem?"

Elizabeth aimed a glare at Caroline. "To answer your question," she said through clenched teeth, nearly vibrating with enough rage to bring down the entire goddamned house, "the last time I saw Wickham, I kneed him in the family jewels. Suffice it to say, we didn't have a second date."

Georgiana abruptly stopped shaking. "Wait... You what?"

Elizabeth pulled back, and despite herself, she couldn't keep from grinning. "Right in the balls," she said. "And then I stepped over him and went to get some Chinese."

Georgiana stared at her for a moment, blinking.

Then threw her head back and burst out laughing. True, hard cackles that shook her shoulders and filled the air until the sound was bouncing off the walls at maximum volume. Georgiana laughed until her face was almost purple and fat tears were tearing down her cheeks, until the sound became wispy and hoarse.

"This is why you're my favorite person!" she bellowed, throwing her arms tight around Elizabeth. "Oh, did he cry? I bet he cried. Big fat man-tears. I don't suppose there's any chance that you recorded this? 'Cause that's one movie I'd pay to own."

"Sadly, I did not think ahead."

"Next time you kick him in the balls, please tape it for me. Or better yet! We can do it together. Take turns."

Elizabeth barked a laugh herself and shook her head, looking back to Will for the first time since Wickham's name had come up. He, too, was on his feet, his gaze fixed on his sister, his mouth drawn and skin a shade paler than normal. He released a long breath and turned to Caroline. Whatever warmth had been in his eyes vanished immediately.

"Never do that again."

Caroline looked alarmed, but lifted her chin. "Do what?"

"Mention him. Not in this house, not in front of Georgiana, and especially not to score points."

"I didn't—"

"Yes, you did. Don't play dumb."

The air in the room grew hot and thick. Elizabeth swallowed and followed his gaze, and tried—really tried—not to smirk at the stricken look on Caroline's face. From the way her brow was pulled and her mouth twisted into a snarl, it seemed she was torn between anger and tears.

"I never meant to upset Georgiana," Caroline said, her voice thick. "It's the last thing I'd want."

Georgiana snorted and rolled her eyes, crashing back into her seat. "Yeah. It shows."

"Georgie—"

"No worries, C. We're cool." The girl popped a strip of bacon in her mouth and grinned. "Actually, hearing that fuckwit might not be able to bring little fuckwits into this world is *exactly* what I wanted for Christmas." She tossed Elizabeth a beaming smile. "So thanks. I'd say you really shouldn't have, but it's just my size and I am so not taking it back to the store."

Charlie, who had more or less spent the past couple minutes looking desperate for an escape hatch, sputtered a laugh and raised his glass of orange juice. "Hear, hear."

"Will, Georgiana..." Caroline pressed her lips together, visibly struggling. "I apologize."

"What part of *best story ever* don't you understand?" Georgiana replied.

"You also owe Elizabeth an apology," Will said.

Caroline blanched like she'd been asked to eat slugs. "What?"

"Elizabeth is a guest in my home and you have been nothing but rude since she joined us for breakfast."

Caroline blanched again, looked up and down the table, then sighed and shook her head. "I think I might head home, Charles," she said instead, pushing back her chair. "I suddenly have a headache."

Charlie shrugged and stuffed a forkful of potato in his mouth before shifting and dragging a set of car keys out of his pocket. "I'll borrow one of Will's cars. See you this afternoon."

Another pause, and this time Caroline looked like she might cry after all at her brother's apparent apathy. But she didn't cry, which Elizabeth respected, albeit begrudgingly. Instead, she gave a haughty nod, took the keys, and left the dining room without another word. No one spoke until the echoes of the front door closing had died.

"We've been fighting since you left campus," Charlie said quietly. "Well, before you left campus. After..." He seemed to catch himself and glanced to Elizabeth, a somewhat pained smile contorting his face. "How *is* Jane?"

"Jane?" Elizabeth looked to Will for help, but he had none to offer. "She's...the last I knew, she was doing well. I talked to her a couple nights ago."

Now that she thought about it, she hadn't checked in with Jane since she'd joined the Darcy household. She frowned, trying to remember when she'd last checked her phone. Then she tried to remember when she'd last *seen* her phone, which proved next to impossible.

Elizabeth shook her head and shifted to Will. "Have I used my phone at all since I've been here?"

"I don't know, but I don't think I've seen you with it."

"Which means it's probably dead." She turned back to Charlie. "Jane was good when I last talked to her."

Charlie offered a small, almost sad smile. "She loves you a lot, doesn't she?"

"She's the sister I always wanted and probably the best person I know." Elizabeth paused, glancing to Will, then to Georgiana, and found herself flooded with warmth. "Well...one of the best people I know, at least."

"Do'h, you're such a sap." Georgiana threw an arm around

Elizabeth and tugged so hard she nearly toppled out of her chair. "But I love you too. And if you and Will don't end up getting married, I'm pretty much going to demand that you adopt me."

Will grunted something unintelligible, his cheeks going pink.

Charlie gave him a long look before turning back to Elizabeth, a sly grin spreading across his face. "So are you two serious?"

Elizabeth swallowed. There was no good way to answer that question, particularly since she had zero idea where she and Will stood right now. Even with the conversations they'd had, they hadn't come close to broaching the subject of what their relationship was now or what would happen when they went back to campus. At one point, not so long ago, Will had told her he loved her, but those words had not resurfaced, either, and Elizabeth was too much of a chickenshit to try and chase them down.

But she wanted to know too.

When the silence shifted from awkward to uncomfortable, she licked her lips and gave herself a mental nudge. "I—"

"Charlie," Will said suddenly, "on the subject of Jane, there's something I've been meaning to tell you."

Charlie jerked his head to Will so rapidly it'd be a miracle if he hadn't given himself whiplash. "What? Is something wrong?"

"No," Will replied. Then hesitated. "Well, *I* was. Wrong, that is."

Elizabeth inhaled, seized her orange juice and took a healthy swig.

"Wrong about what?" Charlie demanded, his voice somewhat manic.

Will hesitated. "I think you should talk to her."

"Okay, but wrong about what?"

There was nothing for a moment but the sound of Georgiana's enthusiastic chewing. The girl was watching the exchange like others might a professional sport.

"I think it's easy for people like me to believe the worst in others," Will said carefully. "After what happened..." He shifted his gaze briefly to his sister and back again. "I can be a little... closed-minded and reactionary."

Georgiana snorted and crunched on a strip of bacon.

Charlie blinked, looked to Elizabeth, to Will, and back again. "Do you know what he's talking about?" he asked bluntly.

Elizabeth hesitated. "I think it's easy to...*infer* certain things, especially if you aren't direct."

"Neither one of you are being very direct at the moment."

"Caroline implied Jane was using you for your connections," Will said. "I didn't disagree with her because I wasn't sure what to think. But what I should have said then, and what I'm saying now, is that you should talk to her and figure out what's true and what's not."

Charlie was quiet for a moment. Then his eyes narrowed. "Seriously? You're telling me this now?"

"To be fair, this seems like something you might have worked out on your own," Elizabeth said.

Charlie, for his part, looked somewhat wounded. He sighed and sank into his seat, giving his half-eaten plate of food a look like it had betrayed him. "I was afraid it might be true." He jerked his head up. "What has Jane said about me?"

Elizabeth smothered a cough. "Um, no."

"What? You can't just dump this on me and not share!"

"I'm sorry. I am prohibited from speaking on the subject by the Best Friend Code of Conduct."

Charlie released a sound that was half moan, half whine. "Can you just tell me if she liked me or not?" he asked in a loud whisper. "It's Christmas! You have to tell me."

"I'm sorry, I'm not a toddler therefore that argument will not work on me."

"Elizabeth!" Charlie shot Will a pleading look. "She's being unreasonable. Make her stop."

Will laughed outright. "You clearly don't know Elizabeth."

"You know that Jane means the world to me." He refocused on Elizabeth, eyes round and pleading. "Jane means *the world* to me. It hasn't gotten better. I miss her so fucking much it's like... poison in my chest."

"Regular poet, you are," Georgiana muttered.

"You love Jane like...poison," Elizabeth repeated dully.

"Yes. No! That's not what I mean at all and..." He looked down now, shoulders slumping. "I've never felt about anyone the way I feel about Jane. Cutting things off with her was the worst decision I ever made."

"If you're looking for ways to grovel, that's a nice start," Georgiana offered. "I mean, I guess. I've never been dumped but as far as lines go, I wouldn't throw you out if you admitted from the get-go that you were a dumbass."

"I was a dumbass," Charlie repeated blandly.

"From what I gather, you had help being a dumbass," Elizabeth said. "If that makes you feel any better."

"It doesn't." He shook his head and for a horrible moment, she thought he might start crying. "But you think there's a chance she'd take me back?"

"I'm not going to speak for Jane at all." She paused. "Except to say that you have a lot of work to do if you want to make things right. And warn you, obviously, that should she decide to take you back and you hurt her again...your body will never be found."

Georgiana snorted again. "Seriously. Favorite person ever right here."

"Can you at least *ask* Jane if she'd be willing to talk to me?"

Charlie asked. "If she's not, I'll leave her alone, but... Elizabeth, for Christmas. Would you at least do that?"

That request was easy enough. She offered a small smile. "That I can do. But if the answer is no, you're on your own."

"Okay." He nodded so emphatically it was a miracle his head didn't pop off. Then he stared at her with marked expectation, until it dawned on her that he was waiting for her to whip out her phone.

"You want me to do this now, then," Elizabeth said.

"Okay," he agreed with a smile.

"It's Christmas—she might not be in the mood to talk ex-boyfriends. Plus, my phone, wherever it is, is dead. I haven't charged it since I got here."

Charlie nodded. "Okay. Well, go charge it."

Will heaved a hard sigh. "Can she at least finish breakfast?"

"It can charge through breakfast," Charlie replied. "Come on. I have to know if there's a chance."

"I hope this Jane chick likes her men extra needy," Georgiana muttered. "Otherwise Charlie's gonna be SOL."

Elizabeth snickered and pushed her chair back. "Fine. I'll be right back."

Charlie relaxed, a dopey, almost drunk smile stretching his mouth wide. "Thanks, Elizabeth. You're the best." He turned to Will and winked. "I love your girlfriend. Hope that's not weird for you."

Will's lips twitched but he didn't say anything, just met Elizabeth's eyes. The uncertainty she felt was thrown back at her, and for the first time since arriving at Pemberley, her gut twisted with something other than excitement.

They needed to figure out what they were doing and if it would last beyond this interlude from real life. If Will still felt any of what he'd shared before, if he wanted to continue seeing her when they returned to Meryton.

If the thing she felt for him was what she thought it was, and if she was brave enough to face it.

"I'll be right back," she said, standing. "Have a phone to charge."

Ten minutes later, when Elizabeth returned to the table, she knew immediately she wouldn't be sitting there for long. Charlie radiated a sort of manic energy that seemed seconds away from combusting. He did, at least, let her get through breakfast before suggesting—or shouting—that she might go check and see if she had enough battery to place a call.

"I'm going, I'm going," she said after she'd polished off her second helping of breakfast potatoes. "You guys start the gift exchange. I don't have anything to contribute, anyway."

"Yet," Charlie told her, rocking on his heels. "You may yet get me the best present of all."

"Then I suppose I'll be returning that tie I picked out for you," Georgiana muttered with an eye-roll. She looked to Elizabeth. "Seriously, woman. Next time learn when to not volunteer information."

"It's fine," Elizabeth replied, pushing in her chair. "Since Charlie's making me break out the chargers, I'll go ahead and power up my laptop and see if any grades have been posted."

Georgiana made a face. "Yuck. That's one way to kill the holiday spirit."

"Some of us make grades we're not ashamed of," Will replied, standing and starting to collect dishes. And for some reason, the sight of him doing something so ordinary, so domestic, made her think things so well beyond the normal range of her thoughts they almost felt like they belonged to someone else.

Maybe because she'd never pictured Will cleaning up after himself or his guests. Still, the house staff had the day off, and someone had to do the dishes.

Which made her aware of something else.

"Did you cook?" Elizabeth blurted.

Will paused, hand outstretched for her plate. "Breakfast? Yes."

"*You* cooked."

"Will knows how to scramble with the best of 'em," Georgiana said. "But breakfast is all he can do."

"You *cooked*."

Will studied her for a moment before a sexy grin took over his mouth. "You don't have to sound so surprised."

"I think I do." Elizabeth stood and handed Will her plate. "And since you cooked, it's kinda criminal that you have to clean up. I'd help, but—"

Charlie mewled in complaint.

"But, that."

Will winked. "Wouldn't let you lift a finger, anyway. Something tells me you could burn down a kitchen just by looking at it."

At that, Elizabeth barked an appreciative laugh, her insides flooding with the sensation she thought could be love. "I'd be offended if it weren't so true. I think you might know me too well."

"Not too well," he replied, his tone dropping. "Don't think that's possible."

A charged beat filled the air until Georgiana began making gagging sounds.

Elizabeth drew back and sighed, the spell, fleeting as it had been, broken. "Right," she said, starting once more for the staircase. "I'll be back in a minute."

"Thank you!" Charlie called after her.

The phone had charged enough to show she had several thousand notifications to surf through—most looking to be texts from Jane, though she also had missed a call from her mom and another from a phone number bearing the Meryton area.

A knot of unease settled in her stomach—small yet potent all the same. Elizabeth swallowed and seized her laptop, her racing brain already seizing the rather sizable list of potential catastrophes for the likelihood rundown. She settled herself on the bed and began scrolling through her texts as her laptop slowly came to life.

Jane: Hey—everything OK? Haven't heard from you in a couple days.

Jane: Did you get my last message?

Jane: Making sure you saw this.

"Shit," she muttered, pressing down on the phone icon with her thumb. There were still rows of messages to read through, but it seemed better to go ahead and get this part out of the way now.

She had just managed to connect her laptop to Will's Wi-Fi —he'd given her his password the first night, which Georgiana had later told her was the modern day equivalent of going steady—and bring up her campus email application when Jane answered.

"Elizabeth?"

"Jane, I am so sorry, I—"

"Oh, *thank god*. Where the heck have you been?"

That was a loaded question. Elizabeth sighed again, her gaze falling on the apparently insanely valuable Jawa situated inside the display case across from the bed. Georgiana was right—this was the Fortress of Geekitude.

But it was all Will, and that made it perfect.

"It's been a crazy couple days. But good crazy. So good I let my phone die and kinda forgot about it until right now."

There was a pause. "You understand that is the lamest

excuse in the history of excuse making and you will be punished for making me worry."

"You are firm but fair."

Finally, her email client opened to a slew of unread messages.

Her world stopped when her eyes landed on the subject line of the first.

ACADEMIC STANDING

"Lizzie, have you heard from Lydia?"

"What?" she asked, her heart at once at a gallop. She clicked the email open and began to read.

"Lydia. Has she contacted you?"

"What?" But she still wasn't listening. All she could do was read that first paragraph again, because what it said couldn't be right. She had a loose wire in her head firing off the wrong synapses. This couldn't be real.

To E. Bennet:

The purpose of this letter is to inform you of the decision reached by the President of Student Affairs at Meryton College, following the previous correspondence sent to you on December 18 regarding our institution's zero tolerance policy for plagiarism. Upon reviewing the evidence provided by Dr. Greenfield, we have scheduled a formal hearing to occur on December 30 to discuss the charges and appropriate disciplinary actions, up to and including expulsion. Please appear in the Dean of Students Office, Oakham Hall, room 304 at 10:00. Failure to attend will result in immediate expulsion.

37

This wasn't real. It couldn't be.

Elizabeth felt her skin heating, her lungs clamoring for air. She felt all these things as a distant observer, detached, a driver who had lost control of the car and was chasing it as it glided toward the freeway. The words on the screen didn't change, no matter how hard she tried to convince herself she'd read wrong.

The car that was her body was about to collide with the interstate at rush-hour and all she could do was watch.

"Elizabeth! What is going on? Did you hear me?"

She released a shaky breath, the rolling sensation in her stomach taking a hard turn toward nausea. "Expelled."

A pause. "What?"

"I... I'm going to be expelled."

"No you aren't."

The response was so immediate, so Jane, that it nearly made her cry.

"I'm looking at the email right now."

"No."

"Jane—"

"That has to be a mistake. Or a joke."

"It's from the President of Student Affairs. I'm facing expulsion." Elizabeth reread the line again, willing it to change. It didn't. "For plagiarism."

"What?" The word came out half breath, half giggle. "No, that's ridiculous. It has to be a prank or something."

Yes, it had to be. Only it wasn't. She shook her head, eyes beginning to burn as she skimmed the rest of the email. "I don't think so. I have a hearing in five days. They'll decide if I'm expelled then."

"So you're not expelled yet. Told you."

"But..." But the words were still there. *Plagiarism. Expelled.* A spark of hope burst but died just as quickly. Things like this didn't just go away.

She hadn't done anything wrong. This had to be a mistake. It just had to be.

"Elizabeth," Jane said softly, her voice bringing her back to earth, "you don't plagiarize."

"I know." Elizabeth swallowed. She glanced to the doorway. The room where she'd spent the happiest nights of her life remained unchanged, and the sound of laughter downstairs told her that Christmas was well underway. But the view from here had been altered. It was no longer her haven, the place outside real life. And when she left, she couldn't take this with her.

Expelled.

"Lizzie? Lizzie, talk to me."

Elizabeth released a breath she hadn't realized she'd been holding, but the awful pressure under her breastbone didn't diminish. "Jane, I think I need to go—"

"Okay. And I know you have this whole other thing on your mind now, but please just tell me if you've heard from Lydia."

She blinked. "Lydia? How in the world could I have heard from Lydia? My phone's been off. Plus, we're not exactly BFFs."

"I have to ask. Kitty's going mad with worry and won't stop

calling."

"Why is Kitty calling you? Why are we worried about Lydia?"

"Right before break, Lydia...did something really stupid."

That was a truly disturbing revelation, because Lydia wasn't exactly known for her forethought. Elizabeth almost hated to ask, but thankfully, she didn't have to. Jane continued the next second.

"Lizzie... She and Wickham...started seeing each other."

Elizabeth's stomach lurched. "What?"

"It started right after you left. I didn't want to upset you," Jane replied miserably. "I knew you'd find out but you were on your vacation and seemed to be having fun and knowing that she was with him would have ruined all that."

Well, it wouldn't have ruined anything, but she certainly would have taken notice. Elizabeth allowed herself a few seconds to absorb this new information before releasing what she hoped was a tempered breath. "Did you at least warn her?"

"Of course I did. I told her he wasn't to be trusted and what he's put you through and... I don't know if she didn't believe it or if she didn't realize how serious it was. You know Lydia. She doesn't always think things through."

That was an understatement.

"Anyway," Jane said a moment later, "she and Wickham went out a few nights ago and never came back. That's why Kitty called me—she thought my dad might be able to do something. I tried to explain that attorneys aren't private investigators, but I don't even know if that got through. I was hoping you might have heard from Lydia—that she might have reached out to you if she was in trouble, since it involved Wickham."

Elizabeth shook her head. Then, upon remembering Jane couldn't see her, said, "Well, my phone's been off and I... No, I haven't heard from her."

"I'm starting to get really worried." Jane swallowed audibly.

"Tell me I'm overreacting and everything is probably fine."

She wished she could, more than anything, but her mind was busy dredging up the things Will had mentioned in his email—how he'd talked Georgiana into running away with him, into sleeping with him. There had at least been a motive there—hurt Will, possibly touch some of the Darcy money, a combination thereof. Lydia didn't make any sense, unless perhaps he believed he could hurt Elizabeth through her dormmate.

Motive or not, Wickham was dangerous. And if Lydia was with him... Well, she was gullible enough to be talked into just about anything. And that much was enough to make Elizabeth feel sick all over again.

"Are you at your parents'?" she asked Jane.

"Yes. We just had breakfast and are about to tackle the present pile. Where are you?"

Elizabeth gave the room another look. God, she didn't want to leave, but she couldn't stay. Not with her expulsion hanging over her head. And while she wasn't sure how she could contribute to the search for Lydia, she knew she needed to try something.

"Nowhere," she said at last. "I'll be on the road within an hour."

"Elizabeth, enjoy your Christmas—"

"I can't. I need to take care of this as soon as possible."

"You know campus is closed, don't you?"

"The administrative office will be open before semester starts. I have to find out what happened."

"But—"

"Jane, there's no way I can turn this off and wait. You know that. I need to be doing something."

There was a long pause, followed by a sigh. "I suppose I do," she said at last. "I'll see if I can get out of the family thing this weekend and come back too."

"No—"

"Elizabeth Bennet, you don't want to argue with me."

She was quiet a moment before giving a sigh of her own. "Okay," she said. "I love you, crazy person that you are."

"I love you too. And you're kind of nuts if you think I'm going to let you stew around the dorm by yourself as we figure this out."

Elizabeth blinked, and without warning, her eyes had begun to sting in that annoyingly familiar way. "I'll see you soon."

"Yeah, I guess you will."

She lowered the phone and ended the call, and her heart sank once again. Downstairs, Christmas was still in full swing, the air full of Georgiana's laughter and Charlie's booming voice. And Will too, his own voice a softer murmur that seemed to thread everything together.

She looked around, taking in Will's bedroom as she hadn't before. The massive bed where they'd made love, the corner where she'd left her duffle, the dresser topped with an assortment of clutter, the display cases featuring Will's various collectibles—this place where she'd been happier than she could remember ever having been before.

What would happen if she truly was expelled? The thought of returning to Meryton had been daunting enough as it was, since they had yet to discuss what their relationship was or if it was anything at all. If she was no longer a student there, her reasons for staying in the area became nonexistent.

If she was no longer a student there…

Elizabeth swallowed and released a shaky breath.

Cross that bridge when we come to it.

For now, she needed to get moving. It was time to pack.

Time to go back to the real world.

~

"Good lord, how long does it take to ask a simple question?"

It was becoming more and more difficult to keep from socking his friend. Had it not been for the eye-rolls that Georgiana shot him every time Charlie complained about Elizabeth's continued absence, he might have done something he regretted.

As much as he wanted Charlie to be happy, he was beginning to question the wisdom of mentioning Jane now. Good intentions being what they were, Will should have anticipated that Charlie would develop a one-track mind and not let the subject go. The better move would have been to wait until they were back on campus, when action made more sense.

Still, Will supposed he couldn't blame his friend—not after the past couple days, at any rate. Being with Elizabeth now was unlike anything he'd experienced—a rush that never ended. There was no crash; there was just the thrill of the present. Of knowing she was here.

Will glanced around the carnage that was their living room. Georgiana and Charlie shared a gusto for gift-receiving. They tore at packages the way a lion might tear at the carcass of a recently felled zebra. Not that Charlie had too much to open here, but the couple gifts he received had been decimated the second he'd claimed his seat.

It was a scene familiar to Pemberley, save Caroline was typically in attendance, but no one seemed to miss her. And it was also easy, frighteningly so, to imagine next year's festivities, only with more presents under the tree and Elizabeth by his side. Or on his lap. Whichever she preferred.

Will released a long breath, doing his best to suppress the jolt of excitement that shuddered down his spine. He wanted that. Today, next year, and forever. Elizabeth belonged here. She made Pemberley feel more like a home than it had in years. She made him...

Well, she made him. Period.

"Seriously," Charlie said again when no one provided him the answer he was looking for. "One little question. She's been up there for over an hour."

"You asked her to call on Christmas," Georgiana said after Charlie grunted and threw another dirty look to the ceiling. "Kind of a dick move. Not gonna lie."

"So it shouldn't have taken so long!"

His sister gave an inelegant snort. "Yeah. Call up your BFF on Christmas to, out of the blue, ask if she'd be willing to talk to her ex. That's not going to require any explanation."

Charlie blinked stupidly and turned to Will. "What kind of explanation?"

"Maybe what she's doing hanging out with said ex," Georgiana volunteered ahead of him. She climbed off the couch and began picking up the debris left from the unwrapping with practiced disaffection. "Especially if she hasn't first told this Jane chick that she's banging my brother."

Will frowned. "Could you not?"

"I could not, but I prefer to."

Charlie barked a laugh. "I want an explanation for that, myself," he said, glancing at his watch. "I never knew you and Elizabeth were a thing. Well, there was that time when Caroline said you were knocking socks, but you said you weren't and I believed you."

"We weren't. Then."

Charlie waggled his brows. "And after *then*?"

"We were discreet."

"I'll say."

"You mean you two know how to be discreet?" Georgiana asked. "'Cause the sounds you make aren't very discreet from my end of the house."

Charlie gave another laugh and the two high-fived.

"It's not too late to put you up for adoption, you know," Will said, face burning.

"Psh. I have girlfriend approval. As long as Elizabeth likes me, I'm golden."

Will's throat tightened, another excited thrill racing through him. Tonight, after the Christmas festivities had come to an end, he'd tell her that he wanted to continue this when they returned to Meryton. He'd leave off the *possibly for the rest of our lives* part until later. Much later.

"Well, I'm going to have to leave," Charlie said, rising to his feet. He shot the ceiling another wistful look as though he could conjure her by will alone. "We have the Bingley Christmas party tonight. Still coming?"

"With bells on," Georgiana chirped.

"If Elizabeth wants to go," Will said. "I forgot to mention. We've been, uhh..."

Georgiana gave another one of her snorts and stage whispered, "F-U-C-K-I—"

Will scrambled to his feet and rushed to cover her mouth before she could finish—not that it made any difference. All he succeeded in doing was earning a look of triumph from his pesky younger sister while Charlie doubled over laughing.

"Well," Charlie said after he got a hold of himself, "I likely have some smoothing over to do with Caroline before she's fit to be around other people."

Will dropped his hand.

"N-G," Georgiana finished.

He ignored her, keeping his gaze on Charlie. "You have her present from us, right?"

His friend snickered, reached into his back pocket and procured the gift card. "Yeah. Think this is going to set her off even more. Thanks, by the way."

Will shrugged. "She told me last year not to make a fuss."

"You know that's Caroline for 'smaller diamonds.'"

"I took her at her word." Plus, she hadn't been very high on his shopping list after the last couple months. "If it turns out Elizabeth doesn't want to get out tonight, I'll make sure she calls you with the verdict on Jane. Okay?"

"Do you think I could just run up there and—"

"Dude." Georgiana made a face and waved her hand in front of her nose. "You reek of desperation. You want to scare Jane off? Continue *this*."

Charlie shook his head, his shoulders dropping as he sighed. "I love her," he said simply. "I've been in love with Jane since the moment I met her and..."

"And you were dumb."

"Your brother—"

"If you love the chick, nothing my brother could or did say should've convinced you to break up with her without talking about this." Georgiana tsked. "I say Elizabeth is still up there because she's trying to convince this poor Jane girl that you're worthy of another shot if you let Will and your sister convince you of anything."

"Again, all I said was Caroline raised a good point. I did not counsel Charlie to break it off with Jane."

"Yeah, but your disapproval is the kind that, like Charlie's desperation, can be smelled at great distances. If you were vibing, he felt it."

Will scowled. "Who's side are you on?"

"Mine. Obvs."

Charlie laughed and ruffled Georgiana's hair in a way she pretended to hate, then slung an arm around her to tug her to his side. "I love you, you little shit."

"Love you too, big shit."

Will rolled his eyes. "I give up."

"Finally," Georgiana said, fist pumping.

Chuckling, Charlie collected his gifts and started for the door. He stopped once he reached the hallway. "The second she gets off the phone, you get *on* the phone and tell me—"

"I'll tell you, I'll tell you."

"I'm not above texting you every three minutes."

"I'm not above turning my cell phone off."

Charlie smirked, flipped him off, and disappeared into the hall. The sound of the front door closing followed.

"Well," Georgiana said, snatching up one of her new video games. "Think I'm gonna break this puppy in."

"Glad you like it." Will tugged his sister into a quick hug, and relaxed when she softened and squeezed him back.

"I love you, turd."

"Love you, brat."

"Thanks for the Christmas awesomeness." She pulled back with a beaming smile. "And seriously, Elizabeth? Best thing that happened to this house in a long time. You gonna put a ring on that?"

Will stepped back, feeling his skin go hot. "What?"

"Dude, come on. It's me."

"It's a bit soon to be talking marriage."

"Maybe for other people, but not you. It's not like you're a spring chicken, anyway."

"Thank you for that."

"Seriously, you're both...you know, marriage age appropriate. It's not too weird to be talking about it."

Will snorted and shook his head. "A little premature considering I don't know how she feels about me, but thank you for rushing me down the altar."

"You don't know how she feels about you?" Georgiana gave him one of those looks designed to make the recipient feel three inches tall. "Bro, I say this with love, but you are really fucking dense sometimes. That girl is nuts for you."

The words had his heart leaping with such hope he thought he might choke on it. He didn't trust himself to reply, and thankfully Georgiana had turned her attention back to her new game, leaving him summarily dismissed. He found himself climbing the stairs before his brain could catch up with him and talk him out of it—even if she wasn't off the phone yet, he wanted...

Well, he wanted to be near her. Now and tomorrow and pretty much forever.

Hopefully tonight they could have the second half of the conversation. Put a name on whatever it was they were doing and make plans for the next few weeks. For the spring semester and the summer and...

Well, Georgiana wasn't too far off the mark. But it was too soon, Will knew; he wasn't ready to go another round with her, even if the odds were better this time.

Still, the difference between what he and Elizabeth had had before and what they had now was worlds apart.

Which made the scene he stumbled upon just short of soul-crushing. Elizabeth was off the phone and doing laps around his room, grabbing random pieces of assorted clothing and stuffing them into her duffle bag. Will felt his stomach drop somewhere within the vicinity of his feet, followed by the wisps of familiar anger until he caught a good look at her face.

"Elizabeth—"

She whipped around, causing long ribbons of brown hair to smack her swollen cheeks. Her eyes rounded, her lips trembled. She was flushed from exertion, but still somehow managed to look pale.

Will swallowed, fear making the hairs on his neck stand on end, but the rest of him hardened. Goddamn, he'd destroy whatever had upset her.

"I have to go," she said, then covered her mouth to hold back a sob.

And that was all he could stand. Will crossed the room and took her into his arms, sighing when she went willingly. She buried her head against his shoulder, shaking, and curled an arm around his neck.

Yeah, he was in love with her—that he'd known, but now he understood why people sometimes used the word *madly* along with it. The way his emotions were jumping made little sense to him, and yet somehow all the sense in the world.

"What happened?" he murmured, doing his best to keep his voice from shaking. "Is it Jane?"

Elizabeth shook her head and pulled away, dragging a hand across her face to wipe away her tears. "No," she said. "I'm... I might be expelled."

Will just stared at her, certain he'd heard wrong. He stared a moment too long—she was back in motion the next second.

"What do you mean, you might be expelled?"

"I mean they're thinking of kicking me out of Meryton."

"But...*why*?"

"They say I plagiarized something."

Will snorted. "Well, they're wrong."

Elizabeth slowed again, meeting his gaze with such uncertainty behind her own. "You believe that?"

"Of course I do."

"Without me having to explain anything?"

"What is there to explain? You don't cheat."

She all but leapt back into his arms at that, kissing him like she depended on him for oxygen. Will stood still for a second before his brain kicked on and caught up with what was happening. She tasted warm and pure and too damn good to be real.

She also tasted of tears and desperation.

Of goodbye.

Goodbye?

Elizabeth pulled away, panting. "Thank you."

"Don't thank me," he said, breathless. "Tell me how to fix it."

"You can't fix this."

"What do they think you plagiarized?"

She shook her head. "I don't know for certain, but I think my term paper. The letter mentioned Professor Greenfield. I have to be on campus on December 30th for a hearing."

"That soon?"

"Yeah, but I have to get started now. I won't be able to think of anything else if I don't *do* something."

"Elizabeth," Will said, grasping her by the shoulders to keep her from moving away from him, "there has to be a reason. Is it possible you forgot to cite a source?"

"I...I guess anything's possible, but I'd think that'd be easy to spot without leaping to the plagiarism conclusion." She pressed her lips together, her brow furrowing. At least she was thinking now. Thinking Elizabeth was much better than Goodbye Elizabeth. "I had to turn it in right before I left. My dad called as I was wrapping it up."

"Is it possible you sent the wrong file?"

"I... No." Her eyes widened, suddenly bright. "I couldn't connect to the internet that night. I was in a rush so I called a Lyft to get me to the airport and saved my paper to a flashdrive, which I gave to Lydia. She was supposed to turn in for me." A few seconds lapsed, filled with only the sound of her breathing. "Shit. *Shit.*"

"Call Lydia."

"I'll try, but..." Elizabeth shook her head. "Jane said they can't find her."

"What? Who can't find her?"

"Jane said that Kitty called to see if Lydia had reached out to her. Apparently..." She closed her eyes and swallowed hard. "From what Jane told me, Lydia took off with Wickham."

Will clenched his hands into tight fists and willed himself not to do something stupid. But of course it was Wickham. Again. Who else would it be?

"Lydia's not the brightest bulb in the box, but I would've thought she'd... Well, you know what he's been saying about me."

Yeah, reason number two to kill the son of a bitch.

"I never mentioned to anyone what happened or why, obviously. But I never thought..." She shook her head again, her face cracking. "It never occurred to me that he might start dating someone I know."

It hadn't occurred to him either, though honestly, it should have. Wickham was vindictive enough to try just about anything to hurt someone he perceived as an enemy. If Elizabeth had indeed kneed him in the balls after rejecting him, Wickham would be out for blood. And Jane was far too intelligent and loyal to fall for his bullshit, leaving a short list of candidates as alternatives.

From what he'd seen of Lydia, she was sweet but, as Elizabeth had said, not what he'd call smart. She had all the markings of a girl from a formerly affluent family who had come to Meryton to husband hunt—she wasn't dedicated in her studies, she didn't contribute much in class, and the few times he'd seen her outside of class, she'd been three sheets to the wind.

To Wickham, she'd be an easy target.

And if he'd learned she was in possession of Elizabeth's final...

But Will didn't say that. It was a radical leap and he didn't want to put the bug in her ear until he had more time to mull it over.

However, from the look of things, time was one thing that wasn't on his side.

"I have to go, Will," Elizabeth said, taking a step back. "I need to be there the second the offices open to see what happened and if there's anything I can do to fix this."

A hard mass took residence in his throat, fortified with a thousand objections and pleas. He couldn't abide the thought of Elizabeth stepping out of his room without knowing when or where he'd see her again, but he was sensible enough to recognize that this wasn't something he could stop.

"I'll come with you." The words were out of his mouth before he could reconsider.

"No. I won't let you leave Georgiana on Christmas."

"Then what can I do? Tell me how to help and I'll do it."

She favored him with another of those heartbreaking smiles. "Thank you, but I don't even know all the details and I need some time to get my head wrapped around this." A pause. "Will, these past couple days—"

"Don't say it."

"What?"

"Whatever it is you want to say now. Wait on that too."

He met her eyes and held.

Don't say goodbye. We're not done.

Elizabeth hesitated but nodded. He wasn't sure what that nod meant and he didn't want to ask.

"Call me when you can," he said.

She nodded again. "I will."

But he knew she wouldn't. There was distance between them now that hadn't been there before. The sort of distance he didn't know how to scale.

All he knew was this wasn't goodbye. Not for him.

He'd do whatever he could to keep her.

38

Elizabeth wouldn't hear a word about Will driving her anywhere. She had her rental, she'd said.

His lips still tingled from the sensation of her parting kiss, and the ache in his chest had yet to abate. The second Elizabeth had closed the door, he'd turned to Georgiana and asked her to give him a few hours to himself.

"Are you going to fix whatever happened?" she'd asked. The light in her eyes had dimmed as well, and it had struck him then just how deep a mark Elizabeth Bennet had left on Pemberley. Not that he was surprised. Elizabeth had an easy way with Georgiana that he envied, and god knows Georgiana could stand to have another woman around.

There were things he knew his sister wouldn't share with him, even now, as close as they were. She needed someone else to rely on, and though it wasn't fair to shove Elizabeth into that role, he could tell it was where Georgiana wanted her.

He couldn't blame her. He wanted her here too. Just this side of forever would be enough.

"Yes," he'd replied, not knowing, in that moment, what exactly he planned to do.

"Then take all the time you need."

The list of resources at his disposal was considerable. Will had contacts in virtually every field, thanks to his father's insistence that he attend networking events with him almost as soon as his voice stopped cracking with puberty. He didn't much care for interrupting them on Christmas Day, but this was important to him—more important than potentially inconveniencing a bunch of his father's old friends.

The quickest thing he could do—the easiest—would be to call the Meryton College board of directors and make a sizable contribution to the college in exchange for expunging Elizabeth's record, but he also knew that would not do anything to endear him to her. Elizabeth was passionate about her education, as she was about everything, but she'd never be satisfied knowing her integrity had been questioned. The only way to make this right in her eyes would be to clear her name of the accusation.

And the only way he could think to help in that regard was to track down Wickham. Hell, even if he had nothing to do with the bomb lobbed at Elizabeth's academic ambitions, it would feel damn good to sock the asshole.

But Wickham had to have something to do with it, particularly if he'd stolen away with the person responsible for turning in the term paper in question.

Will locked himself in his study.

Christmas or not, he had phone calls to make.

Elizabeth experienced a brief rush of guilt before pressing the phone icon on her screen. She brought her cell to her ear as she flipped on the turn signal with her free hand. The debate on whether or not it was appropriate to call a professor on the largest holiday of the year had lasted all of thirty seconds. Enough time for her hasty reply to Professor Greenfield's initial email about the allegation—buried under thirty some-odd other emails—to bounce back with an auto response.

And since the professor had included her cell phone number *for emergencies* in the copy... Well, Elizabeth thought this qualified.

The phone rang four times before someone answered. "Hello?"

"Hello," Elizabeth replied, then cleared her throat, her voice somewhat scratchy. She transitioned into the right lane and tried to wave at the car behind her, but found herself out of hands. "Professor Greenfield? This is Elizabeth Bennet."

The line went silent for an uncomfortable stretch of seconds.

"Professor?"

"Being that you are a reasonably intelligent person, I assume you are in possession of a calendar and know what day it is."

"Yes. I'm sorry to call you now—"

"Somehow I doubt that, Ms. Bennet. If you were sorry, you wouldn't have called."

"Please, Professor, I only now received your email. I'm panicking and couldn't wait."

"Forgive me if I seem unsympathetic, but—"

"I didn't plagiarize anything."

There was another long silence—long enough for Elizabeth to wonder if the call had dropped.

"This isn't exactly my first rodeo, Ms. Bennet," Professor Greenfield said a moment later, her tone cold. "I can expect a few false flags here and there. The software we use isn't perfect and can be overly sensitive, but when I can Google *entire paragraphs* in your paper and hit a perfect match, that's when I stop blaming the software."

"Professor—"

"Please do not insult my intelligence and do not call here again."

"I just want a meeting. I don't know what happened—I had a friend turn it in for me—"

"Yes, I am aware."

She sighed, willing herself to not start screaming. "I left Meryton in a hurry after I received an emergency call from my father."

"I am not interested in excuses."

"I'm not... This isn't an excuse. I saved my paper to my flash-drive and gave it to Lydia to so she could get it to you. I just want to *see* what she turned in—maybe I saved the wrong thing, I don't know." She didn't think so, but she was grasping at straws. Plausible alternatives eluded her for the moment, though something about this whole situation felt off for reasons beyond the obvious. "Professor, I just want to see it. I don't know if there's an explanation—"

"I can think of one."

"In my life, I have never so much as cheated on a pop quiz. I *don't* plagiarize. And if I did, I certainly wouldn't be stupid enough to do it in such a way that a simple Google search could give me up. Let me send you the paper I have on my laptop. I'll screenshot it so you can see when it was created and last modified."

Another pause. She didn't know whether or not that was a good thing.

"Please," she said after a moment. "I don't know what happened but I *need* to. You have nothing to lose. I have *everything*."

"Well, that's certainly dramatic."

"Please—"

"Ms. Bennet, you may cease with the begging." There was a

long sigh. "Email me in the morning and I'll set up an office visit for you so we can discuss this in person."

Relief hit her so hard the car nearly swerved. "Thank you—"

"Now if you don't mind, my wife just finished cooking dinner. I am going back to my holiday."

"Yes, Professor. Merry Christmas!" Elizabeth fumbled so frantically with her cell that she nearly dropped it, but somehow managed to disconnect the call one-handed without causing a pile-up.

It was such a little thing, getting that meeting, but already she felt lighter. The flare of hope that she had done her best to smother sprouted again, and this time she didn't fight it. Right now, it was all she had.

Elizabeth gave her phone, which now rested in the passenger seat, a considering side-eye before redirecting her attention to the relatively empty road ahead of her. Seconds lapsed into minutes, each one making the air grow thicker with silence, contrasting hard against the cacophony happening in her head.

She tapped the steering wheel, fighting off a shiver. It took longer than it should have to identify the new sensation in her gut, the reason she felt the urge to pick up the phone again.

She missed Will.

Shit. It had only been a couple hours since she'd left and she *missed* him. She wanted to give him an update, tell him that she'd managed to get a hold of Greenfield and there was a chance—albeit not a large one—that this could blow over within the next couple days. While she and the professor hadn't had the easiest relationship, Elizabeth had definitely grown to respect Greenfield over the course of the semester. The woman wasn't unreasonable. If a simple error had been made...

But whole paragraphs of plagiarized text? There was no accounting for that.

Elizabeth eyed the phone again but tightened her fingers around the steering wheel. Calling him would accomplish exactly nothing, except to make her want something that might not be logical in a few days. If she lost her position at Meryton, she'd have more to rethink than where she'd sleep, and she couldn't afford to bring Will into that conversation. She couldn't form her future based on a new quasi-relationship, and she couldn't tie herself to this location—which was known primarily for the college—when there might be opportunities elsewhere. Will couldn't be a factor. It wasn't fair to him and it certainly wasn't fair to her—she would not put her life on hold for a man.

No matter how she felt about him.

No matter if she thought she might be in love with him.

No matter if the thought of never seeing him again made her hurt in ways she hadn't known the human body could hurt.

Elizabeth blinked hard, swallowing past the lump in her throat. She gave her head a firm shake and switched on her headlights. She'd be back on campus soon. While she wouldn't have a way of knowing what to look for without Lydia around or the copy of the paper that had been turned in, being at Meryton at the very least provided the illusion of control, and with it, the lingering hope that perhaps she wouldn't have to think about the end of her relationship with Will.

But life had never been in the habit of handing out breaks. After her mother's recent string of exceptional luck, Elizabeth doubted there was any left for the remaining Bennets.

While others might try to play coy, Will would never deny that there were definite perks to being wealthy.

One being that no one yelled at a Darcy for interrupting Christmas dinner. Every phone call he placed had been complete with *yes sirs* and *I'll get on that right away* and *my wife knew I might have to go into the office.* No one paused to question the nature of his requests or even asked if it could wait. He'd had several counterarguments planned, but didn't have to so much as raise his voice.

Will remembered the way his father seemingly got whatever he wanted with as little as a look. That afternoon, he found himself grappling with the uncomfortable reality that the legacy had been well and truly passed on, and that likely no one who spoke to him knew he had returned to complete his education or gave a damn. Money talked plenty for him.

It was his cousin, whom he didn't get to see very much anymore, that got him the information he needed in order to make travel arrangements. They had both been unlucky enough to have been named Fitzwilliam; something over which they'd bonded as children. Fitz was the figurehead-in-training of Darcy Credit International, and though he rarely bent the rules, he'd been all too happy to give Will the information he needed once he'd learned that Wickham was involved.

"Seriously," Fitz had said, his voice thick with anger, "can't this guy just die already?"

"I looked into it. Apparently, it's illegal to kill someone."

"Only if he's human. Not sure George qualifies." There was a moment of silence, filled only with the strokes of a keyboard on the other line. "Aha. Yes, there's a hit. At the Clover Casino and Hotel in Atlantic City."

Which was how, as the sun was setting on Christmas Day, Will found himself behind the wheel and on the road to Raleigh, North Carolina to catch a plane to New Jersey.

He toyed with the idea of phoning Elizabeth as he waited to board, then again once the plane touched down. The urge would hit him with such potency he was certain he'd connect the call, but he never got further than bringing up her number.

After all, he had nothing to tell her—nothing he would, anyway. He couldn't afford to get her hopes up when he wasn't even sure what he would find.

And even then, what would he say? Their relationship remained, as of yet, undefined. Elizabeth wasn't the grand gesture sort of woman to begin with—she wasn't impressed by his money or connections, and the fact that he'd hopped a plane on a possible wild goose chase might cost him ground that he'd regained over the last few days.

Elizabeth was not someone who wanted to be rescued.

And for better or worse, Will wasn't going to let that stop him from trying. Even if he didn't have a plan beyond show up, look around, and find Wickham.

The Clover Casino and Hotel was unremarkable, so far as casinos went. The air was thick with alcohol, whoops of victory and the loud, drunken curses of those not currently riding a lucky streak. The faint hint of cigarette smoke wafted from the areas cordoned off for the casino's nicotine addicts, and almost every square inch of floor was occupied by servers weaving in and out of the clumps comprised of everything from senior citizens to kids that looked far too young to be allowed entrance.

He couldn't explain how, while staring at a sea of faces, his eyes somehow knew where to land. But they did. Will had barely entered the casino area when he spotted her. Had he not been looking for her, he would have never picked her out. She wasn't wearing makeup, her hair was askew, and her eyes had the swollen, puffy look that told anyone plainly that she'd been crying. Never had he seen her anything but giggling and perfectly put together.

Will swallowed and started across the room. She didn't look up once, not even when a server brought her a refill. Rather, she kept her glassy gaze locked on the face of the slot machine, moving only to slap the bet button every few seconds.

He drew in a deep breath as he came to a stop beside her. "Hello, Lydia."

She sluggishly turned her head, her eyes unfocused as they found his. She blinked at him a few times before recognition dawned across her face.

Then, promptly, burst into tears.

39

The casino floor was not the best place to have this conversation. While most slot-machine junkies and career gamblers were well-versed in the art of ignoring things that didn't concern them, the average tourist typically wasn't so focused, and Will didn't think the situation called for rubberneckers.

So he led her awkwardly to the check-in desk, where he managed to reserve a room despite his classmate's increasingly loud wails and sniveling. He wasn't sure what this might look like—a guy taking a sobbing girl to his room, and he didn't want to think about it too much because the answer couldn't be a good one.

Once they were in the elevator and away from the loudest of the casino sounds, Lydia seemed to calm. At least long enough to give her surroundings a good look and ask where they were going.

"I need to talk with you," Will said carefully. "We're going to my room." Then, thinking the better of it, added, "If you'd rather not be in my hotel room alone with me right now, we can go somewhere else."

Lydia gave him an appraising look that made him think she

was likely smarter than most people, himself included, had ever credited. "You're a good guy," she said. "You've always seemed like one, at least." She sniffed and her eyes began to fill once again. "I am in so much trouble."

Will drew his hands into fists in an effort to ground himself. If Wickham had done anything to this girl... "What sort of trouble?"

Lydia couldn't speak for a moment for trembling. The elevator arrived on his floor, and she bolted for freedom the second the doors slid open, dragging in deep breaths. She didn't make it far—just to the edge of the hall that led to the rooms, where she stopped and made a show of looking in either direction.

"Coast is clear." She didn't look at him. "Could...could we stay here? I don't want to go into anyone's room."

"We can stay here," he agreed. "What sort of trouble are you in?"

"It was dumb. So fucking dumb."

"Is this about George Wickham?"

She jerked. "What do you know about it?"

"I know that he's been telling stories about Elizabeth Bennet to anybody who will listen. And I know those stories aren't true."

"How do you know that?"

"Because she told me and I believe her."

"She could be lying. It's all over Facebook."

Will tightened his jaw. Maybe his first assumption had been on the mark after all, and Lydia did have cotton for brains.

But he didn't think so.

"Let's just say I've known George Wickham a very long time. It will be a cold day in Hell before I take his word over someone else's."

Lydia was still for a moment before nodding. "He was so nice to me."

"Yes."

"And I asked him about Elizabeth. I mean, I don't know her very well, but she's always been nice. A little boring, but nice." She wrinkled her nose. "But she's always talking about feminism and sex and I just kinda thought maybe it made sense that she was all hung up on him. He's really nice and cute and funny and I know they'd been flirting and stuff. She gets so..." Lydia gestured vaguely. "*Into* things. He told me she was nuts about him, followed him around campus, memorized his schedule, kept sending nudes and stuff like that. He was worried about dating *me* because he didn't wanna come around Longbourn with Elizabeth there. Thought she might get the wrong idea and start stalking him again."

Will swallowed. "But you came here with him, didn't you? He's here?"

Lydia nodded again. "I was so stupid. I've always been stupid."

Well, that sort of talk certainly wasn't going to help matters. "Lydia—"

"No, I *am*." She broke off with a sob, wiping at her cheeks. "My parents went on a cruise for Christmas. Wickham said he didn't have anywhere to go and wanted to have some fun—kind of an anti-Christmas somewhere else. He said he'd find someone else if I didn't go with him, and I really liked him so that freaked me out and I told him I'd go. We were trying to figure out what to do and...he mentioned he's good at cards. So we decided on Atlantic City...after I told him I could pay for it."

Will edged a step forward. "How?"

Lydia pressed her lips together, her face starting to crumble all over again. "My...student loan money. I thought we'd get here and he'd just win it all back, whatever we spent. He said he could do it."

He could think of nothing to say, so he didn't try for words. All he could do was stare at her.

"Once we got here, he won five hundred dollars almost instantly. And then another three hundred on the slots. He made it look so easy. We'd been here maybe two hours before he had all the money back for the plane tickets and our room." Lydia's lower lip went into full wobble mode. "But he said he could win more. If I let him use more. He said he could win enough to pay for...whatever we wanted to do. And then some." Shaking, she released a long breath and turned to look at him fully. "I am so stupid."

"Do you have anything left?"

She didn't answer—she didn't need to. Her eyes were brimming again, and when she choked out a sob, she couldn't seem to stop herself from losing control entirely. He stood there, watching her cry, thinking of how often he'd seen Georgiana dissolve into a mess over this man. The look on Elizabeth's face when that kid from class had called her a whore during her presentation. And before that—the pain in his father's eyes at learning who had stolen his car. That the boy he'd grown to care for had become a cautionary tale.

"You're not stupid," Will said after a moment. "This is what he does."

"But I'm the one who—"

"No."

"Coming here, using my money—I let him do that."

Will shook his head. "Whatever happened was all on Wickham, Lydia. I promise. He uses people and he's very good at it."

Lydia trembled, considering, but there was something in her eyes that hadn't been there before. After a long moment, she shook her head and looked down, sniffing. "I have three hundred dollars," she said, dragging a wad of bills out of her pocket. "That's all. The rest is gone and I *have* to win it back. My parents are going to murder me."

"Where is Wickham now?"

"I don't know. He took about a thousand dollars to play roulette."

"You let him take that much?"

Her eyes bugged maniacally and she waved her hands, sending a twenty to the ground. Will bent over to collect it.

"I don't know how to play any of these games," she said. "Wickham does. He won a lot of money when we first got here and he's my best shot at getting the money back. All I've done is play the slot machines, and I won, like, forty bucks, but I need a *lot* more than that and he's supposed to be helping me."

"Yes, well, he does nothing if there isn't something in it for himself," Will replied, offering a sympathetic smile as he handed back the wayward twenty. "Don't trust him with your money. I don't care what he says."

Lydia wilted, her eyes swelling again. "I was such an idiot."

"No, you weren't. I told you, Wickham is pretty good at making people believe what he says."

"But Elizabeth didn't. He really *hates* her. I guess she sent some of what he was saying to the faculty and... I don't know what happened, but he was *pissed.*"

Will swallowed. He hadn't heard anything after he'd sent screenshots to the administration—hadn't realized they'd acted at all.

"He had me thinking it was because she wanted to get him kicked out of school because he'd dropped her." Lydia paused, considering. "The way Jane was acting when Wickham kept showing up at Longbourn before break... She believed Elizabeth, but I didn't. Or I thought maybe she was wrong or that it wasn't as bad as they said it was. But she saw through him."

Will was quiet for a moment, unsure of how much to reveal.

His mind took him back to the morning they'd spent on the back porch of Pemberley, Elizabeth's eyes brimming with tears and regret, her voice thick as she related how stupid she felt. How she shouldn't have needed anyone to point out what she now saw as obvious. And then he wondered what she would do if she were here now.

The answer was clear. Elizabeth might not enjoy it, but her compassion far outweighed her pride.

"She didn't see through him," Will said softly.

Lydia shook her head. "Of course she did. Elizabeth's, like, super brainy. He wouldn't have—"

"Elizabeth is smart, that's true," Will agreed, "but that doesn't make her perfect. And I know she didn't see through Wickham, because I'm the one who told her about him."

The words had their desired impact. The self-loathing in Lydia's face melted, exchanged for confused wonder. "You did?"

"Not as quickly as I should have, but yeah, I told her. I told her things that he'd done to me, particularly my sister."

"What kind of things?"

Will pressed his lips together and drew a step back, shaking his head. "My point is, Elizabeth found out before Wickham could take advantage of her, and he lashed out when she called him on it. But even I didn't think he'd take anything this far."

"What do you mean?"

He hesitated. "What happened to the paper you were supposed to turn in for her?"

The change was instant. Lydia's eyes went wide and the color drained from her face. "What do you mean?"

"I think you know exactly what I mean."

"Umm, no, I don't. Sorry."

At that, Lydia broke into a run—or tried to. She made a mad dart toward the elevators, but Will grabbed her wrist and tugged her to a stop, the kinder feelings he'd entertained blinking out of existence.

"Let me go!"

"Not until you answer my question."

"Stop!" Lydia looked around, eyes wild. "Help! This guy's grabbed me!"

Great. That was just what he needed. Will growled but released her wrist and brought up his hands before any of the vacationers could pop out of their hotel rooms and intervene. "Lydia—"

But Lydia was at the bank of elevators again, frantically tapping the *down* button.

"Lydia, Elizabeth's been expelled for plagiarizing her paper."

She almost lost her footing. "What?"

"Well, she has a hearing on the thirtieth. They're going to decide then if her academic career at Meryton is over." He was breathing heavily, taking in her stunned expression. "Plagiarism is a big deal. You do know that, don't you?"

"H-how... How would they even find out?"

Any lingering doubt evaporated. Will exhaled again, slowly, focusing on his breathing rather than on, say, Lydia's neck, which he would very much like to wring at the moment.

"There's software that teachers and professors use," he said through his teeth. "I take it your teachers didn't rely on this in high school?"

Lydia shook her head.

That didn't seem likely. Since that sort of technology had become available to educators, he'd assumed it was utilized all over the place, unless the teacher in question truly didn't care, or if Lydia's parents had shelled out a lot of money to keep her academic missteps quiet. But he knew Lydia's family wasn't particularly well off—one of the older alumni families that likely insisted on Meryton for the sake of tradition rather than practicality.

None of that mattered. Except that Lydia truly looked horrorstruck, and she wasn't what he'd call a superb actress.

"Well," he said after a moment, "it exists. And Greenfield used this software on Elizabeth's paper and the results could have her kicked out of school." A beat. "This is her life, Lydia. Her future. Can you tell me what happened to the paper she gave you?"

"That's..." Lydia turned just as the elevator arrived and slid open. She made no move to step on, every inch of her slumping in defeat. "God, this is so fucked up. He said it wouldn't be a big deal." She cast a longing look at the elevator, which was thankfully empty, but turned her back on it as its doors slid shut again. "He promised me it wouldn't be a big deal."

"Wickham."

She nodded, her face beginning to crack a third time. However, Will was all out of patience.

"What did he say wouldn't be a big deal?"

Lydia flexed her fingers. She looked over her shoulder as though contemplating making another break for it, but the defeat that had been in her face remained. She knew, plain as he did, that there was nowhere to run.

So she turned back to him, inhaled deeply, and told him everything.

40

"Do you want me to go in with you? I will if you think it would help."

Elizabeth flashed Jane a grateful smile, resting her head against the wall at her back. Her left shoulder sagged under the weight of her laptop bag. "Go with me as my emotional support, you mean?"

"More like a character witness. You would never plagiarize and anyone who's had you in class for more than two seconds has to know this."

The conviction in Jane's voice was unwavering, reminding her yet again that she had truly hit the lottery in the best friend department. Not only had Jane rushed back to campus—she'd stuck to Elizabeth like glue, prepared to launch into a rousing pep talk every time she saw an outburst on the horizon. When Elizabeth had announced it was time to make the trip to Greenfield's office, Jane had rolled to her feet and marched to the door without saying a word.

Elizabeth was so used to handling things on her own, she didn't really know how to react to having such reliable support.

She'd considered protesting but hadn't been able to summon the willpower.

Friends like Jane were forever. Even if the worst should happen, Elizabeth couldn't fathom her life without the girl who had become her surrogate sister. No matter what happened, there would always be a way to remain in touch.

That provided some comfort, but also served to remind her of what else she stood to lose. Beyond just the education she'd promised herself, there was Will, and the thing she hadn't known she wanted until a few days ago.

Elizabeth looked down. "I just want this to be over. But I'm terrified of it being over at the same time."

"It'll be fine."

She laughed. "I'd kill for your confidence."

"It's easy to be confident when I'm right."

The sound of footsteps echoed down the corridor, saving Elizabeth from trying to come up with a reply. A few seconds later, Professor Greenfield rounded the corner, dressed in a pair of ratty jeans and an oversized sweatshirt. Her face was fixed in a scowl, and when she met Elizabeth's eyes, her own seemed to darken.

"Do you want me to come in with you?" Jane whispered again. "Tell me now."

"No. I should be fine."

"She doesn't look happy."

No, she didn't. Elizabeth swallowed hard and fought back a surge of rising panic.

"Good morning," she said as Professor Greenfield drew up beside them. "Thank you again for agreeing to meet."

"Yeah," came the gruff response. "Let's just get this thing over with." She pulled a set of keys from her pocket, unlocked the office door, and entered without so much as a backward glance.

Elizabeth breathed in, willing herself to relax.

"I'll be right outside if you need me," Jane said. "And I'm treating you to lunch after this."

She forced a grin, hoping it conveyed everything she couldn't bring herself to say at the moment, then stepped over the threshold into the lion's den and closed the door behind her.

When she turned, she found Professor Greenfield standing behind her desk, holding out a red-marked bundle of paper.

"This is what you wanted to see."

Elizabeth swallowed and forced her feet to move forward. In the period between arriving back on campus and waiting for this meeting, she'd double-checked her term paper as it had been saved on her computer before she'd transferred it to the flashdrive. Aside from a few wonky sentences she hadn't had time to correct, everything looked in order. She'd even tried copying and pasting a few lines into Google to see where the duplication might have occurred, but aside from a few odd near-misses in terms of wording, it had come up blank. The same thing occurred with the few free plagiarism checkers she'd found.

Something was seriously wrong.

"Ms. Bennet, I do not have all day and you are already on my last nerve."

Elizabeth gave her head a shake and stepped forward. "I'm sorry," she said, though not knowing what, exactly, she was apologizing for. She took the paper, scanned the heading, and felt her stomach drop. "I didn't write this."

"I know. That's why you're facing expulsion."

"No. I mean, this isn't the paper I turned in."

Professor Greenfield arched an eyebrow. "That's your name at the top, isn't it?"

"Yes, but..." She was shaking now, so hard it seemed her insides shook with her. "There has to be some mistake. My topic was about the hero archetype and how it reinforces toxic masculinity, not birth control. When I say I didn't write it, I mean I've never seen this before."

The flicker of hope she'd experienced before sparked with new life, but Elizabeth didn't let herself chase it. Not yet.

Professor Greenfield's expression softened, though not by much. "Well," she said after a moment, sinking into her seat, "I'll admit, Ms. Bennet, I can almost always identify the students in my classes who will be problematic for one reason or another. You're hardheaded and opinionated, but smart and well-spoken. I never thought you'd be the type to try and cheat at a grade. And so obviously, too."

Elizabeth lowered her gaze to the paper. "I don't understand what happened," she said, speaking without really meaning to. "I don't suppose you can show me what Lydia turned in, can you?"

Professor Greenfield narrowed her eyes. "What do you think?"

"Hard no." She bit her lower lip. "It's just... I had to leave campus unexpectedly. I didn't have time to go back and check my sources or proofread my paper. Our email was down so I took a flashdrive to Lydia so she could turn it in for me. This is not what was on that flashdrive."

"Are you suggesting Ms. Gardiner did something to your paper? That is a very serious accusation."

"No," she said at once. "I'm not accusing anyone of anything. What I am saying is *I don't know* what happened. Only that I left here having written a paper that I gave to Lydia to turn in and the next thing I know, I'm being accused of plagiarism and my future hinges upon this"—she waved the paper in question —"something I've never seen before, and certainly didn't give to Lydia to turn in. I brought my laptop so you can see the last file saved. See if there was a mix-up."

"I'm sorry, no. I'm not stupid when it comes to computers,

but I'm also not an expert, and I can't open that door or everyone would want to get through. The issue will be determined by academics."

"But if I can prove I had something else saved on my hard-drive, wouldn't you take that into consideration?"

Professor Greenfield pressed her lips together, tilting her head. She was quiet for a moment. "Have you tried asking Ms. Gardiner what happened?" she asked rather than answering.

Elizabeth exhaled slowly. "We can't find her."

"You mean you weren't able to get her to come in over her winter break."

"No, I mean we can't find her. Her roommate says she and another student decided to go off together over Christmas. We've tried calling her, but she didn't let anyone know *where* she was going and hasn't answered her phone at all."

At this, Professor Greenfield frowned, concern leaking into her eyes. "Well, I certainly hope she's all right."

"We all do," Elizabeth agreed.

"And as for this..." She gestured to the paper with a sigh. "Like I said, Ms. Bennet, I wouldn't have expected this of you. But I have been in this profession long enough to have been disappointed by otherwise star students."

"I didn't think you liked me."

"Why is that?"

"Well..." She looked down, wrung her hands. "First day...I kinda jumped all over you for singling out Will Darcy."

The corners of Professor Greenfield's mouth ticked upward. "Oh, that's right. Well, I wasn't exactly being coy that day, myself. No, I think you'll come to find that as you get older, it becomes more work than it's worth to hold a grudge. What I care about is teaching, and you were always a good student." A pause. "I can't make any promises, but I am willing to say as much at your hearing. And if you think it will help, certainly bring your computer so we can see the paper you intended to turn in, along with the time stamp. I don't know if that will make a difference on the outcome, but... It might just be that you're a horse worth betting on."

A thrill shot down her spine. "So...you believe me?"

"I wouldn't go that far, but I will admit the situation is a little more complicated, especially since you didn't actually turn that in to me." Professor Greenfield sighed and rose to her feet. "I'll say I hope you're telling the truth, if nothing else, because I did enjoy having you in class, and it would seriously bum me out if you were a plagiarist."

"Thank you."

She inclined her head. "Now, if you don't mind..." She made her way around the desk. "I have a cranky wife to meet for brunch."

"Tell her I'm sorry for interrupting your time off."

"I will, but that won't make much difference to her." Professor Greenfield stopped by the door. "I'll see you on the thirtieth, Ms. Bennet."

Elizabeth nodded, offered a small, grateful smile, then stepped back into the hall. She was careful not to meet Jane's eyes as her professor followed. It wasn't until Greenfield had disappeared around the corner and down the hall that Elizabeth felt it safe to acknowledge Jane at all.

"Well?" Jane asked, stuffing her cell phone into her pocket. "I couldn't help but notice there was a distinct lack of screaming. Do you have good news for me?"

"She doesn't believe me, but she doesn't *not* believe me, either."

"What does that mean?"

"Best case scenario? If they decide I am a plagiarist, maybe I'm on academic probation rather than outright expelled. But that might be too optimistic."

Jane threw an arm around her shoulder, steering her in for a quick hug. "That's you all over. Miss Half-Full."

"If you go through life expecting the worst, you're never disappointed."

"You should write greeting cards."

"Would you believe they wouldn't hire me?" Elizabeth released a long breath, tension she'd carried with her from Pemberley falling away. It would be back, she knew, but this might be the closest to in control she'd felt since Christmas morning.

Since Will had kissed her lips, grinned at her, then kissed his way down her body and done things with his tongue that made her warm just thinking about it.

She paused and pulled out her phone, charged with a rush of nervous energy that whispered he might have reached out to her. The answering plunge of disappointment left her feeling hollow and isolated.

"What's wrong?" Jane shook her shoulder.

"Huh?"

"You just looked so sad all of a sudden."

Elizabeth forced a smile and shoved her phone back into her pocket. "Nothing. It's nothing."

"This wouldn't have anything to do with why Charlie Bingley started texting me this morning, would it?"

She paused. "What?"

"Apparently you were supposed to tell him something over Christmas and he never heard back from you." Jane tilted her head. "You spent Christmas with the Bingleys?"

"Umm, hardly." Elizabeth gave a short laugh and shuddered. "Well, I guess I kinda did, but Caroline didn't stay long, much to the disappointment of precisely no one."

"What were you doing with the Bingleys?"

"I wasn't with the Bingleys." She paused and rubbed her lips together, an excited but muted flutter taking residence in her belly. And even through her doubts, she didn't think she could stifle the need to talk to someone any longer.

Except talking about it made it real. As long as the words were in her head, they were solely hers, incapable of being twisted or misinterpreted by anyone else. Even if that someone else was Jane.

Hell, maybe *especially* if that someone else was Jane. Because Jane was all rainbows and optimism, even when the world dealt her a shit hand.

But Will was more than her dirty little secret. She wasn't ashamed of the time she'd spent at Pemberley. The only regrets she had were that they hadn't had more time together.

"Elizabeth," Jane said warningly, "you talk or I'll call Caroline."

"You wouldn't."

"Just try me."

Elizabeth rolled her head back, grinning. "On my way back from St. Augustine, my car kinda found itself in Derbyshire."

"Yes, I remember. What does that have to do with anything?"

"Turns out, that's where Pemberley is."

"Pemberley?"

"Yeah...the place where Will Darcy lives."

Jane paused, her eyebrows winging upward. "Darcy. As in the Darcy you pretend to hate but secretly have a thing for."

"That's the one."

"Not denying it now? Woman, talk."

Again, Elizabeth paused, though her heart began to race. She forced herself to meet Jane's eyes and willed herself the courage to say the thing that needed to be said, if only once.

"I think I'm in love with him."

And before she could draw breath, she burst into tears.

41

The night before her hearing went almost exactly as she expected—restless and, when she did manage to fall asleep, nightmare-riddled. She dreamed of a life following her expulsion, of having to live with her mother, whose life, in these dreams, was in the same state of chaos and despair as it had been following the divorce. She dreamed of crawling on her hands and knees to beg Caroline Bingley for a place to stay, of Jane shaking her head and saying she expected so much more from her. And, to be especially cruel, her mind also fed her with dreams of finally falling asleep, then snoozing through her alarm clock and missing the hearing entirely.

Yet when she awoke the next morning, it was with a burst of manic energy, fueled with a combination of fear and cautious hope. And despite the temptation, she didn't bother waking Jane before she left, even though her friend had promised to come with her for moral support. This was one thing she needed to do on her own.

Elizabeth arrived at the administration office twenty minutes early with her computer bag slung over her shoulder, and didn't know what to do with herself to occupy the time, save checking the clock on her phone every few seconds. She didn't let herself play with her phone too long, though, for the nearer her meeting loomed, the more she wanted to text Will. Not that she knew what to say, except that she missed him. She missed him and Georgiana and Pemberley. All of that seemed like such a wonderful dream that she was having trouble believing it had actually happened. She wanted to tell him again how sorry she was that she'd been such a judgmental idiot; if she hadn't been, they might have had more time together.

Though she wasn't sure if wishing for more time was wise; they'd only had three honest days together and they had profoundly reshaped her in ways she'd never thought possible. If they'd had more days, if they had found their footwork as a couple, then the prospect of being expelled would have been elevated to a new level of hell.

If nothing else, this thing with Will had reinvigorated her belief in love. Because if he could still love her after she'd done everything in her power to push him away, they could weather any storm.

With time, at least. And that was something they might not have.

Plus she didn't know if Will was actually still in love with her. And right now, with so much still uncertain, she wasn't sure she wanted to know.

Elizabeth sighed and checked the time again. Only a few minutes had passed. She gave the building another look. It wouldn't hurt her chances any to be ridiculously early—she'd never heard of a student being penalized for that, and maybe it would show the administration just how serious she was about her education. She straightened her shoulders and made her way to the entrance.

It didn't take long to find the route to the room the email had listed. As her feet took her down the hall, her heart thundered loud enough to be heard three counties over. She pressed her lips together and eyed her destination. The door was open and the light was on, which was either very bad or very good. Her skin began to tingle, sweat gathering at the nape of her neck. Closer now, she could make out voices, low and conspiratorial. One belonged to Professor Greenfield, she was certain of it.

The other...

Elizabeth stopped in the doorway and blinked dumbly.

"Lydia?"

Greenfield and Lydia turned on the same beat, neither looking particularly happy, though the professor spared her a soft, tired smile. The room surrounding them wasn't an office, rather a waiting room, complete with its own currently vacant desk and a bank of chairs around a magazine-covered coffee table. The left wall was plastered with awards Meryton had been honored with over the years, while the right featured a board filled with marketing material. A memory sparked, one that felt decades old, but Elizabeth realized belatedly that this was where she'd enrolled. And then she felt stupid, because *obviously* this was where she'd enrolled and a smarter, less frazzled Elizabeth would have recognized it immediately.

If she didn't get expelled today, she was going to sleep until the new term began.

"Lydia," she said again, shaking her head to clear it. "What are you doing here? And when did you get back? We've been trying to reach you."

Lydia flashed a pained grin. "I didn't mean to worry anyone."

Well, that told her precisely nothing. "But what are you doing here?"

Before Lydia could respond, the door at the other end of the room opened, and a young, fresh-faced guy nodded at Professor Greenfield. "She's ready for you."

"Good," she replied, then turned to Elizabeth. "If you would follow us, please."

What the hell is going on here?

Lydia's presence had, if nothing else, distracted her from her fears about expulsion. By the time Elizabeth crossed the threshold into the dean's office, the nerves she'd entertained since Pemberley had taken a full backseat to curiosity. She didn't even flinch when she met the dean's stoic gaze, though that might have been because the dean saved her dirtiest look for Lydia.

"Elizabeth," Professor Greenfield said, "this is Dean Winifred Carrington. I'm not sure if you've met."

They hadn't, but that hardly seemed important at the moment.

Dean Carrington was a severe looking woman. She wore square-rimmed glasses and had her hair pulled into a tight bun, which gave her the appearance of a Professor McGonagall cosplayer. The thought nearly made Elizabeth smirk but she refrained. Now was definitely not the time to get a case of the giggles.

As it was, Dean Carrington didn't seem too interested in Elizabeth. After greeting her with a dismissive nod, she turned her attention to Lydia, and pointed at the document laying face-up on her desk. "Do you stand by this account?"

"I do."

"You understand the seriousness of what you did here."

A pause. "I do. But I didn't think—"

"It's quite clear you *didn't think.*"

Elizabeth shot a look to Greenfield, but the professor's focus was set dead ahead.

Dean Carrington glared at Lydia a moment longer before releasing a long sigh and finally shifting her attention to Elizabeth. "Ms. Bennet. I trust you had an eventful break."

She knew it was unwise, but she couldn't stop herself. "What's going on?"

"I would have Ms. Gardiner explain it. I believe she owes you that much."

Elizabeth blinked and turned to Lydia, whose face was pointed at the floor, tears tracking down her cheeks. But she didn't say anything, and the air in the room grew heavy again.

The dean gave a sigh. "Ms. Gardiner, you have already tested my patience enough for one day."

Lydia released a shaky breath and turned to face Elizabeth, though her gaze remained on the floor. "I...turned in your paper as my own," she said. "And turned in another for you."

Elizabeth's skin went hot. "What?"

"I... A guy I really liked wanted to go away with me. Badly. And I was *so* into him. He told me he'd find someone else to take if I wasn't free." Lydia paused to gulp for air, her tears falling faster now. "And I hadn't written my final. When you gave me yours, I... I changed the name and sent it to Professor Greenfield. I thought I'd have time to write one for you but I wasn't sure, and you're so smart. I couldn't take a hit to my grade but I thought you could and it'd be okay."

Elizabeth forced herself to breathe, curling her hands into fists as hard tremors seized control of her body. The last vestiges of fear had died completely, evolving into a hot, mad rage. "What the *fuck*, Lydia! What the *fuck* is wrong with you?"

Lydia released a wail and buried her face in her hands. "I'm so sorry, Lizzie. I didn't mean for any of this to happen."

"What did you *think* was going to happen?" she snapped. "I can't believe this. Of all the idiotic—"

Dean Carrington held up a hand. "That's enough, Ms. Bennet."

"Is it?" she demanded. "Did you hear what she said?"

"I have two perfectly working ears, so yes, I did hear.

Furthermore, I have her account of what happened right here." The dean waved to the paper on her desk. "I understand you're angry and god knows you have every right to be, but this is not the place to unleash that anger. Ms. Gardiner, please continue."

Lydia parted her lips, a desperate sort of cry sounding between them. "I'm not a good writer," she said, eyes brimming with tears. "Or a good student. I...I tried to write a paper for Elizabeth but I knew it wouldn't sound right. The guy I was with told me I might look online and see if I could find something there. So I did. I copied and pasted a bunch of stuff from articles I found and turned that in." She hesitated, then looked at Elizabeth directly. "I promise I didn't mean for this to happen. Any of it. I just couldn't fail and you're so smart. I didn't know you could get in trouble for this."

"Really?" she snapped. "You didn't know that academic institutions look down on *plagiarism*?"

Lydia shook her head, her face a mess. "I'm not smart, Lizzie. Not like you and Jane. My parents wanted me to come here because they did. I didn't even want to go to college."

"That is the laziest excuse I ever—"

Dean Carrington again held up a hand. "I understand you two might have some more talking to do," she said, rising to her feet, "but this is not the place. Ms. Bennet, you are free to go. Suffice it to say, you are not being expelled today. Professor Greenfield will ensure that your semester grade is adjusted to reflect the work you *did*."

And just like that, it was over. Elizabeth stood in place for what felt like forever, flexing her numb fingers to get circulation going. She looked from her professor to the dean, then to Lydia, who was on the verge of a full-on ugly cry.

It seemed impossible that she could turn and walk out, but when she moved to do just that, no one stopped her. No one followed her, either. When she reached the door, the dean asked her to make sure she closed it behind her, and then her legs were carrying her back through the maze of hallways and to the sitting area where she'd come in.

It wasn't until she was outside the building itself that she released the tension that had kept her fueled the past couple days. At once, she felt boneless, not to mention exhausted. Her mind, however, refused to slow down, and every few seconds her heart gave a jump as though it had yet to receive the memo that the threat was behind them.

Elizabeth inhaled and turned her face to the sky, forcing her muscles to relax.

She wasn't going anywhere.

"Elizabeth."

For a wild moment, she wondered if she'd conjured his voice from sheer want. Now that the crisis was behind her, the need to see Will was surging its way back to the forefront. But then the voice came again, prompting her to open her eyes.

And Will was there. Right in front of her, looking as tired as she felt and then some, but favoring her with the smile she'd come to cherish.

"What are you doing here?"

The smile faltered just a hair. "Just here to drop off next semester's payment," he said, holding up an envelope she hadn't noticed before. "Georgiana hasn't attended a group meeting in person in quite a while, and I thought she might like to before she has to worry about going back to school. There's one in Hertfordshire, not too far from here. I'm running errands until I pick her up."

Elizabeth nodded. "I didn't mean to sound... I just wasn't expecting to see you here."

"Hope it's not an unpleasant surprise."

"What? No, of course not. It's..."

It was just that she had barely processed what had happened

in the dean's office and now she was feet away from the man she knew she loved, and there were no obstacles keeping them apart. Except they were on campus now, and campus meant the real world, not the happy privacy afforded at his home. That place seemed so far away. Had she been at Pemberley, she would have launched herself at him by now. But they weren't at Pemberley, and the rules here hadn't been laid out.

Elizabeth shook her head to clear it. "I haven't been expelled."

He relaxed and gave her a small grin. "I never thought you would be."

Well, that was...unenthusiastic. She swallowed and tried again. "Are you going home tonight then?"

"I think we'll stay," Will said, his tone cautious. "Georgiana is thinking of studying here next year, so I thought I might show her around campus. Take advantage of Netherfield being empty."

"No Charlie or Caroline."

"Charlie came with me, actually, but Caroline stayed behind."

"So when you say Netherfield is empty..."

"Right. Well, would you believe she makes it feel crowded?"

"In a heartbeat."

Will chuckled, shifting his gaze to the building behind her, then edged a step nearer. "See you later?"

"Oh." Her heart dropped and she stepped aside, though there really wasn't a need. "Of course. I won't keep you—"

"No, I mean I'd like to see *you* later." He smiled again, his *just for her* smile, before looking down. "At Netherfield?"

A fresh stab of adrenaline surged through her. "You want to see me?"

"Is that so hard to believe?"

"No. I mean... It's weird, isn't it? Being here?"

"I was hoping we could talk about that." Will stepped back before she could reply and held up the envelope in his hand. "I need to take care of this. Will you come over?"

"Yes. Just text me."

"Will do." Another step back. Will broke his gaze away from hers and offered a sheepish wave. "See you tonight, then."

"Yeah. See you."

She thought he might kiss her, but he didn't. She didn't know whether or not she should read anything into that.

She hoped not, because seeing him again had cinched it. Like it or not, Elizabeth was in love with Will Darcy. A big, sopping messy kind of love that scared the shit out of her, but not half as much as the thought that his feelings had changed.

She had the whole day ahead of her to worry.

42

She had only just entered her dorm room when Jane pounced on her.

"Well?"

Elizabeth blinked at her friend, then snorted. "Have you been just sitting there staring at the door?"

"Yes," Jane replied unapologetically, her eyes wide and her face pale. "What happened? How did it go?"

Elizabeth sighed and closed the door behind her. "I am sorry to say that you are stuck with me for another semester."

The next thing she knew, she had been tackled. Jane had her captured in a rib-cracking hug. "I knew it," she whispered, squeezing. "I knew it."

"Yes, you clearly weren't worried at all," Elizabeth replied, but softened and sank into her friend's arms. "Thank you for being here."

"Like there was anywhere else I'd be." Jane sniffed and pulled back, her lips trembling. And in spite of herself, Elizabeth felt her body warm all over. There were few people in the world like Jane—people who loved with everything they were, stood by their friends in times of need no matter what, and were still unafraid to speak the harsh truths when necessary.

"Can you tell me what happened?" Jane asked, taking a step back and dragging her hand under her eyes. "Or is it confidential?"

"Why would it be confidential?"

"I don't know—I was trying to be polite in case you didn't want to talk about it."

Elizabeth rolled her eyes. "There is nothing I don't tell you."

"Two words: Will Darcy."

Well, she had her there. Elizabeth sighed and ran a hand through her hair, moving to her bed, where she hoped to spend the rest of the day following this conversation. Her adrenaline high was on the fast track to crashing, and her body suddenly craved sleep in a way it hadn't since before Christmas.

"It was Lydia," she said, sitting.

"What was Lydia?"

"Everything, apparently." And she explained the facts as she understood them, the sparks of anger flaring once more. Lydia had always been a bit of a flake, but Elizabeth had never once thought her capable of doing something so stupid. And for what it had nearly cost her, she wasn't sure she'd ever be in a place to forgive her.

"I can't believe that," Jane said, looking thunderstruck. "What in the world was she thinking?"

"She wasn't. That's the nearest I can figure."

Jane pursed her lips, her brow furrowing. "And she was just...there when you showed up?"

"Yeah."

"How did she know about the meeting?"

"Maybe Greenfield got a hold of her."

"After she spent days ignoring texts and calls from me and Kitty? Why would she answer for a professor and not for us?"

"Jane, the girl turned in my paper as hers and submitted a piece of shit under my name. How am I supposed to know how that brain of hers works?"

"I just think it's weird, is all. And timely. You have this meeting set with the dean and Lydia just happens to be there with a statement ready?"

Elizabeth's frown deepened. Yeah, put like that, it was a little weird—a serendipitous kind of weird, but weird all the same. Maybe it would make more sense once she had a little sleep behind her. "I don't know," she said at last. "If I can keep from strangling her long enough when I see her again, I'll be sure to ask."

Jane released a long breath. "I know this won't be easy, but... go easy on her."

Elizabeth barked an incredulous laugh.

"I mean it."

She laughed again.

"Look, what Lydia did was awful, but she didn't have to own up to it. Do you have any idea how difficult that must have been for her?"

"I'm trying really hard to give a damn."

"I'm serious," Jane said, crashing onto her own bed. "Lydia has never been the kind of person to think things through. And no matter how awful what she did was—and I'm not saying it wasn't—I don't think she acted with malicious intent. She might be a little oblivious, but she's not *mean*."

"Honestly, I think that might be worse."

"What?"

"Her general lack of awareness of how other people are affected by her actions," Elizabeth replied. "Mean people at least know what they're doing and why. Lydia just...*didn't think*. And I was almost expelled because of it."

"Almost," Jane agreed. "But you weren't."

"Because she grew a conscience at the eleventh hour."

"But she didn't *have* to do that."

"I'm not going to give her points for being a decent human being after being a pretty damn bad one."

Jane studied her, then broke away with a long sigh. Thankfully, when she spoke again, it was to change the subject. "You probably are wanting to take a nap, huh?"

"What gave it away?"

"The fact that you can barely keep your eyes open. Also, you get super cranky when you're tired."

Elizabeth scowled. "I don't think it's *cranky* to be pissed about nearly getting booted from college."

"I know." Though it looked like she wanted to say more on the subject, she apparently thought the better of it. "I'll leave you with the room, then. Get some shut-eye."

No need to tell her twice. Elizabeth crashed back onto the mattress and closed her eyes. "What are you going to do?"

"Charlie texted me. Again."

She cracked one eye open. "Oh?"

"He's back on campus. Came with Will Darcy." Jane gave Elizabeth a pointed look, but when she didn't take the bait, continued, "He wants to talk and I... Well, I know the smart thing to do would be to ignore him, but..."

"But you miss him."

"Yeah."

Elizabeth offered a smile. "He did a dumb thing, letting you get away."

"Yes, he did." Jane rose to her feet. "But I think I owe it to myself just to give him the opportunity to grovel, don't you think?"

"Absolutely. Are you going to Netherfield, then?"

"No. I told him to meet me at the Meryton Mudhouse. Neutral territory."

Elizabeth nodded. "Smart move."

"I learn only from the best."

"Just be prepared—that boy's nuts about you."

"I'm not taking him back. This is just closure."

"Right. So when you guys get married, I so get dibs on maid of honor."

Jane wrinkled her nose, but her eyes sparked with something that Elizabeth hadn't seen in a while. "You're obviously exhausted. Speaking nonsense. Get some rest."

"At least make him sweat a little before you take him back."

Jane released another long sigh but didn't argue. Which was just as well, as Elizabeth was losing touch with consciousness. The last thing she heard was the door snicking shut, then everything around her dissolved into a blissful sea of nothing.

Elizabeth didn't know how long she slept, but it wasn't enough. Moaning, she twisted onto her side and cracked an eye open. Long shadows were cast along the floor, telling her the sun was well on its way down, which meant it was nearly time for her to make the now familiar trek across campus to see Will.

That thought was enough to wake her up. Elizabeth pressed her face into her pillow and yawned, stretching her arms and legs as best she could. Then the air split with a knock and her heart made a mad leap for freedom.

"Who is it?"

There was a pause. "Lizzie, I know I'm the last person you want to see, but I really need to talk to you."

Elizabeth dragged in a deep breath, her muscles tensing. She wasn't sure yet if she had the patience for Lydia. The burn of anger had yet to fade, even if her sleep-drunk mind kept it from flaring as hot as before. She wasn't ready to forgive and forget, but she also knew herself well enough to grant that if Lydia gave her the time and fuel, she'd simmer to an explosion. And while yelling at her suitemate might feel good in the moment, it wouldn't accomplish much in the end.

"I don't think that's a good idea right now," she decided.

"Please. I won't take long."

"Look," Elizabeth said, throwing her legs over the side of her bed and forcing herself to her feet, "I know you didn't mean for anything bad to happen, but what you did—"

"Please, it will only take a minute."

She hesitated, her shoulders dropping. If the past few months had taught her anything, it was that Lydia was nothing if not persistent. She made her way across the room and unlocked the door.

"If I yell at you, it's not my fault," she warned.

Lydia was a mess, even more so than she had been in the dean's office. Her hair, which had been pulled into a loose braid, looked like it was staging a coup against her head. Her eyes were puffier than before, swollen and pink, and despite everything, Elizabeth felt something inside her twist with sympathy.

Whatever else, Lydia hadn't intended to harm anyone. She hadn't acted out of spite, rather fear, and though that did not excuse what she'd done, it made it easier for Elizabeth to welcome her into her room.

"Lizzie," Lydia said once she was over the threshold, sniffling and wiping at her abused eyes. "Lizzie, I am so, so sorry for all this."

"I know," Elizabeth replied, deflating. "I just don't know what you were thinking."

"I wasn't." She exhaled. "And I know this will make you hate me even more, but the guy I was with… It was Wickham."

"I knew that already."

"You did?"

"Kitty told Jane, who told me."

Lydia said nothing for a few seconds, just stared at her, searching. "I thought you'd be mad about that."

"Because of what he said about me?"

"Well, yeah."

That was a larger issue she didn't particularly care to explore at the moment, involving things that Lydia was in no mood to hear and might not understand. But yes, it did hurt that anyone who knew her would have entertained Wickham at all following the crap he'd spread around campus—that anyone could over-look this behavior or find him attractive in spite of it. That Lydia would devalue herself to such a level that she'd be taken in by a guy like Wickham. He'd already proven himself to be a misogy-nist in word and deed.

Perhaps whatever had happened to Lydia over the past few days would open her eyes, or at least enable her to believe she was worth more than a piece of human garbage like Wickham.

"You are mad," Lydia whispered, her eyes flooding with tears again.

"Well, I'm not doing cartwheels," Elizabeth muttered. "Look... Whatever happened happened, and we can't undo that. But I know confessing what you did was not easy for you, so I appreciate you doing it. In the future, though, if you run off with a guy who's proven to be a creep to at least one of your friends, make sure you answer the phone when people try to call. Kitty was beside herself and so was Jane."

Lydia nodded weakly. "I just didn't know what to say to them. I..." She swallowed. "He made me believe him. I was so dumb to do it."

"That I wouldn't get in trouble?"

"Well, that, yes. But..." She sniffed and wiped at her eyes again. "If it weren't for your boyfriend, I'd be dead."

That sentence made zero sense. "Huh?"

"Will Darcy's your boyfriend, isn't he?"

Elizabeth's pulse began to race. "What about Will?"

Lydia shuffled her feet, looking even less comfortable than she had when Elizabeth had invited her inside. "He told me not to say anything. Made me promise, actually, but he's a good guy, Will. And I feel like you ought to know you're dating someone who's not a complete dipshit now."

"Lydia, what does Will have to do with any of this?"

"He...he found me in Atlantic City."

Elizabeth's legs began to shake. "He...found you. In Atlantic City."

"Wickham had convinced me that he could..." Lydia looked away, and the light from the setting sun hit her face hard, bringing the tear tracks on her cheeks into sharp relief. "I gave him everything in my bank account. All of it. My student loan money. And he lost nearly everything."

Oh holy Jesus. "Shit, Lydia..."

"That's why I didn't pick up the phone. I didn't want to talk to anyone. I was a complete wreck." She met Elizabeth's gaze again, smiling through a mess of tears. "Your boyfriend bailed me out. But he only agreed to do it if I came back and told Professor Greenfield what happened with your paper. And that's what I came here to tell you—that guy's a good guy. And he's *nuts* about you. I don't know anyone who would have paid what Will paid. A-and he made a contribution to Meryton on the terms that they wouldn't expel me. I'm in probation but thanks to him, I'm still a student." Lydia released a long, shaky breath. "And he did make me promise not to tell you any of this, but the guy deserves at least a really good blowjob for everything he did and I don't think he wants me to be the one giving it."

Elizabeth wasn't aware she'd moved until the backs of her legs collided with her mattress. She collapsed without fight, breathing hard, her mind racing and her chest aching with a sensation too raw to be given a name. She tried to think but couldn't—the thoughts were disjointed, in competition with a tidal wave of emotion that would drown her if she sat still. Her skin itself seemed to riot, numb and tingling and feverish.

The fears and doubts she'd entertained since leaving Pemberley vanished in a blink, leaving behind nothing but the desperate need to see Will. Touch Will. Be with Will.

"Fuck," she breathed at last. "Holy...fuck."

"Don't tell him I told you," Lydia said. "He made me promise."

There was no way Elizabeth could pretend she didn't know this. No way.

"I have to go see him," she said, pushing to her feet again. "Right now."

"Lizzie, please—"

"Will won't be angry with you," she said, stuffing her feet into the shoes she'd kicked off earlier. "I'll make sure."

"But—"

"Thank you for telling me." She threw on a hoodie, then lunged into Lydia's arms for a quick hug. "Thank you."

And before Lydia could get out another word, Elizabeth was halfway down the hall, her nerves about ready to riot. A thousand words began flooding her mind, vying for attention, but she couldn't think of what she'd say right now. She could barely think at all.

Will loved her.

And it was time he knew she loved him back.

43

By the time she stood outside Will's dorm room, Elizabeth had worked out a way to bring up the whole Lydia thing in a way that wasn't direct or confrontational. After all, he'd asked to see her, which meant he had something specific he wanted to talk about, and it only seemed fair to let him set the pace of the conversation, especially considering how much of their relationship up until this point had been dictated by her.

Yet the second he opened the door, all good intentions flew out the window.

"Is it true?" Elizabeth blurted, panting. She knew the answer, but she needed to hear him say it.

Will studied her for a moment, his eyes uncertain. But he didn't play dumb or ask her to clarify. Instead, he released a long breath and nodded. "Yes."

"Why?"

"Why?" he repeated, taking a step forward. His familiar scent invaded her senses—soap and aftershave and *home*. "You have to know why."

She swallowed. "Tell me anyway."

"The last time I told you, you didn't seem too happy."

"Things have changed."

"Have they?"

Elizabeth stared at him, barely daring to move. She wanted to be over this part and to the next, but there were things she needed to say—things he needed to hear—before she officially waved the white flag. The fine print that came with being with Elizabeth Bennet. "I don't trust things like this, Will. And I don't like it when other people fight my battles for me."

"I don't like it when I learn that someone has taken advantage of someone I love," he replied. "And if you're looking for me to say I'm sorry, well, I won't because I'm not."

"All that money..."

"I would have given more." Will broke his gaze from hers and tore a hand through his hair, mussing it in the way she loved most. "This is why I told Lydia to keep her mouth shut. I knew it would look like I was trying to buy you, or rescue you, and I know you're the last person in the world that needs to be rescued and that you can't be bought. I know that because those are two of the reasons why I love you, but if you ask me to watch from the sidelines while you get railroaded for something you didn't do when I have the resources to fix it? Elizabeth, I'm damn well going to exhaust every one of those resources. I made a phone call. I got on a plane. I wrote a check. Three very simple things that I could do because I'm a Darcy. And no matter what happens... Even if you walk away now, I will never not think it was the right thing to do."

Elizabeth blinked. "I... I think I can live with that."

"You can?"

"Yeah."

"Good."

Will seized her by her upper arms and pulled her to him, his mouth finding hers. And every nerve in her body burst, her muscles going slack with relief. It was a fight just to keep upright, and she didn't care if she won or not because he was there to catch her. Elizabeth whimpered into his mouth, throwing her arms around his neck as his hands wandered to her waist. The ground beneath her feet shifted as he began walking backward, taking her with him for every fumbling step. The next thing she knew, she was pressed against the mattress, Will over her, above her, cradled between the valley of her thighs and kissing her like she was the elixir of life itself.

"The door," she murmured between kisses. Her hands were several steps ahead of her, already busy dragging his shirt over his head.

"It's closed," he replied, slipping his hand beneath the hem of her hoodie. "And locked."

"And Georgiana?"

"Knew you were coming and will not be knocking anytime soon." He dragged her hoodie over her head and tossed it blindly across the room. "And just for the record, I've said it twice."

"Huh?"

"I love you." He offered her a soft smile, skating his fingers over her stomach, between her breasts, and up her neck until he had her cheek cradled against his palm. "And it's okay if you don't love me. Now, at least. All you need to do is tell me that you want to be here. That *this* is what you want."

Elizabeth was still a long moment, her brain bombarding her with things she wanted to say in a mad jumble, none of which she trusted herself to vocalize. She must have been quiet too long, because the smile on Will's face faded and he pulled back, taking all his wonderful warmth with him.

She groaned inwardly, cursing herself. The words were there —they wanted out—but she was struck with the knowledge that once she spoke them, there would be no turning back. And as wonderful as love was, it was also terrifying. It had nearly killed her mother, and her father had never meant to mold it into a weapon.

But Will...

"I'm sorry," she said hoarsely, sitting up.

"Don't be. If this isn't what you want—"

"It is. But I'm kinda freaked out."

He frowned.

"You know I didn't want a relationship. Ever," she said. "Not a real one. I guess I hadn't ruled out being with someone long-term, but...I always just thought I'd keep the feelings part separate. I don't trust people easily, and trust is kind of a big part of loving someone."

Will held up a hand, understanding warming his eyes. "You don't have to tell me anything—"

"No, I do. I want to. This, at least." She forced a smile before dropping her gaze to a space on the bed between them. "I didn't want a relationship because my expectations are too high, and I didn't think I could live with being let down. The best man in my life crushed me when he left my mother and I don't think he knows that. Because not only was he lying to her—he was lying to me. He made me rethink everything about my childhood and he did it to *protect* me. He stayed with her so I'd have that childhood, and even now he still doesn't see that he took it away from me the second he left. Perfect memories become less perfect when you know the truth, you know? And if my *dad* could do that, what could someone who wasn't biologically programmed to love me do?"

Will didn't reply, and when she looked up, his face betrayed nothing.

"I didn't think I could ever trust anyone to not do that again," she said, forcing herself to maintain eye contact. "A part of me still doesn't and probably never will. Perfect doesn't exist, so what's the use in trying? I figured if I met someone I liked enough...well, maybe we'd do the monogamy thing, but long-term? Marriage? Kids? All things I didn't want. I still don't know if I do."

Will released a long breath, trembling. Still, he didn't speak.

"The point I'm trying to make here is that...that was who I was when I came here. Meeting you...changed that about me, so slowly I didn't even really notice until... Well, right now. And that scares me shitless."

There was nothing for a long beat. She'd run out of things to say, except the one thing she still *needed* to say. But that was a line she couldn't uncross once it was behind her. That she felt it was terrifying enough—handing him the sort of power that had almost destroyed her mother took more faith than she thought she had.

But dammit, he deserved to know. And she wanted him to. He'd given so much without asking for anything in return.

The clouds fogging her mind parted and she forced herself to forge ahead. "I think what scares me the most is I've already done pretty much everything I think I can do to push you away. But you still...do this thing for me. You still love me after all of it."

Will cracked a small grin, and that was enough for her. "If it makes you feel any better, I wasn't wild about it at the time."

"Is it weird that that *does* make me feel better?"

"I don't think so." A pause. "I told you before that I didn't come here looking for anything but a degree. I think part of me felt the same as you, to tell you the truth, except that anyone who would want me would be in it for the money."

"Because women are just like that or because the money is all you have to offer?"

"Either, neither, both. I don't know. How could I tell?"

"Talking helps."

"Yes, and as we all know, everyone is always completely

honest." Will turned and pressed his back to the wall, keeping his gaze on her. "I figured that my life would be pretty boring, apart from Georgiana. I'd get my degree and officially take over my father's company. That was my plan. You railroaded my plan."

"I really didn't mean to."

"I know." He rose up on his knees, edging closer. "But here we are. Despite trying really hard not to, I love you. You crawled inside me that first night, I think, and I am done fighting this. Whatever part of you I can get, I'll take, and I'll be happy for it. If you can't say it now or ever, that's okay. I just want the chance." He paused, a heartbeat away, his attention shifting to her neckline. "But if you do ever say it," he said, running a hand along the collar of her tee, grinning, "I'll know it's real. Because Elizabeth Bennet doesn't say anything she doesn't mean. Ever. You are the most honest person I've ever met."

She released a shaky breath, unable to pull her eyes from his.

His lips quirked into a grin. "Which, I should add, is pretty damn hot."

"It is?"

"Mhmm..." He dropped a kiss on the corner of her mouth, sliding his hands down her sides until he had the material of her tee captured in his fists. "Sexy as hell."

"Will..." Elizabeth tilted her head back, blinking at the ceiling.

"Mmm?"

"I do."

His mouth had wandered farther south and was currently occupied with the exposed flesh of her neck. "Do what?"

"I love you too."

He froze, released a shaky breath that sent a wave of shivers across her skin. Then he pulled back to study her eyes, his own burning. For a moment, she thought he'd ask her to say it again, but he didn't. Instead, he just looked at her and she looked back.

Whatever happened from here happened on new terms.

At last, a wide, silly grin broke across Will's face. He captured her cheeks between his hands again and dragged her mouth to meet his. "I knew it," he whispered against her lips. "I knew it."

"Did you?"

"No, but I really hoped so." Will swallowed her response with the sweetest kiss she'd ever known. He devoured and completed her in the same stroke, his hands framing her face, his thumbs caressing her cheeks with small, loving circles as his tongue slipped between her lips. And finally, Elizabeth collided headfirst with complete and total understanding. Will was kissing her as he never had before—loving her without words.

This was everything. The feel of him against her. The small moans that rumbled through him. The way his kisses grew fevered while maintaining the softness that told her in no uncertain terms how much he loved her.

So she told him again, because why the hell not?

"I love you."

"I love you too," he murmured. "No matter how much you infuriate me."

"Good," she replied. "'Cause I don't think that's gonna stop."

Will grinned. "God, I hope not."

"You're a glutton for punishment."

"Mmm, guess that's true. I do like it when you punish me." He pulled away long enough to whip her shirt over her head—at last—and tear her jeans down her legs. Then they wrestled for a few seconds with getting Will's pants out of the way. By the time he was above her, smiling into her eyes as his cock nudged her sex, Elizabeth was riding a high unlike any other.

Love didn't have to be scary, and it wasn't. With him, it was perfect.

"We still get to fight, don't we?" she asked as he began to push his way inside her.

"Better fucking believe it," he agreed before nipping at her lips.

"Good...'cause you're wrong a lot of the time."

"Am I?"

"Uh huh."

Will grinned and kissed her. "By my count, I've been right about pretty much everything up until now."

"Th-that's because I wasn't really trying."

"Been holding back on me?"

Elizabeth rolled her hips to recapture him as he began to slip away. "I didn't think you could take it."

"I can take anything you can dish, Bennet."

"Famous last words." Elizabeth shoved him back with enough force to surprise him, and by the time he realized her intent, he was already beneath her, watching hungrily as his cock disappeared inside her.

"Are you ready?" she asked. "'Cause this is when I stop holding back."

He snickered and a spark of heat shot through her veins. But there was something else—a sensation she didn't recognize at first bubbling in the pit of her stomach. It was warm and sweet, filled with promise that seemed downright foreign.

And then she knew—she was happy.

Will dragged his gaze back up the length of her body. The wealth of what she saw there made her fall in love with him all over again. "Bring it."

So she did.

EPILOGUE

Three years after graduation

Will could appreciate the appeal of the small cottage, even if he did feel like he was on top of everyone else. But the venue had been the bride's only ask in the whole ceremony. Since the bride should always get what she wanted, no one had tried to talk her out of it.

The home had apparently been in the family for years, from its humble beginnings as a one-room dwelling. Every subsequent generation had put their own stamp on it, making it a patchwork quilt of a house—homey in every sense of the word, but in an oddly charming, mismatched sort of way. The bride's parents, grandparents, and great-grandparents had been married in the living room. Today, in less than an hour, she would follow in their footsteps.

"I thought those things were supposed to be hideous," Will drawled, dragging his gaze down the rosy fabric that made up the maid of honor's dress. It was form-fitting without being snug, revealed enough skin to tantalize but not scandalize. He couldn't wait to get her out of it after the ceremony.

"I keep telling you, sitcoms are not real life," she replied.

Will crossed his arms and met her gaze in the mirror. "Are you forgetting who we live with?"

Elizabeth snorted, then leaned forward as she began applying eyeliner. "There are special rules for Georgiana."

"Mhmm." His eyes, through no fault of his own, landed in the vicinity of her heart-shaped ass, and were quite content to remain there until she turned around and threw a hairbrush at him.

"What? I was enjoying the view."

"You're impossible. Shouldn't you be with the groom, *best man?* Kinda slacking in your duties."

"I have duties?"

"Namely ensuring that said groom doesn't decide to climb out the bathroom window."

Will arched an eyebrow. "You have met Charlie, haven't you? The guy was driving me out of my head asking me again and again why, exactly, Jane decided she'd prefer an evening wedding. He hasn't been able to see her in nearly sixteen hours."

"Probably doesn't help that I've been withholding sex for the past two weeks," Jane said as she brushed past Will into the already-cramped hall bathroom. "As well as cutting back on all displays of affection, private or public."

Will snickered and shook his head. "You're cruel."

"Well, I'm only planning on getting married just this once and forgive me if I'd like our first time as husband and wife to be special." Jane unceremoniously bumped Elizabeth out of the way and began inspecting her reflection. "I broke down and ate a packet of Oreos. Do you see any crumbs anywhere?"

Elizabeth sighed, seized her friend by the shoulders and turned her until they were face-to-face. "Lemme look," she said, leaning forward. "Nope. Just one sexy-ass bride who, by the way, is totally rocking the dress."

Jane beamed prettily and smoothed her hands down her sides. The dress did suit her. It was simple, lacking any of the frills Will had seen on other dresses—namely the monstrosity Caroline had walked down the aisle in two years prior, made up of ribbon, lace, and mountains of silk and bejeweled so ostentatiously she'd been hard to look at. No, Jane's dress was smooth creamy satin. It hit her just below the knee, had a modest neckline, and was held up by a couple straps. She hadn't wanted a big to-do, Elizabeth had told him, and indeed, she hardly looked like the bride of a millionaire, but that was, as Will had discovered over the past few years, Jane to a tee.

Elizabeth had joked that she'd be even less of a traditionalist in the eventuality that there was a wedding in *their* future—a subject that, in itself, had been all but exhausted over the past few years. According to her, should she ever agree to become his wife, they would do it in a quickie ceremony at the courthouse.

This would suit Will just fine. Of course, any future did, so long as she was a part of it.

"Will Darcy." Elizabeth waved a hand in front of his face. "Earth to Will Darcy."

Will shook his head and flashed a sheepish smile at Elizabeth and the bride-to-be. "Sorry. Was just thinking."

"Yes, well, I need you to think somewhere that's else, okay? This is a *no boys allowed* zone until after the ceremony."

He jutted out his lower lip in a pout, one that almost always worked. "Don't make me go back there. He's driving me nuts."

"You're not the one marrying him, so the good news is, he's only going to be your problem for another forty-five minutes." Elizabeth nodded at the bride. "Then he becomes Jane's problem."

"And I don't mind handling him," Jane agreed with a grin.

"And that's more than I ever wanted to hear."

"Then get out of here, dummy." Elizabeth smirked and

pulled him in for a quick kiss. "See you at the altar."

He widened his eyes, grinning. "Promise?"

"Don't push your luck."

"He is going to propose to you tonight," Jane said, meeting Elizabeth's gaze in the mirror as she smoothed out her lipstick. "Are you prepared for that?"

"He's proposed to me twice already since you two got engaged, and that's not counting the four times before that. I'll give him this—the guy is persistent."

"Why don't you want to get married? You're not going to break up with him, are you?"

Elizabeth rolled her eyes, securing the last bobby pin into place. It would take an act of God to get her hair to budge. "I am perfectly happy living in sin, thank you. Not everyone has to get married, Jane."

"So that's a no on breaking up with him, right?"

"Of course that's a no. I do love the man."

"I just do not get you."

"That's okay." Elizabeth shook her head once, twice, then whipped out a brief but intense headbang. Not a strand fell out of place. "Will does get me, and he's secure enough in our relationship not to take it personally when I tell him *no.*"

"You really lucked out in finding someone as crazy as you."

"I know, right?" She whirled around to give Jane one final look before the big march.

Her friend was, as always, the picture of radiance. From her hair to her simple-but-elegant makeup to the amazing dress—Jane rocked the classical beauty look. There was little to no chance of Charlie not bursting into tears the second he saw her, which was good for him, because if Charlie ever gave off a vibe that he didn't know just how lucky he was to have Jane in his life, Elizabeth already knew where she would dump the body.

"You ready to do this thing?"

Jane smiled, all excitement and nerves. "I think so."

"You better *know so* or I'm going to lead you to the getaway car."

"If I'm anxious, it's just because everyone's going to be looking at me."

"Of course they are, doofus. It's your wedding." Elizabeth rolled her eyes, but threw an arm around her friend's shoulder and steered her toward the hallway. "And there are, what, ten people in attendance, half of which is your family."

"I'm going to fall on my face."

"Your dress doesn't have a train."

"I don't need a train to fall on my face."

"That's the spirit." Elizabeth gave her a final squeeze before drawing back. "Come on. Let's go get you hitched."

It was a perfect wedding. Storybook-perfect to the last detail.

Like a good boy, Charlie cried. More accurately, he bawled. The second he saw Jane coming down the makeshift aisle in the living room, he'd dissolved into tears and started blubbering about how gorgeous she was and how he couldn't believe she'd agreed to marry a mess like him. This, naturally, resulted in Jane crying—and Elizabeth giving herself a mental high-five for insisting on waterproof makeup. Jane had sworn she'd make it through the ceremony without so much as shedding a tear, but there was little to no chance that even she'd believed that.

After the happy couple exchanged rings and the ceremonial smooch, the party moved outdoors. There truly weren't too many people in attendance—Charlie's family, including Caroline and spouse, plus the twins they'd spawned in some pact with the devil, Jane's family, which consisted of her parents and a couple cousins with whom she was close, and Elizabeth, Will, and Georgiana. Armed with determination, Pinterest boards, and Charlie's money, Elizabeth had converted the space outside Jane's idyllic cottage into a courtyard, complete with an assortment of tables, a gazebo, a buffet line, and a place for the band. The area was lit with strings of white Christmas lights in conjunction with the lanterns that doubled as table centerpieces.

It was perfect. Everything Jane wanted it to be.

And didn't budge Elizabeth's resolve on the subject of marriage one iota. Though she knew, from the way Will kept looking at her, that Jane had been right, and another proposal was imminent. He'd asked so frequently she'd nearly gotten it down to a science predicting when the next one would come. And every time he asked, she swelled with all the right things—excitement, joy, and love, so much love she thought she might burst. And likewise every time, the first word that came to mind was...*no.*

No, because things were so perfect the way they were. The *exact* way they were. She didn't want to risk ruining it. Not for anything.

"Dance with me?"

Elizabeth started and turned to Will, who had risen from his seat and was holding out his hand. The chords to "In My Life" tickled the air, bringing with them a swell of something she didn't know if she could contain. She smiled and let Will pull her to her feet.

Neither one of them were very confident on the dance floor, which suited her just fine, as Elizabeth had never graduated above the sort of couples' dancing one learned in the eighth grade. Yet there was the familiar feel of him pressed against her, his breath caressing the side of her face, his scent a comfort in itself. And it struck her, as it often did, just how fortunate she was that this man loved her, because picturing her life without him was rather terrifying. The past few years had redefined her in ways she still didn't completely understand, and most days, she was okay with that, because she got to learn alongside him.

"I'm not going to ask."

Elizabeth stiffened. She considered playing dumb, but he knew her too well to fall for it. "You're not?"

"No." He pressed his lips to her shoulder before continuing, "I've been thinking about this a lot recently, and I've realized something."

She waited. He didn't elaborate. She waited some more. Nothing.

Finally, Elizabeth jabbed him. "That is not a place to go quiet."

Will chuckled and drew her closer. "Sorry."

"If you're breaking up with me, it'd be nice if you'd at least wait until after the reception."

He laughed again. "You're not going anywhere. And that's what I realized."

"That you can't get rid of me?"

"That being married might work for some people, but it wouldn't mean you love me any more than you already do. The way I feel about you isn't determined by a license or a ring." He pulled back and smiled into her eyes. "You have every reason to not trust in marriage. But you do trust me, and as long as that's true, I'm a happy guy."

Elizabeth stared at him for a long moment, her throat tight. There were times when it overwhelmed her, the way her life had gone. How a series of missteps had almost cost her the best thing in it, while also leading her where she needed to be.

But most of all, how Will just *got* her. He got her in ways no one ever had or would. How she didn't have to explain herself to him because, somehow, he understood. Every bit of her, even the parts that didn't always make sense.

She swallowed, willing her pulse to stop racing. "Okay."

He nodded, grinning. "Okay."

"No, I mean I'll marry you."

"You...you'll marry me."

Elizabeth pressed forward to kiss him. "I'll marry you, Will Darcy."

"Well, I'm sorry, but it's off the table."

She narrowed her eyes. "Uh huh."

"Seriously. I withdraw my proposal." But he was smiling too widely, too goofily for her to even feign concern. He cupped her face and brought her mouth to his for another kiss. "This is because I said I didn't need it, isn't it?"

"Yeah."

"You're a little psycho, you know that?"

"Duh. But you love me."

"I do." He kissed her again. "God help me, I do."

"And, just for the record, I'm not taking your name."

"Definitely not. I assumed you'd insist on my taking yours."

Elizabeth shrugged. "That works. Oh, and I get two maids of honor. You can't ask me to pick between Jane and Georgiana."

"Technically Jane would be a *matron* of honor."

"Yeah, but that makes her sound really old."

"By the time our wedding comes around, she might be."

She shook her head. "Quickie wedding. Justice of the Peace. That much is the same."

"It sounds perfect. I can be Mr. Elizabeth Bennet by next weekend."

Elizabeth grinned at him, falling again into the endless pools of his eyes. It was a place she'd happily spend the rest of her life. "It's a date."

AFTERWORD

The idea for this book first hit me in 2012—flashes of a modern Darcy and Lizzie arguing with each other on a college campus. I tucked the idea away at the time, too overwhelmed with my current projects and the job I had just accepted at Samhain Publishing as an acquiring developmental editor to tackle anything new. The idea remained for years, a lofty "someday" I'd get around to eventually.

In 2015, I sat down and wrote an outline, which only served to intimidate the hell out of me. Again, I tucked it away, armed with handy excuses about other projects needing attention. Someday had not yet arrived.

Finally, in 2017, after experiencing both professional and personal upheaval, I began writing the book in earnest. My initial intent was to have it finished in three months. I wrote the last words on Christmas Day of that year.

While I haven't read many *Pride & Prejudice* variations or modernizations, if you exclude *Bridget Jones*, I know there is a level of expectation that comes with playing in this particular sandbox. This is intimidating, and I know there is no way I'll have pleased everyone. Hell, I might please no one. But when a book idea has persisted as long as this one did, an author has little choice but to write it. And whether or not you are satisfied at having reached the destination, I thank you for going on the journey with me. It was some of the most fun I've ever had writing.

Until next time, be good to yourself, and to somebody else.

ABOUT THE AUTHOR

Rosalie Stanton is an award winning erotic romance author in the paranormal and contemporary genres. A lifelong enthusiast of larger than life characters, Rosalie enjoys building worlds filled with strong heroes and heroines of all backgrounds.

Rosalie lives in Missouri with her husband and their dog, Luna. At an early age, she discovered a talent for creating worlds, which evolved into a love of words and storytelling. Rosalie graduated with a degree in English. As the granddaughter of an evangelical minister, Rosalie applied herself equally in school in the creative writing and religious studies departments, which had an interesting impact on her writing. When her attention is not engaged by writing or editing, she enjoys spending time with close friends and family.

Sign up for Rosalie's Newsletter for exclusive content, including sneak peeks, announcements, free reads, and other fun stuff.

Find Rosalie Online
www.rosaliestanton.com
rosalie@rosaliestanton.com

ALSO BY ROSALIE STANTON

Currently Available

A Higher Education

Firsts

Hellion

Captive

Blackout

Forbidden Fruit

Moving Target

An Intimate Friendship

Witness

Dark Solace

Sinners and Saints Series

Lost Wages of Sin

Sex, Sin and Scandal

Coming Soon

Sinners and Saints Series

Flip Side of Sin

Sins of the Flesh

Deliverance from Sin

Sins of Omission

Made in the USA
Middletown, DE
29 July 2019